THE
SPLIN
KINC

James Aitcheson was born in Wiltshire and read History at
Emmanuel College, Cambridge, where began his fascination with
the medieval period and the Norman Conquest in particular. *The
Splintered Kingdom* is his second novel.

Also by James Aitcheson

Sworn Sword

JAMES AITCHESON
THE
SPLINTERED
KINGDOM

arrow books

Published by Arrow 2013

10 9 8 7 6 5 4 3 2 1

First published in Great Britain in 2012 by Preface Publishing

20 Vauxhall Bridge Road
London, SW1V 2SA

An imprint of The Random House Group Limited

www.randomhouse.co.uk

Addresses for companies within The Random House Group Limited can be found at www.randomhouse.co.uk

The Random House Group Limited Reg. No. 954009

A CIP catalogue record for this book is available from the British Library

ISBN 978 0 09955 832 3

The Random House Group Limited supports the Forest Stewardship Council® (FSC®), the leading international forest-certification organisation. Our books carrying the FSC label are printed on FSC®-certified paper. FSC is the only forest-certification scheme supported by the leading environmental organisations, including Greenpeace. Our paper procurement policy can be found at www.randomhouse.co.uk/environment

Typeset in Dante MT by Palimpsest Book Production Limited, Falkirk, Stirlingshire
Printed and bound by CPI Group (UK) Ltd, Croydon, CR0 4YY

For Laura

Contents

List of Place-Names

Throughout the novel I have chosen to use contemporary names for the locations involved, as recorded in charters, chronicles and in Domesday Book (1086). Spellings of these names were rarely consistent, however, and often many variations were current at the same time, as for example for Eye in Suffolk, which in this period was rendered as Haia, Hea, Heye and Eia, in addition to the form that I have preferred, Heia. For locations within the British Isles my principal sources have been *A Dictionary of British Place-Names*, edited by A. D. Mills (OUP: Oxford, 2003), and *The Cambridge Dictionary of English Place-Names*, edited by Victor Watts (CUP: Cambridge, 2004).

Alba	Scotland
Amwythic	Shrewsbury, Shropshire (Old Welsh)
Bebbanburh	Bamburgh, Northumberland
Beferlic	Beverley, East Riding of Yorkshire
Brycgstowe	Bristol
Caerswys	Caersŵs, Powys
Ceastre	Chester
Clastburh	Glasbury, Powys
Commines	Comines, France/Belgium
Cornualia	Cornwall
Defnascir	Devon
Deorbi	Derby
Dinant	Dinan, France
Dunholm	Durham
Dyflin	Dublin, Republic of Ireland
Earnford	near Bucknell, Shropshire (fictional)

Eoferwic	York
Estrighoiel	Chepstow, Monmouthshire
Execestre	Exeter, Devon
Gand	Ghent, Belgium
Glowecestre	Gloucester
Hæstinges	Hastings, East Sussex
Hafren	River Severn (Old Welsh)
Heia	Eye, Suffolk
Heldernesse	Holderness, East Riding of Yorkshire
Herefordscir	Herefordshire
Hul	River Hull
Humbre	Humber Estuary
Leomynster	Leominster, Herefordshire
Licedfeld	Lichfield, Staffordshire
Lincolia	Lincoln
Lindisse	Lindsey, Lincolnshire
Lundene	London
Mathrafal	near Meifod, Powys
Montgommeri	Sainte-Foy-de-Montgommery, France
Noruic	Norwich, Norfolk
Rencesvals	Roncesvalles, Spain
Rudum	Rouen, France
Saverna	River Severn (Old English)
Scrobbesburh	Shrewsbury, Shropshire (Old English)
Snotingeham	Nottingham
Stæfford	Stafford
Stratune	Church Stretton, Shropshire
Sudwerca	Southwark, Greater London
Sumorsæte	Somerset
Suthfolc	Suffolk
Temes	River Thames
Use	River Ouse
Wæclinga Stræt	Watling Street
Westmynstre	Westminster, Greater London
Wincestre	Winchester, Hampshire
Wirecestre	Worcester
Yr	River Aire

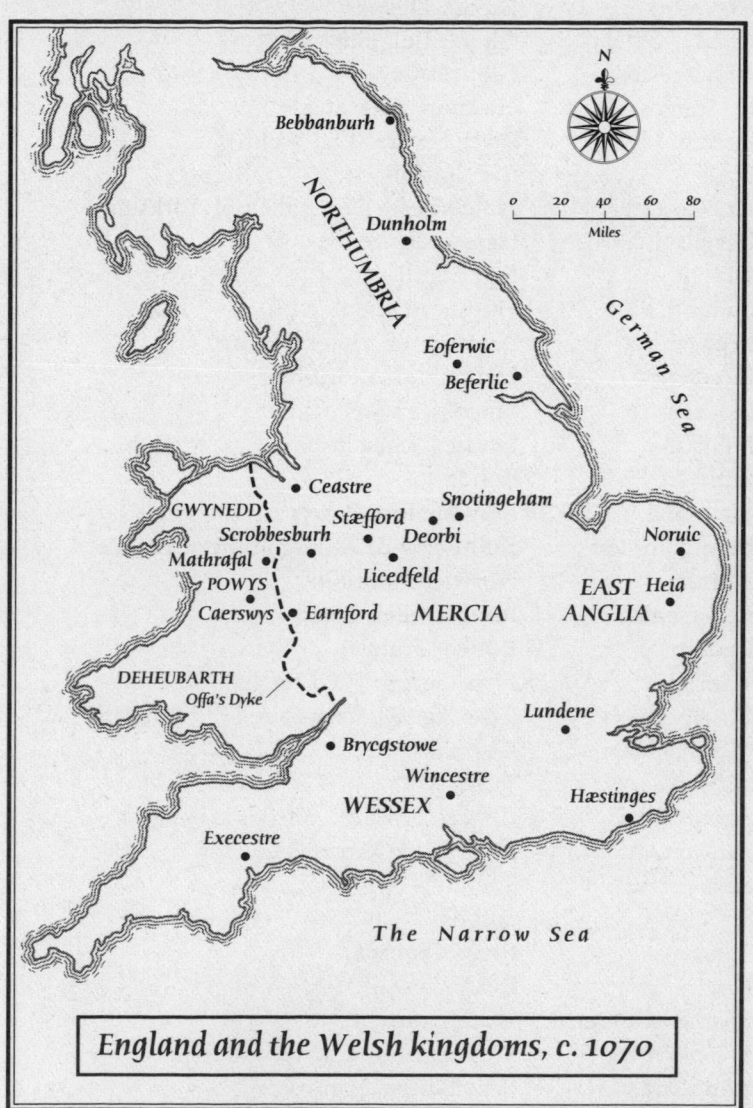

N

0 20 40 60 80
Miles

Bebbanburh

NORTHUMBRIA

Dunholm

German Sea

Eoferwic

Beferlic

Ceastre

GWYNEDD

Snotingeham

Stæfford

Scrobbesburh   Deorbi

Mathrafal

POWYS   Licedfeld

Caerswys   Earnford

Noruic

EAST   Heia
ANGLIA

MERCIA

DEHEUBARTH
Offa's Dyke

Lundene

Brycgstowe

Wincestre

WESSEX   Hæstinges

Execestre

The Narrow Sea

Offa's Dyke

England and the Welsh kingdoms, c. 1070

One

They came at first light, when the eastern skies were still grey and before anyone on the manor had risen. Shadows lay across the land: across the hall upon the mound and the fields surrounding it, across the river and the woods and the great dyke beyond that runs from sea to sea. And it was from those shadows that they came upon Earnford, with swords and knives and axes: a band of men perhaps as few as a dozen in number, perhaps as many as thirty. In truth no one knew, for by the time enough of us had woken, armed ourselves and gathered to stand against them, they had already turned and fled, slipping away amidst the trees, taking seven girls and women from the village with them.

It was the third such raid the Welsh had made in the last month, and the first that had met with any success. Always before now a cry had been raised and we had managed to gather in time to ward them off. For despite their barbarous ways, they were a cowardly race, and it was rare that they chose to fight unless they were sure they had weight of numbers behind them. Every night I'd made sure to place a man on watch, except that this time the sentry must have fallen asleep, for there had been no warning until the screams had begun.

Behind them they left three men slain together with their live-stock, and a cluster of smoking ruins where houses had once stood. And so as the skies lightened over the manor of Earnford, my new-found home, it was to me, Tancred a Dinant, that the villagers turned. They wanted justice; they wanted vengeance; but most of all they wished to see their womenfolk returned safely to them. As their lord I had a duty to their protection, and so I called my knights to me – my faithful followers, my sworn swords – together with as many men as would join me from the village. We buckled our scabbards and knife-sheaths to our belts, donned helmets and mail and jerkins of leather, and those of us who had horses readied them to ride out. Thus with the first glimmer of sun breaking over the hills to the east, we set off in pursuit of the men who had done this.

But now the shadows were lengthening once more; soon it would be evening and we were no closer to finding them or the women they had taken. We had tracked them across winding valleys, through woods so thick with undergrowth that it was often hard to make out their trail, and we were many miles into their country. I no longer recognised the shape of the hills or the curve of the river, and nor, I was sure, would those men of the village who had come with me, most of whom had probably never ventured this far from home in all their lives.

'They're gone,' muttered Serlo, who was riding beside me. 'It'll be dark before long, and we'll never find them then.'

He was the most steadfast of my household knights, one of the three who lived on my manor: built like a bear, and possessed of stout arms and a fierce temper. He was not quick, either in movement or in wits, but there were few who could match his strength and so he was a good man to have at one's side in battle.

I shot him a look, aware of the others following close behind: the dozen men and boys who were depending on us, whose wives' and sisters' honour, not to mention their lives, would be forfeit if we failed.

'We'll find them,' I replied. 'We haven't chased these sons of whores all day just to give up now.'

I tried to sound confident, though I had my doubts. We hadn't stopped since first we set out, but instead had ridden and marched throughout the day, the hottest so far this summer. Yet still I had no idea how close we were, if at all.

Even this late in the afternoon the sun was still strong, the air sticky, as if there were a storm on its way. My shoulders ached under the weight of my hauberk, which felt as if it were made of lead, not steel. Hardly had we ridden a single mile from the manor this morning before I was beginning to regret wearing it, and I'd been half tempted to turn back, but every hour lost was one in which the enemy could be getting ever farther away, and so I had borne it as best I could. My gambeson and tunic clung to my skin, so drenched were they in my sweat, and every time we paused to let the rest of the party catch up I had to fend off the flies which followed me.

I glanced up the path towards the hunched, solidly built figure of Ædda, who had stopped some twenty or so paces further ahead. He was my stableman, the ablest tracker in Earnford and possibly in all of the March. I was relying on him. He had lived in these parts longer than most, and he alone knew where we were. Or so, at least, I hoped.

It wasn't just my own spirit which was failing, either, but those of the villagers too. I couldn't speak much of their tongue, but I didn't need to, for I could sense it in not only their tired eyes, which were turned down towards their feet and the path in front of them, but also in their silence as they trudged onwards for mile after mile.

'Lord,' Ædda called. He was crouching low to the ground, waving towards me.

I frowned. If he had lost the trail, then we would have no choice but to turn back. My first thought was one of relief, and straightaway I despised myself for it. If we arrived back home without the women, I would lose all the respect that I had worked so hard to gain. I had promised that I would find them, which was probably a foolish thing to do, but it was done nonetheless, and I was bound by that promise.

'What is it?' I asked, sliding from the saddle, my boots sinking into the soft earth as I landed. It had rained for a while around midday and under the trees the ground was still damp, which meant that the hoof-prints left by the enemy were easily spotted.

But that was not what he had to show me. Instead he held in his palm a whitish object about the length of his middle finger: a comb, fashioned from antler, decorated with crosses and triangles painted red and green, and at one end, so small as to be barely noticeable, a carved initial letter 'H'.

I took it from him, turning it over and over in my fingers as I examined it, using my nail to scratch some of the dirt from its teeth.

'You think it belongs to one of the women?' I asked, my voice low.

'Who else, lord?' Ædda said. Of all the Englishmen and -women in Earnford, he was one of the few who could speak French. 'We're an hour from the nearest village.'

He gazed at me with his one good eye; the other he had lost in a fight some years ago, or so I had heard. Where it had been only an ugly black scar remained. Indeed he had an unsettling appearance; to add to his missing eye, he had been badly burnt across one side of his face, and the skin that was left was white and raw. Nor was he the friendliest of men: easily goaded, he was prone to fits of anger, and not the kind of man one did well to cross. But while many in Earnford were afraid of him, to me he seemed safe enough, especially compared with some of the men I had fought alongside over the years.

I nodded grimly and placed the comb in my coin-pouch for safekeeping. At least we were on the right trail. But whether the fact that it had been dropped here was a good sign or a bad one, I had no idea.

'Come on,' I called to the others as I returned to my horse. I vaulted up and into the saddle, feeling a fresh determination stir inside me, and gave the animal a kick to start him moving. 'We're close.'

From there the trail led up a steep incline, and so we were forced to dismount and lead our horses on foot. The sun was in front of us, so that whenever the breeze caused the leaves above to part, shafts of golden light would strike us straight in the eyes. The forest was thick with noise: from the chirps of birds as they chased each other between the trees to the buzz of the insects flitting about before my face. Yet despite that it felt strangely quiet, for there was no sign of anyone but us. My sword-arm itched, my fingers curling as if around the hilt of the weapon. I had never much cared for woods. When every direction looked the same, it was so easy to become lost, and between the ferns and the low branches and fallen trunks, there were too many places where an enemy might hide.

'Keep a watch out,' I said to Serlo and my other two knights. To young Turold, eager and willing; and to Pons, whose gaze was as sharp and cold as the steel in his scabbard. They were not the finest swordsmen I had ever known, and were far from being the most natural riders, but together they formed a formidable band of warriors. Even though I had known them but a year, I trusted them with my life. They had made their oaths to me, had sworn themselves to my service, and so we were bound together, our fates inextricably linked.

The sun dropped lower in the sky and the shadows lengthened as orange light slanted between the trunks. Back home the villagers would be wondering where we were, whether we would be returning that night. In the distance an owl could be heard, its own hunt just beginning. Inwardly I was beginning to question whether there was anything to be gained in going on, when suddenly Turold, who was in front of me, stopped still.

'What is it?' I asked.

He didn't meet my eyes but fixed his gaze in the distance, somewhere to our right. 'I thought I heard something.'

'You're imagining things again, whelp,' said Pons. 'It was probably just the wind.'

'Or a deer,' Serlo suggested.

'It wasn't the wind—' Turold began.

'Quiet.' I raised a hand to cut him off. 'Listen.'

I had always thought my own hearing was good, but Turold's was better still; if he thought he had heard something, more often than not he was right. At a mere eighteen years old he wasn't much more than a boy, but though he had few battles behind him he was nonetheless a skilled fighter, and what he lacked in experience he certainly made up for in ambition.

I stood still, my hand upon my horse's flank, scarcely even breathing. At first there was nothing but silence. The air was still and for once this day the birds were quiet, and I was about to give the order to start moving again, when there it was: a voice, or perhaps more than one, and laughter too, faint but unmistakable. How far off, and in what direction, was difficult to tell. The trees had a strange way of masking the sound. Try as I might, I could see nothing through the undergrowth, although I guessed it couldn't have been more than a couple of hundred paces away.

'Do you hear?' asked Turold, his voice low.

I felt my heart pound in my chest. Of course I had no idea if these were indeed the men that we had been pursuing, but it was the first sign of other people we'd had in a good many hours. Again the voices came, a little way to the north, I thought, upon the hill.

'Stay here with the rest until I give the signal,' I said to Ædda.

He nodded but did not speak. Making sure that my sword-belt was firmly fastened, I waved for my knights to follow and left the path in the direction of the voices. Already I could feel myself tensing as I ducked to avoid the low branches and made my way through the bracken, but at the same time I knew we could not make any noise, and so I had to keep reminding myself to slow down, to be careful not to step on fallen branches and other things which might give us away.

We pressed on up the slope. Gradually the voices grew more distinct. Their speech was not one that I was familiar with: not French nor Breton nor Latin. Nor did it sound like English either, from what I'd learnt of that tongue, unless it was a dialect I hadn't heard before.

At last I saw movement. Some twenty or so paces further ahead the trees parted to form a clearing, in the middle of which, gathered around a gently smoking campfire, sat a band of men. I stopped where a tree had fallen across our path, crouching behind it and waving to the others to get down. I laid a hand upon its ridged, flaking bark, the other upon my sword-hilt. The smell of moist earth filled my nose.

'What now?' Serlo whispered.

There were more of them than I had thought: a dozen at least, and I didn't doubt there were others that I couldn't yet see from this vantage. Most of the men had thick moustaches in the style of the majority of the folk who lived in this island, although their chins were clean-shaven and their hair was cut short around their ears. All wore trews in the loose-fitting style that the Welsh favoured. One who was standing had an axe slung across his back, while I could see round shields propped up against the trees on the edge of the clearing. They were warriors, then. But through the branches and with the sun glaring in my eyes, it was difficult to make out much more.

'We need to get closer,' I said.

'Closer?' Pons echoed, forgetting to keep his voice down, and he must have realised that he had spoken too loudly for immediately he looked sheepish.

I glared at him and put my finger to my lips. Without another word I rose and began to skirt around the clearing, picking my way little by little towards the edge of the trees. On the far side I could see the Welshmen's tents pitched in a rough circle, with their horses grazing quietly not far off, and in the middle were seven women. They sat upon the ground, their heads bowed, wrists bound with rope behind their backs.

We had found them. It had taken the whole day – it seemed we had chased them halfway across this island – but we had done it.

We couldn't celebrate yet though, for the hardest part was still to come. And my heart sank, for as I cast my gaze about the clearing I counted no fewer than sixteen Welshmen. Too many to risk facing in open battle, especially when only a handful of us knew how to wield a weapon properly. And so the only way we were going to overcome them was if we could surprise them.

I glanced back the way we had come, but the rest of our party was now out of sight. I turned to Turold. 'Go,' I told him. 'Tell Ædda to bring the others.'

He nodded and set off down the slope, soon disappearing into the undergrowth.

'Now we wait,' I said, crouching low to the ground, trying to keep as still as possible, although it didn't appear as if any of the Welshmen were on watch. Some drank from leather flasks while others were busy cleaning their teeth with green hazel shoots or rubbing them with scraps of wool-cloth. As a race they were meticulous about their appearance, and they obsessed over their teeth more than anything else. From time to time one glanced over his shoulder at the women, or got up from the fire to check on the horses. Most had unbuckled their scabbards or laid their spears down on the ground: something I would never have allowed my men to do, but which might just give us the chance we needed. But then what reason did they have to think there might be trouble? Doubtless they would have expected us to have given up the chase long before now, and that was their mistake.

I glanced about, searching for one who looked like their leader. It wasn't easy, for they were all dressed in similar fashion; none of them had mail, and only a few looked as though they possessed helmets. But then the one with the axe turned about, and I saw a thick silver chain around his neck and a gold ring proudly displayed upon his shield-hand. Liquid that might have been ale dripped from his sodden moustache. He would be the first I would kill.

'Here they come,' Serlo murmured.

I looked up and saw Turold returning. Behind him was Ædda, followed by the rest of our party in single file. I gritted my teeth, praying that they were silent, for the slightest noise could betray us. But the air was filled with the Welshmen's laughter, and they seemed not to hear. One by one the villagers assembled behind me: fourteen spears to add to our four swords. I only hoped it would be enough.

Turold crouched beside me. 'What's our plan?'

'We could come from two sides, trap them in the middle,' Serlo said.

I shook my head. That would need more men than we had, and would take time besides. The longer we spent organising ourselves, the greater the chance we would give ourselves away.

'We all go together,' I said, making sure that all my men could hear me. 'The four of us will lead, killing as many as we can in the first onslaught. By the time they realise what's happening, with any luck we ought to outnumber them.'

It was hardly the most sophisticated of plans, but I could think of nothing better. Neither, it seemed, could any of the others, for they made no objection.

I gave the same instructions to Ædda, who passed them on to his countrymen in their own tongue as they gathered around. My shield hung by its long strap across my back; I brought it over my shoulder and gripped the leather brases firmly in my left hand, at the same time adjusting my helmet, making sure the nasal-piece sat comfortably.

About twenty paces lay between us and the enemy: ground which we'd have to cover quickly if we were to retain the advantage of surprise. I didn't doubt it was possible, since they all had to find their feet and their weapons before they could do anything. But we had to choose the right moment, when the enemy were most off their guard—

'Hild,' said one of the villagers behind me. It was Lyfing, the miller's son, a usually sullen boy of about fifteen with straw-like hair. He rose, looking if he were about to start forwards; I grabbed him by the shoulder, at the same time clamping my other hand across his mouth to stop him speaking.

'Quiet,' I hissed. 'Not yet.'

He tried to struggle, but I was by far the stronger, and he soon gave up. Ædda muttered something in the boy's ear – translating for him, I guessed. I glanced towards the enemy, hoping that none of them had heard, and it was then that I saw what was troubling him. A red-haired Welshman had left the fire and gone over to the circle of women, where he was dragging one of the younger ones to her feet. She must be Hild, then. I recognised her, for she and Lyfing often spent time in each other's company back in Earnford, though until then I wouldn't have been able to say which of the girls she was. Her hair had fallen loose and she was shrieking as she lashed out with her feet. If anything, her oppressor seemed to be enjoying the challenge, for there was a wide grin upon his face. She fell to her knees, only to receive a slap across the cheek, and once more I had to grip the boy's shoulder to keep him back.

One of the older women rushed to help Hild, throwing herself at the Welshman even though her hands were tied, trying to bite him, it seemed, but he pushed her away and she fell face first to the ground, prompting laughter from his friends, who were now turning to see what was happening. All of them were jeering, shouting what must have been insults at the women, as if it were a game. Hild, on her back, tried to scramble away. Laughing, the red-haired one kicked her in the side, and she crumpled.

'Hild,' Lyfing said again, suddenly breaking free of my grip and rushing forward. 'Hild!'

'Lyfing—' I began, but it was too late to stop him. Cursing, I sprang to my feet and the steel rang out as I pulled my sword from its sheath. 'Now!' I called.

As one we rushed from the shadows of the forest, a horde of French and English in common cause, with spears and knives and all manner of blades raised to the sky, gleaming in the late sun.

'Kill them,' I roared. 'Kill them!'

I saw the startled looks on the enemy's faces, and felt a surge of joy, for I knew this would be quick. And I saw their leader, the one with the axe, standing before me, too dumbstruck to draw his weapon or even to move. I was upon him in a heartbeat, running him through, twisting my sword in his stomach, and he was dead before he knew what had happened. Blood spilt from his chest, staining the grass crimson, but no sooner had I freed my blade from his corpse than I was turning, making room for my sword-arm, and as the next one rose to attack me I tore the edge across the side of his face, and with a scream he fell.

The rest were jumping to their feet, snatching up their weapons from where they lay, but it was too late. The battle-calm was upon me and every thrust, every cut, ingrained through long hours of practice, came as if by instinct. Another charged at me, but it was the charge of a desperate man, and I danced easily out of reach before backhanding a blow across his shoulders and neck. Around me all was slaughter. Swords and spears flashed silver; the sound of steel upon steel rang out and the air was filled with the stench of fresh-spilt guts. Five of the enemy lay dead or wounded while only one of our men, so far as I could see, was hurt.

'For St Ouen and King Guillaume,' I shouted. 'For Normandy, for Earnford and for England!'

I saw the gleam of a spearpoint to my right and I turned just in time as another of the enemy rushed at me. I raised my shield to fend off the blow; it glanced off the boss, sending a shudder through my shoulder, but before my assailant could recover for another attack I rushed at him, catching him off balance and sending him crashing to the ground, his weapon falling from his grasp. I stood over him, and it was then that I noticed his red hair. He met my eyes, but only briefly. He didn't even have time to let out a shout before I drove my sword down through his ribs into his heart.

I looked about for my next kill, but the fighting had spread now as the enemy were being forced back, and there was no one, either friend or enemy, who was close. No one except the girl Hild, who was kneeling beside one of the corpses, staring up at me, her wide eyes full of tears. Blood was on her cheek and on her dress, and for a moment I was confused, until I glanced down at the body and saw that it belonged to Lyfing. His eyes were closed and his tunic was soaked crimson where a great gash had been opened in his chest, no doubt by the red-haired one.

'I'm sorry,' I told Hild, though the words would mean nothing to her. I should have protected Lyfing, I thought, protected him from himself. I ought to have known he would try to save his woman first, since in his place I would have done the same.

I had no time to dwell on it, though, for the fighting was not yet over. Beyond the campfire, the enemy's horses, frightened by the noise, were rearing up, tugging at the ropes tethering them to the trees as they tried to free themselves. And the panic was spreading to the Welsh themselves, who had seen their leader and several of their comrades fall and had no wish to be next. Some tried to flee, and were pursued by Serlo along with most of the villagers; others fought on, preferring a heroic death, but they were no match for trained swordsmen such as Pons and Turold, and were soon cut down. That left just six, gathered in a ring with their backs to one another, their spears held before them. But we were many and they were few, and they must have seen the hopelessness of their position, for after exchanging glances they all let their weapons fall to the ground.

I made them form a line and get down on their knees while the villagers rushed to their womenfolk, loosening their bonds and hugging them close. Not an hour ago they must have given up hope of ever seeing them again, yet now they were reunited. I could barely imagine their relief.

Pons nodded towards the ones who had yielded. 'What should we do with them?'

I cast my gaze over each of them in turn, and I saw the fear in their eyes. But they had sent several of my men to their deaths today, and I was not inclined to be merciful.

'Leave them to me,' I said, and then to the Welsh themselves: 'Do any of you speak French?'

At first no one answered, and I was about to repeat myself in the English tongue, when one spoke up. He was probably the youngest of all of them, of an age with Lyfing, I thought: a scrawny lad with lank hair. Possibly this was his first expedition.

'I – I do,' he said, his voice trembling.

I marched across, my mail chinking with each step, and stood over him. 'Whom do you serve?'

He cast his gaze down. 'Rhiwallon ap Cynfyn, lord.'

'Rhiwallon?' I asked. I'd heard that name before; he was foremost among the Welsh princes who held sway in these parts beyond the dyke. Indeed I'd heard it said that he called himself king, though there was precious little in these parts to be king of. Until now I'd never spoken to any who knew him directly. 'He sent you?'

The boy nodded cautiously, as if unsure whether this was the right answer to give or not.

'You took something that didn't belong to you,' I said, slowly enough that he could understand me. 'The death of your companions is the price that you pay.'

He nodded but remained silent. For one so young he did well to keep his composure, when many men twice his age would have crumbled.

'Go back to your master and tell him you failed. Tell him what happened here, and mention to him the name of Tancred a Dinant. If you're lucky he'll spare your life, as I've done. Do you understand?'

'Yes, lord.' I saw a lump form in the boy's throat as he swallowed, but he did not move.

'Then go,' I told him. 'Or else I just might change my mind.'

He scrambled to his feet, hesitating just for a moment while he glanced at his fellow countrymen. The blades of my men were pointed at their backs, their heads were bowed and they didn't speak. He must have seen that he'd suffer the same fate as them if he waited any longer, and so he darted away across the clearing, towards the west and the dying light, into the depths of the forest. I raised a hand to Serlo and Ædda so that they knew to let him go, then went to survey the corpses strewn about the clearing, to see if they had on them anything of worth.

'What about the rest?' Pons called after me. 'Are we going to take them back with us?'

I glanced towards Hild, clutching at Lyfing's limp body, the tears flowing down her cheeks. I thought of all those men back in Earnford whose lives had been cut short earlier that day, and I thought too of their families who would be grieving for them. They had not deserved to die.

And I knew what had to be done.

'Kill them,' I said, without so much as turning around. 'Kill them all.'

They were warriors the same as us, and as such they faced their deaths with dignity. But nevertheless when the end itself came, they screamed as any other man would, and I hoped that the boy running back to his lord would hear those screams and know how fortunate he had been.

Two

We didn't stay there long. There could well be more Welshmen prowling the hills – friends and brothers of those we had killed – and if the boy went back to them rather than to his lord, they would surely come to seek their revenge sooner rather than later. Although we were all weary and it was already late, I knew we could not rest yet.

Before we went, we rounded up the enemy's horses and searched their camp for anything useful or valuable. A man could rightfully claim anything owned by someone he himself had killed, except for silver and anything more precious, which had to be given up to me. In all we managed to find thirty-nine pennies, which I would share out amongst my knights later. Since I had slain the enemy's leader, I claimed for myself his silver chain and gold ring, while the village men found and traded with each other for helmets and knives, shields and weapons, as well as brooches, tunics and even shoes. I saw Ædda donning a fine green cloak trimmed with what looked like otter fur, while another man tried to buckle up a leather corselet that was too small for him.

What food we could gather I divided up into equal parts, though there was little of it: some dozen loaves of bread no bigger than my fist, a handful of small cheeses wrapped in scraps of cloth, and a few berries and nuts. It was not much of a feast, given that we had two dozen empty stomachs to feed, but it was more than any of us had eaten all day, and it came as welcome relief.

With the light fast fading, then, we left that place of slaughter, following our own trail eastwards in the direction of home. As night descended it grew harder to find our way; the moon was new and cloud was beginning to gather, obscuring the little light offered by the stars. We were becoming ever more stretched out, and several times those of us at the front had to stop to let the stragglers catch up.

'They can't go on much longer,' Ædda told me when we paused to drink. 'The women have been through a lot. They need to rest.'

I glanced back at the rest of our party, though it was too dark to make out much more than their shapes. Bringing up the rear were Serlo and Turold, who were doing their best to keep everyone moving; I recognised them by the glint of their mail. In front of them rode the women on their newly acquired mounts, while the men half walked, half stumbled alongside, leading the animals over rocks and trees that had fallen across the way. In the middle was Hild. Her head was bowed, no doubt so the others could not see her tears.

'We can't stop yet,' I said. The longer we stayed in enemy country, the less I liked it. At most we could have made three or four miles, I reckoned, and probably not even that. 'We need to make it to the dyke at least.'

The dyke was the ancient divide between Wales and England, built in the time of a certain King Offa, who had ruled in these parts some three hundred years ago, or so I was told. Beyond it lay friendly country, and while that was no guarantee of safety, I would feel better for reaching it.

'Look at them, lord,' Ædda protested. 'They won't manage that.'

I set my teeth, but deep down I knew that the Englishman was right. Not everyone was strong enough to keep on marching for hour after hour, and no amount of coaxing would change that. The last thing I wanted was to lose anyone now. And so even though I didn't like it, I did not argue with him.

'All right,' I said. 'Across the valley to the next ridge, and then we'll stop.'

Ædda passed on the message to his kinsmen, and as soon as the stragglers had caught up we carried on, crossing the brook and climbing the rise opposite, until we found a good place to set up camp, next to a spring, with a clear view in every direction. The few tents we had taken from the enemy were not large enough to hold everyone, but there was no wind and the night was warm. As long as it did not rain, the trees would be shelter enough.

So far I'd managed to stave off tiredness, but now the day's exertions were beginning to catch up with me. My eyelids felt heavy and my limbs were aching, but I forced myself to stay awake. Someone had to stay on guard, and I trusted no one more than myself. With Serlo for company, I decided to take the first watch.

The night was still. Only the burbling of the spring, and the soft song of steel as Serlo sharpened his sword, broke the silence. Down in the valley, bats flitted between the trees, swooping low and then twisting mid-flight, darting back into the shadows. Otherwise there was no sign of movement. I sat cross-legged upon the ground, still in my mail with my scabbard beside me, drinking ale from one of the leather flasks we had taken from the enemy. It tasted bitter, more so than the sort I was used to, and not entirely to my taste, but I supposed that was the way the Welsh must like it.

'Lord?' said Serlo, after a while. He sat beside me, though he was facing in the other direction, running a whetstone down the edge of his blade.

'Yes?' I asked.

'Those men we killed earlier, the ones who said they were sent by King Rhiwallon.'

'What about them?'

'Do you think they're the same ones who attacked last week?'

He might also have asked whether it was they who had come at full moon a fortnight ago, or last month, or indeed the month before that.

'I don't know,' I said. It was possible, I supposed, although I found it hard to imagine. Wales was a lawless country, where men did as they pleased, where oaths and alliances were made and broken at will; a land where princes rose and fell with the seasons, where a man could count himself a king if he held a single valley. To think that there was any pattern to the attacks was to suggest that there was some plan to them, and that I could not believe. All that most of them were after was sheep and women and, if they could lay their hands on it, silver.

But then why had these ones said they'd been sent by Rhiwallon himself? A mere dozen men was too small a band to cause much disturbance, and if they met with any resistance then all they could do was flee. Unless their purpose was simply to make trouble, to harass our lands this side of the dyke and instil fear amongst their enemies. In which case they had failed. Instead, by killing them, we had sent a warning back to their lord.

'They're growing bolder,' Serlo said, and even though he was turned away from me, I pictured the scowl that would be on his face. 'There's something brewing, something big. Isn't there, lord?'

I hesitated. Apart from the raids, the last year had in truth been fairly settled. While there were often tales of disturbances in one corner of the country or another, for the most part they were local matters, and easily put down. There had been no news of the northern rebels, who were lurking somewhere in the hills and the woods of Northumbria. Nor had anything been heard of Eadgar Ætheling, the man I had sworn to kill, who last year had murdered my former lord in the ambush at Dunholm. He was out there with them, though no one knew where, and while many suspected he would make another attempt to take the crown that he believed was his, there had been no sign of it yet; no word of his men marching or of his ships sailing.

Many months lay between now and winter, though: plenty of time in which to mount a campaign, and I didn't doubt that the ætheling was busy plotting something. And so a part of me couldn't help but share Serlo's suspicions. My sword-arm itched at the very thought. It had been too long since I'd had the chance to test it in battle, and by that I meant a proper fight, not the small raids and skirmishes we were always fighting in this border land. I yearned for the clash of steel upon steel, the blood rushing through my veins, the delight of the charge, the pounding of hooves, the weight of the lance in my hand ready to strike, the cries as we drove into the enemy's lines. The bloodlust. The battle-joy.

'Lord?' Serlo said again.

But I had no answer for him. Instead I passed him the flask I'd been drinking from. 'Here. Try some of this. I need a piss.'

I ventured down the hill, towards the willows by the stream, though not so far that I lost sight of the tents upon the rise. My right leg had gone numb from the way I had been sitting and I tried to stretch it out, limping slightly as I went.

I reached the stream and was just about to unlace my braies when, carrying on the faint breeze, I heard what sounded like sobbing. Frowning, I ducked beneath the branches and the drooping leaves, fending them away from my face as I made my way towards the noise. I did not have to go far. Barely ten paces away from me, kneeling down by the stream with her head in her hands, was Hild.

How had she managed to slip away without either Serlo or I noticing? Probably while we were speaking, I thought, and silently I castigated myself for not being more careful. If I couldn't keep close watch over our own camp, how easy would it be for the enemy to take us by surprise?

She saw me standing there, and straightaway scrambled to her feet, brushing dirt from her skirts, speaking quickly in words I didn't understand. She was a thin girl, short of stature; not yet married, for her hair was uncovered and unbound, and not unattractive either, despite the graze to her cheek where she had been struck.

'It's all right,' I said, raising my hands and opening my palms to show that I meant her no harm. She was probably only about sixteen or seventeen summers old, though I was never much good at guessing ages. I tried to remember whose daughter she was, but I could not.

She did not move, as if her feet had taken root where she stood. I felt I ought to say something more. In the past year I'd learnt to speak some English, but at that moment few words came to mind.

'It's all right,' I said again, though I was not prepared for what was to come, as she spluttered into tears and threw her arms around me. I was too surprised to do anything but stand there as she clutched at me, her face buried in my cloak.

'Lyfing,' she said, between sobs. 'Lyfing.'

I felt a stab of regret. There was no way we could have carried his body with us so many miles back to Earnford, and we'd had no time to dig a proper grave either, and so we'd had little choice but to leave him for the crows and the wolves to feed upon.

And yet I knew what it meant to lose someone so close. The same night that my lord had died at the Northumbrians' hands, I'd also lost Oswynn. I had not even had the chance to say farewell, nor to tell her how much she had truly meant to me, and now that chance was gone for ever. She still came to me in my dreams from time to time: her black hair unbound and unkempt, falling loose to her breasts; her embrace as tender as I remembered. But what I missed above all else was not her dark beauty but her strength of will, her lack of fear even in the face of the proudest of my fellow knights. The world may be governed by men, but it is women who govern our hearts, and I had never known another woman like Oswynn. Even though our time together had been short, and many things had changed for me since then, one thing remained the same, for still I missed her.

It was then that I remembered the comb with the initial 'H' carved into it that Ædda had found on the path, which I still carried in my coin-pouch. Gently I prised first Hild's hands, then the rest of her away from me and drew out the small piece of antler.

'This is yours, I think.'

Her eyes, heavy from so many tears, opened wide. She took it from me, clasping it in both hands close to her chest, before pressing it to her lips. I wondered whether it was Lyfing who had given her that comb, and, if so, how hard he must have worked and how long he must have saved his few silver pennies to be able to afford it, to help win her affections. Though it had all come to nothing. Perhaps he would be waiting for her at the end of days, just as I hoped Oswynn was waiting for me.

She murmured something: a thanks, perhaps, or else a prayer. In the distance a wolf howled, and its call was answered by a second and then a third. A pack returning from the hunt, I thought, just like us.

'Come,' I said. 'It's not safe here.'

She was looking towards the stream, gazing into the broken

waters tumbling over the stones. I didn't know if she had even heard me, but I placed a hand on her shoulder and she met my eyes.

'We've got a long day's travel ahead of us,' I said. 'You should get some rest.'

Unspeaking, she nodded. After a final, forlorn glance at me, she bowed her head and was gone.

It was growing late when we arrived back the next day. Now that our numbers had swollen, we travelled more slowly than I would have liked, but at last around sunset the summit of Read Dun – the Red Hill, as it was known to the people who lived at its foot – came into sight. Its forbidding and thickly wooded slopes marked the western bounds of my land, and I knew we did not have far to travel. Before long we had emerged from its shadow, and in front of us lay fields thick with green wheat, with the silver ribbon of the river winding its way between them. Cottages and hovels nestled by its banks, with spires of smoke rising from the thatch. Beyond them on the higher ground stood stables and granaries, the slaughtering shed and the hen coop and the still-empty house that formed the steward's lodgings, with the great hall at their centre, all of it enclosed by a simple ditch and timber stockade.

Earnford. The manor given to me by my new lord, Robert Malet. The place that I called home, strange though it seems when I look back upon those times now. Of course I couldn't have known then what lay ahead, what path fate and God had chosen for me, so perhaps it was not so strange at the time. Besides, by that summer – my twenty-seventh, and the one thousand and seventieth since our Lord's Incarnation – I'd already held the manor for the better part of a year. Indeed it was fifteen months since King Guillaume had been victorious at Eoferwic: since we had routed the English rebels under their leader, the pretender Eadgar, and driven them from the city back to their halls in the north. Back then I had been but a knight in my lord's service, oath-sworn and hungry for battle, for redemption and vengeance and the chance to prove myself. Now I was a lord in my own right, with lands and a hall and a gatehouse, with loyal knights to lead under my banner.

The wind was rising, gusting from the west. From the gable of the hall flew my device: a black hawk on a white field. It had once been the symbol of my old lord, the Earl of Northumbria, before he met his end at the hands of the rebels, and I'd kept it as my own out of respect to him. He had taught me the way of the sword, had been like a father to me, had helped to make me the man I was. In return I had sworn to serve him unto death, and in the same way I hoped that by taking on the hawk banner I could serve his memory still.

Pons gave a blast upon the horn, so that the villagers would not see our shadows in the distance and think we were the enemy coming back for another attack. A shout went up as we approached and young and old alike came rushing from the fields and their houses, abandoning cart and oxen and spindle and distaff to greet us. Children raced to their mothers, shrieking as they threw their arms around their legs, while the girls we had rescued ran to their fathers and husbands: the ones who had been too old or infirm to come with us. Everywhere men and women held each other, crying tears of happiness, crying with the joy of being alive.

Turold smiled at me, and I smiled back. Families were something of a mystery to me. I had never really known my own; both my mother and my father had died when I was young. But it was hard not to be touched by such a sight.

Men clutched at our sleeves and cloaks as we rode through the throng. Others knelt down in the dirt before us, bursting forth with what I imagined to be thanks, until there were so many of them surrounding us, reaching out to clasp our hands, that my mount could barely move, and I had to slide down from the saddle to lead him on foot.

'*Hlaford* Tancred!' Ædda cried out loud, raising his fist to the sky. His words were taken up by the rest of the men, until they were all chanting as if with one voice: 'Hlaford Tancred!'

And then through the midst of the crowd, I glimpsed Leofrun. Her auburn hair fell loosely across her shoulders as I liked her to wear it, shining in the late sun. She smiled softly, and there was a tear of gladness in her eye. I left the reins of my horse for someone else to take as she rushed towards me. Taking her in my arms, I held her close.

'You were gone so long,' she said in French. 'I thought—' She stopped herself. 'I'm glad you're safe.'

'Me too,' I replied with a grin.

Her cheeks glowed. Her belly looked even more swollen than I remembered, even though we'd been gone but two days. Already she was several months with child, and I reckoned it could not be long now before her time: another couple of months at most. I was nervous, as I knew she was herself. Although I think she cared for me more than I did for her, she made me happy enough, and I did not want to lose her. She was strong both in body and in mind, with wide hips that would make the birth easier, but even so I was uneasy.

Placing one hand on her belly, and with the other wiping the tear that had rolled down her soft cheek, I kissed her.

'Those men who came,' she said. 'Are they—?'

'Yes.'

'All of them?'

'All of them.'

She nodded, as if contemplating this fact, then closed her eyes and threw her arms around me. 'I'm glad you're safe.'

Before all else we buried the three who had been killed in the Welsh attack: a father and both his sons. We laid them in the ground in the same place where his wife also lay, having died of the pox last autumn. Erchembald the priest performed the rites while the villagers watched, and afterwards he spoke a few words for Lyfing, offering consolation to Nothmund the miller, to his wife Gode and to Hild, for all that it was worth. It would not bring him back to them.

While it was only right that we remembered those who had died, however, there was also reason to be happy. And so as day turned to dusk, the rest of Earnford celebrated our safe return. A great fire was built by the banks of the river, and everyone gathered around it. I had a haunch of salted beef brought down from the hall and laid out on a long trestle table, along with platters of smoked fish caught at the weir, rounds of cheese, loaves of that day's bread, pots of honey from the beehives on my demesne, pitchers of ale and mead, casks of cider brought across from Normandy and barrels of wine from Burgundy. Thus we feasted, filling the air with our laughter and the joy of hard-earned victory.

Children chased each other around the flames, wrestled upon the ground and played in the ford, splashing water in each other's faces, soaking their clothes and their hair. Men danced with their women as a cheerful song sounded out across the valley, led by the aged swineherd Garwulf on a kind of lyre known as a *crwth*, which his Welsh father had taught him how to play. His fingers darted furiously up and down the strings; with every stroke of his bow he stamped his foot upon the ground. Shortly he was joined by another man on a wooden flute, who added soft flourishes and flurries to the swineherd's rhythms, and then someone else brought out a drum and began to beat a steady time on it. Their music rose to the heavens and I led my smiling Leofrun by the hand beneath the arches made by the others' arms, holding her gaze all the while, looking deep into those grey-blue eyes and thinking that I did not deserve a woman so devoted and caring as she.

Ale flowed and spirits soared. But I could not keep from my mind those who were not there: the miller and his wife, not to mention those the Welsh had slain. As the dance quickened and men took different partners, I slipped away from Leofrun and all those people into the shadows. It had grown dark by then and so no one saw me retreat to the grassy slopes beneath the stockade. For a long while I simply sat there, swigging from the flagon I'd brought with me as I watched the flames writhing into the sky. Two of the field labourers – Odgar and Rædwulf – cast another log on to the pile, throwing up plumes of dark smoke that twisted about each other and billowed with thick clouds of sparks.

Still I couldn't shake the feeling that Lyfing's death was my fault. An image rose unbidden to my mind of his limp, crimson-stained body, and of his woman looking up at me with those helpless eyes. He was no warrior, just a mill-hand, but nevertheless he hadn't hesitated to take up arms, to follow me into battle, to risk his neck for me, for his kin, for his woman. He hadn't needed to fight, but he had chosen to do so out of loyalty and love, and because of that he had lost everything.

More than a decade had passed since I set out on the sword-path, since I had first given my oath, and in those years I had seen countless comrades fall. Many I could no longer recall by face or by name, but many more had been close friends of mine, and I would have been lying if I said that their deaths had not affected me. Lyfing, on the other hand, I had hardly known at all, even though he was one of my people, one of those I was sworn to defend. Perhaps that was why I was taking his loss hard, for it meant that I had failed in my duty, not just to him but to his family as well, to Hild and to the whole of Earnford.

'It isn't good for you to spend so much time alone, lord.'

The voice came from behind, startling me, and I turned to find Father Erchembald. A Norman, he was a stout man, short of stature, with a youthful face that belied his years and his wisdom. After the events of last year and the business with the chaplain Ælfwold, I had grown more wary around men of the cloth, but I could not help but like this man, who always seemed in good humour.

'I'm not alone now,' I replied. The flagon by my side was almost empty but I offered it to him anyway.

He waved it away as he sat down, cross-legged, on the grass beside me. I shrugged and drank down the few drops that were left, while he watched me with a look that was somewhere between concern and disapproval.

'What is it?' I asked.

'You should be down there, with them,' he said. 'With Leofrun.'

I didn't know what to say to that, and after a few moments of silence had passed between us, he sighed and tried again: 'It is because of you that Earnford rejoices rather than mourns tonight.'

Down by the fire some of the village girls approached Turold and Pons and Serlo, taking them each by the hand and pulling them into the circle as a new song began. French and English making merry together: I hadn't thought I would live to see it happen. Even now, somewhere in the north, the rebels could be gathering their forces, preparing to march. But when I watched the village men drinking and singing and dancing in the last light, I found it hard to imagine any of them taking up arms under Eadgar's banner. All they wanted was to tend their animals and plough their fields, to sow their crops and feed their families. They cared nothing for the kingdom. What did it matter to them whether a foreigner wore the crown, or one of their own race? As long as they were governed by a lord who would protect them from the Welsh who came with fire and sword across the hills, they had everything they needed.

Except that this time I had not protected them, and four men had died needlessly.

'It is because of me that a boy was killed yesterday.' I could not meet the priest's eyes but instead stared down at the ground. 'I ought to have stopped him. Instead all I could think about was my own glory.'

'We must all make our own choices,' Father Erchembald said, 'and young Lyfing chose to fight. He knew the risks, and I'm sure you did all that you could for him. You cannot blame yourself for his death.'

I gazed at the blazing fire, remembering the way the flames had swept through the town, through the fastness and the mead-hall that winter's night at Dunholm. For a long time I had blamed myself for what had happened there too, before swearing instead to kill the man who was responsible. Lyfing's killer already lay dead, and so in that sense the blood-price was paid, though I was no happier for it.

'Those women wouldn't be here were it not for you,' the priest said, gesturing at the figures dancing down by the river. 'You did a good thing, Tancred, and you must not forget that. They are indebted to you. Let them show you their thanks.'

'Perhaps.'

'It is for the best,' said Erchembald. 'It seems to me that a man can spend so much time in his own head that he forgets the world around him. The things which are truly important.'

'What do you mean, father?'

'I know that you still seek vengeance. You long to be with your old comrades, to ride into battle once more, to hunt down the man who murdered your former lord.'

He knew me too well by now for me to deny it, and so I said nothing.

'I cannot blame you for wanting these things,' he went on, 'but your place is here, and you shouldn't lose sight of the fact that in Earnford you have men who are loyal to you, folk who respect you. A woman who loves you, and soon a child as well.'

That last surprised me. Erchembald had never been especially fond of Leofrun, perhaps because she was with child but we were unwed, something that the Church frowned upon, although it was not such an uncommon arrangement.

'It's not enough,' I said, and only after the words had left my tongue did I realise how selfish they sounded.

If the priest was at all shocked, he did well to hide it. 'When does any of us ever have enough?' he asked gently. 'Try not to dwell upon the past, nor on what the future might hold, for those are things beyond your control. Instead be thankful for what you have in the present, and, if you can do that, you will find contentment. I know it.'

I was not entirely convinced, but I nodded nonetheless. Father Erchembald got to his feet, and then without another word he left me. I watched him as he made his way down the knoll, across the timber bridge that led over the stream, towards the fire where, like Serlo and Pons and Turold before him, he found himself suddenly dragged into the dancing-ring, to squeals of delight from the women.

I sat by myself, mulling over his words, eventually coming to the conclusion that, as usual, he was right, though I did not like to admit it. In those days I was ever stubborn, and once I had made up my mind about something, it was difficult to make me change it, as anyone who knew me well would attest. Yet the truth was that I ought to have been happy, for I had more than most men could ever dream of.

Music and laughter floated on the breeze, along with the smell of roasting meat. I heard Leofrun calling my name, asking around the rest of the revellers in case they knew where I had gone.

'Have you seen him?' she said, to which they could only shake their heads.

There she stood, silhouetted against the fire, the orange glow playing across her cheeks, biting her lip as she did whenever she was worried. Indeed she cared for me, probably more than I deserved. To say that she was pleasing to look upon was something of an understatement, for she was truly a creature of beauty and I was lucky to have a woman like her. With her tumbling auburn hair, her soft, songful laugh and her firm breasts, there were few girls in all the world who could match her.

Few girls, perhaps, except for one. Try as I might, even after more than a year I could not put her from my mind.

Again I heard Leofrun calling, and whether it was out of guilt or affection or something else, this time I found myself getting to my feet and going to join her.

Three

Nothing more was heard or seen of the Welsh in the days that followed. Each morning Ædda and I saddled horses and headed off into the country about Earnford, searching for signs of them: for burnt-out campfires, or tracks where a scouting-band might have passed, or anything else that would have suggested they had been roaming nearby. What I planned to do if we ever found anything I didn't know, but at the very least it made me feel as though I was making myself useful.

Even after a year I hadn't grown entirely comfortable with the duties that came with being a lord, as Father Erchembald knew well. I was much happier in the saddle, with my scabbard and knife-sheath buckled to my belt and my shield resting upon my back. It was how I had spent most of the past thirteen years, and it was how I meant to spend the next thirteen at least. Some lords, once they had acquired manors and wealth and servants and retainers, forgot how to wield a blade or lead the charge. Instead they grew fat on rich food and ale, barely leaving their halls or seeing anything of the world beyond the bounds of their estates. I was determined not to follow that path, and that was why, day after day, I rose at the break of dawn, donned my helmet and jerkin of leather, and rode out into the wilds.

Yet for all the time we spent scouring those same hills, those same woods, we never saw any sign of the enemy. Clearly Rhiwallon, their so-called king, must have thought the better of sending another expedition against us. Perhaps by now he'd heard the tale of how I had dealt with the last raiding-band, or perhaps not. Either way, he had made the right choice, for I'd resolved that the next time he thought to threaten my manor, I would not be so forgiving. Next time I would not leave even one man alive. I told Ædda as much as we were riding back from one of our morning expeditions.

'And if you're not here, lord, what then?'

'What do you mean?' I asked, frowning, for it seemed to me there was a barb hidden in his words.

'When you and your men are called away to serve your king, to join his wars, who will defend us?'

In the years since the invasion I had grown to trust few Englishmen. Ædda was one of those that I had taken a liking to, and I confess that I was taken aback by his tone. The stableman was a solemn and private character who rarely showed much cheer, but this was the first time I could remember that he had challenged me so openly.

He was around ten years older than me, I reckoned, though he had long since lost count. His skin was weathered from many seasons spent in the sun, the wind and the rain, and he had the look of one who had witnessed many hardships. In fact he might once have been a warrior, for while he was not especially tall he was ideally built for the shield-wall, with broad shoulders and powerful forearms that I imagined could once have sent many foemen to their graves.

'You could defend them,' I said. From the little I had seen, he was a capable fighter, if not an exceptional one. He was at ease in armour and helmet, and proficient, too, with both the spear and the long style of knife called the *seax* that the English favoured, which was more than most men could claim.

'You would abandon us,' Ædda said.

I bridled at his directness, but managed to hold my temper and instead cast him a warning glare. 'If the summons comes for me to fight, then I have no choice but to go. You know that.'

His one good eye bored into me defiantly, but I held his gaze and eventually he turned away.

'You fought well the other day,' I said, and again I spoke honestly. He had killed more than his share of Welshmen that evening. 'If it came to it, the villagers would follow you.'

Indeed he commanded a strange sort of respect among the peasants of Earnford, partly on account of his missing eye and disfigured face, which seemed to intrigue and intimidate them in equal measure. But he was also single-minded and forever had an air of determination about him that inspired confidence, much as they feared him.

'They would not follow a cripple,' Ædda said. 'They scorn me.'

'They would if I told them to. Who else could lead them as well as you?'

The Englishman gave a snort of derision. 'Those days are behind me, lord.'

I regarded him for a moment, wondering what he meant. If he had led men into battle before, it was the first he had told me about it, though it would not surprise me if he had. Perhaps that was how he had come to lose his eye, too; so far as I knew he had never let the whole story be known, and no one had ever dared to ask. Nor was I to find out then, either, since he did not speak after that, but instead spent every mile of the journey back home in silence, as if he had already told me too much.

For the first time in a while, then, life in Earnford began to return to something like normal, until the memory of the Welsh raids seemed as distant as a dream. The villagers took care of their animals and tended their crops, which were growing taller by the week; it would not be all that long until the harvest. A week before midsummer, a pedlar came by way of the bumpy tracks from Leomynster and Hereford. With him he brought his tired, grey mule and a shaky cart decorated with streamers of cloth in scarlet and green. As usual it came laden with more than it seemed it should be able to bear: timber planks, fishhooks, iron cooking-pots, flasks of oil, stout candles and other useful things, as well as jars of honey and spices, casks of wine, pots of ointment and herbs and other remedies, which he said would cure all manner of complaints.

The pedlar's name was Byrhtwald and he was well known both to me and to the people of Earnford, for he had visited the manor

30

many times in the past year. As well as the various goods he brought on his cart and in his pack, he often carried smaller trinkets on his person, among which this time was a bronze pendant inlaid with a golden cross, which hung by a leather thong around his neck.

'This?' he said, when I asked him what it was. He looped the string over his head and held it out to me. 'I bought it some years ago from a Flemish merchant who acquired it on pilgrimage in the Holy Land. I like to think it has given me protection on my many travels.'

Carefully I undid the catch and opened the two halves of the pendant. Into my palm fell a bundle of cloth little larger than an acorn, with some kind of hard object inside. A thin strip of parchment was attached to the cloth, which was finely woven and might even have been silk, and on it in tiny letters something had been written, though the script was difficult to read.

The question had just formed in my mind when Byrhtwald answered it: 'The toe-bone of St Ignatius.'

I had no idea who that was or when he had lived, so I sent one of my servants to find Father Erchembald, who had more knowledge on such matters.

'Bishop Ignatius of Antioch,' he murmured to me when the relic-bundle was shown to him. Awe-stricken, he turned it over slowly in his hand, squinting at the tiny writing. 'He was blessed as a child by Christ, and later martyred by the pagan emperor of Rome, who had him fed to lions, as I recall. He was among the holiest of holy men.' He eyed Byrhtwald closely. 'How much do you want for it?'

'Surely you're not asking me to part with so treasured a possession?' the pedlar asked. 'I have borne St Ignatius with me everywhere I go for seven years and more.'

'Spare us,' I said. He wouldn't have allowed myself or the priest to examine it so closely if he had no intention of selling it. Nor had I seen him wearing the pendant in all the times he had come to Earnford before now, which suggested, despite his story about the Flemish merchant, that it had come into his possession recently. 'How much?'

'Two pounds of silver are all I ask for.'

'Two whole pounds?' I repeated. A good riding horse would cost as much, and in fact probably less. 'For all I know this could be nothing but a sheep-bone.'

Byrhtwald looked affronted. 'Have I ever cheated you before, lord?'

That was no answer, and both of us knew it. But I supposed he had been honest in all the dealings I'd had with him thus far, and so perhaps he spoke truthfully this time as well. I turned away to confer again with the priest.

'Tancred,' said Erchembald, keeping his voice low in an effort to contain his obvious excitement, 'a relic this ancient would have tremendous power. And to think that the saint was touched by Christ Himself.' He paused. 'Our friend might not know how much this is truly worth.'

I had to suppress a laugh. 'I'll wager he knows exactly what it's worth.' Although if Byrhtwald were sincere about its provenance, then the protection such an object would lend whoever possessed it would be more than worth the cost.

I opened the coin-purse which hung from my belt. 'I'll give you half a pound,' I said to the trader.

'Half a pound? You would rob me and let me and my poor wife and children starve!'

'The last time we met, you told me your wife was dead.'

His cheeks turned red. 'She recovered,' he mumbled.

'She recovered?'

'Thanks to St Ignatius!' he said, and looked pleased with himself for having thought of this answer. 'It turned out she had only fallen into the deepest of sleeps, brought on by her ravaging illness. All of us thought her dead, but on the day that she was to be buried she miraculously awoke, thanks to the blessed saint's favour.'

That he was lying was clear, but exactly which parts of his tale were false and which were true I could not say. Still, I admired his nerve and his quick mind. As always I found myself entertained by him, even as he frustrated me.

'Two-thirds,' I said. 'No more.'

He hesitated as if considering, and then smiled, holding up his hands to show that I had beaten him. 'Two-thirds,' he conceded. 'Provided that I can have a bed in your hall tonight, a warm meal and a flagon of your best ale.'

That seemed only fair, and so we settled it, weighing up the amount both on his scales and on the ones kept by the priest in his house until we could agree on the correct measure. Thus the toe-bone of the martyr St Ignatius belonged to me. If Byrhtwald had got less than he had hoped for, he did not seem overly disappointed. He tore into that evening's meal and drank until he could barely stand. At the same time Father Erchembald remained convinced that we had secured a good price, and so everyone was happy.

As well as his wares, Byrhtwald often brought news of happenings elsewhere in the kingdom, and so far as I could tell he was usually reliable. He shared what knowledge he had the following morning while we broke our fast. Considering how much ale had vanished down his throat the night before, he seemed little the worse for wear. Certainly his appetite hadn't diminished; the way he stuffed the bread into his mouth, one would have thought he hadn't eaten in days.

'They say', he said in between mouthfuls, 'that Wild Eadric is once more on the warpath.'

He looked at me meaningfully, as if expecting me to know who that was, and then took a gulp of goat's milk from his cup. That was the first I had heard of any man of that name.

'Who is he?' I asked.

Byrhtwald spluttered. 'You've never heard of him?' White droplets dribbled down his chin, running into his beard. 'Eadric, whom they call *se wilda*, the Wild One?'

'Should I have?'

'He was one of the leading English thegns who held land in these parts under the old king. A formidable man and a vengeful one too, or so I'm told by those who have met him; I've never had the pleasure myself. He raised an army in rebellion against King Guillaume three years ago, led his men along the March south of here, ravaging much of the country before he was met in battle at the crossing-point at Hereford and driven into exile.'

That would have been the year one thousand and sixty-seven: the first after we had landed upon these shores. There had been a host of small risings that summer: too many for me to recall them all. Most had been crushed almost as soon as they had begun, the leaders put to the sword and their followers made to submit. Guillaume fitz Osbern was the one who had quelled them; the king's closest friend and adviser, he had been left to govern the realm while the king himself had returned to Normandy.

'Where did this Eadric go?' I asked.

'Across the dyke. They say he joined the Welshmen, that he swore his oath to the brother-kings Bleddyn of Gwynedd and Rhiwallon of Powys. Nothing has been heard of him in the last three years.'

'Until now,' I said.

'That's right.'

I waited in case the pedlar willingly divulged any more, but he did not. Knowing what he wanted, I called for someone to fetch my coin-pouch from my chamber.

As soon as a silver penny had made its way into his palm, he went on: 'The rumour is that they plan to march this summer. Together they're said to be raising an army larger even than the one the ætheling led against Eoferwic last year. An army thousands strong.'

At that I couldn't help but laugh. 'The Welsh are nothing more than raiders and sheep-stealers. They couldn't raise an army worth the name.'

'Nonetheless, it is happening. I will tell you something else as well, and I offer this freely, because we are friends and because you will no doubt learn it soon enough anyway. Eadric is looking for you.'

'For me?'

'From what I hear, the ætheling has been offering a handsome gift of silver and gold for the man who delivers you to him. It seems he bears a grudge against you, for some reason I do not fully understand, but which perhaps you do.'

He looked at me quizzically. I suspected he had some idea why, and merely wanted confirmation. But this was a game that two could play at, and I had no more intention of giving out free information than he had.

'Tell me what you think.'

'Very well,' he said, shrugging as though it were of little consequence. 'This is why I think he wants you. It's said you're the man who won the gates at Eoferwic, who led the charge against the ætheling, who fought him in single combat upon the bridge, who shed his blood and almost killed him.'

He paused, perhaps waiting for me to agree. In its essentials the story was true, although the details had grown somewhat exaggerated in the weeks following the battle. I had not taken the gates on my own, but with my sworn brothers Eudo and Wace by my side and others too. And while I had crossed swords with Eadgar and even wounded him, it was folly and battle-rage that had driven me to fight him. I was the one who had nearly been killed, not him. Were it not for the help of my friends, I would probably not be here now, and the tales would be very different.

'Now,' Byrhtwald went on, 'perhaps I am mistaken, and they speak of a different Tancred entirely, though yours is not such a common name that that seems likely to me.'

There was no use denying it any longer. 'You know you're right.'

He shook his head sadly and bit his lip. 'Nevertheless, it shames me that I did not make the connection sooner. For some reason I imagined that a man of such feats would be taller.'

'Taller?' No one would have described me as towering, but I was hardly short.

'I jest,' the Englishman said. 'But let us speak seriously for a moment, lord. Your fame goes before you. Your name is whispered in the halls of the north; the ætheling himself trembles at its sound. He remembers only too well how you embarrassed him before, and he punishes most cruelly any who dare speak of you in his presence. That is why he has offered this prize for your capture. Wild Eadric is not the only one seeking it, but he is the one you should fear.'

'What do you mean by that?'

'Only that he is a powerful man, and dangerous too, especially to those who get on the wrong side of him. He is more cunning than you know, and unrelenting in pursuit of his ends. Do not think to underestimate him, especially now that he has the Welshmen as his allies.'

'If the Welsh really were planning an attack as you say, I would know of it already,' I said. 'The summons would have come for me, and we would at this moment be mustering our own army to fight them.'

'Ignore me if you wish, for I am only the bearer of news. Whether you choose to heed it or not is none of my concern. But let it be known that I have never sold you an untruth.'

I wasn't so sure of that, and I was even less convinced by his rumours of a Welsh host gathering. Nevertheless I kept quiet, and talk soon moved on to other things. Of the rebels in the north or the Danes across the sea, Byrhtwald had nothing to relate. That worried me, for the less we heard, the more I began to wonder if Serlo had been right: if perhaps the enemy were biding their time as they gathered their forces for a bigger assault. Something was afoot, even if we did not yet know what.

Until the enemy showed themselves, though, we could do nothing. Nothing except wait, and that was the part of the warrior's life I had always liked least. In the heat of the mêlée, with the clash of blades all around, the crash of shield-bosses ringing in one's ears, there was no time for fear or doubt, but the hours and days before a battle were when those things crept into one's mind. Every man who made his living by the sword felt the same, no matter how seasoned he was, how many campaigns he had fought or how many men he had killed. With every day that went by I grew ever more restless.

As it happened we didn't have long to wait. By then just over a month had passed since the Welsh raid, though somehow it felt longer. Already the crops were growing tall in the fields, ripening under the summer sun, while new houses of wattle and cob were being built not far from where the old ones had been razed.

On the day that the news came, Pons and Turold had gone scouting with Ædda while I remained in Earnford, hearing the villagers' grievances with one another and passing judgment. One of the swineherd's boars had escaped its pen, knocked over his neighbour's water-butt and uprooted half the vegetables in the garden behind his cottage, and for that he was to pay two piglets to the injured party. Gode the miller's wife had been caught collecting armfuls of sticks and fallen timber from the woods without my permission, and she was forced to surrender the lot as well as give me three sacks of her finest flour. Since Lyfing's death she and her husband, Nothmund, had been hard worked, having added their son's share of the burden to their own. She had never been able to bear another child, for reasons that neither they nor Father Erchembald, who knew something of the various ailments that afflicted people, could fathom. Lyfing's death had left them distraught and tired and desperate, especially as the dry weather continued and the river ran low, which meant that there were days when the flow was not enough to turn the mill-wheel. But none of that excused what she had done, and so justice had to be dispensed.

In the usual course of affairs much of this would have been left to my steward, Alberic, except that he had fled my service in the week before Easter. A boor of a man whom I had never taken to, he was guilty of having while drunk begun a brawl with one of the village men whose daughter he'd taken a fancy to. After beating the father to the ground and leaving him for dead, Alberic took one of my best stallions and as much silver as he could carry, riding away before anyone could stop him. That was the last that anyone had seen of him. We'd sent word out to the towns and markets nearby seeking his arrest, but he had never been caught. As a result his lands became forfeit to me and his tearful wife was forced to take another husband, but I had not yet found anyone to replace him as steward. And so the business of the manorial court was left to me.

It was late that afternoon when the horsemen, some two dozen or so in number, were first spotted in the distance. Their banner was divided into alternating stripes of black and yellow, and the yellow was trimmed with golden thread that caught the light. Those colours I knew well, for not so long ago I had fought under them myself. They were the colours of the Malet family, and of Robert, my lord. He was rarely seen in these parts; most of his estates lay on the other side of this island, in the shire of Suthfolc, and most of his time was spent there or else in Normandy, at his family home of Graville. Which meant that it was something of a surprise to find the black and gold flying there in the valley of Earnford that summer's evening.

Straightaway I sent word for Serlo and at the same time called for my sword, which was shortly brought to me by one of the twins, Snocca and Cnebba, boys of around fourteen who worked with Ædda in the stables. Even after a year I found I could not always tell them apart. Whichever one it was, I thanked him as I buckled the belt around my waist. I'd had a new blade forged some months ago from the best steel that I could afford, with two blood-red gems adorning the hilt, and a scabbard to go with it: one that reflected my new-found standing. Reinforced with bands of copper, which were inlaid with lines of silver in twisting plant-like designs, it showed that I had wealth to spend, gold to give to men who would follow me. It was that same promise of riches that had drawn my three knights to my service in the first place.

I could see Robert himself now, riding at the head of the conroi, flanked on either side by a dozen knights, with his banner-bearer alongside him. Unlike his knights, who all wore helmets and coifs, his head was bare, and I could see his face clearly: his angular features, his high brow, his prominent nose. Beneath his hauberk he was dressed all in black from his tunic to his trews: an affectation which he considered fashionable but which I found a little odd, though of course I would never say so openly.

They made their way past the mill and the fish-weirs and the hay-meadows, following the cart-track that led to the ford, then past the church. Field labourers looked on as the column of horsemen rode in single file, along the baulks that marked the divisions between the furlongs, up the slope towards the hall. With Serlo at my side I strode down the path to greet them.

Robert grinned broadly as he saw me. 'Tancred,' he said as they drew to a halt and he swung down from his saddle. 'It's good to see you. It has been too long.'

'It has, lord,' I replied, and found that I was grinning too. It was several months since I had seen him: not since the winter, in fact, when he had come here after attending the king's Christmas court at Glowecestre.

He was then in his twenty-seventh summer, the same age as myself. He embraced me like a brother, and brothers we were, if not in blood then in arms, for the previous year we had ridden and fought alongside one another in the great battle against the ætheling, and had survived.

'You should have sent word ahead,' I said. 'I didn't know you were visiting these parts.'

His smile faded, and all of a sudden his face bore a grim expression. 'You haven't heard the news, then?'

I frowned as the thought crossed my mind: had the pedlar Byrhtwald been right after all?

'What news, lord?'

'Come,' Robert said. 'Let us not discuss it here. We've been in the saddle since before dawn. Let us eat and drink first, and then we'll talk.'

I held his gaze for a moment, searching for some clue in his expression, but none was forthcoming.

'Of course.'

The villagers had come in from the fields to see what was happening. Amongst the crowd I caught sight of Snocca and his brother, and I signalled for them to show Robert's men to the paddock beyond the hall where their mounts could graze. They were a diverse lot: some of them fresh-faced and eager for plunder and glory; others more weathered, with scars upon their faces marking their years of service. More than a few I recognised from the battle at Eoferwic, and some I had even led in the charge, though I did not know all of their names. But I did recall young Urse, he of the ruddy face and wide nostrils that always put me in mind of a pig's snout, as well as Ansculf, the captain of Robert's household knights. Neither ever had much liking for me, though I had no particular quarrel with them. Both regarded me with cold expressions as they rode past.

If truth be told, there was something magnificent in seeing so many warriors in gleaming mail, so many men of the sword gathered in Earnford, and the villagers clearly shared that feeling. In the faces of the onlookers could be read a mixture of curiosity and apprehension and awe.

'You are a fortunate man, Tancred,' Robert said, breaking into my thoughts.

'How so, lord?'

Our boots squelched in the soft earth. Above the distant woods a pair of kites circled.

'To have been spared so far the unrest and bloodshed that plagues the rest of the realm,' he said. 'I envy you.'

I gave him a wry look. If he thought that we didn't have our own troubles here, then he was sorely mistaken.

Either he didn't notice, though, or else he ignored me, for he went on, shaking his head: 'It amazes me that nearly four years have passed since we came across the Narrow Sea, since the usurper was killed at Hæstinges, and still it seems not a month goes by without risings in one part of the kingdom or another.'

His father, Guillaume Malet, had said something similar, I remembered, when I had entered his service last year. For a moment as I looked at Robert it almost seemed as if I were back there in the vicomte's palace, and I felt the same sudden sense of foreboding.

'This is nothing new, lord.'

'Perhaps not, but it is unsettling,' Robert replied, and his expression was still grim. 'Every week we hear of Normans being waylaid on the road or murdered in their halls out in the shires. Tales come to us of bands of armed men gathering in the woods and the marshlands, numbering in their scores and their hundreds, building strongholds as they prepare to rise against us, to drive us from this island for good.'

'And you believe those rumours?' I asked, meaning it as a jibe. Robert did not rise to it.

'I don't know,' he admitted. 'Still, can we afford to ignore them? If we pay them no heed and they turn out to be right, then we stand to lose everything we have fought so hard to gain.'

Of course the stories that had reached him would have grown greatly embellished in the telling and the retelling. All the same, I knew just as well as he that buried among the roots of each of those tales would be a seed of something that resembled the truth.

For a moment silence passed between us, and then I asked: 'What about the ætheling? Has there been any word of him?'

'Not yet,' Robert said. 'He continues to hide in the wilds of the north, though no one knows where.'

From that at least I drew some relief, though it was slight. Eadgar Ætheling was the only figure I could see who was capable of rallying the disparate noble families of Northumbria and uniting them in rebellion against us. The last surviving heir in the old English royal line, he had tried to claim the crown twice already: once in the wake of the defeat at Hæstinges, though he'd lacked the support of the earls and had been forced to submit to King Guillaume; and again last year, when with the aid of the northerners and a host of swords-for-hire from abroad he had tried to take Eoferwic. Already his followers proclaimed him king, and not just of Northumbria but of the whole of England.

But as long as the ætheling stayed in the north, it seemed to me that the kingdom was in little danger. For no one else had either the reputation or the standing to lead the size of army which would be needed to defeat us. The last who had come near to doing so had been Harold Godwineson, and at Hæstinges he had nearly succeeded, despite what the poets who have written songs about that battle would have one believe. Since his death there had been only Eadgar, and unless and until he marched, all the rumours Robert had heard would remain just that: rumours.

We passed beneath the gatehouse and came to the hall. I let Robert enter first and followed behind him. There were no window-slits of horn to let in the light, and the hearth-fire would not be lit until much later, so it took my eyes some time to adjust to the gloom after the brightness of outside. Along one side stood a long oak table and benches which could be brought out for meals or the rare occasions when we had guests. On the walls were hangings to keep out the draughts, though these were no lavish embroideries depicting scenes from folklore, of battle or of the hunt, with warriors and ships and fantastic beasts, for such things were beyond my means, but rather plain cloths of scarlet and green.

Robert cast his gaze about the hall. 'You have a fine place here,' he said. His tone held genuine appreciation, although compared with the kind of living he was no doubt accustomed to, mine must seem like a modest existence. But what need had I for expensive wall-decorations, for jewelled chalices, silver plates or gilded candle-sticks? Such things were, after all, only baubles, and did not by themselves lend a man any more status or influence. And something Father Erchembald had said came back to me: what mattered in the end was that I had around me men I could trust, sworn to my service. Men who would follow me into the heart of battle, into the gravest of peril. Their oaths were worth more than gold or silver or any number of precious stones.

'Tancred,' came a voice, and I turned. Serlo had not come in with us but had paused out in the yard and was looking back out through the gates, down the slope towards the fields and the cottages, his expression one of concern.

At that moment I heard shouts from outside, followed by cries of distress. I glanced at Robert, who looked as confused as I was, and we hurried out.

There was some sort of commotion, though at first as I gazed out into the low sun I could not see what was happening. But then I spotted Pons and Turold close by the sheepfolds. They were on foot, their arms beneath the shoulders of a third man whose weight they were bearing between them as they staggered forward. Pons called for help, and some of the villagers rushed towards them, taking the burden and helping to lay the man down upon a heap of straw.

I broke into a run across the yard, out towards the swelling crowd, pushing my way through until I stood over the man and could see his face more clearly. Even then it took me a moment to recognise him, so dirtied were his features. His tunic was bloodied and there was an arrowhead lodged in his side, while his face and his beard streamed with blood that even now he was coughing up. Then I saw his burnt face and the black scar where his left eye should have been.

It was Ædda.

Four

I crouched down beside the Englishman. He was alive, but his eyes were closed and every breath seemed laboured, as if there were a great weight pressing down upon his chest.

'Someone find the priest,' I shouted to those who were watching. 'Fetch him here now.'

Father Erchembald was the best-practised of anyone in the valley when it came to healing. In his house he often kept a store of herbs and draughts and other remedies. He would know what to do.

Ædda groaned, and it seemed a pitiful sound from one so solidly built. His eyelids trembled and then his whole body convulsed as he spluttered. There was fresh blood on his lips and his mouth. His eyes opened, only slightly and only for a moment.

'Lord?' he managed to utter, as if he wasn't quite sure it was me. He looked so weak: not at all like the man whose mere presence was often enough to make a room go silent.

I glanced up at Turold and Pons. 'What happened?'

'The Welshmen happened,' Pons answered. 'They came upon us by surprise in the next valley. We'd just turned for home when suddenly there were arrows flying at us from out of the woods. Ædda was struck and we fled straightaway.'

Another raiding-party, I suspected. 'Do you know how many of them there were?'

'We didn't see, lord,' said Turold. 'It all happened too quickly. We didn't stop to count. All we wanted to do was get away from there.'

Ædda coughed again. His tunic stuck to his skin. I started to peel back the cloth around his wounded side, hoping to get a better look at where the arrow had struck. At my touch he recoiled, his face twisted in agony. Sensibly neither Turold nor Pons had tried to pull it free, which could have worsened his injury. Gripping it firmly, I snapped off the shaft so that only the steel head was left buried in his flesh.

I turned to Pons. 'Bring me water.'

Much of my youth had been spent in a monastery, where the infirmarian had taught me a little about wounds and how to treat them. Among other things I knew how important it was to keep them clean to prevent them suppurating, and for that knowledge alone I was grateful, since it had saved not only others' lives but also my own on more than one occasion.

'Hold him still,' I said to Turold.

I cut away part of the Englishman's tunic with my knife so I could see his injury more clearly. The arrow had struck about halfway up his torso, just below his ribs. Thankfully it didn't look as though it had penetrated all that deep; certainly I had seen worse. At the same time, however, I remembered losing comrades and friends to wounds which on first sight looked far less severe.

Pons returned with a pail of water and also a scrap of cloth, which I soaked and then pressed to the stableman's wound, trying to dab away some of the blood and the dirt which had congealed around the gash. Ædda tried to pull away but Turold kept a firm hold on his shoulder, pinning him down until I'd cleared away as much of the blood as I could, though even as I did so I saw that more was flowing, dark and warm, clinging thickly to my fingers.

'How is he?' called a voice from behind, and I turned my head to see the stout figure of Father Erchembald hustling towards us.

'Not good,' I said and got to my feet, making way for him to have a closer look.

He knelt down and took the cloth from me, wringing it out and pressing it to the side of the big Englishman, trying to staunch the bleeding, before wrapping it around his torso to make a kind of bandage.

'What do we do?' I asked.

The priest rose to his feet. 'First we need to get him back to my house,' he replied. 'I can't do anything for him here.'

I didn't need to be told twice. 'Come on,' I said to Turold. 'Help me carry him.'

Ædda was not a small man by any means, but even so he was heavier than I had expected, and straightaway I felt the strain upon my shoulders and back. Together, though, we managed to lift him up. He was barely conscious; there was no question of him being able to walk even with our help, and so we staggered forward across the yard and out of the gates, with Robert and the rest of my knights making sure that the villagers stayed out of our way. Some of Robert's men must have heard the noise and had left their horses while they tried to find out what was happening, but someone else would have to tell them, for at that moment I was thinking only about getting Ædda to the priest's house.

It was less than a hundred paces down the cart-track, but it felt much further. Erchembald was waiting when we arrived, with a stool beside him and an open box at his feet, inside which were all the implements leech-doctors use to weigh and crush and mix different remedies: pewter spoons, pestles made of bone and steel spatulas. He gestured towards a bed with a mattress of straw that stood against the wall on the other side of the room.

'Lay him down there,' he said.

I gritted my teeth. Turold and I managed to haul the stableman's limp form across the room and on to the mattress. He groaned, and this time he sounded even weaker than before.

'I'll need to remove the arrow before anything else,' Erchembald said. 'Here, take this.'

He was speaking to me, I realised, and he was holding out a small glass bottle no larger than the width of my palm, which contained some clear liquid.

I took it from him, frowning. 'What is it?'

'Extract of nightshade and poppy dissolved in spirit,' he replied as he went to the shelf on the wall and retrieved a bone needle, which he began to thread. 'Mix one part of it with three parts wine. There's a flagon and bowl on the table there.' He glanced at Turold. 'Fetch me the tongs and piece of wood from the chest under those blankets.'

I did as he asked, unstoppering the bottle and pouring in the clear liquid until the bowl was one-quarter full, or as near as I could manage, then adding the wine. Only a few last dregs were left in the flagon, but it was enough.

'Now what?' I asked.

'Now stir it,' Erchembald replied. 'Then he must drink. With any luck it will help to alleviate the pain. And you' – he gestured again to Turold and handed him another cloth – 'come and stand here. When I say, you must press this against the wound to staunch the flow of blood.'

Taking one of the spatulas from the box at the priest's feet, I stirred the mixture until it was the same colour throughout, then carried it across to the bed. I knelt down beside Ædda, cradling his head in one hand while I lifted the bowl to his lips. At first he resisted and would not drink, but I saw Robert standing just outside the door and I called him over to help hold him still while I grabbed the Englishman's nose. He tried to draw away, but very soon he had to breathe, and when he did I was ready with the bowl. I tipped some of the mixture into his open mouth; he spluttered but I clamped his jaw shut with my free hand until he swallowed. He gasped and mumbled something that might have been an insult, but if it was I could not make it out, and then his head sank back on to the mattress.

'Fetch me some more wine,' said Erchembald, to no one in particular, as he rolled up the sleeves of his robe. 'The stronger, the better. He'll need it.'

'I'll see to it,' Robert said.

'And send everyone else away,' the priest called after him. 'I need to be able to see what I'm doing.'

I glanced towards the door, and saw the faces of Serlo and Pons, with a number of the villagers pressing behind them, straining their necks in an effort to see what was going on. Together they were blocking the priest's light.

Erchembald peered at the arrow. 'There are no barbs that I can see. With any luck that should make this easier.' He turned to me. 'Hold him still. Otherwise this will only take longer. Give him that piece of wood to bite down on.'

He pointed to the block that Turold had brought him, which rested on the floor just behind me. On each side there were marks where previous patients had buried their teeth.

'Here,' I said to the Englishman as I placed it between his jaws.

Outside I could hear Robert shouting at the gathering crowd, driving them away from the house, and suddenly bright sunlight flooded into the room.

I pressed down on both of Ædda's shoulders with all my weight, pinning him to the bed as I met his gaze. The look of steely determination that I had grown used to had all but vanished; instead there were tears in his good eye, tears rolling down his bruised cheek, though he was trying to hold them back, and I could feel his fear.

And then it began. First the priest worked two long-handled spoons into the wound, which he cupped around either side of the arrowhead before extracting it with great care. Ædda grunted and clenched his teeth firmly around the woodblock, but this was not even the hard part.

'The cloth,' Erchembald said, as a trickle of fresh blood ran down the Englishman's side.

While Turold did as instructed, the priest set aside the arrowhead, then he inspected the wound.

'No shards of wood or steel left inside.' He lifted up a steel pin, fearsomely sharp, from the stool next to him, and I saw the whites of Ædda's eyes. To Turold he said: 'Take those tongs. When I say, you must hold the flesh either side of the wound while I make the holes. Grip tightly and don't let go unless I tell you to.' He turned to me. 'Are you ready? He will struggle, but for this I need you to make sure he doesn't move.'

'I'm ready.'

While Turold gripped Ædda's flesh with the tongs, the priest drove the steel pin through the skin, making the holes where he would later sew the linen sutures to bind the two sides of the wound together. I had seen it done before, but never so deftly or so quickly.

Not that it made it any easier for Ædda, who roared through

it all. He roared every time the pin penetrated his flesh and he roared every time it came out again. He yelled through gritted teeth, biting down so hard on the wood that I thought it might split, his whole body shaking with agony. His cries filled the air, so loud that when Father Erchembald told Turold to grip the flesh tighter with the tongs, he had to shout so as to be heard. But I did not relent as I held the stableman down, leaning on his shoulders with all my weight, preventing him from struggling. I did not want to cause him pain, but I knew that if we didn't do this, his suffering would only be worse.

Robert returned with two wineskins as the priest was about to begin stitching, although there was little need for them by then for Ædda had passed out. It was probably just as well, since it meant Erchembald could finish what he needed to do without further difficulty, and I could rest my arms. Even so, I stayed until it was done, crouching by the Englishman's bedside in case by some chance he came to. But he did not, and when at last the priest laid down his needle and tied off the final suture, Ædda was asleep, his chest rising and falling in even rhythm.

'It is done,' Erchembald said. His brow glistened with sweat as he stood up, wiping his hands with a dirtied cloth. There was blood on his fingers and on his forearms, and his sleeves and his robe were stained a deep crimson.

Without another word he went outside, and I followed him to the stream which ran beside the herb-patch behind his house. The sun was almost at its highest, and I was struck by the heat; it must have been cool inside, though I hadn't been aware of it. Flies darted about us, attracted by the stench of fresh-spilt blood, and I had to fend them away from my face.

'Will he live?' I asked.

The priest did not reply straightaway, and I wondered if he had heard me. He crouched down by the edge of the brook, cleaning his hands in its clear waters and rinsing out some of the cloths he had used.

'Father?'

He splashed some water into his face and, blinking, stood up.

'God alone has the answer to that question,' he said, his expression solemn. 'I have done what I can for him, but so often it is hard to tell. Some live; others die. While I can close the wound and stop the bleeding, much depends on the extent of the damage done to his innards and that I cannot help.'

Exactly what I was expecting to hear I didn't know, but that was not it. A numbness overcame me. I knew he was only being honest, but I would have thought that a man of the Church would also try to offer some manner of consolation, some hope.

He must have seen what I was thinking, for he added quickly: 'He is strong, I will say that much. For most men the pain is too much and they pass out straightaway, but he held on and almost saw it through. If God grants him that same strength over the days to come, then there is a good chance he will survive.'

'And what do we do in the meantime?'

'In the meantime the best you can do is pray,' Erchembald said. 'Now, I must prepare a poultice for that wound. The sutures will prevent it from bleeding further, but it will not heal well otherwise.'

'Let me help,' I said.

'There is nothing you can help with, lord, except ensure that no one disturbs me. I know the villagers mean well, but I cannot have them getting in my way.'

Indeed I could see a group of men and women gathering close by the church, glancing nervously towards us. They would want to know what was happening.

'I will make sure of it,' I said.

'In that case, if you will forgive me, I must go.'

He hastened back inside, leaving me to gaze into the stream. The cloths he had left to soak in the water, and I watched pink tendrils twist and coil around each other, forming eddies in the current.

I was not alone for long, as shortly I felt a hand on my shoulder and turned to see Robert. 'I'm sorry for the Englishman,' he said. 'You know him well?'

Better than most in Earnford, I liked to think. 'He is my stableman,' I said. 'The ablest tracker I've known, and a good friend too.'

'He will survive, Tancred. I'm sure of it.'

He meant well, but after what Father Erchembald had said his words sounded hollow to my ears. 'You don't know that, lord.'

'No,' he said after a moment's pause, and he sighed. 'I don't.'

'You saw no sign of any raiders on your way to Earnford this afternoon?'

'None,' he replied. 'But that doesn't mean they weren't there. They could well have fled when they saw us approaching.'

That was more than possible. If they were a small band, they would have been easily hidden.

'I'll take a dozen men out to scout the country,' Robert said, grim-faced, as he gazed out across the fields along the edge of the woods. 'If the enemy are close by, we'll find them.'

That I doubted, though I did not say so. Whoever had attacked the stableman, Pons and Turold was probably long gone by now, and Robert would have little chance of catching up with them.

Yet as he began to marshal his knights and they prepared to ride out once more, I had the unsettling feeling that Byrhtwald had been right; that somewhere in that wilderness beyond the dyke the Welsh were lurking, and in numbers too. Like eagles circling high overhead, they watched, waiting for the moment when they could stoop and catch their prey unawares.

For the moment to strike again, and this time to kill.

My doubts were borne out when Robert and his men returned a few hours later. Dusk was upon us and I'd retreated to my hall, having spent much of the afternoon trying to calm the men and women of Earnford. They had seen what had happened to Ædda and now feared for their own lives as well as those of their children.

Leofrun had joined me for a time to try and lift me from my darkened mood, and while I was grateful for her presence and her efforts, I was not much cheered. Now she had retired to our chambers and I was alone. I sat on a stool before the hearth-fire, drawing a whetstone up my knife-edge, not because it needed it but because I did not know what else to do. My first lord had given this blade to me when I entered his service at the age of thirteen. It had shed some of its weight since then, so many times had I sharpened it, and it was no longer as well balanced as a fighting blade ought to be, but I could never bring myself to use any other and so it had stayed by my side all these years.

I was holding the edge up to the firelight, examining it for any nicks, when the doors to the hall were flung open and Robert strode in, bringing a burst of cool air with him.

I got to my feet, sheathing the knife and setting it down on the floor. 'Did you see anything?'

He shook his head as he untied his helmet-strap. 'There were some pony tracks leading away from where your men said the attack took place. We followed the trail over the hills, and for a short way into the forest, but there we lost it. As soon as that happened we turned back; it was too dangerous to linger there longer than we had to, especially with the light fading.'

'How many sets of tracks were there?'

'Only two or three, we reckoned, with perhaps a couple more on foot, although it was hard to tell.'

Ædda would have known, I thought; he would have been able to stay on their trail. The irony was not lost on me. And what if those few were merely the advance party for a larger raiding-band?

'How does the Englishman fare?'

'He lives,' I replied. 'He's still in much pain, but no longer bleeding.'

Robert was silent for a moment, then said, 'I hear this isn't the first time that the Welsh have attacked in recent weeks.'

'No, lord.'

'I was speaking with your man Serlo, who told me the story of how you hunted down the ones who came raiding last month. Didn't you consider that by killing them all you might only end up provoking the enemy?'

'I didn't kill them all,' I protested. 'One of them I spared.'

'One to tell the tale. Yes, I know.'

'What choice did I have?' I asked, rounding on him. 'They sent several of my people to their graves, butchered their livestock and burnt their cottages to the ground. Death was no more than they deserved.'

'I'm only suggesting that if you had let those men live, the Welsh might not have come seeking vengeance, and the Englishman would not lie injured and perhaps dying.'

'The Welsh are always raiding, looking for opportunities to steal and wreak their violence,' I countered. 'It wasn't vengeance that brought them here today. Besides, if I'd let those who came last time live, they would only have returned in greater numbers. They are a savage people; they have no understanding of honour as we do.'

'The sword is not the answer to every problem,' Robert said, seemingly not listening to what I was saying. 'Sometimes it is better to keep it sheathed and stay your hand. You would be wise to remember that.'

'Don't tell me what to do,' I said. 'This is my manor. I am lord here.'

The blood was hot in my veins, my heart thumping in my chest as I glared at him. He might have been my liege, but even so he had no right to appear as if out of nowhere, to ask for food and drink and shelter, and then to tell me how I should run affairs on my own lands.

'You forget yourself, Tancred,' Robert said, and there was a note of warning in his voice. As long as I had known him I had regarded him as a man of even temper, who was patient and rarely moved to anger. But every man had his limits, beyond which his patience ran out, and I sensed that I was testing those limits now.

He was neither the tallest nor the most imposing of men, but he always had an air of confidence about him: a confidence which some would say came close to arrogance, and he could be every bit as stubborn as myself. He met my stare, but I was not about to back down.

'Tell me, lord,' I said. 'Why have you come here?'

At least two hundred miles lay between Suthfolc and here, and I doubted he would have travelled so far for any small reason. He hadn't yet told me what news he bore, which worried me, for that probably meant I was not going to like it.

For a moment he did nothing but stare back at me, but eventually he broke off.

'Still as headstrong as ever,' he said with a sigh of frustration or amusement: I didn't know which. Perhaps it was a mixture of both. 'Very well. You have to hear this anyway, and I suppose there is no better time than now.'

He motioned to the stool I had been sitting on when he entered, while he brought across another from the dais at the far end of the hall. The seriousness of his manner unnerved me a little, but I did as he bade without argument, taking my seat beside the hearth-fire.

'You ask me why I have come,' Robert said. 'And I will admit that I have not been entirely frank with you thus far.'

That did not surprise me. Like many noblemen I had known, Robert rarely gave much away that he did not have to. In that respect, I thought, he was every bit his father's son. Except that his father's secrecy and half-truths had given rise to considerably worse consequences, for they had almost cost us the kingdom.

'What do you mean?' I asked.

'I have told you about Eadgar and the rebels,' Robert said. 'All that I have said is true, at least so far as we can tell. The king has his spies in Northumbria, but they cannot be everywhere at once, and the news when it reaches us is often as much a week old, or more.'

'You aren't calling me away to fight in the north, then.'

'No,' he said. 'But there are matters more pressing that you must know about. Stirrings on the other side of the dyke.'

This was what Byrhtwald had spoken of, although I'd dismissed it at the time.

'Go on,' I said.

'For countless years there has been enmity between the two peoples who dwell in this island. The Welsh have always hated the English, who they say overran Britain and stole it from them after the Romans departed centuries ago.'

'I know this—'

'Just listen for a moment,' he said harshly. 'Since that time they have forever been trying to win back this kingdom, and have often sent great hosts to try to conquer the lands they believe belong to them. It is why the great dyke that lies to the west of here was built in the first place: so that the Mercian kings could keep the Welsh out.'

Some of this I hadn't heard before, but a great deal of it I had, and in any case I was not sure what he meant by mentioning it.

'Why is this important?' I asked.

'It is important so that you understand the significance of what I'm about to tell you,' Robert said in an admonishing tone. 'Since the invasion all this has changed. You know that the English thegns who fought alongside the usurper at Hæstinges were all exiled, and their estates forfeited to King Guillaume. Well, it seems that many of those who used to hold land in these parts, rather than fleeing into the north or across the sea, went over the dyke instead. Now we learn that they are binding themselves with oaths to the Welsh kings in an effort to regain their lands. For the first time the two peoples are making common cause.'

'Among these thegns,' I asked, 'is there one who goes by the name of Wild Eadric?'

'That's right,' Robert replied with some surprise. 'You have heard of him.'

'Only recently.'

'In that case you already understand what I have to say,' he said. 'We have an army gathering at Scrobbesburh ready to fight the enemy. You must leave Earnford and come with me.'

His words hung like smoke in the air. For all the times in the past year that I had longed to lead my conroi into battle, I had never thought that when the summons came it would feel like this. Earnford was my home; it was everything I had fought for so many years to gain. A hall of my own, with retainers who swore their oaths to me: since my very first battle I had dreamt of this.

'No.' I rose and turned towards the fire. 'I can't leave. Not now.'

'This is not a matter of choice, Tancred.'

This was exactly what Ædda had feared when we had spoken only a few days ago. Now those fears had come true, though he might not live to know it.

'A man has been grievously wounded today,' I said. 'The enemy are afield, and you expect me to leave my manor to their mercy?'

'Would that things were different,' Robert replied. 'But unfortunately they are not. This summons comes from Guillaume fitz Osbern himself.'

Fitz Osbern. The same man who had put down Wild Eadric's rebellion three years ago. His writ carried more authority in the realm than that of anyone but the king himself. By any measure the most powerful of Guillaume's vassals, Fitz Osbern had responsibility for governing the whole of the March. A seasoned warrior and an able commander of men, he had led the right wing of our army at Hæstinges. I had met him more than once and knew he was not the sort of man whom one did well to defy. If the summons had come from him then I could not ignore it.

I was silent for a moment while I considered what to say, but no words came to mind.

'You will come, then,' Robert said.

He made it sound like a question, even though I knew it wasn't. 'To Scrobbesburh?'

'That's right. Even as we speak, word is going out to all the barons in the shires along the borderlands. They will muster there while Fitz Osbern decides what to do. Already he is moving north from his castle at Hereford, with an advance guard of more than one hundred knights.'

Things were certainly moving fast. The fact that Fitz Osbern was marching so soon suggested that this latest threat was no small disturbance but a serious threat.

'When do we leave?' I asked.

'As soon as possible. Tomorrow at sunrise.'

Outside, the skies were growing dark; it was too late to set out that night. We would need time to provision ourselves for the road, and for battle. Food had to be packed, weapons sharpened, horses made ready and more besides.

The past year had been more or less peaceful. Now, however, it seemed as though that peace was coming to an end.

Five

Before leaving there was one last thing I needed to do. Waking early, I went while it was still dark and I went alone, leaving the warmth of my bed where Leofrun still slept, slipping out of the gates with hardly a word to the sentry on watch. With night as my shroud I rode west, splashing across the ford and past the scattered houses on the other bank, hooves pounding the narrow track that led from the village into the woods, towards the forbidding shadow that was Read Dun.

Few of the village folk dared to even approach the hill, let alone climb it. Long ago a great battle had been fought there, or so it was said: a brutal encounter between rival princes in which many hundreds of men had fallen, their corpses littering the field like leaves in autumn. So much blood was spilt that day that it ran in crimson streams, staining the earth itself, and that was what gave the hill its name. Since then no crops had ever grown there, or so it was claimed. Indeed the folk of Earnford considered it unlucky to drink from its springs or so much as set foot on its slopes.

The ground was uneven and in places had slipped away entirely, leaving severe precipices with only rocks below. After a while I had to lead my mare on foot, for the way had grown too steep to ride up, the paths uneven and strewn with loose pebbles, but as I emerged on the other side of the woods it seemed to level off again, and after that it was but a short ride along the ridge to the summit and the upright stone which stood there, like a sentinel keeping watch over the land.

The first grey light was beginning to bleed over the eastern horizon, and in the gloom I could just about make out Earnford and the fields about it. And there was my hall, ringed by its timber walls, standing within the loop formed by the river, rising ghost-like out of the mist that hung in the valley. White tendrils wrapped themselves around the willows, around the church and the mill, veiling the hay-meadows and the pasturelands. How small it all looked, I thought, and how insignificant.

After what had happened to Ædda only the day before, it was probably not the wisest idea to venture out alone. From up here, though, I had a clear view in every direction; even in the half-light I could easily see anyone approaching, friendly or otherwise. Besides, I had both my sword and my knife, and so even if somehow the enemy did stumble upon me, I had no doubt that they would find me more than a match for them.

Down amongst the trees the world was already waking: the branches were alive with birdsong, heralding the new day. Up here it was silent. It was still too early for most people to have risen and not a single spire of smoke could yet be seen. Nothing moved, not even the wind. In every direction the country lay deathly still.

I dismounted and dug into my saddlebag, where I found a carrot to feed my mount. After hobbling her to prevent her wandering, I approached the standing stone, which towered above me, nine or ten feet tall, like a column supporting some invisible roof. It had been erected here by the ancient folk, it was said: the ones who had lived in these parts before even the Romans, the first conquerors of this island, had arrived. Perhaps it was meant as a boundary marker, or perhaps this had been a place of gathering, where they had come to feast and dance, to perform strange ceremonies in the manner of the old religion. Father Erchembald said this place was the Devil's work and disapproved of my coming here, where the servants of evil supposedly dwelt and where by night the spectres of the dead fed upon the souls of unwitting travellers they had waylaid. But in all the times I'd come here I'd never sensed any malevolence. Instead what I felt that morning was a stillness of a kind I had not known in some time, and wonder too at the men who had toiled to bear such a massive thing all the way up this hillside.

I ran my hand over the stone's surface. Cold to the touch, it had been worn smooth by the elements over so many years. And yet as I explored it further, my fingers found small pits and other blemishes, and as I moved around it I saw that down one side ran a deep cleft, like a wound, and out of that wound green lichen was growing like pus, feeding off the rigid corpse. Not even stone could survive unbroken for ever. Some day this would fall, as the halls and the cities of the Romans had already done; just as our castles with their towers and ditches and walls would too, and the great vaults of the minster churches that we were building across this land.

Everything came to an end eventually; there was no greater truth than that. After a year and more, my time in Earnford was likewise drawing to a close. Today I would have to leave this place I had grown to know so well, and I didn't know when I might be back.

A shiver ran through me, but this was not the time to feel sorry for myself. Drawing my cloak closer around my shoulders, I returned to my mount to unhitch the two saddlebags I had brought: the reason for my coming up here. Inside was silver and gold: some of which had come from the raiding-party we had pursued only a month before; the rest from other expeditions, from the grain and fish and fleeces that were sometimes sold at market or to passing travellers and traders. In all it amounted to a few pounds: not a large hoard, but too much to take with me. If the Welsh did come while we were gone I couldn't let it fall into their hands. And so I had no option other than to bury it.

Around the standing stone was a ring of smaller boulders, each of them a different shape and none taller than my knee, though they were all as firmly rooted in the ground as the central pillar. All, that was, except for one. Smaller and flatter than the rest, it was almost hidden in the long grass. I searched around its base for the crevice I knew was there, where I could slide my hand under the rock. It took all my strength, but I managed to prise it free of the soft ground, using one edge as a pivot and rolling it to one side, revealing the hollow beneath. At the bottom lay a leather pouch filled with coins that I had placed there some months before, together with a pair of gilded brooches for fastening one's cloak, and three silver arm-rings inscribed with pagan symbols that no one could decipher, not even the priest, who was able to read the letters of many languages. In addition to that treasure there were also three seaxes, long-bladed English knives that I had taken in another battle, as well as another sword that I had no use for. Finely wrought, it had served me well on campaigns previous, but now I had better-balanced, quicker blades, both of which I was taking with me.

Into that hollow I lowered the two bags, though not before stuffing a handful of the coins into my purse. I had kept some back already, but it was always better to have a little too much silver than not enough; besides, one never knew when it might prove useful. Then I hauled the boulder back over the space so that it was left exactly as I had found it, or as near as I could manage, so that the hoard was completely hidden from sight.

Already the skies were growing lighter; day was fast approaching and I could not linger here. Earnford would soon be waking, and Robert and his men would be ready to ride. I returned to the mare, untied the hobble from around her legs and vaulted up into the saddle.

'Come on,' I murmured to her as I kicked on. 'Time to go.'

Father Erchembald found me as I was returning along the cart-track which ran beside the church. He did not show any surprise that I was out so early, since he knew of my hoard, though he knew better than to ask exactly where it was hidden.

'He's awake, for the present at least,' he said, and I guessed he meant Ædda. 'He's been asking for you. He's weak and in great pain, but if you want to speak to him before you leave, this is your chance.'

The priest showed me inside his house to where the Englishman was lying on the bed, so quiet and still that at first I thought Erchembald was mistaken. Ædda must have heard me come in, though, since his eye opened. At first he stared blankly, as if he couldn't quite work out who I was or how he had come to be here. Whether he was just tired, or whether it was due to the wine and infusion of poppy that Father Erchembald had been giving him, I couldn't tell. But then after a few moments he recognised me.

'Lord.' He lifted one arm from the fleece covering him and offered his hand.

I clasped it in mine and crouched down at his side. 'Ædda,' I replied. 'I'm glad to see you're still with us.'

'And I, lord.' His voice was quiet, little more than a croak. 'And I.'

'How are you feeling?'

'Better.' He tried to smile, and I caught a flash of his crooked and yellow teeth. 'Give me a spear and shield and I'll ride with you.'

His humour caught me by surprise, for Ædda rarely joked, if ever. I didn't know if it was a good sign that he was recovering, or if it meant he had been struck on the head as well as in the side.

I smiled back at him. 'We'd only slow you down.'

He made a sound that was somewhere between a grunt and a laugh. The effort of speaking was taking its toll on him. I would not stay for long.

'The priest says you're going away to fight the Welsh,' he said.

'We are,' I replied, wondering how much Erchembald had told him. Did he know that we were leaving to join Fitz Osbern's army, or did he think we were going after the ones who had attacked him?

'Kill a couple of the bastards for me,' he said. 'Show them no mercy.'

His face creased in discomfort and he began to cough. I helped him to sit up. There was a wine-cup standing on the stool beside his head, and I raised it to his lips while he sipped at it. He nodded when he'd had enough, then lay back down again, drawing the blanket up over his shivering shoulders, clutching at the hem as he closed his eyes.

'No mercy,' I said. 'I promise.'

But he was already asleep, his chest rising and falling in even rhythm. I heard movement behind me and glanced over my shoulder to find the priest standing in the doorway.

'He'll sleep through most of the day, I should expect,' he said.

'You did well to get so much from him. He woke a few times during the night but he was far from lucid.'

To see such a bear of a man lying so still, as fragile as a child, sent a shudder of discomfort through me. If someone like Ædda could be so easily laid low, what did that say about the rest of us?

'He kept murmuring something in his sleep,' Erchembald continued. 'The same few words again and again. At first I couldn't make out what he was saying, but as he repeated it I started to write it down.'

He went to his writing-desk, on which rested a sheet of parchment with a single line of neat script in black ink at its head. I got to my feet and he handed it to me. The sheet was dry as bone and curling at the edges.

'This at least is what I made out, though I can only guess what he meant by it.'

Ten words. That was all there were, though they were not ones that I recognised. From having seen similar writings before I supposed that it was English.

'"*Crungon walo wide; cwoman woldagas, swylt eall fornom secgrofra wera,*"' I read aloud, pronouncing the strange combinations of letters as best I could, at the same time trying to work out what they meant in French.

'"Far and wide men were slaughtered; days of pestilence came, and death took all the brave men away,"' said the priest. 'That is the best translation I have been able to manage.'

I glanced first at him, then at Ædda, unconscious on the bed. 'I don't understand.'

'Nor do I,' said Erchembald. 'To begin with I thought it was probably just the effects of the poppy; its juice can do strange things to a man's mind. The more that he repeated it, though, the more I wondered if there might be something else in what he was saying.'

Far and wide men were slaughtered; days of pestilence came, and death took all the brave men away. Merely repeating the words in my own mind sent a chill through me. Indeed they had a portentous note to them that seemed to me could only bode ill. I touched the cross which hung around my neck, as if doing so would somehow shield me from them.

'Is it from Scripture?' I asked.

'Not from any verse that I have heard before. But I concede that there are several books that even I have not read, so it is not impossible.'

'Do you think he was trying to warn us of something?'

'Who can tell?' Erchembald sighed. 'He clearly did not know where he was even when he came to, and we cannot hope to know what he was seeing in his dreams. Perhaps it is only nonsense, and we should not take anything more from it than that.'

It did not sound like nonsense to me. But I couldn't think what the Englishman might have meant by it. Who were the brave men he had spoken of? Did he mean myself and my knights?

'In any case I shouldn't delay you any longer,' the priest said, interrupting my thoughts. 'I know you have a long way to travel if you are to reach Scrobbesburh by nightfall.'

'Before I go there is one more thing,' I said. 'I want you to act as my steward while I'm away. To take care of Earnford, and of Leofrun.'

'I will.' He did not seem surprised; he had probably been expecting this. But then he was the obvious choice: I could think of no one better suited to taking on such a responsibility, and he had not only my trust but also that of the people too, which was all-important.

'Post men on lookout day and night,' I instructed him. 'If you see the enemy, don't try to fight them but get everyone inside the fastness.'

'Yes, lord.'

I clasped his hand, and hoped that it would not be for the last time. I hoped too that when all this was over and the Welsh were defeated, there would still be an Earnford to come back to.

'I almost forgot,' he said. 'There's something I wish you to take with you.'

He led me inside the church and to the strongbox that was kept beneath the altar, from which he produced the bronze relic-pendant with the gold cross that we had purchased from Byrhtwald.

'May St Ignatius guard you through everything to come,' he said firmly, pressing the cold metal into my palm and closing my fingers around it.

I swallowed, knowing how much power the priest ascribed to the bone contained inside, even if I could not quite bring myself to believe in its authenticity. He wore an earnest expression: the kind that I knew meant that he had made his decision, and would not be swayed.

'Thank you,' I said, passing the leather thong by which the pendant hung over my head. 'I'll take good care of it, and will bring it back safely.'

He nodded, and after he had locked the chest once more we stepped out into the breaking dawn, where at last we made our farewells.

'Be safe, father,' I said.

'And you,' he called after me. 'God be with you, Tancred.'

I turned and tried to smile, but my heart was not truly in it, and with that I left him.

The skies were aflame with the morning light when I arrived back at the hall. Robert's men were striking the camp they had made in the bailey and the paddock, tying blankets into rolls and making ready to leave, while my own knights were at the stables saddling their horses. We were each taking two: our destriers, which were our war-mounts, vigorous and lightning-footed, trained to the mêlée and the charge; and also rounceys, hardy and dependable animals which would carry our packs, our tents and our provisions, as well as cloaks and spare tunics, lances and spare knives, flint and steel and bunches of kindling for making campfires, and pots and spoons with which to cook.

I let the two stable-hands, Snocca and his twin brother Cnebba, take care of my mare, while I donned my gambeson and my mail, buckling up my hauberk and tying the laces which bound my chausses around my thighs. My saddlebags were packed and waiting, and they attached them to her harness. Both boys would be coming with us, for we needed someone to look after the animals and make sure that they were fed and groomed, to help polish mail and sharpen blades. Neither of them said a word. Perhaps they sensed my mood, or perhaps they were lost in their own thoughts. This was their home, after all, as much as it was mine.

My destrier, Nihtfeax, was already saddled. His name meant night-mane or shadow-hair, I was told by the owner of the stud where I had purchased him, and it was fitting, for his coat and his mane were as black as pitch, a white star between his eyes being the only marking. Strong-willed and hot in temper, he had been with me for the better part of a year. He would have the chance to prove himself before long.

That was when I spotted Leofrun watching from the entrance to the hall. Forgetting about the horses for a moment, I ran to her. She threw her hands around me and, sobbing, buried her face in my shoulder.

I held her close, knowing that it would be my last chance to do so for a good while. 'You know that if I could stay, I would.'

'I understand,' she replied in a quiet voice. 'How long will it be before you return?'

'I don't know,' I said. 'It might be weeks or it might be months, depending on how long it takes for the Welsh to show themselves.'

'When you do come back, you will have a newborn son to hold in your arms.'

'I look forward to it,' I said, smiling gently as I placed a hand upon her belly. Of course whether it was a boy or girl only God could know. She was hoping for the latter, whereas I wanted a son whom I could one day teach swordcraft and horsemanship and the pleasures of the hunt.

'I wish I could ride with you,' Leofrun said.

'No, you don't,' I said, and laughed gently. 'If you'd ever seen a marching-camp you would know that it's not a safe place for a woman. Spirits run high, tempers flare and men will not hesitate in killing to get what they want, to slake their desires. If you came with me, I wouldn't be able to sleep since I would forever be fighting off all the others lusting after you. You wouldn't enjoy it.'

She blushed at that and, in spite of her tears, even managed a smile. 'I wouldn't be afraid,' she said. 'I would bear it if it meant I could stay with you.'

Even had she been fit enough to ride with us, I wouldn't have wanted her to come. Only too well did I remember what had happened the last time I'd taken my woman with me on campaign, and I was determined not to let the same thing happen again. I would not risk losing Leofrun as I had lost Oswynn.

'But I would be afraid,' I said. 'Trust me when I say that it's safer for you here.'

She knew I was right, though she wouldn't admit it. She bowed her head; tears spilt down her cheeks and again I held her to me, stroking to one side a strand of hair that had fallen before her eyes, feeling her warmth, breathing in the scent of her, drinking in everything I could of this moment so that I would not forget it in the weeks to come.

I didn't want that embrace ever to end, but the others were waiting for me, and so eventually I had to break off. There was time for one final kiss before Snocca brought me Nihtfeax and I mounted up.

'I'll be praying for your safety every morning and every night,' Leofrun said.

'And I for you.'

Robert rode towards us. In each hand he held a lance to which had been nailed a banner. One displayed his colours of black and gold, while the other was embroidered with the familiar black hawk on white field, which he handed to me.

'You have everything you need?' he asked, glancing first at me, then at Leofrun. He looked anxious to leave, and I suppose he was right to be, since Scrobbesburh lay a full day's ride from here, and that at a good pace. The days were long but we still had to make best use of them.

I leant down from the saddle, clasping Leofrun's hand. 'I shall return. I promise.'

'I know that you will,' she said.

She followed us as far as the gates. Outside the palisade, on the slopes that led up to the hall, some of the villagers had risen and were waiting. A few bowed their heads as we approached; others stared back at me with plaintive eyes, unspeaking; others still could not fight back the tears. Children clung to their fathers' trews or to their mothers' skirts, confused and frightened at the sight of so large a conroi. We rode past them, crossing the ford, turning to follow the winding river eastwards. The wind was at our backs, the sun rising over the hills, casting its warmth upon the new day, but it did little to cheer me, for inside I felt numb and cold. On the opposite bank rose the mound, ringed by the tall wooden stakes of the palisade, with the hall standing proudly atop it, though from below all I could see was the gable and the thatch. Too soon we were past it, past the woods where the pigs were often taken to forage, past the meadows where the cattle grazed, past the mill with its slowly turning wheel, which marked the edge of my manor. Earnford was behind us.

A sick feeling rose in my stomach and my gut, but I did not pause or even slow. And not once did I look back.

We struck out north, following the rutted and uneven track towards the town of Stratune, which lay on the road to Scrobbesburh. The sun rose above the trees lining the eastern hills, and as it did so the mist lifted from the valleys and the day's heat grew. There was no breeze to speak of, nor any cloud to offer shelter from the sun; before long my brow was running with sweat and I had to remove my helmet and coif. Most Norman men had their hair cut in the French style, short on top and shaved at the back, but in the last year I'd found it easier to let mine grow. It fell in ragged fashion almost to my nape, just past my ears: not as long as many Englishmen wore it, but then I had no wish to be confused for one of them. Now, though, it was matted to my head, and when I rubbed a hand across the back of my neck it came away slick with moisture.

I rode with Robert at the head of the column, with our conroi strung out in pairs, threes and fours some distance behind us. Down in the valleys we had kept formation in case of ambush, but after an hour or so we found ourselves in open country, with wheatfields on one flank and open pastures on the other. If anyone were to try to attack us here, it would be easy to see them coming.

Behind me Serlo laughed: a throaty guffaw that I knew well. He and the others seemed to be enjoying the company of Robert's men: a good thing, for these could well be the same men who before too long would be riding beside them in the charge.

'Fitz Osbern will be glad to have your services again,' Robert said.

It took me a moment to realise that he was speaking to me. He had not said a word since we had left Earnford, though the manor was several miles behind us now.

'Fitz Osbern, lord?'

'Of course.' Grinning, he clapped a hand upon my shoulder. 'You are the man, after all, who captured the gates at Eoferwic and opened the city to King Guillaume's army. You're the one who made that victory possible.'

Byrhtwald had said much the same thing. Nonetheless I found it hard to believe that my deeds, such as they were, were spoken of so highly.

'Is that what Fitz Osbern thinks?' I asked, casting Robert a sardonic look.

'Probably not,' he replied. 'But it's what many men have been saying. Your reputation grows, Tancred.'

At that I couldn't help but laugh. Many knights dream of plunder, of silver and gold and sword-hilts inlaid with precious stones, but most of all they want reputation and fame – for when we die and our souls flee this world, that is the only thing that remains of us on earth. We aspire for songs to be written about us: songs of the battles we have fought, of the men we've slain and the things we have achieved; songs that will be sung around campfires and in the halls and palaces of Christendom for years to come; songs that will live on through the ages, like that of the knight Rollant and his ill-fated stand at Rencesvals.

I was no different. But at the same time I knew full well that on the field of battle a man's reputation counted for nothing; the only thing that mattered was the strength of his sword-arm. I supposed if tales of my efforts won me respect from those who before had offered me none, then it could only be a good thing, but that was as much as I was prepared to admit.

'I'm sure Beatrice will be glad to see you, too,' said Robert. 'It must be some while since you last saw her.'

At the mention of his sister I turned in surprise. 'Beatrice?'

I had not thought about her in longer than I cared to remember. Last year I had been charged by their father with her protection, and had escorted her to the safety of Lundene. It was there that we had shared a kiss: the first touch of a woman that I had known since Oswynn's death. If truth be told, she was part of the reason I had sworn my oath to Robert rather than take my sword elsewhere, as I clung to the foolish hope of somehow seeing her again.

Since the end of the rebellion last year, however, she had returned to Normandy, and I had been in Earnford, and slowly, almost without my realising it, the memory had faded from my mind. I had found Leofrun, and in so doing had forgotten about Beatrice. Forgotten, that was, until now.

Of course Robert knew none of this. No one did, except his sister and myself, and I trusted that she would not have mentioned our tryst to anyone.

'She's travelling with Fitz Osbern's conroi,' Robert said. 'They were due to leave yesterday morning. She's probably waiting for us in Scrobbesburh even now. I meant to tell you sooner, but with everything that happened there wasn't the time. Why did you think I was the one who brought you the summons, rather than one of Fitz Osbern's messengers? She's the reason I'm here in the Marches.'

I'd assumed he had been visiting relations or some of his vassals who lived in these parts: private business, at any rate, which it was not my place to know.

'What do you mean, lord?'

'She's to be married again, or so we hope.'

At those words I felt a pang in my heart of something unexpected, that I could neither account for nor quite describe. Not love or jealousy, but something else that had no name.

'Married?' I asked. 'To whom?'

Robert was looking straight ahead and so did not seem to notice my disquiet, for which I thanked God.

'To Fitz Osbern's son,' he said. 'I accompanied Beatrice to Hereford so that I could propose the union in person, to strengthen the bond between our two houses.'

Fitz Osbern had several sons, not that I could at that time recall their faces, even though I must have crossed paths with them. Nevertheless, I could see that such a marriage would make for a powerful alliance. Just as Fitz Osbern held sway over much of the south and west of the kingdom, so the Malets were one of the most powerful noble families in the north and the east.

'When?'

'Not for some time,' Robert said. 'Barely had we arrived when the word came that the enemy were gathering their host beyond the dyke. I have spoken privately with Fitz Osbern and he has given his approval to the match, although as yet no formal arrangements have been made. As long as the Welsh continue to threaten the kingdom, I suppose talk of marriage will have to wait.'

I did not know what to say to that, or even what to feel. The thought that she was to be wed was like a weight upon my heart, and that surprised me. I hadn't so much as seen her in over a year, nor at the time had she given any clue as to the depth of her own feelings. And I remembered all too well the instant when her lips had left mine and she had twisted away from my embrace: as if she were somehow ashamed. In the months that followed I'd often dwelt upon that moment, and the more I did so, the easier it had been to put her out of my mind.

'What about you?' Robert said, breaking me out of my thoughts. 'You must have considered taking a wife, fathering sons to continue your line.'

'I have Leofrun.'

'That's not what I mean,' he said. 'We all have needs, and there is no shame in fulfilling them. However much you enjoy her company, though, she's hardly of noble stock.'

'She is my woman.' For some reason I felt defensive, even though there was truth in what he said. Even if the child Leofrun carried turned out to be a boy, he would not necessarily be able to inherit, being bastard-born.

Robert shrugged as if indifferent. 'It's none of my business, I'm certain.'

'I'm married to my sword,' I said. 'For now that's enough for me.'

Except that it wasn't. Even as the words left my lips I realised how false they were. As much as I cared for Leofrun, a part of my heart still yearned for another, a woman who had been dead for a year and more. And then there was Beatrice, who ever since I'd first met her had frustrated and intrigued me in equal measure. The nearer we grew to Scrobbesburh, the nearer I was to her, and the more anxious I became. For this would be the first time our paths had crossed since that kiss, when so much had changed.

Six

We reached Scrobbesburh at dusk. The castle was the first thing we saw, the whitewashed timbers of its tower and palisade gleaming in the late sun and dazzling us even from several miles away. The Saverna curved around in a great circle here, almost turning back on itself, and the castle stood at the neck of the loop that it made, overlooking the river and the wharves which ran along its banks. I saw merchant ships, their crews busy unloading whatever goods they had brought upstream, from Wirecestre and Glowecestre and places more distant than that: from Normandy and Dyflin and even Denmark, I didn't wonder.

The western skies were burning orange, fading to a pinkish hue where feathery wisps of cloud drifted slowly overhead. On the almost-island which lay inside the river-loop were encamped the first men who would make up our host. The banks of the Saverna were thick with willows and other trees, but through the gaps between them I glimpsed clusters of tents arrayed around glowing campfires. Smoke wafted across the river on what little breeze there was, and with it came the smell of roasting meat. Men laughed; some sang, though from so far away I could not make out their words, and in any case it was not a tune that I recognised.

'Look,' said Robert. He was pointing to the centre of the camp, where a banner stood suspended between two sturdy poles outside a long pavilion. In the evening glare it was difficult to make out the symbol upon it, but I squinted and then it became clear: the wolf, white as snow, on a field the colour of blood.

Fitz Osbern's device. He had already arrived, then, and presumably that meant Beatrice had too.

'I see it, lord.' I tried to keep the tension from entering my voice, but I could not keep my fingers from tightening around the reins.

This was only the second time I had visited Scrobbesburh since first I'd come to the Marches. Little had changed so far as I could see, except that where before the only approach to the town from the south had been across a narrow ford, now the fast-flowing waters were spanned by the five arches of a newly built bridge. Around it stood storehouses and wattle and thatch hovels where craftsmen worked and tried to sell their wares to passing travellers. Familiar smells wafted towards me: cattle dung and piss that meant a tanner's place was near.

A handful of beggars were waiting by the bridge and we had to slow as they crowded about with outstretched hands and plaintive eyes. They knew that men of the sword like us usually had silver to spare, and unlike many of their kinsmen they were not afraid to approach us, though our swords and our helmets and our polished hauberks should have marked us out as men who were not to be crossed.

Our mounts' iron-shod hooves raised a clatter against the timbers. On the open ground on the opposite bank lay the camp. Several men rose to their feet as we approached; Robert called a greeting to them and in return they lifted their fists and their wooden flasks to the sky.

'The black hawk!' one cried out, recognising the pennon nailed to my lance. 'It's Tancred a Dinant!'

A cheer rose up. Robert was right about my fame going before me, although I hadn't believed it until then. Unsure what else to do, I raised a hand, acknowledging them as we passed by.

Along the riverbank, where the grass was lush and plentiful, paddocks had been marked out with wooden stockades and horses grazed contentedly, or else drank their fill at shallow inlets. In the shade of a broad-bellied oak a dozen men were training with cudgels and wooden practice swords, circling patiently about each other, each one looking for an opening, waiting for his opponent to make a mistake before they came together, raining blows against each other's shields and then backing away once more.

At a guess I would have said there were probably fewer than five hundred fighting men encamped there, with as many horses. It was not much of a host, not yet at any rate, though it would grow as more of Fitz Osbern's vassals arrived over the coming days. Robert had said the summons had gone out all along the borderlands, which meant there could be men coming from as far afield as Ceastre in the north and Estrighoiel in the south. It would take time for them all to muster, and I could only hope that they did so before the Welsh and their English allies began to march.

Ahead, Robert gave a shout, and he spurred his mount into a canter. I turned to see what the noise was about, shielding my eyes against the glare. The flaps to the pavilion were drawn apart, and a figure emerged. She stood beneath the wolf banner, and with the light behind her she was almost entirely in shadow, but it took only a moment for me to recognise her. Her hair shone like filaments of gold, and her face was full of warmth, her cheeks radiant as the sun.

Robert reined in his horse in front of her, leaping down to the ground and striding forwards to throw his arms around her. I followed slowly behind.

'Sister,' he said. 'I'm glad to see you safe.'

'And you, Robert,' Beatrice replied, as they broke off the embrace.

She was exactly as I had remembered, from her large eyes to her milky-pale cheeks and her fair hair, which was bound and all but covered by a wimple. Tall for a woman, she was also slender, with a good figure that it was hard to tear one's eyes from, and delicate features that many men would have given anything short of their lives to hold and to caress. A silver band decorated her wrist, and she wore a simple linen gown, loosely draped in the English fashion and a perfect white in colour.

All of a sudden I was there in her chambers in Lundene again, feeling her pressed against me, the warmth of her breath upon my cheek, the softness of her lips upon mine. I felt that pang again, and tried to bury it, but it would not go away.

'You remember Tancred, don't you?' Robert asked, clapping a hand on my shoulder as I dismounted and joined him.

Smiling, she turned to me. 'Of course,' she said. 'Although it's been some time since we last met.'

My throat was dry all of a sudden and I swallowed to moisten it. 'You look well.'

'As do you,' she said, glancing up and down, from my helmet to my boots. 'You look like a lord.'

'Lord and defender of Earnford,' Robert put in. 'Last month he pursued a Welsh raiding-party for an entire day just to avenge the men they had killed. Ten of the enemy were slain by his hand alone.'

I regarded him with a questioning look. Only last night he had sought to chastise me for my actions, yet now he made light of it.

'Is that so?' Beatrice asked, in a way that left me unsure whether she was impressed by that, or whether she believed it at all.

'He exaggerates, my lady. It was only four.'

Robert laughed. 'You are as modest a man as I have ever known.'

'Not modest, lord,' I said. 'It's the truth, that's all.'

I glanced at Beatrice and her eyes, chestnut-brown, met mine. I gazed into them, searching for I knew not what. Some hint that she acknowledged what had happened between us all those months ago, maybe. But there was nothing.

She turned to Robert. 'Fitz Osbern asked to see you as soon as you arrived. There is some business he wishes to discuss.'

Robert nodded. 'Where is he?'

'At the hall in the castle,' she replied. 'He and the castellan have been in council for the past hour at least.'

'I'll join them straightaway and see what it is he wishes,' Robert said.

'Let me take you to him.' Beatrice gave a flick of her hand, and suddenly I noticed two maidservants waiting behind her at the entrance to the pavilion. One was plump and in her middle years, while the other was younger, probably not more than thirteen or fourteen summers old, with brown hair that fell loosely past her shoulders, and it was she who hastened away.

'Has there been any further word about the Welsh?' I asked Beatrice.

'Nothing yet,' she said. 'At least, not as far as I've heard. But then people rarely think to tell me much about what's happening.'

'Fitz Osbern will know,' said Robert. 'I'll find out from him, and when I do, I'll make sure to tell you.'

The girl returned with a dappled grey mare. Without a word to her, Beatrice took the reins and climbed up into the saddle.

'It has been good to see you, Tancred,' she said. 'I trust it won't be so long before we meet again.'

'I trust not, my lady,' I said.

She smiled once more, warmly but without the affection that I had grown used to. It was as if we had barely met, as if she had forgotten everything that had passed between us, or else buried those memories so deep that they could no longer be raised up. It shouldn't have mattered to me, and yet for some reason it did.

Beside her, Robert had also mounted up. 'I'll be back before long,' he told me. 'Keep a pot of stew and a jug of ale waiting for me.'

With that, brother and sister rode away. I watched them as they made their way from the camp towards the castle on the hill, and I was left standing there alone, numb with a strange sense of hurt and disappointment.

Ansculf was marshalling Robert's men, sending some to take care of the horses while directing others to fill wineskins from the river. Some of Robert's servants had travelled ahead with Beatrice and Fitz Osbern, and had set up camp in a good location, in the lee of a clump of birches not far from the water's edge.

I signalled to Serlo and the others, who were pacing about, stretching their legs. Together we followed Robert's men to their fire, where already a pot of water was boiling. The smell of carrots and fish filled my nose, but I did not feel hungry.

'Start putting those tents up,' I said to my knights as I unhitched my saddlebags from our horses, and then to the twins Snocca and Cnebba: 'Fetch some more wood for the fire.'

We would need it, I reckoned: the wind was rising, changing direction, and the skies were clear. Even though the day had been warm, the night ahead would be a cold one.

Shaking my head to clear it, I got to work.

We retired almost as soon as it was dark. Robert came back from the castle shortly after that, though all I heard was his voice as he bade good night to the few of his men who were still drinking and playing dice in the dying light of the flames. I did not try to get up. By then I was bone-tired and barely able to keep my eyes open. Whatever news he had, it could wait until the morning, I decided, and that was the last thought to cross my mind before at last I fell asleep.

When next I stirred it was still night. Morning was some way off, for the birds had not yet begun to sing. All was silent, and at first I could not work out what had roused me. I strained my ears but could make nothing out, and I was about to roll over and try to get back to sleep, but then I heard movement: the muffled sound of feet upon grass.

Staying as still as I could, hardly breathing, I listened. There was someone just outside the tent, close by the fire, I reckoned, though it was hard to tell. They circled about, moving slowly, softly, as if trying not to be heard. It was unlikely to be any of my men or Robert's, but who else would be lurking around our camp at this time of night?

Whilst on the march we usually slept two men to a tent, except that as a lord and a leader of men I always made sure I had one to myself. Whereas many barons were accustomed to taking whores and camp-followers to their tents, I had not shared mine with anyone since Oswynn. In those days my only bed-companions were my sword, which lay on the blanket at my side, and my knife, which rested beneath the rolled-up cloak I used for a pillow. Slowly, so as not to alarm whoever was out there, I reached for the latter, sliding the blade silently from its sheath. If it came to a fight at close quarters, a short blade was better than a long one.

Trying not to make a sound, I made for the entrance to the tent. The flaps were closed over but not laced up, and I opened them just enough to be able to see through. The stars were out but the moon was behind a cloud; the campfire had died long ago, leaving only gently smoking ash. Of whoever had been here there was no sign. Brandishing my knife in front of me, I ducked my head and ventured out.

The night was indeed cold. I was wearing just my tunic and my trews; I could move more quietly in bare feet and so I left my boots behind. Keeping low, I looked around. Eight tents stood around the fire, of which mine was one, but a few were pitched a short way back from it, and as I rounded the side of my own, I saw a short figure dressed in a black cloak, crouching in the shadows outside Serlo and Pons's tent not half a dozen paces away.

The figure reached for the flaps, and as he did so I rushed forwards. He heard me coming and started to turn, but I was on him before he could do so, dragging him to his feet, reaching one hand around his torso and clamping it across his mouth, while with the other I brought my blade up towards his throat. The steel gleamed softly in the starlight.

He struggled and tried to cry out, but I was by far the stronger and I held firm, wrenching his head back so that the flat of my blade rested against his skin.

'Make a sound and I will slit your throat,' I said.

He couldn't have been much more than a child, and a scrawny one at that, slight of build and half starved too, I didn't wonder. A thief, most probably, or else one of the beggars we had passed by the bridge. Either way he had some nerve if he thought to try to steal from men like us.

'Who are you?' I demanded. 'What are you doing here?'

His breath came in stutters as he shuddered, too afraid to answer, and then those shudders turned to tears as he began to sob.

'Stop crying, boy.' If he thought he was going to get any sympathy from me, then he was sorely mistaken. 'Speak.'

'Don't k-kill me, lord, p-please.'

I froze in surprise. That was a girl's voice. I lowered my knife and spun the child around, and as I did so her hood fell from her head and I saw her face. She was the young maidservant who had been with Beatrice earlier, her brown hair shining in the faint light.

'P-please, lord,' she said, her face streaming with tears, not daring to meet my eyes.

'Why are you here?'

But she was sobbing so much that she did not answer. Still in shock, I didn't doubt. We could not stay here, or someone would soon hear us. With my free hand I grabbed her wrist as I made for the river glittering under the stars. She did not resist, but let me pull her along, until I thought we'd put enough distance between ourselves and the camp that we could talk freely, without having to lower our voices.

'I'm sorry, lord,' she said as soon as we had stopped. 'I didn't know which one was yours. I didn't mean to—'

The words came tumbling out and I raised my hand to quiet her. 'It's all right. I'm not going to hurt you. What's your name?'

She bowed her head. 'Papia.'

'You're one of Lady Beatrice's maidservants.'

She nodded, still trembling, although at least her tears had ceased flowing now.

'Do you know who I am?' I asked.

'Tancred a Dinant,' she said, and I saw a lump form in her throat as she swallowed. 'Seigneur of Earnford and once knight of the Earl of Northumbria, Robert de Commines, may God rest his soul.'

Clearly she knew my face; she must have recognised me from earlier. But my fame was not so widespread that every serving-girl would naturally have heard that I had once served Robert de Commines.

'Did Lady Beatrice send you?'

Again the girl nodded. 'She would meet with you tonight, if you wish to see her.'

'Tonight?'

'Even as I speak she is waiting for you at the church of St Ealhmund.'

That she would send for me so soon seemed more than a little strange. Even as my heart stirred, suspicions were already forming in my mind. How could I know that this wasn't some kind of trick?

'Is she alone?' I asked Papia.

'She is alone, lord.'

Of course it was a pointless question, and that was no answer at all, for it was exactly what she would tell me if this were indeed a ruse designed to trap me.

'We must go now if at all, lord,' the girl said. 'The longer my lady is out, the greater the risk she takes that someone will find her missing.'

I closed my eyes and offered a silent prayer for guidance, but none was forthcoming. The decision was mine to make, and God would not try to sway me.

'All right,' I said. 'Wait here while I fetch my cloak.'

It was not especially cold out, but I could hardly go to meet Beatrice in clothes that were covered in dust from the road, and I had brought no better tunic to wear instead.

I returned to my tent, found the sheath for my knife and buckled my copper-bound scabbard on my waist. I did not know Scrobbesburh, but all towns were dangerous places by night and I wanted to be ready for whatever danger might be lurking. Besides, I felt naked if I went anywhere without some manner of blade with which to defend myself. I lived by the sword, someone had told me once: probably the truest words I had ever heard.

After putting on my boots and my cloak I slipped away again, down to the spot by the river where I'd left Papia. At first I thought she had gone, but then I found her sitting on the ground, her back resting against the trunk of a birch. She stood up as I approached, brushing grass and dirt from her cloak. Her tears had dried and her composure had returned.

'Come on,' I told her. 'Show me the way.'

We headed up the rise towards the maze of shadows and narrow streets, of squat timber houses and long merchants' halls that made up Scrobbesburh. The only sound I could discern was of men laughing and shouting drunkenly on the other side of town, probably out enjoying the many pleasures of the night.

A dark alleyway branched off from the main thoroughfare, and Papia led me down it. Some of those voices were nearer now, and I heard English words as well as French. Dogs were barking and infants, woken by the noise, began to wail. I wondered what the commotion was about. The girl did not stop, though, but hurried onwards, bunching her skirts in her hands, raising them so that they did not trail in the mud and the clods of cattle dung that littered the street. We turned a corner and then I saw the church. Its stone belfry rose before me, so tall that from the top it must be possible to see for miles in every direction.

'Lady Beatrice is waiting inside,' Papia said as we reached the door by the nave. 'I will keep watch here in case anyone comes.'

I nodded but could not speak as I stared at the door: the only thing now keeping me from Beatrice. I felt a lurch in my stomach, of sickness mixed with anticipation. Taking a deep breath, trying to still my beating heart, I grasped the ring that served as a handle, curling my fingers around the twisted rods of cold iron, turning it until I felt the catch lift.

I pushed. The door opened easily, without so much as a murmur, and before I could think twice, I stepped inside.

Seven

She knelt in front of the altar, her hood drawn back. A small lantern rested on the flagstones beside her, its light falling upon her hair, which shone like spun gold. I pushed the door to behind me, and at the sound of the catch falling into place she glanced over her shoulder. Seeing me, she got hurriedly to her feet, as if startled, nearly knocking over her lantern as she did so.

'Beatrice,' I said.

'I thought you might not come.'

To tell the truth it was not quite the greeting I had been expecting. My footsteps sounded loudly upon the floor-tiles as I crossed the nave towards her. Every heartbeat felt like an eternity.

'You sent for me and so here I am, my lady,' I replied in just as neutral a tone. The blood was pounding in my head, making it hard to think properly. Even now I wasn't entirely sure why I was here. I stopped a few paces short of her. 'Are we safe?'

I glanced about at the painted stone pillars and the arches between them, searching in the shadows of the side aisle flanking the nave for signs of movement. A narrow gallery ran along one wall, where it would be all to easy to hide. Probably I was being over-anxious, but a part of me still wondered whether this was a snare and I was the unwitting victim who had fallen into it. Even were that not the case, I couldn't shake the feeling that we were being watched.

'Of course we're safe,' Beatrice said. 'Do you take me for a fool? Only Papia knows that we are here, and she will say nothing of this to anyone.'

'Can you be sure of that?' I asked, though even as I did so

I realised it was too late. The time for those kinds of questions had passed.

'She is the most loyal of all my maidservants,' Beatrice replied indignantly. 'I trust her as far as it is possible to trust anyone on this earth.'

I had the feeling that she had said something much like that before, when I had last seen her back in Lundene all those months ago, though I could not recall exactly.

'You clearly have faith in the girl,' I said. 'She is little more than a child, yet you sent her into an army camp by night. Didn't you think what might happen if someone else found her before me?'

She had been lucky indeed, for if I hadn't woken when I did, then things might have been very different.

'Questions would have been asked, I know,' she said. 'Still, I would have found some way to answer them.'

'There would have been more than questions.' Most knights were men of honour, but for every dozen of them there was bound to be one who, depraved or drunk enough, would not think twice about forcing himself on a girl like Papia, no matter her age.

'You would rather I hadn't sent her, then?' Beatrice said, rounding on me. 'I did what I did because I had to.'

I frowned. 'Because you had to?'

She looked away, suddenly embarrassed. 'Besides,' she said hurriedly, 'no harm has been done, and you are here.'

I had not come here to begin a quarrel, yet that was what I had found.

'Why did you send for me, my lady?'

She looked away, towards the altar. In place of the white gown she had been wearing earlier, she had on a dark blue one under a black cloak trimmed with fur: the better for blending into the night. In that respect at least she had come prepared.

'I had to speak with you,' she said. 'To tell you, although perhaps by now you have already heard the news. I don't know when it will be. Perhaps not for some weeks or even months yet, with everything that's happening. Fitz Osbern has agreed to Robert's proposal—'

'I know,' I said with some impatience. 'Robert told me so himself.'

Stung by my interruption, she turned to face me again, and as the faint light of the lantern-flame shone upon her face I saw tears glistening in the corners of her eyes. Yet she was the one who, in Lundene last year, had turned her back on me. In that moment I realised that whatever her reason for bringing me here tonight, I was not prepared to play these games with her. What love I might have felt for her had been fleeting, sincere at the time but now diminished, a ghost of what it once was.

'It's been more than a year since I last saw you,' she said. 'You could have come back after Eoferwic. Why didn't you?'

'Why?' I choked back a laugh. 'You are the sister of my lord. Is that not enough of a reason?'

'That didn't stop you before.'

That was true. I had been stupid, and so had she. As in many ways we both were this very night, merely by being in this place together.

'If we were discovered it would bring disgrace upon the both of us,' I said, although doubtless it would be worse for her than for me. 'You know this now, just as you knew it then.'

Even now I kept thinking that someone would come upon us. It wouldn't have been difficult for someone to follow us here if they had been careful: this town had so many dark corners in which one could hide. If anyone found out we had met here, word would soon get back to Robert, and what might happen then didn't bear dwelling upon.

Knowing that I was right, she gazed down at the floor-tiles, shaking her head. She had come here holding on to the faintest of hopes, without knowing whether or not they would be fulfilled; without knowing how I would respond. She had taken a chance in more ways than one.

'It's strange,' she said quietly. 'You're exactly as I remember you and yet somehow different.'

Whether she meant that as an observation or a slight, I wasn't sure, although I could see the truth in it. She might have changed little, but I was not the same person as I had been that day in Lundene. Back then it had been only a short while after Dunholm, where I had lost everything. My lord, my woman and many of my closest comrades had been killed, and without them, without my sword and my horse and my silver, I was nothing. Little more than a year later, however, I had land and a hall and knights of my own. Whereas before I'd had naught to lose and all to gain, now the opposite held true.

I sighed, not knowing what to say. Somehow I had to tell her that this could not go on, that what had once passed between us was now faded into memory, yet the glimmer of affection I still held for her was enough to give me pause while I considered my exact words.

'Beatrice—'

Before I could continue, a piercing noise from outside broke the stillness: a noise that sounded for all the world like a scream. At the same time there were men's voices, laughing and shouting loudly enough to wake the whole town. My hand instinctively reached for the knife-hilt at my waist as I turned towards the door, expecting it to open at any moment, waiting for men to come charging in with swords in hand, but they did not.

'Papia,' Beatrice whispered, and there was fear in her eyes.

Someone must have followed us, I thought, and now they had found the girl. I cursed myself for not having been more careful even as, blade already in hand, I rushed to the door and flung it open, searching out into the night.

I saw them straightaway. There were five of them, some forty or so paces down the street, barely more than shadows in the darkness. And in their midst I glimpsed the smaller form of the maidservant. She was on the ground, desperately lashing out with her fists and her legs as they tried to pin her down. Two of them were trying to tear her dress from her, while another stood over her, unlacing his braies. The others looked on, swigging from flagons and leather bottles, jeering at the girl and shouting insults in French.

Even as I stood there, feet rooted to the ground as I tried to work out what to do, Beatrice was pushing past me. She darted out into the street, almost tripping over her skirts, shouting her maidservant's name. Almost as one, the men heard her and turned, some of them already casting aside their flagons and reaching for their weapons.

'Beatrice!' I shouted. I broke into a run after her, gripping my knife-hilt firmly, my feet pounding the soft earth. After a few paces I had caught her, grabbing her waist to hold her back.

'Papia,' she called, trying to wriggle free from my hold, but I was too strong for her and she soon gave up.

The girl was on the ground still, though now that the men's attention was elsewhere she was backing away in crab fashion, pulling her skirts back down over her legs, trying to regain her modesty.

'Who's this, then?' their lord shouted, and I took him for such not just because he had spoken first but also because of the gold rings which adorned his fingers. 'Another man and his whore?'

They looked drunk, and not entirely steady on their feet, but that did not mean they were any less dangerous. Ale dulled men's sword-skills but it also made them more reckless and unpredictable, and I knew from experience that a man with little regard for his own life could be a fearsome foe.

'Stay away from the girl,' I called back. 'Otherwise you'll have my blade to answer to.'

How I planned to take on five men on my own I didn't know, but I could hardly stand by and do nothing, and besides my blood was rising, my sword-hand itching.

'You hear that?' the lord said. 'He thinks he can fight us!'

He laughed aloud, and some of the others began to snigger. They were all sizes and shapes, I saw now as they came out into the middle of the street: short and tall, some broad-shouldered and squat, others rangy and long-limbed. All had swords, which meant they were almost certainly knights, yet none was wearing anything more than a loose tunic and trews. Five well-aimed blows was all it would take to fell them. I hoped it would not come to that.

'Tancred,' Beatrice said. She placed a hand on my shoulder but I shook it off as I strode forward, passing my knife into my left hand and pulling my sword free of its scabbard with the other. Rarely did I fight with two blades, but I had no shield or mail or even helmet with which to protect myself, and so I had no choice.

I fixed my gaze on the lord. His face was pitted with pockmarks and lined with the scars of battle, his nose was broken, and his thick eyebrows made his eyes appear mere shadows.

'Leave now,' I said.

I was hoping that they would see sense and realise there was no point in risking their lives. They exchanged glances, but they must have had confidence in their numbers, for they did not move.

Their lord snorted. 'Or what?'

'Or else I will kill every one of you and leave your corpses for the dogs to feed on.'

'You and what army?' he asked, prompting a fresh bout of laughter from his men. 'I suggest that you walk away, friend, unless you enjoy the taste of steel.'

Those who had not already drawn their weapons slid them with barely a whisper of steel from sheaths and scabbards. Blades flashed in the starlight. Barely ten paces separated me from the first of them. If they all came at me together they would soon have me surrounded, and Beatrice as well, with no hope of escape. But I could not back down now. I would not leave Papia to her fate.

'Look at his woman,' one of them said, gesturing with his free hand towards Beatrice. 'She's a fine one. I'd like to plough that furrow.'

'You'll get your chance, Gisulf,' said another, a thickset man with large ears that stuck out from his head. 'I reckon we'd all like a go with her.'

I glanced at Beatrice, who was shrinking back under their stares, slowly retreating towards the church door and the faint orange glow coming from within, though I knew she would find no sanctuary there. It had been a mistake for us to meet here. This whole night had been a mistake from the moment that I had chosen to follow the girl to her mistress, and I had only made it worse by challenging these men. Now they would kill me, and probably Beatrice too once they had finished with her.

'She's certainly a pretty one,' the broken-nosed one called, joining in with the rest of his men. They were enjoying this, I saw. 'Not like the rest of the whores in this godforsaken town. Not like this one either.' He stepped to Papia's side, grabbing her arm just as she was getting to her feet and jerking her off-balance so that she lost her footing and fell on her face in the mud. 'Where did you find her?'

'She's not a whore,' I said, tightening my grip upon my sword-hilt. Anger swelled inside me; my blood was boiling in my veins, and it was all I could do to hold myself back as I waited for the opening, waited for them to let down their guard just for a moment.

'She'll scream like one when I'm inside her,' he replied, smirking as if already picturing it in his mind. 'I'll rut her harder than she's ever been rutted. I'll—'

I didn't give him the chance to finish. In that moment the battle-rage took me, and I was rushing forward, roaring as the bloodlust filled me, thinking only of wiping that smirk from his face.

The first of them stood before me, sword in hand, grinning with the anticipation of easy blood, but I was upon him before he knew it. All he could do was raise his blade to meet mine, and they clashed with a great screech of steel upon steel. Out of the corner of my eye I glimpsed the one they had called Gisulf coming at my flank. Turning the blade, I spun away from the first man, carving the air with my sword-edge. It tore into Gisulf's tunic, slicing across his upper arm, and his weapon fell from his grasp as he clutched at the wound, crying out in pain.

The others were shouting, but I was amongst them now, swinging both my blades in a wide arc about me, to try to keep them at bay.

'I don't want to have to kill you,' I shouted. 'Go now and no one else has to feel my sword-edge.'

They were not listening. One, bolder than the rest, yelled in anger and rushed at me, backhanding a wild, drunken swing towards my head. In doing so he left himself exposed. Ducking easily beneath the path made by his sword-edge, I thrust my knife deep into his thigh, leaving it there as blood, dark and warm and sticky, spurted forth over my hand. At once the man doubled over, and as he did so I landed a kick on his chest, sending him falling backwards. He landed on top of a screaming Papia, who was still on the ground.

'Get up,' I shouted to her. 'Get up!'

The other three formed a ring around me, but having seen two of their companions wounded, they were no longer as confident as they had been. Uncertain whether to keep their distance or to attack, they hesitated, though not for long. Their broken-nosed lord charged, his eyes filled with fury and hatred and thoughts of revenge.

'You'll pay,' he snarled, even as I saw the other two glance nervously at each other. 'You'll pay for what you've done.'

He threw himself at me, his sword flashing across my path. Thinking to come around his flank, I tried to dance to one side, but he was quicker than I had imagined, and I was still in mid-step when his sword-point found my right shoulder. Pain seared through me and I stumbled sideways, my sword falling out of position as with my free hand I clutched at the wound. But I had no time to pause and gather myself as my attacker came at me again.

'Die, damn you,' he said. 'Die, you whoreson!'

Gritting my teeth, I forced myself to lift my blade once more, ready for his next strike and the next and the next, as he began to rain blows upon me. It was all I could do to parry them as he pressed me back towards the houses at the side of the street. My back came up against something hard, and I realised then that I had nowhere to go.

I met his gaze and saw the look of victory in his eyes. He raised his sword high, preparing for one final blow, when from behind there came a cry of agony. Except that this time it did not sound like a girl's scream, but that of a man. It was enough to make their lord hesitate, just for a heartbeat, but it was all the chance I needed. Head down, I barrelled into his lower half, grabbing hold of his tunic and wrestling him from his feet. The street rushed up to meet us, and then together we struck the ground. There was blood in my mouth, and dirt as well, but even as he tried to scramble for his sword-hilt, which lay beyond reach of his outstretched hand, I was getting to my feet again, levelling my blade at his neck.

'Move and I will kill you,' I said.

He froze at once, his eyes wide as he saw the steel and realised that in a single stroke his life would be over. 'Mercy,' he said. 'Mercy, please, I beg of you.'

Breathless, my brow and my underarms running with sweat, I stood in the stillness of night. All I could hear was the thumping of my own heart. Of the other two men who had been left, one lay crumpled in a puddle. Blood pooled around him, flowing from a wound in his side that even at a glance I knew could not be staunched. Papia stood over the body, tears streaming down her cheeks, and in her hand was a knife. My knife, I realised, for I would have recognised it anywhere. She did not move, as if her feet had taken root – in some shock, I didn't wonder, at herself and what she had done.

The last one stood numbly in the middle of the road, his square jaw hanging agape as he glanced first at his dying friend, then at me standing over his lord, then finally at his two injured drinking-companions: the one named Gisulf with the gash to his arm, and the other writhing on the ground, cursing violently as he clutched his wounded thigh.

'Go,' I called to the square-jawed man and to Gisulf: the only two left standing. 'Unless, that is, you want to suffer the same fate as them or see your lord perish.'

Each stared at me as if uncomprehending, then back at their comrades, before finally their senses returned and the two of them fled into one of the narrow alleyways. I heard their footsteps receding into the night, but before long they were gone.

I turned my attention back to their lord. All the man's earlier arrogance had vanished and now he lay at the point of my sword, whimpering, still pleading for mercy.

'Why should I spare you?' I asked him. 'You tried to rape the girl. You tried to kill me.'

He had no answer to that, and instead he closed his eyes, muttering a prayer to God and shivering as he waited for the strike that would end his life. I left him there to lie in the dirt and hurried to Papia's side, carefully taking the knife from her still-shaking hand and wiping its blade on the corpse's cloak before sheathing it. At the same time I was joined by Beatrice, who, now that the danger had passed, had come rushing from the churchyard and threw her arms around the sobbing girl, hugging her tight.

'I'm sorry,' she said as she smoothed down Papia's hair. 'I'm so sorry. Are you hurt?'

Papia shook her head, but I knew it straightaway for a lie. Even if she had not been visibly harmed, she had seen things this night that no woman should ever have to see, and certainly no girl her age. And it was my fault, since it was because of me that she was here in the first place.

I looked away, gripping my shoulder where I'd been struck. I couldn't see the wound but I could feel it, for every time I moved my arm a fresh bolt of pain shot through it.

'You're bleeding,' Beatrice said.

'I'll live.' After all, it could have been much worse: had I been but a fraction slower, my opponent's sword-edge would have found my face or my chest, and I might not be standing here. I tried to put it from my mind.

Dogs barked and I heard voices coming from inside some of the houses. It would not be long before the townsmen mustered enough courage to venture out and see what had happened, and when they did I wanted to be far away from here.

'We can't stay here,' I said. 'Those men will return, and when they do they'll bring others with them.'

At that moment, though, there came a grunt, followed by heavy footsteps, and I turned. The lord had risen to his feet and, brandishing his sword before him, he came slowly towards me, except that he must have come down hard on his ankle when he fell or otherwise have hurt himself in the fight, for he was hobbling.

'Get back,' I said to the two women. 'Behind me, now!'

They did not need telling a second time, but obeyed without question. I fixed my gaze upon the man and his twisted, scarred face, and he stared back at me, his broken teeth clenched.

'It's over,' I said. 'You don't have to fight me. Throw down your sword and I'll let you run.'

He halted about ten paces from me. 'I won't run, you bastard,' he said, and he spat upon the ground. 'Your whore killed one of my men. He did nothing to any of you.'

I almost laughed. It wasn't my fault that they had failed to kill me, nor that that man had wasted his life in pursuit of slaking his lust.

'Take my advice and go,' I said. 'Otherwise I will kill you too.'

He did not listen, but with a howl of rage he rushed towards me, wielding his blade in both hands, his eyes wild with madness as if he were the Devil's own son. He was slowed by his injured leg but I didn't risk making the same mistake as before, instead meeting him face to face. He aimed a cut towards my neck and I raised my sword to parry his, ignoring the protests from my injured shoulder, trusting in the steel not to break as I forced his blade to one side. He stumbled and, as he tried to recover, I suddenly had the opening I needed.

Before he could bring his weapon to bear again I gritted my teeth and lunged forward, thrusting my sword towards his chest. He saw it coming and desperately tried to twist out of the way. It was too late. All at once my blade-point was penetrating cloth and flesh, burying itself in his gut. My attacker screamed out in a greater agony than I could begin to imagine as I twisted the blade and wrenched it free.

Still he clutched his weapon, though he must have known that it was useless to him now. His breath came in stutters as he looked up at me despairingly, then collapsed backwards into a puddle. From down the hill came shouting and the sound of hooves, and as I glanced up I thought I could make out the flicker of lantern-light coming from around the corner, though I was not sure. Men were on their way, at any rate, and I didn't want to have to spill any more blood this night. We could not stay here much longer.

'Who are you?' the man managed, his voice barely more than a croak. He was not long for this life.

I crouched down beside him. 'My name is Tancred,' I said. 'And I am your death.'

He stared back at me, his eyes moist as he saw the last moments of his life slipping by and knew that he would never wield a sword, never feel a woman's touch, never so much as eat or drink or breathe again.

'Do it,' he whispered. 'Make it quick.'

I nodded, lifting my sword in both hands so that I held it like a dagger over his chest, then in one clean blow drove it between his ribs, thrusting it deeper until it found his heart. One final gasp escaped his lips, and then his eyes closed and his head rolled to one side. I wrested my blade free, rising without another glance at him, leaving him there as I bolted back in the direction of the church, to Beatrice and Papia. Those shouts were louder now, closer than before, and if we delayed any further then all this would have been for nothing.

'This way,' I said, sheathing my sword at last, gesturing towards one of the side streets that led back towards the river. 'Quickly!'

Beatrice did not move. She was staring at the bodies which now lay strewn across the way, and I thought she was about to vomit, but I grabbed her hand, tugging her away from there, and then at last she seemed to wake from her thoughts.

'Come on,' I told her. 'Now!'

She did not need telling again, and as I broke into a run, so did she, with Papia not far behind us: the three of us darting through the narrow alleyways, past inns and pig-sheds and crumbling hovels, slipping into the shadows.

Eight

Twice I glanced behind to see if we were being pursued. I saw no one, but nonetheless we kept running until I saw the river ahead, glittering faintly under the light of the stars. By then the cries of panic and the sound of hooves had faded almost to nothing. Now there was only the sound of rats scurrying along the wharfside and on to the boats moored there, the calls of a moorhen disturbed from its sleep, and our own breathing.

We ducked into a narrow alley which ran behind a large storehouse, where we could not be easily spotted from the river. Shipmasters usually left some of their crew behind to guard whatever cargo was left on board, or even defend the boat itself against those who might try to steal it, and I decided it was better that they did not see us.

Even now I could scarcely believe that I was still alive, that we had all three of us managed to escape unharmed. Unharmed, that was, except for the cut to my shoulder. Now that the rush of battle was gone, it had begun to throb: like tiny arrows of fire shooting through my flesh. A trickle of blood ran down my arm and I clutched at it, at the same time glancing out into the street, looking back the way we came. The belfry of St Ealhmund's church stood on top of the hill, rising above the houses, with faint lantern-light flickering across its stonework, and when I stilled my breathing and listened carefully I could make out voices. Mercifully, though, there was no sign of anyone following us.

Relief came over me and I closed my eyes as I leant back against the wall of the storehouse, letting the night's cool air fill my chest, doing my best to ignore the pain. The stink of putrid fish, offal and ox dung filled my nose.

'Here,' said Beatrice, and she pressed a bundle of dark cloth against my shoulder in an effort to stem the flow of blood. I grimaced at the sting but did not pull away. She rolled up my sleeve and began to wipe some of the blood from around the wound. 'Can I use your knife?'

I nodded wordlessly.

'Hold this,' she said and placed my hand on top of the bundle of cloth. I kept it pressed to the wound while she reached down to the sheath on my belt and carefully drew out the blade, which was still covered with blood. Taking her cloak from me, she used the knife to hack a long strip from it to serve as a bandage. Now that I could see the wound better, it did not look nearly as bad as I had imagined, though knowing that did nothing to ease the pain. First folding it so that it formed a double layer, Beatrice passed the bandage under my arm and then tied the two ends together, tightly enough that it would bind the gash and, at the very least, keep it from bleeding further.

'Thank you,' I said when she had finished.

'Will you be all right?'

'I'll be fine,' I said, grimacing in spite of myself as another bolt of agony stabbed through my shoulder.

'I can't afford to stay out any longer,' she said. 'We have to get back before we're missed. If anyone were to notice that I'm gone . . .'

She did not finish, but I knew what she was thinking. At the very least there would be talk: about what she was doing out so late and by herself, with only her maidservant to help protect her.

'I'll come with you,' I said. 'The streets aren't safe.'

'No, it's better if you don't. We can't risk being seen together.'

It was a little late to be worrying about that, I thought. Indeed, if she had made that decision an hour ago, then she would not have sent the girl to me in the first place; I would still be asleep in my tent and two men would not have lost their lives in needless bloodshed.

I was too tired to argue, though. I needed to find water or, better, spirits to put on the gash, and the sooner the better. A slight cut such as it was would heal by itself without any need for stitches, but I had to keep it clean.

She took my hand in hers, squeezing it tenderly, and I realised that with everything that had happened, I'd failed to divest her of this notion that there could exist something between us. Before I could say anything, though, she had let go, turning her attention to Papia, who was sitting huddled on the ground with her back against a stack of barrels, shivering with cold and with fear, her knees drawn up towards her face, which was buried in her hands. There was blood on her fingers, blood staining her dress.

Beatrice crouched down in front of her. 'We have to go.'

Sobbing, the maidservant shook her head. Her hair fell in disarray over her eyes, and gently Beatrice pushed it aside and hugged the girl tightly to her chest. 'Come,' she said.

This time the girl nodded and got to her feet. Not once did she look at me. Beatrice held her hand as the three of us made for the far end of the alleyway, where it opened out on to one of the main streets.

I glanced out into the road to make sure that no one was watching. One way headed up the hill, towards the heart of the town; the other led back in the direction of the camp. Both were deserted.

'This is where we part, then,' I said.

'Be safe, Tancred.'

'And you, my lady.'

She held my eyes, but only for a moment, before she and the girl were hurrying away up the rutted street. The skies were cloudy and there was little light from either moon or stars. It wasn't long before they had vanished into the night.

I woke the next day to find the sun shining in through the flaps at the entrance to my tent, confusing me, for in my dreams it had been night and I was in my hall at Earnford, with Ædda and Erchembald and all the rest. But then I recalled where we were: Scrobbesburh.

Blinking at the light, I rolled over on to my side, remembering my wound too late. Sharp heat flashed through my shoulder and I clutched at it, wincing and cursing at the same time, and sat up. Thankfully the cut had long since stopped bleeding; the bandage that Beatrice had tied around it had helped see to that. I loosened the knot she had made, hoping to get a better look at the wound now that it was day, though there was not much to see. A narrow line of dried blood ran down my upper arm, about the length of my little finger: proof that last night had been real and I had not just imagined it. Proof that I had fought those men, that I had met Beatrice in the church. I retied the cloth and rolled my sleeve back down, covering it lest anyone should see.

A fire was already burning when I emerged from the tent. Serlo, Turold and Pons were sitting around it, together with Snocca and Cnebba and several of Robert's men, as well as his own servants: resting their shields on their knees and using them as tables, passing around bottles filled with water fetched from the river.

But among all those faces was one I hadn't expected to be there. Someone I hadn't seen in a long time, but whom I recognised at a glance: rangy and long-limbed, with a thin face, thick eyebrows and dark hair.

'Eudo!' I let out a laugh at the sight of my old friend and comrade.

'Tancred,' he said, likewise grinning as he leapt to his feet. 'I was wondering when you'd wake.'

For more than a dozen years we had served the same lord, fought under the same banner in the same conroi. Shoulder to shoulder we had stood in the shield-wall; knee to knee we had ridden alongside each other in the charge. Together we had lived through so many battles that I had long since lost count, and in so doing we had forged a bond stronger even than that of kinship: a bond that could never be broken.

'It's been a while,' he said.

'It has,' I agreed. Indeed the last time I'd seen him was the previous summer, when the king had gathered his host to stand against the great Danish fleet that had been supposed to sail. The fleet that we had been waiting all year for, but which in the end never came. 'What are you doing here?'

'The same as you,' Eudo said. 'I was in Hereford with Lord Robert when we heard the news about the Welsh. We got here the day before yesterday, although my men and I were all out on sentry duty last night, so I didn't hear you'd arrived until this morning.'

He had come with Robert all the way from the other end of the kingdom, then. While I had been given Earnford, both Eudo and Wace had been granted demesnes from Robert's holdings in distant Suthfolc, close to where the land ended and the marshes that bordered the sea began: a region that was no less troubled than these parts, since that coast was often plagued by pirates and raiders from across the German Sea.

'Robert didn't say you were with him,' I said.

Eudo shrugged. 'With everything that's been happening he probably forgot. His mind has been on other things lately: first the arrangements for his sister's marriage, and now the threat from across the dyke. Did you know that Lady Beatrice is to be married again?'

'I had heard,' I said, and it came out more stiffly than I had meant.

Not that Eudo seemed to notice. Even if he had, I doubted he would have made anything of it. 'It's strange to think it's already more than a year since we were all fleeing Eoferwic together,' he said. 'You, me, Wace, the ladies. Malet's chaplain.'

Indeed it was more than a year since the business with Ælfwold: since we had fought him and his hired swords beside the Temes; since he had tried to kill me upon the cliff-top and had fallen to his death. A breaker of oaths, he had remained a treacherous man to the end. Eudo would not speak of any of this openly, of course, yet I knew he was thinking it.

'More than a year since the battle, too,' I added. 'Since Dunholm.'

At once I regretted having said it as Eudo fell quiet. I hadn't meant to darken the mood, though it was difficult to think upon the events of last year and not to remember what had taken place there that cold winter's night.

Eudo was the one to break the silence. 'Still,' he said, sighing, 'after all that, here we are. Soon to ride together once more.'

'Is Wace with you?'

'He was, at least until yesterday. Fitz Osbern sent him ahead to Cestre to bear the summons to Earl Hugues there.'

'He must be worried if he's looking for help from the Wolf,' I said.

'The Wolf?'

'Hugues Lupus,' I explained. 'That's how he's known, here on the March at least. It's Latin.'

It was fitting, too. Hugues d'Avranches, the Earl of Ceastre, was known for his wild nature and his fierce temper, as well as for the brutality with which he dealt with anyone who crossed him: all in all a man to be feared and respected, though it was said he was only twenty in years. As with most bynames, he had first been called the Wolf in jest, but after learning of it he had grown to like it, so much so that he soon adopted the animal as his symbol, much to the anger of Fitz Osbern, whose own banner bore the same device. The two had been at odds ever since, and I took the fact that Fitz Osbern was now calling upon Hugues for aid as a clear sign of how serious he considered the threat posed by the Welsh.

'Did you hear what happened last night?' Eudo asked.

'No,' I said. 'What?'

'Two men were murdered in the town. They were out whoring with three others of their company when they were set upon in the streets. Cut down in cold blood, they were.'

I froze. To hear the tale from someone else's lips was strange to say the least.

'The word is it was the doing of one man alone,' Pons put in. 'Or that's what I've heard anyway.'

'One against five?' asked Turold.

'That's what those who survived say,' Pons replied as he stuffed more bread into his mouth. 'They claim their attacker was lying in wait for them; that he came on them like a shadow out of the night, slew their comrades before they could even draw their swords.'

Serlo snorted in disdain. 'You'd choose to believe the words of cowards? They clearly abandoned their friends to save their own skin. It's exactly the kind of yarn you would expect them to spin.'

'It sounds unlikely, doesn't it?' Eudo agreed. 'Probably they'd been drinking and managed to get into a brawl, and were just unlucky to be on the wrong side.'

My throat was dry. I realised I hadn't yet said anything, and forced myself to speak. 'Did they see their attacker's face?'

'They say not,' Pons replied. 'It all happened too quickly, their heads and bellies were filled with ale, and it was dark besides.'

'Another reason to think they're lying,' Serlo muttered. 'Probably they got into some fight between themselves over a girl, and ended up killing each other.'

'There could be a hundred different explanations,' said Turold. 'Maybe there was money involved, or else the killings were part of some feud that none of them wish to speak about.'

At least it seemed I didn't have to worry about those men recognising me. That thought had been plaguing me in the hours since. Not that I recalled particularly what they looked like either, apart from the one named Gisulf, with the large ears, so it wasn't as if I could even take much care to prevent our paths crossing.

'Whatever happened and whatever the reason behind it, Fitz Osbern is furious,' Eudo said. 'He's ordered all the bawdy houses closed to stop something like this happening again.'

'Who knows?' Pons said, with a mischievous look in his eyes. 'There could be a rogue killer lurking in our midst, waiting to strike again even as we speak. It might be anyone. Maybe he's sitting with us right now.' He glanced about mock warily, before his gaze eventually settled on Serlo, who was sitting next to him, and he grinned. 'Maybe his name is Serlo.'

The big man scowled back at him. 'I know who I'd stick my knife in first, if he doesn't shut his mouth soon.' He lifted an end of cheese from his shield and threw it at Pons, who raised a hand to defend himself, in vain as it turned out, for it hit him on the cheek.

'Hey,' he said. 'I don't want your mouldy food.' He retrieved the end and hurled it back, striking Serlo in the eye before he could turn away.

'What was that for?' the other man said, rubbing the spot where the cheese had hit him.

'Because you're a humourless goat-turd who doesn't know a joke when it hits him in the face, that's what.'

Straightaway Serlo flung himself at Pons, sending their shields with their knives and bread and lumps of cheese clattering to the ground. Grabbing hold of the other's shoulder, he tried to wrestle him to the ground, but Pons was too quick for him, twisting free so that even though Serlo's hand was still on his collar, it was he who was on top and pinning the big man.

'Do you give up yet?' Pons asked as he pressed down on Serlo's neck.

'Hardly.' Serlo gritted his teeth and rose, using all his great strength to throw Pons off him. Each holding the other's tunic, they rolled through a puddle towards a clump of blackberry bushes. The rest of the men scrambled out of the way, cheering one or the other on, calling to their friends nearby to come and watch, and suddenly there were twenty, thirty men pushing forward, trying to get a better view of the tussle.

'Should we do something?' Eudo asked.

'Let them be,' I said as first Serlo and then Pons found themselves amongst the brambles, much to the laughter of all those who had gathered. Between the curses I heard the ripping of cloth, but still neither of them would give in.

As long as I had known him Pons had been the most restless of all my knights, and when there was no fighting to be done he often liked to provoke his sword-brothers. In particular he seemed to enjoy baiting Serlo, who, far from being the dour soul that others often took him for, had something of a playful streak to his character, and was usually all too eager for a fight if one came looking for him.

A boy of no more than thirteen pushed past me, trying to edge his way towards a better view. There were now so many men in front of me that even though I could hear Serlo and Pons I could no longer see them. Still, I had watched them brawl before, and I was fairly certain this wouldn't be the last time either.

'Anyway,' Eudo went on, 'I didn't come here to spread rumours. There are enough of them as it is, if not about the Welsh or the ætheling, then about the Danes.'

'The Danes?' I echoed. That was new information to me, though of course Eudo, with his hall by the wind-battered coast on the other side of the kingdom, would have better sources than I. Not only that, but he would have an interest in knowing what was happening across the sea, since his lands were among those most vulnerable should any ship-band ever come raiding.

'We don't know much for certain,' Eudo said. 'Still, the merchants who frequent those ports have been telling us that the order has gone out from King Sweyn for his fleet to assemble once again, and that he means to sail this autumn.'

After his plans to invade last year had come to nothing, I had assumed that Sweyn had given up pursuing his claim to the English crown. But perhaps the schisms within the royal household and the squabbling between the jarls – his warlords and noblemen – that together had prevented him leaving his kingdom last year were now resolved, or were less severe than many had been saying. Or else those same warlords had heard tell of what was happening else-where in England and were now swayed by the prospect of easy plunder: eager all of a sudden for silver, for adventure, and for the chance to win renown in foreign lands.

The men who had crowded to watch Serlo and Pons gave another cheer as the two of them emerged from the brambles, having clearly decided to make a truce at last. Their tunics were torn and covered in leaves and grime and thorny twigs, and each had taken cuts and grazes to his face and arms, but they were both grinning widely, no doubt enjoying the attention.

Gradually the crowd began to return to their own campfires, and I turned back to Eudo. 'How much do you trust these merchants?'

'Not a lot,' he admitted. 'But some are more reliable than others, and we've been hearing much the same stories for weeks now, so there's likely to be some truth in them.'

First the Northumbrians, then the Welsh, and now it sounded like the Danes as well. If what Eudo was saying turned out to be true, I didn't see how we could fight them all. A shiver passed through me in spite of the warmth of the morning, and I had a hollow feeling in my stomach.

'Not that any of this is likely to happen for some months yet,' Eudo went on, more brightly. 'If it happens at all. And anyway, in the meantime we have other battles to fight first.'

Other battles, other enemies. I glanced around us at the sea of tents, at the banners in all their colours fluttering as the wind rose, at the sheep and the cattle in their pens, at the chickens that some lords had brought to help feed their retinues, darting about in pursuit of the seed being thrown to them. At the many scores of men who had gathered with their swords and their shields, their spears and their helmets and their hauberks of mail, ready to test their sword-arms against the enemy.

Already it was a formidable host, and of course hundreds more would come in the days to follow as Hugues the Wolf and others responded to Fitz Osbern's call to arms. Yet even as I gazed across the camp, I could not stop doubt from creeping into my mind. For the first time I began to wonder if it would be enough.

Nine

The days grew hotter and tempers became ever more frayed as we waited for the rest of Fitz Osbern's barons to respond to the summons, for the Wolf to arrive from Ceastre and Wace with him. Men always grow restive when they have nothing to do, and never was that more true than when speaking of men of the sword. Over the week that followed I could sense a growing agitation amongst our army. Almost every day fights broke out: by the wharves, on the streets, in the alehouses and even at times in the middle of the camp itself; sometimes between English and Norman but more often between Frenchmen themselves.

I often likened the March to a patchwork made from scraps of land from hundreds of different lordships, stitched together by grants made in charters and writs, by oaths and by a common desire to keep out the Welsh who threatened their lands. Such a patchwork, however, was only as strong as the threads that joined its various pieces, and since those threads were woven from words alone, they were easily broken. While many of the holdings belonged to newly endowed men like myself, who had won their lordships in the years since the invasion, by and large those who held greatest influence on the borderlands belonged to the old families of Normandy: lineages which in more than a few cases harked back as far as the days of Charlemagne, who had been king of the Franks some two and a half centuries before. They saw the newcomers as troublesome and ambitious upstarts, hungry for wealth and adventure and power, and as such not to be trusted. In return they were greeted with, if not hostility, then at the very least frosty indifference.

Now that both sides were brought together in one place, though, their petty squabbles and jealousies boiled over into open confrontation. A dozen men were killed in that week alone; on one particular morning three bodies were found floating face-down in the river, so bloated with water that their features were unrecognisable and no one was able to say who they were. Still more were injured: one man lost his hand when a brawl over a game of dice ended in swords being drawn; another was badly burnt when he was pushed into a brazier for lying with someone else's woman; and others I had witnessed and heard of were missing ears and fingers in retribution for slights both real and imagined.

Amongst my own men, too, tension was growing. At first it was nothing more than the usual exchange of snide remarks and lewd jokes at each other's expense: the sort of thing that I had long since grown used to. But all too soon the thrill of at last being on campaign and amongst fellow warriors wore off, and it became ever harder for them to hold their tongues. Even I had to fight hard to restrain the resentment simmering within me: resentment towards Robert, towards Guillaume fitz Osbern, but most of all towards the Welsh, whose fault it was that we had been dragged here. We had left Earnford in such a rush, yet until Fitz Osbern decided what should be done, we could only sit on our backsides and wait. Altogether it only served to put me more on edge, and over those few days I confess I was not an easy man to be around.

To that Eudo would also attest, after I nearly took his head off in a training fight. We were using oak cudgels rather than swords, but even so a blow from one of those could hurt if it struck home; I knew from experience. When Eudo followed too far through a stroke, instinct took over. While he struggled to recover, I saw my chance, backhanding a swing towards his head with all the strength I could muster. He saw it coming just in time to twist and duck beneath it, losing his balance and landing on his face in the mud, prompting sniggers from those who happened to be watching.

Cursing, he got to his feet, ignoring the hand I extended to help him up, and stood red-faced before me. 'God's teeth, Tancred. Are you trying to kill me?'

'Are you hurt?'

'I'll live, though no thanks to you.' He spat on the ground, his face twisted into an expression of distaste, and he wiped some of the dirt from his cheek, rubbing it on his tunic and his trews.

'I don't know what I was thinking.'

'Well, next time think harder. The way you came at me, anyone would think it was Eadgar Ætheling you were fighting.'

The sun was almost upon the horizon by then and Eudo wasn't in the mood to fight any more, so we left the practice yard, making our way past paddocks where the horses grazed contentedly, towards the black and gold. Carts drawn by teams of oxen trundled past, laden with hay or barrels of ale and bundles of straw. The smell of stewed vegetables and roasting meat drifted on the breeze. From down by the river floated the soft notes of a flute, soon joined by drunken voices singing a song of distant lands.

'I'm frustrated, that's all,' I said as we walked. 'The longer we stay here, the worse it gets. Sometimes I wish the Welsh would attack now, if they're going to come at all.'

'What you need is to feel the warmth of a good woman,' said Eudo. 'That'll soon see to your frustration. Fitz Osbern might have ordered the stews closed but if you go with good silver to some of the alehouses they'll see that your needs are satisfied. There's one not far from the town gates where the girls are pretty and none too expensive either.'

'The cost isn't what worries me,' I said. 'It's more your idea of pretty. Last time I remember ending up with a great sow of a girl who smelt as if she hadn't washed in about ten years.'

He laughed. 'You always did have an eye for the slim ones. I'll keep a lookout next time I'm there and see if there are any you might like.'

'In any case,' I said, 'what happened to Censwith?'

Of all the girls Eudo had known, she was the only one he had kept going back to; the very fact that he had often spoken of her by name marked her out. As long as I had known him he had never cared much for matters of the heart, and I had thought nothing about it at the time, but since Eoferwic last year he had often spoken of buying her freedom from the man in Sudwerca who owned her, and even of taking her for his wife.

'She died is what happened,' Eudo said. 'Caught a fever last spring and never recovered. I saw her for the last time as she lay on her deathbed. I'll never forget how weak she looked and how fragile, though I'm not sure she even recognised who I was.'

'I'm sorry.' I could not think of anything else to say.

Eudo sighed. 'I never did get the chance to free her. Still, if there are whorehouses in heaven then I hope to find her there someday.'

I rested my hand on his shoulder in sympathy. We were nearing the great pavilion when from behind came the blast of a war-horn. I turned to see a column of men approaching on the other side of the river but making for the bridge, towards our camp: several hundred of them, most riding what looked like short draught horses or else sturdy ponies, and flying a banner I did not recognise, depicting a yellow-gold serpent on a green field.

'Whose device is that?' Eudo asked.

'I'm not sure.' It didn't belong to Earl Hugues; that much was certain. In fact I couldn't think of any of the Marcher lords who used a snake as their device. To be able to raise a host numbering in the hundreds such as they had brought, they must hold a great deal of power, with estates and vassals spread across several shires. And yet were that the case then I was fairly certain I would have heard of them before now.

They halted on the open ground on the approach to the river; again their horns sounded. A few dismounted and waved to the knights guarding the crossing, who had already formed a shield-wall several men deep across the bridge in case they should try to attack. It did not look to me as if they had come to fight, though, but rather as if they were requesting a parley.

Two of them rode forwards from the ranks with their banner-bearer a short way behind them, waving the green and yellow flag high for all to see. From so far away it was hard to make out much, but even so I could see that both men had come dressed for war, with sword-hilts inlaid with glittering rubies, helmets with nasal-pieces and cheek-plates inlaid with shining gold. Evidently they were men of some wealth, and they were not afraid to flaunt it either.

'Fitz Osbern,' one of them called out, cupping his hands around his mouth. 'We wish to speak with Fitz Osbern!'

His French was halting, as if it were not his natural tongue, and I wondered if they were Englishmen: some of those thegns, perhaps, who had submitted to King Guillaume instead of continuing the struggle in the weeks after Hæstinges. In return for being allowed to keep their lands they were required to fight against their countrymen, and they often joined us on campaign, though as turncoats they were held in little regard, and the oaths they had given were seen by many as less than worthless. But their names and the colours of their banners were commonly known, and the golden snake was not one of them.

Fitz Osbern was not in his pavilion and a message had to be sent to the castle where he was in council with the castellan – a kinsman of his by the name of Roger de Montgommeri, who was also a vicomte in Normandy – as well as some of the other nobles, Lord Robert among them. It was some time before he appeared but eventually I spied him, and I knew it was him because of his balding pate and greying hair. He rode at the head of a score of mailed knights to meet the two men upon the bridge. What was said I could not make out, but they knelt down before him, removing their gilded helms and bowing their heads. After a while Fitz Osbern motioned them to their feet and the two men, each accompanied by a dozen spearmen, followed him on horse to the castle.

'They're Welshmen,' Robert told us when he returned a few hours later.

'Welshmen?' I echoed, disbelieving. I could see that I spoke for everyone else warming themselves by the dwindling campfire too. 'What do they want with Fitz Osbern?'

'They've come to join us, or so they say. Their names are Maredudd and Ithel; they're the sons of the great King Gruffydd who used to hold sway over all of Wales, until he was overthrown and slain by the hand of a certain Harold Godwineson some seven years ago.'

'Harold the usurper?' asked Turold.

'The very same,' Robert replied. 'Although this was long before he seized the crown, when he was merely earl of Hereford and Wessex, although he was a powerful man even then. They say that the kingdoms of Powys and Gwynedd belong to them by right; that they were deprived of their inheritance by the brothers Bleddyn and Rhiwallon whom Harold set up as rulers in the wake of his campaign.'

'I don't like it,' I said. 'If they truly wanted to win back their inheritance then why have they waited seven years before finally marching?'

'Until recently it seems they lacked the support of the other highborn families,' Robert replied. 'But since Bleddyn and Rhiwallon made common cause with the exiled English thegns it seems that there has been growing discontent. Many of those families remember Harold's campaign and the slaughter that the English visited upon their lands. Many lost their homes and their sons to the sword-edges of those same men who now seek help from them.'

'Any enemy of the usurper is surely a friend of ours,' put in Turold. 'As long as they bring men, what does it matter?'

At the very least I supposed they were taking away men who might otherwise have filled out the ranks of the enemy shield-wall. But though I could well believe the extent of their hatred for the English, it was hard to imagine they would simply swear their allegiance to another foreign lord without some design of their own.

'There must be more to it than that; some other prize on offer,' I said. 'Otherwise why would they take up arms against their own countrymen and in doing so risk losing the lands they already hold?'

'You're quite right,' said Robert. 'In return for them bringing their men to fight under our banners, Gruffydd's sons want nothing less than our help in regaining their birthright and restoring their titles to them.'

Serlo spluttered; droplets of wine dribbled down his chin and he dried it on his sleeve. 'For the sake of a few hundred spears they would have us deliver them an entire kingdom?'

'Two kingdoms,' Pons said sourly. 'Powys and Gwynedd both.'

Of course if Maredudd and Ithel succeeded, then those who had sided with them would be generously rewarded. Not only must they have great faith in Gruffydd's sons, then, but they must be very confident too that we would accept their price, steep though it was.

'Fitz Osbern will never agree to that,' Serlo muttered. 'Only a fool makes a bargain with a Welshman. They have no sense of honour; they're oath-breakers, every one of them.'

Usually I would have sided with Serlo; experience of living on the March this past year had taught me to trust the Welsh even less than the English. But at the same time I understood that this was about far more than just inheritance or power. For if Fitz Osbern could ensure that the rulers across the dyke were friendly to us, sworn to him personally through the giving of hostages and by oaths of fealty, and that they paid tribute to King Guillaume, then we might never need to fear raids by the Welsh again. At a time when the realm was beset with threats on all sides, it would give us the respite we sorely needed to quell our other enemies.

'If it can buy us peace on the March, maybe that's a bargain worth making,' I said. 'Even if that peace lasts only for a while. And God knows we need the men.'

We had been in Scrobbesburh five days already; in that time we had received no word from Ceastre, and I knew that Fitz Osbern was growing anxious about whether Earl Hugues would come at all. Nor had the spies he had sent to scout the lands beyond the dyke yet returned, which meant we had no way of knowing how soon it would be before the enemy marched in force.

'I don't trust them,' Serlo said. 'Who's to say their coming here isn't part of some ruse designed to trap us?'

'Why go to so much trouble, though?' I asked him. 'Why bring such an army all this way if there's a chance that Fitz Osbern will just send them away?'

Serlo gave a shrug but didn't answer. Instead he said: 'I'll tell you what's going to happen. First they'll try to worm their way into our confidence and then at the first chance they get they'll turn on us. Far better for Fitz Osbern to kill them now and be done with it.'

'In that case,' Robert said sharply, 'it's probably as well that the decision rests with him and not with you.'

Indeed, for the time being at least Fitz Osbern seemed willing to trust them, since in spite of the open displeasure of several of the leading barons, Maredudd and Ithel were allowed to stay, setting up their camp at his direction on the other side of the river where there was less chance of their men clashing with our own, most of whom held the Welsh in as little regard as Serlo and were all too ready for a fight.

Still, they did not have too long to wait for better news. It came the next day in the form of Hugues d'Avranches, the Wolf of Ceastre, whose black banner and pennons were first sighted approaching on the northern road around midday. He arrived at the head of a contingent of fifty knights and another one hundred and twenty foot-soldiers, with many more due to follow in the days to come as his vassals and tenants left their feasting-halls and rode out from their strongholds.

Accompanying him was Wace together with his three household knights. It was the first that I had seen of him since the previous summer, although he had not changed much in that time. Indeed he was as I had always known him: broad-shouldered and thickset, with arms like a smith's. Below his eye was the scar from the blow that he had taken at Hæstinges, which had left him able only to half open it, though he could still see nearly as well as before. Well enough, at least, that he had sent countless foemen to their deaths in the years since.

'You should see a barber,' were his first words when he saw me. 'With all that hair you look like one of them.'

He meant the English, of course, and straightaway I found myself on edge. But then Wace often had a way of doing that to people: it was the sort of remark that was typical of him, and I should have known better than to expect anything else. His blunt manner had often brought him trouble over the years, not to mention Eudo and myself as well at times. Together the three of us had grown up, trained at arms and learnt the art of horsemanship; together we had fought our first battles and ridden on campaign across the length and the breadth of Christendom. And now of all the knights who had once served beneath the hawk banner of Robert de Commines, the one-time Earl of Northumbria, we three were the only ones left alive.

'We were wondering when you'd arrive,' I said. 'There was talk that the Wolf might ignore the summons altogether.'

'He's not here out of any especial loyalty to Guillaume fitz Osbern, that much is for certain,' Wace replied in his usual flat tone. 'He made us wait two full days and nights before he eventually came to a decision. I was starting to think he'd never give us an answer and that we'd have no choice but to return without him.'

Despite Hugues's youth he was evidently far from guileless. He knew that the tale would spread, and in refusing to respond to the summons immediately he was making a clear assertion of his power. I suspected that Fitz Osbern would not be best pleased when it reached his ears, though in truth there was little he could do about it. He was wise and experienced enough to understand that they did not have to like each other as individuals, so long as their men could be trusted to stand shoulder to shoulder in the shield-wall and protect each other's flanks in the charge; that was all that mattered. Kingdoms had been won and lost before on little more than the strength of the bond between those fighting on one side or the other, and there was no sense in further kindling the flames of their quarrel if that led to ruin on the field of battle.

'I'm surprised he came at all,' Eudo said. 'There's no love lost between those two.'

Wace's face was grim. 'To tell the truth, I don't think it was an easy decision for Earl Hugues to make. The same rumours about the Welsh have been heard in Ceastre; they fear an attack by the men of Gwynedd along the coast. Earl Hugues has had to leave several hundred men to garrison the city.'

That was a setback, certainly, though I supposed he had little choice when his own earldom was at risk. No one could say yet what the enemy planned, and I supposed that by gathering all his forces in one place Fitz Osbern hoped to be prepared for whatever happened, since he could not hope to defend the entire length of the March at once.

After a while talk moved on from news of the Welsh. I asked Wace about his manor in Suthfolc and he introduced me to his men, who were busying themselves setting up tents and building a fire close by the black and gold. But all the while my thoughts kept returning to Earl Hugues and his fears of attack upon his lands. For as concerned as the Wolf was for Ceastre, so I was for Earnford. I wondered how Father Erchembald was managing in my absence, and how Ædda was faring under his care. I supposed that if anything had happened that was worth hearing about, news of it would already have reached us. But then again, if the enemy moved quickly enough, we might not know until it was too late. All I could do was pray that no harm would come to them, and pray too that I would be able to keep the promise I had made.

Ten

I t rained that night, rained so hard that the gutters outside the houses overflowed and the winding streets of Scrobbesburh ran like rivers, carrying dirt and fragments of straw mixed with cattle shit. The drops bounced off the cobbles in the market square; they pooled in the cart-tracks along the shambles, in one place forming a vast lake that we had no choice but to ride on through, our horses' hooves kicking up mud and the putrid remains of whatever animals had been slaughtered there that day. All the while the wind lashed at the town with furious gusts, threatening to tear the thatch from the roofs, to lift trees from their very roots. Branches creaked as Wace and Eudo and I passed beneath them, the three of us riding in single file through the narrow ways towards the castle and the timber hall huddled within the protection of its walls.

Almost one hundred barons had already gathered there by the time we had seen to our horses and entered, our cloaks and tunics sodden, our trews clinging to our legs and our hair plastered against our heads. The musty smell of damp cloth mixed with sweat hung in the air. A peat fire was smouldering in the hearth while in the middle of the floor stood a charcoal brazier. Several men were gathered around them, trying to dry themselves. Others sat on benches around the edge with wine-cups in hand, making subdued conversation, no doubt sharing the latest rumours they had heard while they waited for Fitz Osbern and Earl Hugues to appear.

Some of those faces I recognised from previous campaigns or else from times when our paths had crossed at the king's court, even if I did not know them by name. But there were many more

I hadn't seen before, and that was no wonder, since by then it seemed that almost the entire March was in Scrobbesburh. Certainly all its foremost men were in that hall: young and old, seasoned warriors and richly dressed nobles, sword-brothers and rivals alike. A low murmur filled the air, lifting to the rafters along which mice scuttled, flickers of grey in the gloom, disturbed by the rain and by the presence of so many men. Though not much larger than my own hall at Earnford, in decoration it was far grander, with tapestries and hangings upon the wall in stripes of white and pear green: the colours of the castellan.

I looked for Robert, but perhaps he had been called upon to confer privately with Fitz Osbern and Earl Hugues, for I could not see him. Servants hustled through the throng, bringing hot food out on wooden platters from the kitchens and laying it down on the long tables in front of the hearth, to a chorus of cheers from the men who were standing nearby.

'I can't remember the last time I saw so many barons in one place,' I said.

'Neither can I,' said Eudo, who had managed to find a pitcher from somewhere. He took a swig and then passed it to me. I lifted it to my lips, letting the smell of barley fill my nose before drinking deeply. It was better ale than I had enjoyed in a while, and stronger stuff too than the kind that we usually had in Earnford.

'Leave some for the rest of us,' said Wace.

I swallowed. 'Here,' I said, holding the jug out to him. 'Take it.'

No sooner had he done so than I spotted a hint of movement towards the front of the hall. Anxious for a clearer view, I edged my way through the crowd. On the far side behind the dais hung long embroidered drapes, all but concealing a doorway to an ante-chamber, and from between those drapes several figures now stepped. The hall fell quiet as first came Fitz Osbern, in an expensive-looking tunic of blue cloth trimmed with golden thread, with his wife on his arm, a lady of considerable size with a turned-up, piggish nose and a fierce look in her eyes. Behind them followed the fair-haired and broad-chested Hugues d'Avranches, striding in with a self-confidence that I often saw in young warriors. Next was the castellan Roger de Montgommeri, a small man with a fidgety manner and narrow eyes, and last of all came Lord Robert, dressed in black as he always was, with Beatrice at his side.

I hadn't seen her in a week. Of all places this was the last in which I had expected to find her – this council of barons – but there she was, wearing a dark green gown in the English style, loose-fitting with bunched sleeves, and a necklace and bracelets of silver. Fitz Osbern motioned for both ladies, for Robert and the other nobles to be seated on the chairs set out on the dais, and she smiled politely. Her eyes passed over the crowd, and it seemed that they lingered on me, if only for a heartbeat. Her expression was serene, her manner relaxed.

Fitz Osbern himself sat in the middle of the dais, on what one could only describe as a throne: high-backed with wide armrests, with intricate animal-like designs carved into its dark wood, polished so that the surfaces gleamed in the soft glow of the hearth-fire and the rushlights in their iron stands.

'Welcome,' he said. There was little warmth in his voice, which carried the tones of one well used to authority. 'I thank you all for coming to Scrobbesburh, though naturally I wish that the circumstances were happier. As you know, I have called you here because of the threat we face from the Welsh and the English across the dyke. A threat that grows greater by the day as Bleddyn and Rhiwallon muster their forces; one that as far as the kingdom is concerned could not have come at a worse time.'

He paused, making sure that he had the full attention of everyone, allowing them a moment to dwell upon the significance of his words. 'By now I am sure many of you will have heard tell of King Sweyn's movements across the sea in Denmark. Fewer, perhaps, will know what is taking place in the north, where the followers of the ætheling are once again rising and this time sending messengers across the kingdom to stir up rebellion.'

'What about Eadgar himself?' someone called out, though I could not spot who and it was not a voice I recognised. 'Has he dared show himself yet, or is he still cowering behind the shield of the Scots' king?'

At that there was laughter. Following his last defeat, it was said that he had slunk into the bleak wildlands beyond Northumbria that were known as Alba, whose king was his brother-by-marriage and no friend of ours. Indeed he had lent the ætheling many men and ships to support his endeavours before, and would probably do so again.

'Of his movements we know nothing for certain,' Fitz Osbern answered mildly, fixing a cold stare upon the man who had interrupted him. 'From what we gather, however, there have been envoys sent across the German Sea between him and the Danish king. We suspect, although we remain unsure, that the two may be in alliance.'

A murmur of disquiet went up around the hall and Fitz Osbern raised a hand to still it.

'There will be a chance for you all to speak in time if you so wish,' he said. 'But first listen to me. As I am sure you are all aware, we have received an offer of help from an unexpected quarter: the brothers Maredudd and Ithel, sons of the late King Gruffydd, who in return for bringing four hundred men to our cause seek the restoration of their lands—'

'I'd sooner rot in hell than do any Welshman a favour,' another man shouted from the back of the hall. Nor was he alone in his feelings, since several of the nobles around him added their voices in support. One, more enthusiastic or perhaps simply more drunk than the rest, raised his fist into the air, startling a passing servant-girl, who dropped the jug she was carrying. It fell with a crash to the floor, sending a spray of wine across the man's cloak.

'Quiet!' Earl Hugues rose to his feet, his young face red with fury. 'Otherwise I will have you expelled from here, and see to it that your lands are confiscated forthwith.'

Slowly the murmurs subsided. Red-faced and close to tears, the girl knelt upon the floor, trying to gather up the pieces of the broken jug from amidst the soaking rushes, and she was soon joined by some of the other servants as the lords cleared a circle around them.

'Let me remind you that Lord Guillaume is speaking,' the Wolf added. 'You would do well to pay heed to what he has to say, unless you want to find yourselves at the wrong end of the enemy's spears.'

Despite his youth, he had a certain presence about him. In fact in many ways he reminded me of Eadgar, who was around the same age: a couple of years younger in fact, for the ætheling was said to be only eighteen. Both were solidly built and so far as I could judge shared a similar character, bold of speech and unafraid of confrontation in a way that belied their cunning.

'Thank you, Hugues,' Fitz Osbern said, though I sensed he did not entirely appreciate the younger man's intervention. The hall began to settle once more as the servants clearing up the remains of the wine-jug disappeared back into the kitchens.

The Wolf inclined his head politely, with a solemnity that would have befitted a grey-bearded archbishop performing the holy sacrament, not a man of twenty. On the other side of the dais I noticed Beatrice lean across and whisper something in Robert's ear. Whatever it was she said, it caused a smile to break out across his face, though he did not say anything in reply.

'As I was saying,' Fitz Osbern went on, 'the princes Maredudd and Ithel have come seeking our help, and I intend to offer it to them. Not only are they enemies of those who would destroy us and everything we have fought these past four years to gain, but they are also enemies of the usurper, for it was Harold Godwineson who slew their father.'

He waited in case there was any further dissent, but this time none was forthcoming.

'Now,' he said, 'the only question left is about the best means of taking the fight to the enemy across the dyke. To that end I have deliberated in council with these men sitting here with me, and with the Welsh princes also. At our reckoning we have now between us an army three thousand strong with which to defend the March.'

I glanced uncertainly at Wace and Eudo, who had found me in the middle of the crowd, and they returned the same look. It was a significantly smaller host than we'd had at Eoferwic last year.

'These three thousand, lord,' said a man in a scarlet tunic, a stout figure with a thick beard. 'Are they all fighting men?'

The question was worth asking, for not all of those who travelled with a host were warriors. As well as knights, spearmen and archers every lord brought several members of his own household: servants such as the twins Snocca and Cnebba I had brought with me, grooms and stable-hands, shield-carriers, leech-doctors, chaplains, armourers and bladesmiths to fix broken hauberks and shattered swords. While many of them could probably hold a spear and stand in the shield-wall if called to, that was not where their skills lay, and they could not be relied upon.

The hall fell silent for the first time as we waited for Fitz Osbern to answer. But he did not speak, not to begin with at any rate, instead exchanging glances with the other men on the dais.

'Are they all fighting men, lord?' repeated the bearded man.

If Fitz Osbern took offence at the prompt, he did not show it. 'No, Berengar,' he replied flatly, his gaze unflinching. 'No, they are not.'

All at once the barons were up in arms; those who had been sitting on the benches at the sides were on their feet. The Wolf was shouting, demanding silence, while Robert stood with arms outstretched in a calming gesture. But Fitz Osbern simply sat there upon his throne, with the composure and patience of a king before his subjects, waiting for the uproar to die away once more.

At a guess that meant we had no more than fifteen hundred spearmen at our disposal, around half that many knights, and perhaps two hundred archers. I turned to Eudo and Wace, who were standing beside me. 'How does he expect us to fight off the enemy with so few?'

'Maybe he doesn't,' Wace suggested. 'Maybe he's waiting for reinforcements to arrive from Lundene.'

'I doubt King Guillaume will be able to send him any,' Eudo said. 'With the Danes about to sail in the next months he'll need every man he can muster defending the coast along the German Sea.'

That was where he and Wace would have preferred to be, too, I didn't wonder: close to their estates that not only provided the source of their wealth but were also their homes, as Earnford was mine. Instead they could only hope to God that no harm came to them, and trust that if the Danes did come the king could repulse them swiftly, before they could wreak any significant damage.

'How then, lord,' said the one called Berengar, 'do you propose we defend our manors against an enemy that some are saying have mustered a greater host than anyone since the usurper himself?'

'Our spies have been tracking both Rhiwallon and Bleddyn in the last few weeks while they've travelled from place to place, mustering support amongst their people,' Fitz Osbern said. 'They believe the enemy have no more than fifteen hundred men ready to march.'

'Your spies be damned!' Berengar spat upon the rushes. 'If you believed that then you would not have brought us here from all quarters of the March. What about those raiding-parties that are already afield, that have been harassing our lands for months? Do your spies know how many they number?'

I waited for the moment when Fitz Osbern's fury would spill over, when he would order his knights to remove this man from the hall, but it never came.

'No, they don't,' he said calmly. 'But they know a lot more than you, Berengar, so believe me when I tell you this. And believe me, too, when I tell you that the next time you open your mouth out of turn, I will not be so forbearing. Hold your tongue from now on, unless you wish to see it cut from your mouth.' He looked around at the rest of us. 'Dare I ask whether any of you have more to add, or may I now speak?'

As I saw it, though, Berengar's only mistake had been to let his temper get the better of him. His point was well made, yet Fitz Osbern had failed to answer it. He would not have gathered us here in this hall if he truly thought we faced a host of only fifteen hundred.

'I wish to say something,' I called out, almost without realising it. I found myself striding forward, forcing my way through to the front of the crowd. Men grumbled as I pushed them aside.

'Tancred,' Robert said warningly, half rising from his chair. I was not about to listen to him, or anyone.

'Lord,' I said, addressing Fitz Osbern directly in spite of the disquiet rippling about the hall. Suddenly I was aware of everyone's gazes resting upon me. Blood pounded in my skull and my heart-beat sounded through my entire body, but I would not back down now. 'Many of us here hold land along the dyke. Our manors will be the first the enemy lay waste. How are we supposed to defend the whole length of the borderland with so few men?'

A hush fell across the hall, but he did not answer, not at first. Instead he looked at me, frowning as the torchlight reflected off his balding pate. 'I know you. Or at least, your face is familiar, which means we have no doubt met before.' He glanced at Robert. 'He is one of your vassals, I assume.'

'Yes, lord,' Robert answered. 'This is Tancred a Dinant: the man who led the band that opened the gates to us at Eoferwic, who faced Eadgar Ætheling single-handedly upon the bridge and almost killed him.'

'Tancred,' Fitz Osbern repeated, as if mulling it over. 'The Breton. Of course, I remember now. Your exploits are well known to me. As I recall, you used to be sworn to the Earl of Northumbria before his death last year.'

'I was,' I replied, though I did not see how that was important.

He paused as if in thought, leaning on one of the throne's gleaming armrests and resting his chin on top of his fist. 'You say that we do not have the men to defend the entire March, and I think that you are right. Nonetheless, here in Scrobbesburh we are less than three days from Hereford, and two at most from Ceastre. Wherever the enemy decide to attack, as soon as they cross the dyke we will hear of it. When that happens, we will march straightaway and come upon them in force before they even know it.'

'In the few days it would take us to catch up with them they could have ravaged half the March, burnt our halls and butchered our livestock,' I countered. 'You would let them do that while we sit here on our arses?'

Fitz Osbern narrowed his eyes. 'Do I take it that you have some-thing better in mind?'

It was not my place to argue with him, and so far he had indulged my interruption, but I could sense he was tiring now. If I wanted to make myself heard, I would have to be quick about it.

'Yes, lord,' I said, meeting his gaze. 'I say we attack them, and attack them now.'

For a moment no one spoke, either unable to believe what I had just said or else stunned by my lack of respect. Outside the doors, the rain could still be heard pounding down upon the bailey; the thatch of that great hall rustled and the wind whistled as it passed through the cracks in the timber walls, causing a cold draught that the hangings could not keep out, which made the torch-flames gutter.

'Attack them?' someone said at last, and as I turned to face him I saw that it was Berengar.

'Why not?' I asked. 'If they're still waiting for their full force to gather, then at the very least we should be harrying them, not waiting for them to come to us.'

'Enough, Tancred,' said Robert. 'This is not the time—'

Fitz Osbern raised a hand to silence him. 'I would hear what he has to say. What do you suggest we do?'

This last was directed at me. I had not thought this far. But I could feel the weight of a hundred pairs of eyes upon me, and a hundred sets of ears were waiting to find out what I would say next.

'Speak!' a man said, and I didn't know whether he was encouraging or goading me.

Another chimed in: 'Perhaps he's lost his voice!'

At that there was laughter. Usually I did not much care for being mocked, but I resisted the urge to challenge those men, for it gave me the moment I needed to think.

'I suggest a double-pronged campaign,' I answered as the laughter began to die away, raising my voice so that everyone could hear me. 'We separate our host into three: one part to remain here, guarding Scrobbesburh, while the other two cross into Wales, raiding north and south of where the enemy have their camp, distracting them and forcing them to do battle before they're ready.'

That provoked a murmur. It was often said that only a fool chose to divide his forces, and indeed it was a risky strategy, for each part was then weakened and thus easier to defeat individually. But those who had seen as many battles as I had knew that often that risk could turn to advantage, since few commanders were ever so adventurous as to attempt such a strategy, and as a result the enemy rarely expected it.

'This is ridiculous,' said Berengar. 'We don't have to put up with this nonsense.'

I stared at him, uncomprehending, since I'd thought that we were of one mind in this. His comrades roared in agreement, while others jeered and hurled insults at me, saying that I knew nothing, calling me reckless and a worthless son of a whore and many other things that I could only partly make out.

'We divided our forces at Eoferwic,' I pointed out, having to shout to make myself heard. 'It brought us victory there.'

With luck that ought to make Fitz Osbern listen. He was the one who had led the second assault on the city, and had made it work, too. In so doing he'd turned what had been a desperate struggle into a rout for the ætheling and his host. And it seemed that many present had also been in that battle, since from the back of the hall at last came some cheers of support, which quickly spread as Wace and Eudo added their voices to the din, and suddenly the entire hall was rising, lending their support to my cause or else shouting in protest, and in the centre of it all I found myself smiling.

Fitz Osbern conversed with the Wolf, who was sitting at his right hand, though I could not hear what was being said, and then Robert added something to which the other two nodded. I glanced at Beatrice, who until now had merely sat and listened, showing not so much as a flicker of a reaction. Now she was smiling too, no doubt amused at the sight of so many full-grown men squabbling like children.

Fitz Osbern rose to his feet, bringing the council to order at last. 'We shall now discuss this matter in confidence,' he said, gesturing at the men sitting to either side of him. 'Tomorrow I will send further word, but in the meantime you may return to your men and tell them everything that has been said here tonight.'

Had I lost or won? I stood, confused, as the other lords made for the great doors at the far end of the hall, grumbling amongst themselves. I was about to follow when I heard Robert calling my name.

I turned. 'What, lord?'

'You will come with us.'

His face was stern, his mouth set in displeasure, and a sinking feeling overcame me. Presumably this was my punishment for having spoken so rashly. Out of the corner of my eye I glimpsed Berengar smirking, but his satisfaction was short-lived.

'And you,' Robert said to him sharply. 'Fitz Osbern wishes to speak with you both.'

This time I was the one to smirk at him, and he returned a cold stare, as if this were somehow all my fault.

'We'll see you back at the camp,' Wace called, to which Eudo added with a laugh: 'If Fitz Osbern doesn't eat you alive, that is.'

I shot them a sarcastic look, but no retort came to my tongue. Robert was beckoning for us to follow him and the other great lords through the embroidered drapes behind the dais, and I had no choice but to leave Eudo and Wace.

Beatrice was standing by the curtain. 'That was foolishness if I ever saw it,' she said, falling into step beside me. Her admonition was betrayed by her smile, and that cheered me a little, though not quite enough to bring one to my own face, since I knew that behind that smile lay hope. Hope that could only lead to hurt, for I could not return what she felt.

'At least I entertain you,' I answered stiffly as we ducked beneath the hanging drapes into the small antechamber behind the hall.

She must have noticed the coldness in my manner for she regarded me with a questioning look.

'The hour is growing late,' she said. 'I should retire. Hopefully our paths will cross again soon.'

'I'm sure of it, my lady,' I replied in as neutral a tone as I could manage.

She bade a quick farewell to her brother, making her apologies to Earl Hugues, the castellan Roger and Fitz Osbern before taking her cloak from her maidservant who must have been waiting: not Papia this time, I noticed, but a plumper girl with dark features and a sullen look about her.

And then she was gone. I felt a stab of anger at myself. I hadn't meant to seem unfriendly, but what else could I have said?

Fitz Osbern bade his wife a good night and then gestured for us to be seated. A round table stood in the middle of the chamber with several chairs arranged around it. Berengar took one, as did I, making sure that I sat opposite from him where I could keep a close watch over him. No doubt he was thinking likewise, since his narrow eyes were fixed upon me.

'What?' I asked, but he said nothing.

Fitz Osbern was still standing, his hands planted firmly on the table in front of him. 'Now,' he said to myself and Berengar. 'Under other circumstances I would reproach the two of you for your outbursts. However, since there are more pressing matters at hand, on this occasion I am willing to forgive such indiscretions, providing that you listen to what I have to say.'

He paused, making sure that we had heard, before addressing everyone: 'I believe a suggestion was put forward for a twin-pronged campaign against the Welsh. What we must all agree upon is how we should proceed from here, and how our forces are best to be divided.'

For a moment I was taken by surprise. I had assumed that my proposal was to go unheard.

Berengar was the first to speak. 'I don't believe this, lord. Why are you listening to him? What right does he have to dictate how our host should be disposed?'

'None at all,' Fitz Osbern replied. 'But I do. I am persuaded of the plan's merits and that, as far as you are concerned, is all that need matter. I will gladly listen to any alternative proposals if you have them, but as I see it our best approach is this: for one smaller party to move quickly from the south, the aim being to penetrate deep into Powys and raid far and wide across their country, to seize cattle and burn their crops and so deprive them of resources, and to otherwise divide their attention. Meanwhile a second, larger host will march into Gwynedd to the north, descending upon the enemy while, with any luck, they are distracted.'

'How many men do you intend to send on each of these expeditions?' asked the castellan, Roger de Montgommeri: the first words I had heard emerge from his lips all evening. He spoke slowly, but not in a dim-witted way; rather in a calculating manner, which lent him a certain presence in spite of his less-than-imposing stature.

'No more than a thousand and a half in the northern party, and five hundred in the southern,' Fitz Osbern answered. 'Among the latter will be the brothers Maredudd and Ithel together with a contingent of their own men. They will have their kingdoms eventually, but before they do, they must first prove their worth to us. Their knowledge of the land will prove invaluable besides.'

'Which means you plan to leave around another four hundred in reserve this side of the dyke,' said the castellan, frowning slightly as if musing aloud.

'I believe that ought to be sufficient to defend Scrobbesburh if required.'

Sufficient to hold the castle, probably, but whether it would be enough to prevent the enemy from taking the town, I was less certain. Still, it seemed unlikely that the Welsh would march upon Scrobbesburh itself, since they would surely need to rout both of our other forces first, or else they would leave themselves with an enemy in their rear.

'And who do you suggest should lead these attacks?' asked Robert.

The question was meant for Fitz Osbern but it was Earl Hugues who spoke first. 'I will head the northern advance,' he said, glancing about the table as if daring anyone to defy him. 'Gwynedd borders upon my earldom; it is my responsibility if it is anyone's.'

'I have no objection,' said Fitz Osbern. He would, I suspected, be more than glad to send the Wolf hunting elsewhere – far enough away at least that the younger man would not be constantly barking at his heels. 'As for the command of the other raiding-party, I invite any of the rest of you to put yourselves forward if you so wish.'

There was silence, and I could see why. Should the plan succeed and the Welsh be defeated, the honour conferred upon the men commanding each raiding-party would be considerable. And yet of the two, this one carried by far the greater risk, since it would be marching into the enemy heartland, many miles from any castle or other fastness, far even beyond the safety of the dyke. Not only that, but such a small band could easily find itself exposed with little hope of retreat, and in such a situation one's very life might well be forfeit.

And yet if I'd learnt anything in my years it was that life was rarely without danger in one form or another. Oftimes the best thing a man could do was embrace it.

'I will lead them,' I said.

Eleven

Only after I'd spoken did it strike me how self-important those words made me sound, and how foolish too. Next to me Robert was frowning, shaking his head slowly. Once more, all eyes were upon me.

'You?' Berengar asked. 'What makes you think you can command such a force?'

'Peace, Berengar,' said Fitz Osbern from the head of the table. 'I can think of no one better suited for the task.'

But Berengar would not listen. He rose to his feet, his expression one of indignance and disgust. 'You would have *him* lead this raiding-band?'

'I see no reason why not,' Fitz Osbern said mildly, as if the matter were of little account, and the idea that anyone else should take charge were ridiculous.

'Surely someone with more experience is needed for an undertaking such as this,' Berengar said. 'What has he done to merit this?'

To tell the truth his doubts were well placed, though he could not have known it. Never before in all my years of campaigning had I ridden at the head of such an army. Under my old lord I had commanded a whole conroi, and sometimes more than one; when his horse was killed beneath him during the feigned flight at Hæstinges I was the one who had rallied his men, all threescore of them, and held off the enemy hordes who pursued us. That was not quite the same thing, admittedly, yet even so I had no doubt that I was capable.

'Do you have someone better in mind?' Fitz Osbern asked Berengar. 'Perhaps you would be willing to take charge of the expedition yourself?'

Berengar opened his mouth as if to protest, but then obviously thought better of it and shut it again. I could see he was torn: on the one hand was the promise of honour and fame, while on the other was the knowledge that should he fail, whatever reputation he had would be tarnished for ever. He gazed down at the table, hardly blinking, his lips set firm.

Fitz Osbern was not about to let him back down so easily. 'Well, what is your answer?'

'Lord . . .' Berengar said, and I could see from the frown on his face that he was having to choose his words carefully. 'If I may say, this whole idea is foolishness. You would send close to two thousand men out into the wilds beyond the dyke, into country that few Frenchmen have ever dared set foot in. If those men are lost, what then?'

'With every week that passes the Welsh are gathering their strength,' Earl Hugues put in. 'If we simply wait for them to come to us then there is no guarantee that we'll be able to hold them off. Were you not the first to point that out?'

Fitz Osbern nodded, for once it seemed agreeing with the Wolf. 'Certainly this will be no easy task, Berengar, but I think you rather overestimate the enemy. Since you will not put yourself forward, though, it is of little consequence.' He turned his attention to me. 'I believe that Tancred has experience enough. Indeed for the hero of Eoferwic – the man who led the charge against Eadgar Ætheling, who dared to fight him in single combat – I imagine that the command of a small raiding-party such as this should be a straightforward proposition.'

It seemed I would be forever branded with that feat, despite the fact that it had been borne not from courage but from stupidity, even if I were the only one who understood that. Nevertheless, I sensed a challenge in Fitz Osbern's words; one that was difficult to back down from. It was only due to his sufferance that I'd been allowed to speak at all this evening. Now I was being presented with the chance for honour and glory greater than any I had won before. Yet if I withdrew my offer then I would be seen as a coward and would lose all the respect I had worked so hard to gain.

'It is your choice,' said Fitz Osbern, perhaps sensing my hesitance. 'Should you wish to decline then I am sure I can find other men who would be only too willing to carry out this task.'

His manner suggested indifference, but I knew he meant it not as a reassurance but as an incitement. There would be no other opportunity like this for some time, if ever. A year spent out here on the Marches had not dulled my yearning for battle. Far from it: the hunger raged inside me and my sword-hand itched with the prospect of adventure.

'You don't have to do this, Tancred,' Robert warned. 'Remember, you are under no obligation to accept.'

'Robert is right,' said Fitz Osbern, his eyes boring into me. 'You do not owe me anything.'

Nevertheless my mind was set. This was my chance to take the attack to the enemy, to help put an end to the ceaseless raids which had troubled Earnford and everywhere else along the borderlands; a chance, too, to see the black hawk soar proudly as it had not done in over a year, and to lead conrois beneath its wings. Knowing all that, there was only one answer I could give.

'I will do this, lord,' I said.

Again a flicker of a smile crossed his face, which surprised me, for Guillaume fitz Osbern was not a man generally known for his humour. Still, his was not a friendly smile but rather one of satisfaction, as if he had expected nothing less from me. As if he had somehow known that I alone of everyone in this chamber would be willing to accept this responsibility, perilous as it was.

A smile that somehow told, in a manner I could not quite understand, of quiet victory.

We made ready to march the next day as soon as first light graced the eastern skies. The last thing Fitz Osbern wanted was for the enemy to get wind of our strategy, which meant that the sooner we could strike, the better. Across the camp men were waking, fires were being lit, horses were being fed. All this I watched from the other side of the river, by the barrow mound that I had chosen as our mustering point. The morning was chill, the wind rising, and I pulled my cloak more tightly around me, folding my arms in front of my chest as I paced about with Serlo and Pons and Turold, waiting for the rest of my party to assemble.

In all I was to be given command of half a thousand fighting men: a conroi of forty from Fitz Osbern's household, as well as countless lesser lords together with their followers, many of whom I recognised for those who had lent their voices in my support the previous night. Included in that number were half the troops brought by the exiled Welsh brothers Maredudd and Ithel. As armies went it was far from the largest I had ever ridden in, but then our purpose was not to face the enemy in open battle if we could possibly avoid it. Instead we would travel quickly, laying waste as widely as possible, with any luck distracting the enemy while Earl Hugues's host marched upon them in force from the north.

That, at least, was the plan; we would soon see how successful it proved. Nonetheless, I had confidence in the Wolf in spite of his age. No sooner had Fitz Osbern dismissed us all from his council than the earl had come over in person to wish me luck.

'You are a brave man,' he told me. 'Few would dare accept such a risky enterprise. I wanted to let it be known that you have my respect.'

To hear such words from one so young seemed strange, and were he not already one of the kingdom's foremost barons and an accomplished leader of men, I might have laughed. Instead I fought against the urge, knowing that it would do me no favours.

'Thank you, lord.'

He clasped my hand. 'God willing, one day we will ride together. You can tell me the stories of your exploits then. With luck there will be many more to tell once this is over.'

I managed a smile. 'I look forward to it,' I said, though at the same time I wasn't sure if I quite meant it. There was something that unnerved me about him, though exactly what was difficult to say. Was it his brashness, his self-assurance? Perhaps, but then those were traits shared by many men who lived by the sword. Was it that he reminded me of what I had been like at the same age?

That was the previous night. Now the sun would soon be rising, and when it did I wanted to be ready to march. Not far from where I was standing our Welsh allies were busy striking camp, though I had sent word that they should leave behind whatever they did not need, which in most cases meant everything except for their clothes, a few provisions, their armour and their weapons. I wanted us to travel as light as possible, for then we could cover more ground, and for the same reason I had ordered that there were to be no camp-followers who might slow us down.

The Welsh brothers had spotted me by then, and now they strode over to greet me. Both of them spoke French – enough at least that they could make themselves understood – which was just as well, since I knew barely any Welsh and I was of no mind to start learning now.

'You're the man we have heard so much about, then,' Maredudd said after we had made our introductions. He was the taller of the two and, I guessed, the older, although in truth it was hard to tell. His cheeks were freckled and, unlike most Welshmen I had met, his top lip was unadorned with any trace of a moustache. 'The Breton.'

'That's right.' It was so long since I had been back to the land of my birth that most of the time I regarded myself as French, so it was always strange to hear someone call me that. On the other hand I knew that the Bretons as a people were said to be kinsfolk to the Welsh, and perhaps that slight link counted for something with them. Certainly I had heard it mentioned that our two tongues were closely related, and I had come across more than one Breton merchant who claimed to be able to converse freely with people of the various ports they frequented in Wales. Perhaps they possessed a better ear for language than I did, however, for while I could sometimes pick out a word or two that sounded familiar, and others the meaning of which I might be able to guess, the Welsh had a strange way of pronouncing everything that seemed harsh to my ear and which I still found largely impenetrable, despite having often crossed paths with their kind in the past year.

'Fitz Osbern has told us a great deal about you,' said Ithel. He was slightly rounder, with a ruddy complexion and ears that stuck out from the side of his head.

'Only good things, I trust,' I replied, managing a smile. In all the time I'd spent in these parts I hadn't known anyone from across the dyke who was not my enemy, and I couldn't help but be suspicious of them, even though outwardly they seemed honest enough.

Roughly speaking both were of an age with myself, I reckoned, though at first glance one would have been forgiven for thinking that they were some years older, for their stony expressions and cold gazes seemed to me those of men who had trodden the sword-path for several years. Their faces were lined with the scars of battle: scars that spoke to me of faded glories, of victories long-forgotten, of kingdoms stolen and birthrights denied.

Even if I hadn't known beforehand, I would have guessed that they were brothers. As well as being similarly featured, both were dark-haired and possessed the broad shoulders and thick arms of a blacksmith. They wore their hair short, as did most of their men, who came in all sizes and ages, from long-limbed youths to large-bellied men of forty, armed with all kinds of weapons from simple knives, hunting bows and short-handled wood-axes to long spears and swords. A diverse band if ever I saw one, though what mattered most of all was their temperament in the heat of the mêlée, and that I could not know. Still, they looked like men who could acquit themselves in a fight, which was more than I had been expecting.

Before we left Lord Robert came to wish me luck. He was equipped for war, ready to ride out under the Wolf's banner: dressed in hauberk and chausses, the chain links newly polished and gleaming in the light of the morning. For all that, though, he did not look entirely comfortable. Whilst he was proficient enough at arms, he was not a warrior by nature. He lacked the battle-hunger of a man whose living was made by the sword as mine was, and we both knew it.

'I hope you realise what it is you are undertaking,' he said. 'Beatrice said before that you were foolish, and she was right. You didn't have to put yourself forward.'

'If you'd wanted, you could have prevented me.' He would have been within his rights as my lord to do so. The fact that he hadn't I took as a sign of his respect for me.

'I have no desire to lose you or any of my vassals,' he said. 'But I won't deny you this opportunity, so long as you understand that by accepting this task you take your fate into your own hands. This is not as simple as hunting down a pack of raiders as you did last month. The Wolf, Fitz Osbern and I need to rely on you if we are to succeed.'

'I know that, and I understand.'

'Be sure that you do.' His expression was stern. 'If I have one piece of advice to offer, it is this: be wary of the princes Ithel and Maredudd. They will remain loyal only as long as they have something to gain by doing so, regardless of what oaths they might have made. Keep a close watch over them, and trust them only as far as you have to.'

'I will, lord.'

'Don't underestimate the enemy, either. The Welsh are more cunning than I think even Fitz Osbern realises, and with Wild Eadric and the English rebels on their side as well, they will be more confident than ever.'

If he thought I didn't already know this, he was mistaken, but I listened patiently regardless. There was a certain anxiety in his demeanour that I rarely saw, although it was impossible to know whether he was nervous for my sake or because he was mindful of the challenges facing him also. Whichever it was, it sent a chill through me. Only then did I realise the immensity of the responsibility I was about to shoulder.

'God be with you, Tancred,' Robert said.

'And with you, lord.'

We bade each other farewell and he returned to where Earl Hugues was mustering his forces across the river, leaving me a conroi of his knights and Wace and Eudo too. The three of us had not ridden together in so long, and my mood lightened, though only briefly, as from the other direction I glimpsed the stout figure of Berengar with more than a dozen men beneath a banner decorated in horizontal stripes of scarlet and sky blue. He stopped his snorting destrier in front of me, though he did not deign to dismount.

'What are you doing here?' I asked, more out of surprise than anything else.

'Rest assured I haven't come out of choice, if that's what you mean,' Berengar replied sourly. 'Fitz Osbern in his wisdom has decided I should accompany you on this reckless enterprise, though God only knows why he thinks I'd wish to take orders from the likes of you.'

To say that his abruptness didn't rankle would have been a lie, but if we were to fight alongside one another then somehow his quarrel with me, whatever it was, had to be settled. 'Berengar, if I've offended you—'

He cut me off. 'Don't waste your breath trying to win me over, either. I'll do my part, have no fears about that. But let me warn you from the beginning that you'll get no favours from me.'

Before I could say anything in reply, he gave a signal to his men and then rode off in the direction of a group of lords who were gathering by the banks of the river where they had planted their pennons.

'What was that about?' asked Wace as he and Eudo joined me.

I shrugged; he had about as much notion as I did. 'You tell me.'

'You always were quick to make enemies,' Eudo said with a grin. 'What did you do this time?'

When first we had met as boys, Eudo had not much liked me either, although that was due to the bloodied nose I had given him, and the wound to his pride.

'If only I knew,' I muttered, casting a glance towards the river, where Berengar was laughing at a joke told by one of his knights, in better spirits all of a sudden. Whatever the cause of his ill humour, it seemed it was reserved for me alone. Already in spite of myself I was taking a dislike to his pudgy face and his ridiculous beard.

I changed the subject, not wishing to dwell on it any longer. 'Are these the last of the men who'll be joining us?' I asked, nodding towards the conroi that had recently arrived.

'As far as I know,' Eudo said.

I called for Snocca to bring me my helmet with its newly attached strips of scarlet cloth – the tail that signified that I was the leader of this expedition – and then vaulted up into Nihtfeax's saddle. After waving to Pons, who promptly gave the two sharp blasts upon the horn that were the signal for the rest of our host to rally, I beckoned to Eudo and Wace to join me as I rode to the head of the column. The new day was already upon us, the bright disc of the sun breaking over the clustered rooftops of Scrobbesburh, and as it did so a thrill stirred within me: a thrill that I had not felt in many months.

For the black hawk was flying proudly in the breeze, its wings spread wide, its talons outstretched as if stooping upon its prey, and Tancred a Dinant was at last riding to war.

Our route led us south at first. We could have followed the wide valley of the river Saverna, since that presented the easiest country for riding, but the enemy would be expecting that, and it was known they often sent out scouts down either bank to keep watch for any sign of horsemen and to carry back warnings of impending attack. By taking the Roman way towards Hereford instead, I hoped that we might fool them into thinking that we were simply sending reinforcements to the castles that held the southern end of the March.

We kept a steady pace for half the day, maintaining the ruse for long enough that even the wariest of the enemy scouts who might be watching should have abandoned their suspicions. A few miles after Stratune, then, we left the road and made for the long mountain that rose to the west. Up steep-sided vales we climbed, through dense woods and across clear-tumbling streams. The paths were narrow and ill travelled, overhung by thick branches that forced us to dismount, and often we had no choice but to go in single file: a long string of men and horses stretching for as much as a mile and possibly more. Whenever we found ourselves in open ground I called a halt so that the rearguard could catch up, and so we did not make nearly as much progress as I would have liked, but it was progress nonetheless, and I tried to be content with that.

By dusk we found ourselves leading our horses across high heath-lands, bright with purple flowers that matched the colour of the sky. Valley after valley stretched out before us: creases and folds in the fabric of the earth, endlessly rising and falling all the way to the distant horizon. Rocky outcrops rose like islands out of the sea of heather, and as the light faded we set up camp in the lee of one of those tors, not because it was especially sheltered, but for want of anywhere better, and because at least there was forage enough for our horses. We had some way to go before reaching the plains on the other side of this mountain, and I thought it better not to risk our mounts' necks descending the slopes in the dark. At the very least I hoped that there we would have some protection from the wind, which swept across the land in fierce gusts from the west: a sure sign of worse weather to come.

If truth be told it was far from the best sleep I'd ever had; the ground was hard and littered with jagged stones, making it hard to settle. Nor did the tor offer as much respite from the elements as I had hoped; some of the men lost their tents entirely and were forced to share, sleeping four or five together, which did nothing to improve their moods the next day.

No sooner had we left Scrobbesburh behind us, in fact, than quarrels began to break out between the Welsh and the French parts of our host, who resented being made to march together, and while few of those came to blows, the further we travelled, the more frequent they grew. Thankfully Maredudd and Ithel were as eager as I was to foster a closer spirit between the two camps, and to set an example we made sure to ride together in the vanguard when we set out that second day: myself with my conroi, which included my knights as well as those that Robert had placed under my charge; and they with their *teulu*, which was almost the same thing, being the name they gave to their hearth-troops, their house-hold warriors, their ablest and staunchest fighters; men who would give their lives in the service of their lords. It did not stop each side hurling insults at the other, but at the very least there was no more fighting after that, and that was enough to satisfy me. I only hoped the peace would last.

'Once they sniff enemy blood, they will be much happier,' said Maredudd confidently. 'There will be less trouble then, I think.'

I cast him a sceptical look but said nothing. In my experience once men discovered the bloodlust within themselves it was a hard thing to shake. I had seen with my own eyes many occasions when as many men had died fighting between themselves over the spoils of victory as had been slain in their pursuit.

Within a few hours of breaking camp we had left the mountain behind us, eventually crossing the dyke shortly before midday. The deeper we marched into Powys, the more familiar the princes grew with the country, and the more swiftly we were able to travel. They knew not only which landmarks we ought to watch out for but also the best places to ford each river, whether to skirt around or else to cut through the woods that clung to the sharply rising slopes. We foraged as we went, filling our wineskins at springs and streams, sending small bands of men out to hunt deer or to steal cattle and sheep from the villages and farms we passed, all the while taking care to conceal our true numbers. News would quickly spread that a Norman raiding-party was afield, and that was all part of Fitz Osbern's intention, but our exact strength I wanted to remain a secret, since that way the enemy would be kept guessing.

Not that we saw much sign of them; not, that was, until late on the second day. The brothers and I had sent out our fastest riders to scout out the land ahead and to our flanks to determine what our next move should be, and one of those returned that afternoon saying that he had spied a band of Welshmen one hundred strong mustering inside some ramparts not an hour's ride upriver.

'Caerswys,' Ithel said as he wiped some of the sweat from his brow, and his brother nodded sagely.

'You know of it?' I asked them.

'Know of it?' Maredudd echoed. 'We fought there once against the English many years ago, and won ourselves a great victory, short-lived though it was.'

Ithel nodded solemnly, and in his eyes I saw sadness. 'Not a month after that our father lay dead, our once-proud army was shattered and our kingdom was stolen from us.'

Much as I felt for their plight, this was not the time for reminiscences. What mattered was those hundred Welshmen, and what we planned to do about them. 'What about the place itself?'

'It's one of the forts left behind by the Romans,' Ithel replied. 'When we were there we erected a stockade on top of the ramparts and set sharpened stakes in the ditches, but even if those are no longer standing, it is a hard place to capture.'

Of that I had no doubt, but then I had little intention of trying to take it. The likelihood was that the enemy did not mean to garrison the fort in any case: if the scout's estimate of their numbers was reliable, they had too few men for that, and besides there seemed little reason to defend this spot when it lay so many miles from the borderlands. Instead I guessed they were merely stopping there, and that tomorrow they would march northwards to join the rest of Bleddyn and Rhiwallon's host.

Any lingering hopes I might have held of storming that stronghold faded when first I glimpsed it. Night was fast approaching by then and it was hard to discern much in the gloom and the mist settling over the flood plain, but they had made campfires inside the stronghold and their faint glow was enough for my eyes to make out a series of earthen banks and ditches arranged in a rough rectangle, with the remains of what looked like a stone gatehouse at the eastern end. A timber palisade did indeed run along the top of the earthworks, although from such a distance it was impossible to tell its condition: whether it had been repaired in the years since Ithel and Maredudd had made their stand there, or whether it was already rotten, in which case all that would be needed were a few swift axe blows before it fell.

'There's a breach on its northern side,' said Eudo, whose sight was better than mine. 'Too narrow to make an attack, though.'

Not that any of the other approaches looked more promising, for Caerswys stood at the meeting-point of two fast-flowing rivers, meaning that it was protected by water to south and west, and while the Welsh brothers assured me that both were fordable I knew it would be all too easy for the enemy to see us coming and hold us at those crossings. The only other choice we had, then, was to try to assault the gatehouse, but that would be well defended and would surely mean the loss of many lives, which we could ill afford, especially when we had other choices at hand.

'What do you suggest?' asked Wace.

'We wait until morning,' I said. 'They'll leave sooner or later, and when they do, we'll be ready for them.'

After posting sentries to keep a lookout for any signs of movement, I returned to where the rest of our host were waiting. From there we marched along the ridge that rose to the north of the fort, travelling in groups of no more than twenty at a time so that we would be less easily seen. Shadows shrouded the hills and cloud obscured the skies, and so it seemed doubtful that the enemy would spot us, but even so, one could never be too careful.

Several cart-tracks led out from the fort, heading in all directions along the two river valleys as well as into the hills, but only one led north. Suspecting that was the one that the enemy would take, I left Maredudd around half a mile from the fort with a contingent of spearmen and the forty or so archers we possessed. The gorse was thick enough there that they could easily lie hidden within arrow-shot of the road. At the same time his brother Ithel and I took the rest of our host – some three hundred men, most of them mounted – over to a clump of trees that stood a further quarter-mile away on the other side of the track, on the highest part of the ridge, where we might see the enemy but they would find it difficult to see us.

And there, with our trap set, we waited. By the time our whole host was in place, though, I reckoned it could only be a few hours until first light. My eyes stabbed with tiredness but I knew that I would not be able to sleep even if I tried; already I could feel my heart beginning to pound, my sword-arm tensing, though the prospect of battle lay some while off still. My feelings were shared by Eudo and Wace, as well as my own knights, and so in order to keep them busy I sent them all to keep watch whilst I did the rounds of the men, conferring with the other barons and making sure that they all knew what they were supposed to do. We held the advantage not just in numbers but also in position, and so it ought to be a simple victory, but all the same I knew better than to get complacent. When it came to war I was only too aware that things were never quite as easy as one imagined.

'Your plan had better work,' Berengar said when my path brought me to him and his companions. 'Otherwise I'll see that you pay for each one of my men who loses his life fighting in your cause.'

I shrugged. 'If it doesn't work, we'll all be dead men.'

He scowled, but evidently could think of nothing else to say, and I moved on. Yet even as I walked away I could feel the weight of his gaze pressing upon my back, and I shivered in spite of myself, sensing that if I were not careful his knife might be in there before too long. Straightaway I castigated myself for the thought. Whatever grievance he harboured, surely it was not so serious that he would wish me dead because of it?

Still, as I sat sharpening my sword that night I made sure to keep a close watch over him, at the same time promising myself that if he or his men ever came for me, I would be ready. And if at any point it came down to a choice between my life and his, I knew where my decision lay.

Twelve

The enemy were later leaving Caerswys than I had expected; it had already been light for some while when we first received word that they had been spotted filing out from the fort's gatehouse. The skies were grey and a steady drizzle had been falling since before daybreak, dampening the men's spirits with every hour that passed and also, I imagined, frustrating Maredudd's archers, who needed to keep their bowstrings dry or else the sinews would stretch and be useless. I could only hope that, huddled low amidst the gorse bushes and the heather, they had found some shelter from the damp.

In any case it was too late now to do anything about that, as through the trees and the bracken I glimpsed the first few Welshmen, albeit still several hundred paces off. Their spearpoints bobbed as they climbed the track that led up the hill towards us, and though they had no way of knowing it, towards their deaths. I'd been right insofar as they were heading north, although already it seemed to me that they numbered more than the one hundred our scouts had told me yesterday. Indeed I would have said they had half that many again, though any exact count was impossible; they did not ride or march in ordered lines but rather in groups of as few as five men or as many as twenty. Not all of them were warriors either, for among them I spied more than a few women: soldiers' wives and other camp-followers; gatherers of wood, tenders of stew-pots, stitchers of wounds and menders of cloth.

'Remember who's beside you in the charge,' I said to my conroi and the rest of the knights around me. 'Stay close and watch your flanks; don't break from the line.'

Of course they knew all of this already, but battle does strange things to one's mind. Many times I had seen men whom I usually considered clear-headed become blinded by rage, by the bloodlust, by dreams of glory. Forgetting themselves and where they were, they would ride gladly to their deaths, only realising their folly when it was already too late. I had no wish to see any of my men succumb to that fate – friends and sword-brothers whom I had grown to know so well – and so I gave them this reminder, regardless of whether or not they thought they needed it.

Already the enemy vanguard was approaching the place where Maredudd lay waiting. My grip upon the reins tightened as I waited for him to give the signal to his archers to let their arrows fly. Surely it would not be long now. It didn't help that the enemy were not all in one column, as I had been hoping, but rather strung out along the track, since that made them harder targets. Nihtfeax pawed restlessly at the ground and I patted his neck to keep him calm. Like men, horses grow anxious before a fight; whether they can feel the apprehension in the air or sense when danger is near, I have never been able to tell, but at the very least they know when they are about to be called upon, and so it was then.

He wasn't the only one who was anxious. I was too, partly because this would be the first time I had led so many men in the charge and partly because somewhere lost amidst the darkness of the woods to my rear was Berengar. I would have preferred to have him where I could see him, but I didn't trust him enough to put him and his comrades in my conroi or even in the first line, and so he lurked in the ranks, no doubt stirring up resentment against me, for he seemed to me the kind of man who would do that, even in these moments before the charge. My blood rose as I pictured his hard-eyed scowl: about the only expression I had seen him show in the short while I had known him. Still, I couldn't let my anger get the better of me; all I could do was trust that he and his comrades would do their part, as he had promised. Until victory was assured I couldn't afford to waste time on petty distractions such as him, no matter how much he tried my patience.

I closed my eyes, inhaling deeply, letting the moist smell of the earth and the leaves fill my nose, imagining what I would do when we met the Welsh lines, rehearsing in my mind each swing of my sword. Behind me Pons swore, too loudly for my liking, and I shot him a glance over my shoulder as he wiped glistening white droppings from his mailed arm. Above our heads, a colony of jackdaws cawed as they squabbled; the last thing I wanted to do was startle them and cause them to fly up, since there could be no clearer sign to the enemy that something was wrong, and our plans, so carefully set in place, would be scattered to the winds.

'Quiet,' I told him.

He spat on the ground, and then glanced up, face screwed into a look of disgust as he searched the rustling branches for the offending creature. 'Bloody birds,' he said.

'They can shit on you all day long for all that I care. Now shut up.'

It would not be long now. The stragglers in the enemy train were making their way up the track, these ones on foot rather than mounted, the men carrying packs while the women bore their shields, carrying them by their long guige straps across their backs.

'Any man who so much as lays a finger on any of those women will know my sword-edge,' I said, making sure that the message was passed on down the line.

Eudo was beside me. 'So that you can have them first, you mean?' he asked with a smirk.

'So that they can go and tell their countrymen of the slaughter we wrought here,' I replied.

It was partly true, but it was not the main reason, which was that I wanted to make sure that I had discipline. We were here for a purpose, and I was confident that allowing men to slake their lusts at every opportunity was not a part of what Fitz Osbern had in mind. Nor could we take any captives with us, since they would only slow us down.

Besides, I knew all too well what could happen when men were given rein to do as they would. If all those who had gone looting and drinking at Dunholm had held themselves back, perhaps they would have been ready when the Northumbrians had come. Were that the case, we would surely have won that victory and so many good men would not now lie dead, their corpses left to rot in a wild and distant land. It was pointless to wonder about what might have been, since what was done could not be changed, but I was determined not to allow the same thing to happen again. And so if I said that no women were to be touched, then that was how it would be, and any who dared ignore me would face my wrath.

I turned my attention back towards the road, where, having now climbed to the top of the ridge, the enemy vanguard had drawn to a halt. I froze, thinking for a moment that they had seen something and our plan was discovered, until I realised that they were only waiting for the rest to catch up. In so doing they could not know that they were making themselves easy targets for Maredudd's archers.

Even as that thought entered my head, it happened. A flash of movement amidst the gorse beyond the road, and suddenly a cluster of dark lines shot silently up into the grey skies, followed by another and another and yet more still. They sailed high, their silver heads glinting dully in the dim light, before arcing down, plunging back towards the earth. Men and women called to one another in warning, but it was in vain. One man dropped as he took a shaft in his chest; another yelled as one ran through his shoulder; behind him a horse screamed and reared up, hooves raised high as it tossed its rider to the dirt.

And so it had begun.

I held up a hand to stall my knights, who were glancing at me, ready for the signal. 'Wait,' I said. 'Not yet.'

I spied the dark forms of Maredudd's archers standing in a line a hundred paces to the other side of the enemy, who were in sudden disarray. Another volley was let loose, and another, as fast as the men could draw the shafts from their arrow-bags. So spread out were their targets, however, that most of them fell harmlessly on to the path or amongst the heather. It was enough to startle the ponies, some of which were bolting, one trailing a man who had not managed to free his foot from the stirrup. His cries were in vain as the animal galloped back down the way that they had come, and several times his head bounced off the ground before he struck a rock, and then he was still.

'*Ysgwydeu!*' one of the enemy shouted, amidst the cries of panic. I could not tell whether or not he was their leader, since from this distance they all looked the same, but the call was taken up by some of the other men, who were at last starting to rally: '*Ysgwydeu! Ysgwydeu!*'

Almost as one their women ran to their menfolk's sides, unlooping the long straps from around their shoulders and passing them the shields before just as quickly rushing back to lead their animals out of arrow-shot. Steel continued to spit down from the sky, but the enemy did not think to form a line, to raise the shield-wall and protect their faces. Instead, driven to rage by the deaths of their comrades, they charged headlong upon Maredudd's men, crashing through the heather and the gorse, not keeping to their ranks but simply running as fast as their legs could manage. They roared with one voice, shouting out in their tongue as they brandished their weapons high: their spears and their knives and their axes.

This was the moment I had been waiting for: the moment for which I had been longing for so many months. I gripped the brases of my tall kite shield in my left hand, wrapping my fingers around the lance-haft in my right. My heart leapt in my chest, and I could feel the blood surging through my veins, growing hotter and hotter—

A war-horn bellowed out, deep-throated and baleful like the call of some monstrous beast: the signal from Maredudd.

'Now,' I yelled, not just for my own knights to hear but for every other conroi that was with me too. 'For St Ouen and Normandy, for Fitz Osbern and King Guillaume!'

The jackdaws flapped and screeched at the suddenness of the sound, rising in their dozens from the branches as all around me the answering cry came: 'For King Guillaume!'

Raising my hawk pennon high, I spurred Nihtfeax forward, controlling him with my legs alone as we burst out from the trees on to the heath, my sword-brothers by my flanks, hooves pounding the soft ground, and it seemed that the earth itself trembled under the weight of our charge as more than a hundred horsemen rode knee to knee, and now I couched my lance under my arm, ready for the moment when we would meet the enemy. Behind me I heard Ithel raise a battle-cry in Welsh: a cry that was echoed by his spearmen who were following, but their voices were soon lost amidst the thunder of the blood in my ears.

Less than two hundred paces before us were the enemy, chasing down Maredudd's now-fleeing archers. So lost were they in thoughts of avenging their fallen comrades that they failed to notice us bearing down upon them. Made clumsy by the shields on their arms and the weapons in their hands, they stumbled over some of the lower bushes, sprawling as they met the hidden ditches and pits that we had dug last night and covered over with branches and long grass. All the while they grew ever more spread out; Maredudd was waving to his men, sending them in all directions, and the enemy did not know which ones to chase.

Those of the womenfolk who had seen what was happening screamed warnings from further down the road, but their husbands and their brothers did not seem to hear, or else if they did, they did not heed them. Not, at least, until it was too late.

The ground disappeared beneath us as I pushed Nihtfeax into a gallop. Out of the corner of my eye I saw some of the knights at the end of the line falling a little behind and I yelled at them to keep formation. Not that I had time to see whether in fact they'd listened, since then we were upon the enemy. Some of them had awoken to the danger from their rear and were turning, but they were too few and too dispersed to make much of a stand against us. I glimpsed my first foe standing before me, eyes wide as he saw a hundred mailed horsemen and more bearing down upon him. Struck dumb with fear, he knew not whether to fight or whether to flee, and in the end he did neither. I drove my lance into his shoulder, knocking him to the ground where his body was crushed under the weight of so many hooves.

Within an instant he was forgotten; already I was moving on, keeping up the momentum of the charge. One man, seeing his death before him, hurled his spear towards me; I ducked low and it sailed past my head. Screaming his final words, he ran at us with knife in hand. But if he thought he might take one of us with him, he was wrong, as the point of my lance found his chest, striking ribs and puncturing his heart. Blood spurted forth, spattering my chausses, and as he toppled backwards I left the weapon lodged in his torso as I drew my sword instead.

'No mercy!' I shouted.

We were among the enemy now and panic was spreading through them. To my left Wace and his men battered down upon shields, burying their blades in the flesh of their foes, while to my right a tide of men and horses and naked steel rolled across the heath, sweeping all before it, engulfing the enemy and driving them down. Shouts of panic filled the air, as they saw themselves trapped between us on the one hand and, on the other, Maredudd's archers, who were rallying once more and picking off any who tried to flee. Corpses littered the field of battle, lying in the ditches or else scattered amidst the undergrowth: some with feathered shafts protruding from their backs and sides; others with bright gashes across the backs of their skulls, their tunics torn, their faces marked with crimson streaks.

'On,' I said. 'On! On!'

My shield and sword felt light in my hands; my mail no longer weighed upon my shoulders. Each breath brought a fresh surge of vigour to my limbs, and my blade-edge sang with the song of battle, ringing out with each strike, with each foeman it sent to his death. Around me the world itself seemed to slow: I could sense every swing of their weapons, every movement of their shields even before they happened, and all of a sudden I was laughing with the ease of it all, laughing with the joy of the fight and the delight of the kill. Victory was at hand; I could almost grasp it, and with that knowledge in mind I spurred Nihtfeax onwards, no longer caring about keeping formation. All that concerned me now was finding the next man who would meet his end upon my sword-point. The enemy fell before me, and for the first time in a long while I felt free. The battle-calm was upon me, and I was lost to the will of my blade, bringing it down again and again and again as I clove a path through my foes, swinging and parrying and thrusting, falling into a rhythm so familiar it had become instinctive, sending them to hell.

All too soon it was over. One last strike of my blade, tearing through the throat of a flaxen-haired youth, and I found myself alone with no one else to kill. Sweat rolled off my brow and I wiped it from my eyes while the bloodlust faded and I recovered my breath and glanced about. All the rest of the enemy had turned to flight, most of them turning back down the hill, following their womenfolk who were already halfway back towards the fort. A few tried to escape across the heath, evidently hoping to lose their pursuers amidst the clumps of gorse, although their attempts were in vain for they were soon ridden down, their broken and bloodied bodies trampled into the dirt. They had been routed, and now the field of battle belonged to us.

'For Normandy,' I called out, raising my sword to the heavens. The cheer was taken up by the rest of our knights, all chanting as one with me: 'For Normandy!'

'*Cymry!*' another shout went up, and I saw that it was Ithel, leading the cry as he rallied his foot-warriors about him, and his words were echoed by his brother's men on the other side of the field.

We had lost few men so far as I could tell, which was to be expected given our advantage in numbers. Perhaps a dozen of Maredudd's men had fallen, and around the same number of Ithel's too. As I scanned about I counted at least seven mailed corpses that probably belonged to Frenchmen, which to my mind was seven too many. Next to some of them lay their horses, some dead but the rest wounded, shrieking in pain as they writhed on the ground, guts half spilling from their bellies. I marshalled my conroi to me, making sure that they were all present. None seemed to have been injured that I could see, and that was as well, since far sterner challenges awaited than this.

Pons had retrieved my lance with its hawk pennon from the chest of the man it had been buried in, and he handed it to me. Where the cloth had once been white, now its corners were stained pink.

'A good victory, lord,' said Serlo. There was blood on his face and spattered across his mail, but he did not seem to care. For once his serious expression had vanished, and in its place was a broad smile.

'The first of many,' Turold added as he sheathed his blade.

'So long as God is willing,' I replied, likewise grinning. All my life I had known nothing like the taste of a successful day's fighting for putting men in good humour, and so it was then. They slapped one another on the back and embraced as if drunk, whooping with delight as they congratulated their comrades on all the foemen they had slain. Others set about looting the corpses of those who had fallen on both sides, many of them fighting amongst themselves for the most valuable things as they claimed coin-purses, corselets of leather, helmets, knife-sheaths, brooches and even shoes, until some of those bodies lay all but naked.

I ought to have intervened, since by right a large part of that loot belonged to myself as the leader of the expedition. But in truth my attention was elsewhere. Close by the road I had spotted Berengar. He was still in the saddle, which was how I was able to spot him, though for whatever reason he was some way off from where most of the fighting had taken place, surrounded by some twenty or so of his comrades and retainers. Their pennons, decorated in his colours of scarlet and blue, hung damp and still from their lances. Even though I could not make out what they were doing there, something about the way they were gathered aroused my suspicions.

'Come with me,' I said, gesturing to Pons, Turold and Serlo.

They glanced at each other with confused expressions but they did not question me, instead leaving their animals to the care of the rest of our conroi and following me as I strode across the heath. Men raised their fists and their swords when they caught sight of me, clamouring my name, and I acknowledged them with a wave as we passed, though as I knew well it took more than one man to win a battle: this was more their victory than mine, and it was they who deserved the cheers, not I.

Berengar had dismounted by the time we approached, and his friends had formed a ring around him, jeering loudly and calling out insults, although through the press of men and horses I couldn't see at whom they were directed. As I got closer I heard what sounded like a woman's voice, though her words were not ones I could understand, closely followed by the wail of an infant.

'What's going on here?' I asked. So intent were Berengar's companions on whatever was happening that they did not hear me. Shouting for them to make way, I forced myself through their midst, ignoring their curses.

'Hey,' one protested as I tried to push past. 'You're not the only one who wants to see, friend.'

I stared back into his close-set eyes, though he stood more than half a head taller than me. 'You'd do well to show some respect,' I said, jabbing a finger into his chest. 'Especially when you clearly don't know to whom you're speaking.'

'Listen to what he says,' Serlo added, loudly enough so that everyone else could hear too. 'Or don't you recognise Lord Tancred?'

That, at least, provoked a murmur, and as the word passed around the circle, one by one their gazes turned towards us.

The one who had challenged me bowed his head, saying: 'I'm sorry, lord, I didn't mean—'

I wasn't about to wait for the rest of his apology. 'Out of my way,' I said, barging past.

The rest were more obliging and quickly made way. Berengar stood in the middle of the circle, a knife in one hand and a bundle of frayed cloth in the crook of his other arm. At his feet, prevented from rising by two stout knights who held her shoulders, knelt one of the Welshwomen. Slight of build and fair of complexion, she could have been no more than about sixteen or seventeen in years. Her dress and hood were muddied, her sleeves torn, her auburn hair in disarray. From her lips came a stream of words I could not understand, though there was no mistaking her tone, which was one of desperation. Tears flooded her eyes, streaming down her face, and her hands were clasped together as if she were pleading with him.

Again I heard those infant's wails, and this time I saw where they were coming from. For almost buried within the cloth held by

Berengar was the fragile form of a child: one so small that it could barely have been born.

'What are you doing?' I asked Berengar, who had not moved. His naked blade was poised; for what purpose I could not quite make out – or rather I had some inkling, but the thought horrified me and I did not want to believe it.

'What do you think?' he retorted. 'Making sure her son doesn't live to hold a spear in the enemy's shield-wall.'

I stared at him in disbelief. For all his foul temper, I had not imagined him the kind of man given to such cruelty.

'We don't slaughter children,' I said.

'What do you care?'

'For the love of Christ, Berengar, he's only a baby.'

'For now, yes. But what happens when he grows up, when in years to come he decides to take up arms against us? How many Frenchmen would you let him kill?'

I didn't deign to answer, for that would only dignify his question. 'Give him to me,' I said instead.

'Why? So you can let him and his whore of a mother go free?'

I stepped towards him, aware of more than twenty pairs of eyes watching us, and aware too of the silence that had fallen around us. He backed away, bringing the edge of his knife closer to the infant's chest. The girl screamed, struggling against the grip of the two who held her.

'So that no one has to die who doesn't have to,' I said. 'This woman and her child are not our enemies.'

'Maybe you should do as he suggests, lord,' said one of the two sturdy-looking men restraining the Welshwoman. His face was familiar, for I had seen him in Berengar's company before, though I could not recall his name – if ever I had learnt it. One of his household knights, I suspected.

'Maybe you should shut up, Frederic,' Berengar shot back. 'Your oath is to me. You owe nothing to this man.'

Affronted, the one called Frederic fell silent.

'I'm tired of taking orders from him,' Berengar went on, pointing a grimy finger in my direction. 'He is no better than any of us; he is only our leader because he has Fitz Osbern's favour. And yet what has he done to deserve that honour?'

I clenched my fist, trying to restrain my temper. If he had misgivings about my leadership, he should have spoken with me in private. By letting his grievances spill out into the open air, he made it clear that he sought to undermine me.

'Tancred was at Eoferwic,' another man called out, though I did not recognise him. 'If it weren't for him, we could never have taken the city.'

There was a roar of agreement, and I noticed Frederic exchanging uncertain glances with some of Berengar's other knights.

But the man himself was not swayed. 'So we keep hearing,' he said with a snort. 'But were any of you there? Did any of you actually see him fight the ætheling, as he claims to have done?'

I started forward, speaking almost through gritted teeth: 'Berengar—'

'No,' he said, cutting me off. 'You will not tell me what to do any longer. These people are our enemies, and this is justice.' For a second time he withdrew, this time turning so that his back was to me, as if trying to protect the howling child, though I knew that was not what he had in mind. He lifted his blade, the flat side gleaming dully in the grey morning light, the edge wickedly sharp.

Again the Welshwoman shrieked, and suddenly it seemed she had managed to shake off the hold of her captors, or perhaps they had decided after all to let her go. Either way it mattered little as she darted forward, almost tripping over the ragged hem of her skirt, making for Berengar, but he had seen her coming. Turning, he backhanded a slash with his knife, but he was too quick through the stroke. The steel passed inches from her face as instead the back of his hand connected with her cheek and her nose, sending her sprawling to the ground.

Before he could do anything more, however, I was upon him. While his attention was on her I rushed forward, seizing hold of his knife-arm, twisting it back so sharply that he had no choice but to drop the weapon. In the same moment I drew my own blade with my left hand and, grabbing him from behind, held it up to his neck.

'Give the boy to his mother,' I said. 'Do it slowly, or else I swear my knife-edge will meet your throat.'

Dazed, the woman had managed to rise no further than her knees. Blood was running from her nostrils, mixing with her tears. Tenderly she pressed her hand to the place where she had been struck; her palm and fingers came away red.

'Help her,' I said to the circle of men who were looking on. 'Someone help her.'

But they did not move, and I realised that their eyes were not upon the Welshwoman but on me, and on my blade, pressed to the neck of a fellow baron. A man who was lord and master to many of them.

I swallowed, realising what I had just done, but I could not undo it, nor could I waver. 'Serlo, take the child from him. Turold, Pons, get the girl to her feet.'

The child's wails rang in my ears. One becomes used to the cries of the dying, but the cries of those at the beginning of their lives are a different thing entirely. To speak truthfully, hearing them there, in that place, unsettled me in a way that I could not have imagined.

This child had been born into slaughter, into a world of hatred and bloodshed and cruelty. Even if he survived plague and famine and the sword, he would grow up hearing tales of what we had done here and elsewhere. Desiring of vengeance, he would most likely end his days in the same place they had begun. This was how it had happened before, and in the same way it would happen again, over and over through my lifetime and for centuries to come until the hour of reckoning itself.

But that was not what most shook my soul. Rather it was the realisation of how fragile were these bodies that kept our souls upon this earth; how but for good fortune an infant's entire future could be taken away; how finely balanced was the blade-edge that separated death from life.

And there stood I, Tancred a Dinant: the bringer of both. The guardian of the weak and the killer of men. The shield and the scourge. The arbiter of fates. With one hand I gave life and hope, while with the other I took it away and in its place dealt slaughter and pain.

Sweat rolled off my brow, stinging my eyes, blurring my sight, and I blinked to try to clear it. Berengar let out a grunt, and only then did I realise how close my knife was to the vein in his neck: barely a hair's breadth from his skin. He neither moved nor spoke as he allowed Serlo to gently lift the infant from his grasp, no doubt aware how close he was to spending an eternity in hell.

Pons and Turold helped the Welshwoman up. Spluttering, she received her child, cradling him in her arms, holding him tight to her chest as she caressed his tiny head.

'Now go,' I said to her, and to the rest of the men: 'Make a path; let her through.'

This time they did as instructed, without question or hesitation. For a moment the girl stared at me, as if expecting some sort of trick.

'Go,' I said again, more forcefully this time, taking my hand off Berengar's arm momentarily so that I could gesture down the hill, back towards Caerswys. Even then he knew better than to try anything; indeed he would have to be a brave man to do so, or else a stupid one, and he did not seem to me like either of those.

At last the girl seemed to understand what I was saying. Keeping her head down, not once looking back, she hurried as quickly as she could away from there, following the road. A group of three men were busy looting corpses not far off and they started forward when they saw her, but I shouted to them to let her alone, and thankfully they listened, instead returning to fight between themselves over a battered helmet that one of them had found.

Slowly I withdrew my knife from Berengar's neck and replaced it in its sheath. No sooner had I done so than he wrested free of my grip, whirling about to face me, his eyes suffused with rage.

'You bastard,' he said, his hand flying to his sword-hilt. 'You Devil-turd, you son of a whore!'

He stopped short of actually drawing his weapon, and I saw why, for Wace and Eudo as well as others were riding up, having seen what was happening. He must have realised that even if he managed to strike me down he would still have their lances to answer to, and judged that his life was worth more than that.

'I ought to kill you now,' he said, his voice low. His words were for me alone. 'You're lucky that you have your friends to protect you, but in future you'd better keep a watch out, for I'll be waiting. Waiting until you make a mistake, and when you do, I'll be there to make sure you know it.'

He spat on the ground at his feet, and with a final glare turned and marched away, waving without a word for his men and his comrades to follow him.

'Don't even think to cross me, Berengar,' I yelled as he went. 'Do you hear me?'

He did, of course, but he neither said anything nor even looked in my direction. His horse was brought to him by a retainer, he mounted up, and then he was riding away, and I was left standing there, my blood boiling, my anger barely subsiding. All around me there was silence, as the other barons waited for my next instruction: none wanted to be the first to speak for fear of incurring my wrath.

'Gather your men,' I said to them. 'Let's leave this place.'

That done, I turned and made for a stunted ash tree beneath which the Welsh brothers Maredudd and Ithel were embracing and congratulating each other on a well-won victory.

'Was that wise?' Wace asked as he fell into step beside me. 'Threatening him in front of his own men, I mean.'

'We'll soon see, won't we?' I wanted to think no more about Berengar.

'And for the sake of a single child too. You realise that after all that he'll probably die of a fever next week. Either that or starvation; he looked that thin.'

'He didn't deserve death,' I said. 'And nor did she. Berengar wouldn't have stopped at the baby.' Admittedly that was a guess, though I could well imagine what might have happened. He would have made sure to draw it out, too. Only when he had finished with her would he finally have stuck his knife in her breast.

'If you keep provoking him, it will simply turn others against you too. Soon you'll find you have more enemies than you can even count.'

'He's hated me from the moment we met,' I said. 'What I want to know is why.'

'And how are you going to find out?'

'Have some of your knights, or else some of Eudo's, talk to those who are closest to him and find out what they know.'

'Why not your own men?' he asked, frowning, and there was a hint of indignation in his tone.

'They recognise Serlo, Turold and Pons,' I said. 'They've seen them in my company too often; they'll be wary of them.'

Wace paused as if considering. 'If you find out, what will you do then?'

I shook my head. 'I don't know.'

'You cannot expect everyone in this world to be your friend, Tancred. Nor will this injury be healed any time soon. Whatever Berengar holds against you, you will not be able to sway him to your side. Not now.'

Wace was one of my longest-serving friends; I had always trusted his judgement. He was more level-headed than Eudo, and as long as I had known him he had always made sure to speak his mind, something that many men did not take kindly to, and which had often caused him trouble over the years, but which I respected. Even so, for all his well-meaning advice, on this occasion I could not help but feel that he was wrong. Only by knowing why Berengar held me in such contempt could I begin to understand what I might be able to do about it.

'Will you do this for me?' I asked.

He fixed his eyes, both the good and the crippled one, sternly upon me, and pursed his lips: a sign that his patience was being tried. 'I think you'd do better to forget what has happened, and hope that he does the same.' He spoke slowly, as if addressing a stubborn child.

'That's no answer.'

Wace sighed. 'If you wish it, I'll see what I can manage. But for what it's worth, I think you should leave well alone.'

He walked away, clearly unhappy, and I sensed that there was something more to his discontent that he was not telling me, though I could not work out what.

When I look back on those times now, after so many years, I realise that I was fortunate to have such friends as him, though perhaps I did not always appreciate it at the time. Indeed Wace and Eudo were to me as brothers; the closest thing to kin that I had, and the years that we'd spent training at arms, feasting and drinking in the hall of the castle at Commines, fighting together under the same banner, were among the best I had known. Yet ever since our lord's death it seemed that much had changed. After all, we were no longer merely sworn swords but barons in our own right; we had retainers of our own, and we had duties to them now as well as to each other. While those old bonds of companionship would continue to hold, none of us could deny that they were weaker than once they had been, and for that reason I confess to feeling a strange sort of sadness as I watched Wace striding to greet his own men.

Nor was that the only thing weighing upon my mind. Though I would not admit it to anyone, Berengar's threats made me wary. Why that was, I wasn't sure. Many men had sworn to kill me over the years, but usually that had been in the heat of battle, and I had been able to see them coming at me. This was different, and the more that I dwelt upon it, the more anxious I grew.

The rain began to fall more heavily. I drew my cloak closer about me and pulled my hood up over my head. And, despite myself, I shivered.

Thirteen

B efore we left that place I ordered all the enemy dead dragged from where they had been cut down amongst the heather to be heaped in the middle of the road, on the very crest of the ridge where they could be seen for miles around. There was little wind and a putrid stench hung in the air of entrails and shit all intermingled. In the ground beside all those broken corpses and severed limbs I planted a spear with the crimson-stained hawk pennon nailed just beneath its head, in the hope that any of their countrymen who passed this way would see it and know who had done this. The fame of the hawk of Earnford was not yet so widespread that every Welshman would recognise it. Still, I was determined that if they hadn't heard the name of Tancred a Dinant before now, they would learn it soon.

The few of the enemy who had chosen to lay down their weapons rather than fight on or flee were brought before me. There were only ten, but then there had not been that many of them to begin with. Among them were men of all ages, shapes and heights. Each had his hands tied behind his back and wore the same wide-eyed expression, as if amidst the expectation of death there remained the faintest flicker of hope that he might be spared. A single stroke of a sword across each of their necks was all it would take to finish their lives and allow them to join their fallen comrades. I had only to give the word and it would be done.

But I had no intention of killing them. Not yet, in any case. First they would tell us what they knew of the movements of the enemy host, or at the very least the whereabouts of their main camp, for that had to be where this band were marching: that much seemed clear to me.

'Mathrafal,' Ithel told me after he had spoken to them. He was translating while his brother marshalled the rest of our men and made ready to ride once more. His face was even ruddier than usual, if that were possible, flushed as he was after the exertion and the thrill of the fight. He was a good deal sturdier than most warriors I'd known, and even though I hadn't seen how he'd acquitted himself, I trusted him to have played his part.

'Mathrafal?' I repeated, making sure that I had heard him correctly. It did not seem like a word at all, but rather the kind of noise one might make when drawing forth phlegm to spit. An evil-sounding name, for certain.

'That is where the usurpers are mustering their forces,' Ithel replied. 'Or at least so they say.'

I had no fears regarding their honesty. Knowing that their very lives depended on giving us the answers we wanted, these men would not think to lie. 'How far is it from here?'

He shrugged. 'A full day's march by the old road, I should think, and longer if we strike out across the hills. I have never been there, though I have heard of it, so I cannot say for certain.'

'Then find me someone who has,' I said.

The morning's skirmish had not quenched my thirst for battle, and though I would not admit it I was contemplating riding ahead to this place Mathrafal, if only to see for myself the enemy camp and find out how many they truly numbered.

One of the captured foemen was soon dragged before me. Unlike most of his countrymen, who took care of their appearance and usually went clean-shaven, he wore a straggling beard, and most of his top row of teeth was either broken or missing, so that when he did speak it was with something of a lisp. He was decked out in mail, although it was too big for his frame, and I guessed he had won it as plunder, for he did not look rich enough to be able to afford it otherwise.

'Who is this?' I asked.

'He calls himself Haerarddur,' said Ithel. 'He was the leader of this war-band.'

I raised an eyebrow. Their leader he might have been, but he was a poor one if he had thrown down his sword while around him his countrymen had continued to fight. From the way that he trembled as he was forced to his knees in front of me, certainly I would not trust him to hold the shield-wall or to rally a battle-line.

'Tell him to describe Mathrafal for me,' I said.

I waited while Ithel put the question to him and the answer was given.

'He says it is some years since he was last there,' said the ruddy-faced Welshman. 'As he remembers, though, it is little more than a village. It sits at the bottom of a broad river plain, surrounded all about by pastureland and hay-meadows, with a great hall at its centre.'

'Then why muster there?' I mused aloud. It did not sound like a place that would be easily defensible.

'It is the stronghold and ancestral home of Bleddyn and Rhiwallon. The heart of the kingdom of Powys, and, some would say, of Wales itself.'

A natural rallying point, from the sounds of it. 'This hall,' I said as my own back at Earnford rose to mind, 'how well is it protected? Is there a wall, a rampart, a stockade?'

He frowned. 'You aren't thinking of attacking them, surely?'

'Just ask him,' I said, though I knew that Ithel was right. Regardless of what defences the enemy might or might not possess, we lacked the men to go marching straight into the heart of their camp. Besides, somewhere to the north Earl Hugues's army would be beginning to march; his scouts would be watching them, waiting for the most opportune moment when he could make his attack. All I had to do was distract the enemy enough to divide their attention and draw them out. That was the task that Fitz Osbern had presented me with, and even though I did not much like it, that was what I had sworn to do.

'A stockade, yes,' Ithel again came back with the answer. 'A water channel runs around the entire circuit, fed by the nearby river.

There are two gates: one at the southern end and the other at the western side where the road descends from the village.'

I turned my gaze towards Haerarddur himself, trying to discern whether or not he was speaking the truth. There had been no mention of a tower or a mound, or anything more substantial than that. It was beginning to sound less like the castle that I imagined than a simple holdfast, a refuge in times of need. The trickiest obstacle to any potential attacker would be the moat, and yet depending on how wide and deep it proved, even that need not necessarily pose much of a problem. Still, useful though it was to have, none of that information was enough to tempt me: there was nothing to be had in risking our party unless victory could be all but assured, as it had been today.

'Very well,' I said to Ithel. 'Unbind the others and let them go.'

'And this one?'

'We'll bring him with us. If we discover that he's been lying to us, then his life will be forfeit.'

Ithel nodded, then barked something at Haerarddur, who got to his feet, if somewhat clumsily, due to his bound wrists. He lifted his head proudly as he did so, challenging any who looked in his direction with a stare, though I didn't see that he had much to be proud about.

I left him to the care of the Welshmen under the serpent banner while I returned to my conroi and to Nihtfeax. Already the crows were flocking in their scores to where we had piled the enemy's bodies, their savage beaks digging into the open wounds, scratching at skin, tearing flesh from faces and gouging eyes from their sockets, as if they had not fed in a month or more. Others wheeled about above our heads, cawing in chorus, calling more of their kind from far and wide to partake of the feast that in kindness we had laid out for them. Their share in the spoils was our parting gift; they would finish what we had begun, and if we happened to pass by here again some days from now, not one of those corpses would be recognisable as the men they had once been. In death was every man made equal.

Only when Serlo offered me my banner did I manage to tear my gaze away. Unfurling the cloth, I raised it high for all to see at the same time as Pons sounded the horn and we started on our way.

Yet even many hours later, still it seemed as though the stench of that place remained with me, rising off the blood spattered across my helmet and my hair, the blood that even now was congealing upon my mail, soaking through the chain links, staining my tunic, clinging to my skin. And somehow I sensed that, this time, it would take more than water to cleanse myself of that smell.

We did not make for Mathrafal; not straightaway at any rate. Instead of following the old road north we struck out west along the ridge above the wide river plains, where the brothers had assured me the raiding would be good and we might send further warnings to the enemy. True to their word, an hour after we had left Caerswys behind us we came upon a modest village, perhaps thirteen or fourteen hovels in all, which made it only slightly smaller than Earnford. Around it the fields grew thick with barley, while higher up the slopes sheep grazed: white specks against the green.

Perhaps they mistook us for some of their kinsfolk, or perhaps they simply refused to believe that any raiding-army would venture so far beyond the dyke, for at first the villagers did nothing. Only once we had ridden down from the ridge and approached close enough that they could see our banners, our hauberks, the devices painted on our shields, was the cry finally raised. All across the valley men abandoned their oxen and their flocks, threw down their spades and their pails, while their wives and daughters scooped the younger ones up into their arms as they scattered, some making for the safety of the woods, others for the collapsed mill that stood by the river: anywhere they could escape our swords.

No more than half a dozen remained to fight us – the brave and the foolhardy – and they were the ones who fell. They were few and we were many, and whereas they armed themselves with sickles and hayforks and one with an axe, we came upon them with lances and swords and mail. There was little glory to be had in killing peasants and few knights took much pleasure in doing so. Nonetheless, in choosing to make a stand rather than flee with their families they understood that they were also choosing to die. A part of me admired them, for in spite of their meagre numbers and their lack of skill they were fearless fighters, between them managing to unhorse two of our knights as well as wound another on his sword-arm, which was no small feat.

Quickly, however, they were overwhelmed and we set to work, tearing thatch from roof-beams and pulling up floorboards in search of anything of value the people might have hidden there, putting to slaughter the hogs in their sties and the sheep in their folds, laying the torch to storehouses and to the mill. The village was not large and we did not take long to scour it, and when we had finished there was little left of that place save for a trail of animal carcasses, broken fences, collapsed timbers and blackened ruins. Plumes of smoke and ash billowed in the breeze, blowing in my face, choking my lungs, the heat and the dust stinging my eyes and forcing an unwelcome tear that I quickly blinked away.

The people who once had lived here would not return. Instead, if they had any sense, they would go on to the next village and spread word to their kinsfolk of what had happened here, so that in time Rhiwallon, Bleddyn, Wild Eadric and all their men would also hear and know that we were coming for them.

Before long broad river plains gave way to steep-sided hills, which in turn became sharp-ridged mountains whose peaks I could not see for the cloud. The going was rougher now, the paths less well travelled and harder to follow amidst the tufts of long grasses and the woods that clung to the slopes. In all my travels across Christendom I had not known country like this. Certainly it was not the sort of place in which I would have liked to fight a pitched battle, for there was not much open ground in which to make a mounted charge, and that which there was was by turns either too soft or too uneven, crossed by small rivulets and riddled with holes where badgers and other animals had made their homes. All the while I kept watching the woods for signs of movement. I never saw anything, but one could not be too careful, and as much as possible I tried to keep our column out of arrowshot of the trees.

'Once we reach the pass at the top of the valley the country will be easier,' Maredudd assured me.

Ithel sounded less certain, but being the younger of the two he was content to defer to his brother. I would have asked Haerarddur, who seemed to know these parts well, but the longer the day went on the less I trusted what he said. Indeed now that the threat of death no longer seemed imminent he seemed to have found his confidence again. His earlier fear had diminished, and despite the fact that he was supposed to be our hostage, he kept trying to make conversation with the men guarding him, even at one point sharing what must have been a joke, for afterwards none of them could stop laughing. I soon put a stop to that, instead placing the Welshman with Eudo, under whose charge I hoped he would prove less talkative.

We came upon a number of other villages that afternoon, and for the most part we left them alone, sometimes harrying their cattle or else stealing sheep that we could kill that evening for meat, but no more than that. An army of several hundred men quickly grows hungry, and what supplies we had brought with us from Scrobbesburh were dwindling, so we had little choice but to live off what we could find. Besides, the more smoke spires we sent up, the more easily the enemy would find us, and I wanted to avoid meeting them in battle if at all possible, for almost without question they would outnumber us. So long as they knew we were roaming, it was better that they did not know our exact movements, since then we could appear to be everywhere at once.

We raided in the same fashion for the better part of a week, making what I trusted was a great circle west of the valley of Mathrafal. But for all the miles that passed beneath our horses' hooves, for all the woods we circled, the hills we crossed and the rivers we forded, none of the enemy ever showed themselves. There was growing discontent among our men, many of whom were tiring of wandering with seemingly no purpose in a land they did not recognise, especially since the higher we ventured into those hills and the further from the dyke we found ourselves, the fewer people we saw and the less plunder there was to be had. For, as I had learnt, a man will follow you anywhere so long as he has meat and drink enough to satisfy his stomach and the promise of silver to fill his coin-pouch. Take away either one of those things and he soon grows restless, and a restless ally is often as good as an enemy: dangerous and unpredictable.

And so it proved then. It didn't help that Berengar was still seeking to stir up resentment, although many of the barons were beginning to grow tired of his remarks and jibes, which I supposed was reason to be thankful. Whenever we stopped to fill our water bottles I could hear him. No longer content to voice his disquiet behind my back, instead he made sure that whenever he spoke out I was within earshot, as if taunting me. For a while after Caerswys he had said hardly a word in my presence, and I'd wondered if what had happened had finally cowed him into silence. Clearly that had been wishful thinking.

'From what I've heard he used to be held in high favour by both the king and Fitz Osbern,' Wace told me when next I saw him. 'He won his fame at Hæstinges. His was the hand that slew the usurper's brother Gyrth; the one who rallied the English forces after Harold himself fell.'

That part of the battle had been among the hardest fought, as I remembered. It had been late in the day; we had managed to force our way on to the ridge above the field of blood, but still their shield-wall had held. Thousands of their countrymen lay dead and yet Gyrth and his huscarls continued to fight on, defending his family's wyvern banner to the last. Only after he had fallen to the charge did their line crumble and the rout finally begin. But that Berengar was the man who made that happen – round-bellied, pudgy-faced Berengar – I found hard to believe.

'Are you sure?' I asked.

'It's what they say.'

'You mentioned that the king used to hold him in favour. What happened?'

'It seems he was rewarded generously with lands and for the next couple of years there he sat, growing ever fatter on the wealth of his estates. The next time he was called upon to fight, apparently his arse was so large that his horse collapsed under his weight. Some months after that he somehow managed to kill his two young nephews in a training match and was made to forfeit most of his lands in recompense. All he has left now is one manor near to Hereford, and not a rich one at that.'

'That still doesn't explain why he hates me so much.'

'It ought to,' Wace said. 'Don't you see? He's you, except that you haven't yet eaten your own weight in mutton or beaten your sister's sons to death. He used to be the one who was lauded. Now he finds himself ridiculed and shouted down in council, while you've taken his place. Of course he hates you.'

'Because of that?'

Wace shrugged. 'Men have killed each other for less.'

He'd been right; none of that brought me closer to working out what I could do to repair the damage that had been wrought. If unpleasant words were the worst Berengar could offer, I wouldn't have been concerned, but he had slain two of his own kinsfolk, and the way that Wace had spoken of it suggested it was no mere accident. Nor had I forgotten how he had almost killed that mother and child. If their lives were worth nothing to him, what did that say about mine?

The next day I sent Eudo and Ithel ahead at the head of a party of ten men, with Haerarddur as well, both to explore the land around Mathrafal and, if they managed to get close enough, to catch a glimpse of the enemy encampment. They were gone longer than I had expected, and by the time they arrived back it had already been dark for several hours. We had pitched our tents within the ringworks of an ancient hill fort, and I was pacing their circuit, anxiously keeping a lookout for Eudo's return, when I heard a shout of greeting from the men on watch by the eastern ramparts. I hurried across the enclosure to find, emerging from out of the black, the dark forms of thirteen horsemen climbing the slope towards the causewayed entrance. The skies were clouded that night, and at first I could not make out their faces, but I knew it was them.

'They're gone,' was the first thing Eudo said once he had reached me and let someone take care of his mount.

'What do you mean?' I asked.

'We saw the hall with its moat, and the village as well, but the enemy weren't there,' he said with a sigh. His shoulders hung low and he looked bone-tired, but then I supposed he must have been riding hard since daybreak. 'Their campfires were still smouldering, so they couldn't have left long before we arrived. A few hours, perhaps; no more than half a day.'

Not for the first time I wished that Ædda were with us. He would have been able to tell us.

'The place looks to be defended by barely fifty spears,' Ithel added, and there was an eagerness to his tone that I had not heard before. 'We could storm the palisade and take the fastness; it would not be all that difficult.'

Eudo snorted. 'You would try to capture it?' he asked, as if the mere suggestion was a ridiculous idea, a sentiment that I shared.

Ithel looked taken aback. 'We have the numbers,' he said defensively. 'Why not?'

I'd had my doubts before about his ability and experience as a war leader, and what he had said only served to strengthen them. 'Even if we manage to take it,' I said, 'what would we do with it?'

Eudo nodded in agreement. We both knew that there was nothing to be gained in wasting time and men trying to capture such a place when we had little need of it, when we could just as easily skirt around it.

'It is Mathrafal,' Ithel replied, as if it were as simple as that; as if that were all he need say. When he saw that we were waiting for more he went on: 'It has been the seat of their house for a hundred years and more; it is where they hold their court, where their treasure hoard lies. If we strike at the heart, the head will fall soon after. How can their vassals and followers continue to brave the shield-wall for men who cannot even protect their own halls?'

All this had come out in an excitable rush, and despite his years I saw Ithel now for the youth that he was. A noble youth, for certain, and by no means stupid, but rash nonetheless and as yet lacking in knowledge of how wars were waged. The hour was late and I was too weary to listen to his ramblings.

Ignoring him, I turned to Eudo instead. 'Was there any sign of which way the enemy went?'

'There were tracks leading away downriver,' he said. 'I can only guess that they received word that the Wolf was afield to the north and marched to head them off. Why else would they have left so suddenly?'

Which either meant that they did not consider us a significant threat, or else that they still knew nothing of our presence, which seemed more likely, given that only a fool would choose to leave an enemy in his rear. Either way, we had a chance to catch them by surprise. I only hoped that Earl Hugues was ready for them, for if he was not, we would all be riding to our deaths.

Ithel called to his brother, who had come out from his tent to join us, and the two exchanged some words in Welsh. Maredudd's eyes were bleary, as if he had not slept well, and as he spoke his expression quickly turned from gladness to anger.

'What is this?' he asked as he rounded on me. 'Mathrafal lies all but undefended and yet I am told you would have us march past it without so much as a glance in its direction.'

'To attack would be folly,' I said. 'Only by seizing this opportunity and pursuing the enemy can we hope to rout them.'

If we abandoned the two-pronged strategy then we would have divided our forces for nothing, and the Wolf would be left to face the enemy alone. How could these two not see this?

'Your lord Fitz Osbern promised us a kingdom,' he said. 'Mathrafal is the heart of that kingdom. There will be no better chance than this to take it.'

'You will have your chance once the enemy are defeated,' I said, trying as best I could to keep frustration from entering my voice.

'We have brought you this far, across hills and moors,' Ithel put in. 'We have fought for you, and without us you would all have been dead long ago. Now there is silver for the taking and you would deny it us.'

So that was it. In the end all they really desired was what every man wished for: coin enough to fill their purses, chests of gold to furnish their halls, circlets inlaid with precious stones with which to crown themselves.

'And you think that the enemy will not have taken any of it with them?' I asked, and I was unable to contain my laughter. 'You think they would be so dim-witted as to leave it all in the care of just fifty spearmen?'

They had no answer to that, nor did I expect them to. Of course they needed silver, as any lord did, not just for themselves but also for their retainers, to reward them for their service. Nevertheless, they were fools if they thought they would find it in Mathrafal, which to judge by everything I had heard was hardly a palace befitting of kings but rather a fortified dwelling not much larger than my own hall at Earnford.

'We will not suffer to be mocked,' Maredudd said. 'We were promised a kingdom. It is our birthright as the sons of Gruffydd ap Llywelyn!'

'And you will have it,' I said. 'In time you will have Mathrafal and all of Wales too, just as Fitz Osbern promised, but not yet.'

In truth I cared little for their supposed birthright, or who their father was, or whether their claims were just or legitimate or fair. They were enemies of our enemy and that was the only thing that mattered: the fact that they would lend their support in fighting those who threatened to destroy us. The number of spears and shields they could bring to our aid was all I was interested in.

Neither of the brothers had anything more to say, which was just as well, since I could not trust myself to hold my temper much longer. With everything that had happened these last few days, I wanted nothing more than to be away from here, to be back in Scrobbesburh or, better still, the comfort of my own manor at Earnford, where Leofrun was waiting for my return.

'Wake your men,' I said to Ithel and Maredudd. 'We march as soon as we can.'

'Now?' Eudo asked. 'We've been in the saddle since dawn. We've ridden probably more than thirty miles. You can't expect us to start out on the road without resting first.'

'We have to if we're to have any hope of catching the enemy.

You said they'd already been gone several hours by the time you reached Mathrafal. By now they could be as much as a day's march ahead of us, on their way to do battle with the Wolf.'

Grudgingly Maredudd and Ithel made for their half of the camp, shouting to rouse their troops. Torches were lit as the message was passed from tent to tent, and one by one bleary-eyed faces began to emerge, angry at having been woken so early. I didn't doubt that the brothers would blame me for that, but what else could I do? Earl Hugues had been relying on us to fulfil our part of the strategy, but since our raiding had failed to tempt the Welsh kings out, somehow we had to make sure that we could bring our small force to bear when the two sides clashed. For all that any of us knew, our five hundred men could make the difference between failure and triumph.

I turned to Eudo, who was fixing me with a stare as cold as I had ever seen from him. Only too well did I understand his exasperation, and feel for his tiredness. Didn't he see, though, that the longer we delayed, the less chance we had of catching up with the enemy?

'What more do you want from me?' I asked.

His lips were set firm in disapproval, or disgust; I could not tell which. 'This is unwise, Tancred,' he said, keeping his voice low as he glanced towards the Welsh brothers, although they were far enough away by then that I doubted they would hear. 'With every day we're venturing further into unknown country. More and more we depend on what they tell us, and yet I trust them less and less.'

'Fitz Osbern trusts them,' I said, though I knew it wasn't much of an answer.

Eudo knew it too, for he gave me a sardonic look. 'They have as many spears under their banner on this expedition as we do. If they turn on us—'

'They won't.' I tried to sound confident, as much to convince myself as him, for I was only too aware of how vulnerable we all were, and how much we needed the Welshmen. As, I hoped, they needed us too.

'You can't know that,' he said. 'They have something in mind, I'm sure of it.'

'If they'd wanted to lead us into a trap, they could have done so long ago,' I replied. 'Why wait until now?'

'I don't know,' he said. 'And the not knowing is what I like least about it.'

Eudo was not the kind of man usually prone to such suspicions, and the fact that he would express his sentiments so openly suggested to me that I ought to take him seriously. Yet the time to voice those kinds of doubts had long passed. Whether we liked it or not, we had to trust Maredudd and Ithel. Not only that, but somehow I would have to repair the damage that had been wrought this night, to make sure that they would trust me in turn.

'What else can we do but follow them?' I asked. 'If they're leading us to our deaths, then we'll know it soon enough. But if we start sowing mistrust between us and them, they'll only turn on us all the sooner.'

It was scant consolation, and Eudo did not look satisfied by it, but I could offer him nothing better. If our years of friendship counted for anything then he would accept my judgement on this, as he had on countless occasions before.

Shaking his head, he said, 'Fitz Osbern might have placed you in charge, but that doesn't mean you have all the answers, Tancred. Remember that.'

'Eudo—'

He didn't give me the chance to reply as he swung up into the saddle and rode off.

A group of foot-warriors had stopped to see what was going on. 'What are you looking at?' I snapped at them. 'Fetch your belongings and ready your horses. We ride as soon as we can.'

I made my way to the other side of the hill fort where the French tents stood. Already my thoughts were turning to other things: to the battle that lay ahead; to Rhiwallon and Bleddyn, whose men had raided my lands so many times this past year; and to Eadric and all the Englishmen who had joined them. To the conquest of the Marches, of the Welsh kingdoms, and to glory.

Fourteen

We came upon Mathrafal around mid-morning, skirting the fields to its west, keeping our distance in case Eudo and his patrol had been mistaken and there were more of them lying in wait than they had been able to see. The place was just as he and Haerarddur had described: a cluster of halls and storehouses within a square enclosure around one hundred paces on each side, with stout ramparts and a moat surrounding it, and a scattering of houses beyond that.

Hearth-smoke rose from the buildings; from our vantage on the hillside I spied flashes of movement within the fort as men rushed back and forth, climbing the ladders on to the catwalk behind the palisade. They had seen us, though they needn't have feared, for I had no intention of approaching them. Their spearpoints and shield-bosses gleamed dully under overcast skies: I counted three dozen men at least, and those were just the ones I could see. Enough, probably, to hold the walls for hours, especially if they also had bows with arrows, and javelins that they could throw down at us. Even though we'd overwhelm them eventually, it would cost the lives of more men than we could spare.

Out of the corner of my eye I saw Ithel and Maredudd exchange a look, though they knew better than to try to challenge me again. My mind was set and they would not change it.

Leading away from that camp, following the river valley to the north, were several cart-tracks. Riding hard, we followed them, stopping only to give our horses drink, keeping well away from any sign of settlement where we could. I did not want the men to become distracted with ideas of plunder.

That didn't stop the folk who lived in those places running like rabbits at the very sight of us, driving their animals and carrying those children who were too small to run towards the safety of the trees or the hills on the other side of the river. Once, I sent Serlo out with a handful of men to cut off a few of the stragglers. He returned having captured a family of five, all of them curly-haired and with a thin, wasted look about them. They told us of a great army that had marched through only the previous evening, whose vanguard had borne the banner of a scarlet lion with an azure tongue, upon a straw-coloured field.

'The banner of the house of Cynfyn. Of Rhiwallon and Bleddyn,' said Ithel, who was again translating for me. As the day had gone on his mood had lightened somewhat, though his brother still kept his distance, and regarded with me hostility whenever I happened to glance his way.

'How many passed this way?' I asked.

The question was put to the father of the family, a man of more than forty years with iron-grey hair. Gazing at his feet, shivering with fear, he mumbled something so quietly as to be incomprehensible.

'*Pa niuer ynt wy?*' Ithel barked. The man hesitated before speaking, and I saw the lump in his throat as he swallowed. Eventually he answered, more loudly this time, though still he could not muster the courage to look up from the ground.

'Hundreds upon hundreds,' Ithel said. 'Two thousand, or possibly more.'

I swore under my breath. Were that true, they outnumbered Earl Hugues's force by some margin, which made it all the more crucial that we found some way to add our men to his in the battle to come, either by reaching him beforehand or, failing that, by trailing the enemy until the fighting started, at which point we might catch them in the rear.

'He doesn't know for certain,' Ithel said. 'He begs that you have mercy upon him and his family.'

I glanced at the wretched man standing with his family gathered close around him. His two young daughters clutched at the skirts and the sleeves of their mother, who was doing her best to comfort them. I met her eyes, grey-blue like Leofrun's. With all that had happened recently, I had thought little about her or my unborn child, who very soon would be making his way into this world. Guilt filled me, but it was a guilt tinged with anger. Anger at the Welsh and their English allies for having torn me away from them and from Earnford. At myself, too, for having abandoned them, for having allowed my foolish desire for respect and renown to get the better of me, to bring me to this point.

I tore my gaze from those eyes, unable to look at them any longer.

'Send them away,' I said. 'We ride on.'

The skies grew darker as heavy cloud swept in from across the mountains. Rain followed, hammering at us in furious bursts, driven by a piercing wind that buffeted our flanks. Soon we were soaked to the skin, our tunics and packs heavy with water. By then we must have been marching for some twelve hours. With every mile our pace was slackening, although it was the animals that were tiring more than the men. They had toiled hard for several days, and I was starting to worry whether they would be fresh enough for the battle to come.

A little after noon the river was joined by a smaller stream that we had to ford. Here another set of tracks joined those we had been following, although whether the two bands had met here, or whether one had passed through before the other, was impossible to tell. Both sets looked newly laid, with ox dung that stank as if it were fresh.

'How recently do you think they were here?' I asked Serlo, who crouched beside me as we took a closer look at the tracks.

'Not more than half a day ago, if you're asking me.'

Neither of us were especially knowledgeable about such things, but that was roughly what I had been thinking too. We were gaining ground on them, quicker than I would have expected, though I supposed they would be slowed down by the carts carrying their baggage and supplies.

Again I had sent scouts ahead of the main party to find out

where the enemy were and, if possible, to seek out the Wolf and carry word to him of where we were, for he had to be close now also. If he had any sense he would be waiting for them to come to him, presumably standing his ground where the country afforded good protection: perhaps within the ringworks of some hill fort, like the one we had found the previous night. Somewhere obvious, at any rate, where the sight of his banners flying would be sure to incite the enemy and draw them into attacking him. I asked the princes if there was any such place close by.

'None that I can think of in Mechain,' Maredudd replied with a shrug of his shoulders.

I frowned, not recognising the name. 'Mechain?'

'That's what they call this part of Powys,' his brother explained. 'There is good grazing here but it has never been especially prosperous, and there is little that is worth defending.'

I sincerely hoped that the Wolf knew what he was doing, and that he was ready for the enemy advance. In the meantime we marched on, waiting for our scouts to return. After another hour, one did. He had seen forty horsemen taking shelter from the rain in the ruins of an old mill at a river bend not two miles ahead of us along the valley.

'They had eight carts with them, each led by two oxen,' said Giro, for that was his name. 'Probably a dozen barrels in each cart.'

Supplies for the main host, I guessed; perhaps part of the baggage train that was lagging behind the rest. 'How are they armed?'

'Four appeared to have swords; those ones wore mail shirts, but no coifs or chausses. The rest had only knives; a handful had helmets.'

'Not a war-band, then,' I said. 'If they were, they'd be better armed than that.'

Giro shrugged. 'I don't know, lord.'

Easy prey, I thought. And if we could capture a few, we might find out how the rest of their army was disposed.

'Time for the hunt to begin,' I said.

The rain had eased a little by the time we caught sight of them an hour later, though they seemed in no hurry to move off. Their oxen had been unhitched from the carts and were grazing contentedly, while the horses were tethered to stakes not far from the mill. The building had been abandoned some time ago, to judge by the state of the timbers and the clumps of brambles and nettles growing around it. The roof had mostly collapsed, and I wondered that they should have chosen this place to shelter, especially when there were woods nearby. Running parallel to the river about a hundred paces from its banks was a low stone wall, although it looked in poor repair, with several gaps.

'What's your plan, lord?' Giro asked. He had shown me to the crest from where he had first spotted the horsemen, where a copse concealed us from view.

I'd hoped to weaken them with a volley from Maredudd's archers, but the ruins gave them enough protection that it would be a waste of arrows. At the same time if we charged upon them, they would easily see us coming in time to get away. But as I gazed down the valley, suddenly a strategy presented itself.

'Do you see the thicket on that rise?' I asked Giro, pointing to a spot about a mile and a half to the north. There the valley's slopes fell away sharply towards the river, forming a natural gap of flat ground less than a hundred paces wide through which we might drive the enemy, as if through the neck of a bottle. 'Take word back to the princes Ithel and Maredudd. Tell them to take a hundred of their spearmen and all their archers along the ridge and to wait at that spot. We will drive the enemy towards them.'

A continuous line of trees ran along the top of the ridge to that rise, which would help provide cover for the Welshmen as they moved into position, and would with any luck prevent them being spotted from the mill.

'And the others, lord?' Giro asked.

'They're to join us here. We will trap the enemy with the river at their backs.'

There was no bridge close by, and the waters looked too deep and fast-running to be fordable. We would drive the horsemen into a corner, or else further up the valley, into the ranks of the Welsh shield-wall. Either way they would be forced to surrender.

That, at least, was the plan. No sooner had the rest of our host assembled in that copse than Berengar was barging through the ranks towards me, his face a picture of fury.

'Out of my way,' he said as he shouldered his way past Pons and Turold.

'Quiet,' I hissed. 'What do you want now?'

'What kind of a fool are you, sending the Welshmen on ahead? How do you expect to be able keep an eye on them now?'

I bridled, but somehow managed to keep my calm. 'Keep an eye on them?'

'Don't you realise what will happen? Or are you blind as well as stupid?'

'Berengar—'

'They will betray us,' he snarled, his face so close to mine that spittle struck my cheek. 'And it will be your fault. Fitz Osbern made a mistake when he made you leader of this expedition, but we are the ones who will pay for it.'

'That's enough,' Turold said. 'Know your place—'

But Berengar wasn't listening. 'You will kill us,' he said. 'You will kill us all with your foolishness! Am I the only one who sees it?'

Serlo clamped a hand on his shoulder. Berengar whirled about, faster than I would have thought a man of his size could manage, thrusting his elbow in Serlo's face. Suddenly the knight was reeling, clutching at his nose as blood spilt through his fingers.

Without pausing to think I lunged at Berengar. He wasn't expecting it and in spite of his weight I managed to topple him. The two of us crashed to the ground, and I was on top with both hands gripping his throat, throttling him, until suddenly I felt hands on my arms and around my torso, tearing me away and dragging me to my feet.

'Tancred!' someone shouted in my ear, and in the other, 'Forget him, lord. He's worth less than a goat's turd.'

I struggled, but it was no use. Slowly I came to my senses to find Wace and Pons either side of me, pinning my arms and preventing me from moving. Berengar lay on the ground, red-faced with anger, breathlessness and, I suspected, more than a touch of embarrassment. He struggled to get up, helped by his knights. He spat in my direction, his eyes filled with a look of such hatred and vengeance as I had rarely seen.

'You go too far, Breton,' he said. 'Too far!'

I was about to reply, when something else caught my attention. About forty paces away, some of the knights had left their horses and broken from the line and were pursuing another figure through the undergrowth. They had mail and shields to slow them down, however, whereas he had none, and I saw that they would not catch him.

'Hey,' one said. 'Get back here!'

It took me a moment to realise what had happened. While the men guarding him had been distracted, Haerarddur, the Welshman we had captured at Caerswys, had managed to get away from them. Now he was crashing through nettles and branches, half stumbling over exposed roots, making for the open ground beyond the woods.

Swearing, I shook off the hands of Pons and Wace. 'Fetch me Nihtfeax!' I said, in an instant forgetting about Berengar.

Already Haerarddur had reached the fields that lay between the copse and the mill, and now he began waving his arms wildly, shouting something in Welsh. A warning, I guessed, for through the leaves and the branches suddenly I spied movement by the ruined mill as men came to see what was going on. So much for our surprise attack, I thought.

My destrier was brought to me by Snocca. I took the reins and a javelin from Cnebba as I worked my feet through the stirrups and gripped the crossed straps of my shield in my palm.

'Go! Go now!' I shouted to my conroi and to all the other lords. 'Ride!'

We burst out from the trees in pursuit of the Welshman, who for all his years was a fast runner. The enemy had been slow to react, at first seemingly bemused at the sight of one of their countrymen flailing down the hill, but suddenly they understood. They rushed to their horses, mounting up and hacking with knives and swords at the ropes that tethered them. They had seen our numbers, and none among them wished to fight.

Behind me our war-horn blasted out. At its bellow Haerarddur risked a wide-eyed glance over his shoulder. He saw us bearing down on him but he did not stop running; in fact if anything it seemed to spur him on, though he must have known that he could not hope to outpace us.

I hefted my javelin tightly, drew it back, then hurled it at his exposed back. It sailed through the air, wobbling in the air as it descended before striking home. The steel point drove through his ribs and out the other side. He sank to his knees, gasping for breath that would not come, clutching in vain at the spearhead protruding from his chest. Eudo was not far behind. He swerved to the left to give his sword-arm room, and then it was just as if he were practising against cabbages at the stakes in the training yard. He swung the blade down; the edge sliced through the Welshman's neck, in one blow severing the head with its lank hair and gaping mouth, sending it flying. It landed amidst the long grass at the same time as the rest of the corpse collapsed forward.

Ahead of us stood the low stone wall, and beyond that the mill and the river. The last few enemy horsemen were making their escape, and in their hurry to get away they left behind their carts and their oxen. The animals had been spooked by the sound of the horn and the sight of us riding hard towards them, and now they were scattering in all directions, lolloping in ungainly fashion.

The enemy had a couple of hundred paces on us, but as long as Ithel and Maredudd were ready for them that should not matter. We would drive the enemy into range of the Welshmen's bows. Between the two halves of our host they would find themselves trapped with no place to go.

Blood pounded through my skull as I yelled out, 'On, on, on; for Normandy!'

The cry was passed down the line as we spurred on across the meadows. A few pulled ahead of me, their mounts enjoying the feeling of open ground beneath their hooves. Normally I would have called on them to keep formation, but the only thing that mattered now was speed. Most of the enemy were not burdened by hauberks and chausses as we were, which meant that even though their horses were smaller than ours, they were beginning to open the distance. Already they had almost reached the bottom of the rise where I had sent Maredudd and Ithel with their men. I hoped they were in place; any moment now a flurry of arrows should be let loose from out of those trees, the spearmen would march out from their hiding place and form a shield-wall to block off the valley floor, and we would fall upon the enemy from behind.

Except that the arrows did not come. Nor was there any sign of the spearmen, and still the enemy were drawing away from us.

'Faster!' I shouted, for all the good that it would do. 'Faster! Ride harder!'

The enemy passed beneath the rise, not one hundred paces from the thicket where our Welsh allies were supposed to be waiting. I gripped the straps of my shield in one hand, the reins in the other, as silently I prayed to God and all the saints: let the arrows fly. But still they did not. Where were they? Unless they had found a better position further ahead, though I couldn't work out where. Beyond that thicket, the valley broadened out and the only cover was provided by the thorny briar patches beside the riverbank.

Hooves thudded upon the soft ground, kicking up turf and stones. Nihtfeax's mane whipped in the wind; my cheeks were wet from the drizzle blowing in my face. I dug my heels in, drawing every last ounce of strength that I could from his legs.

'For Normandy,' someone shouted close by my flank. I risked a glance and saw that it was Eudo, his eyes filled with the battle-joy and the thrill of the charge, fixed on the horsemen ahead of us. 'For King Guillaume!'

And that was when it happened, so quickly that at first I could not quite comprehend it. A cluster of black lines shot out from the thicket, their silver points bearing down not upon the enemy but upon us. There was a sharp whistle of air as one passed no more than a hand's span by my helmet, another dropped just in front of Nihtfeax's hooves, and then they were everywhere, raining down in their dozens and their scores.

'Shields!' I heard someone cry, and it might even have been me except that it sounded somehow distant, and I couldn't remember having willed myself to speak.

After that all was confusion. Even when it was all over, still I struggled to recall exactly the order of things. Whoever gave the warning, it came too late. Horses shrieked as steel pierced their flanks and their riders were thrown from the saddle. Some of the knights had slowed, uncertain what to do, but that only made them easier targets. Others tried to turn their mounts too quickly; the beasts went down in a writhing mess of hooves and grass, earth and blood, falling upon their masters and crushing them. Not ten paces ahead of me, one of Wace's men caught an arrow in the neck, the point piercing his ventail. He tumbled backwards across his horse's flank, dead even before he hit the ground.

'Retreat,' Wace was shouting, 'Retreat!'

Another volley of arrows shot out from the trees, arcing over the meadows that sloped down from the rise. From out of the clump emerged spearmen in their scores, beating their spear-hafts and their sword-hilts upon the rims of their shields, raising the battle-thunder as they marched to meet us.

My first thought was that Berengar had been right: that the princes had indeed betrayed us. After everything, I ought to have listened to him. A furious heat rose up inside me: at the brothers for having deceived us for so long; at myself for having failed to see it.

'Back,' I called, waving to catch the attention of my knights. Some dozen or so lay on the ground, blood coursing from wounds that would not be healed. 'Conroi with me!'

On either side of me shafts thudded into the sodden turf. Nihtfeax wheeled about and then we were galloping back in the direction we had come, towards the mill, where the rest of our host were now rallying, drawing up in their ranks and their conrois.

That was when I saw Ithel and Maredudd together with their teulu galloping down from the ridge: forty or fifty men on horse-back with pennons of gold and green on their lances. Behind them, running and stumbling over the tussocks, came an assort-ment of foot-soldiers with leather jerkins, bows in hand or else slung over their shoulders, and a few with bucklers strapped to their arms.

Except that it didn't seem as if they were coming to attack us, but rather as though they were in flight. I soon saw why. From the woods that ran along the ridge emerged an array of shield-bosses and spearpoints: too many to count, but at a guess I'd have said there were easily more than a thousand. In the centre of the line flew two identical banners that I recognised in an instant, even though I had never before seen them with my own eyes. Banners in pale yellow, each emblazoned with a scarlet lion that had a tongue of blue. The symbol of the house of Cynfyn. Of the self-proclaimed kings Rhiwallon and Bleddyn.

A chill ran through me as I stared at it, my mouth too dry even to let out a curse. I had thought to trap some of the enemy horsemen, when in fact they themselves had been but the morsel in a larger snare.

And I had taken it. Like a fish to a hook I had been drawn in, and now we faced a battle if ever I had known one. A battle from which we would now be lucky to escape with our lives. For they commanded both the ridge and the valley north of the mill, and already they were sending a party of foot-warriors to cut off our withdrawal back south. At the same time we had the river at our backs, and while there was a chance we could swim it if we divested ourselves of our mail, we would make ourselves easy targets for the enemy's archers, and it would mean surrendering most of our animals besides.

'We're trapped,' said Turold as I rallied my conroi in front of the mill. I could see the panic spreading across his face, as it was among the men in our shield-wall. 'They will drive us into the water, drown us without mercy.'

'Shut up,' I told him. 'Let me think.'

Turold was young; he had never faced a fight like this before. Yet there must have been countless occasions when I had fought against odds worse than these and still had made it through. Not that I could recall them then. The enemy probably had at least three men to every one of ours, and while numbers were not everything, they counted for a lot.

All along the ridge they thumped their spear-hafts against the ground, hollering out curses and insults. Rather than attacking straightaway, instead they were holding back while their full army drew up in its battle-lines, waiting either for us to surrender or for fear to engulf our ranks. Only once they thought us too disheartened to fight properly would they finally come and tear us apart. Had I been them, I would probably have done the same, for it was a strategy that I had seen work before, and indeed it was working now. Among our own host, men were jostling so as not to find themselves in the first line of the wall, despite their lords' efforts to keep them under control.

'Keep your ranks!' I bellowed at them as I rode along the front of the line, untying my chin-strap, unhooking my ventail, taking off my helmet with its red tails and drawing back my coif so that they could see my face clearly. 'Stand firm and hold the line!'

I saw Snocca and Cnebba standing by the packhorses not far off and signalled for them to bring me the hawk banner, which I had entrusted to them. They did so, and I gave it flight for all our host to see, before driving the pole into the soft earth.

'Here,' I said. 'This is where we fight. Bring your men forward; defend the banner!'

As it was, our back rank was almost standing in the river, and that was where we would all quickly end up if we didn't leave at least some open ground behind us.

The barons glanced at each other nervously but did not move until Eudo joined me.

'Do it,' he shouted as he showed them his blade. 'Unless you wish to feel my sword-edge, do it now!'

He spoke with such force that for a moment I almost believed he would make good on his threat, and perhaps the barons did too, since one by one they began to marshal their retainers, exhorting them with threats and curses, and gradually the line shuffled forward. On the other side of the mill the Welsh brothers were dismounting, not far from where Wace was rallying the right wing of our battle-line, roaring at them to hold their positions.

'Take charge here,' I said to Eudo as I leapt down from the saddle and broke into a jog towards the Welshmen. The ground was boggier downstream of the mill, where the blocked leats had over-flowed, and within a few paces my boots were sinking through the long grass into the mud.

'They were waiting for us,' Maredudd said breathlessly when I reached him. There were bright thorn-scratches upon his body, and there was a pained expression on his face as he clutched at the lower part of his shield-arm where it was unprotected by his hauberk, which came only to his elbow. 'They came upon us by surprise in the woods. We had no chance.'

'Are these all the men you have left?' I asked, gesturing at the small band he had brought. I'd sent them with around one hundred and fifty men, of whom half remained. A few were doubled over, vomiting, while others were too shocked even to stand, and had collapsed on the ground.

'Get up!' Wace was saying to them, and when they did not respond, Ithel joined him, yelling: '*Kyuodwch chwi!*'

Maredudd nodded. 'This is all we have.'

I cursed aloud, but we had no time to waste standing around if any of us we were to survive this day. The enemy would not hold back for ever; soon their battle-hunger would outweigh their patience and they would come streaming down from the woods upon that ridge, swords and spears in hand, death in their eyes.

Until they did, however, we had work to do.

'Rally your men,' I told the brothers. 'Their spears will be needed before long.'

Even as I left them an idea was forming in my mind: one that might just give us a chance. It wasn't much, but we had nothing to lose by it, and if it worked we could at the very least be sure of taking a good number of the enemy with us.

Fifteen

S nocca and Cnebba were waiting when I returned to the head of our host. Other boys were attending to their lords, bringing them spears and shields, leading their destriers away and corralling them with the packhorses on the open ground behind our lines. This battle would not be won in the charge but in the clash and grind of shield-bosses, the crush of men, the struggle of wills. Not with swordcraft but with the grim, close work of spears and knives.

'Come with me,' I said to the twins, and then to a group of sturdy lads carrying bundles of spears under their arms: 'You too.'

I would need strong arms for what I had in mind, and so I called over Pons and Turold and Serlo too.

'See those carts, the ones the enemy left behind? I want them laid on their side, blocking the gaps in that wall.'

The wall ran along the firmer ground on our left wing, coming to an end where the mill-pool had once been. It rose only to waist-height in most places and chest-height in some, and so on its own hardly presented much of an obstacle. Together with the carts, though, I hoped it would be enough to frustrate the enemy's approach and present them with a choice. Either they could waste time and lives trying to clear the obstruction before they could meet our shield-wall, or else they would have to attack across the marshier ground on our right, where Wace and our Welsh allies were positioned.

We got to work without delay. The carts were heavy things, and it took several men to pull them, and to turn them over on to their sides. Other men, seeing what we intended, pulled timbers from the ruined mill and added them to our crude barricade. It wasn't much, but it all helped. Had we more time, I would have tried to find some way to set fire to the whole thing, but we didn't, and so it was a futile thought.

'Quickly!' I shouted, at the same time throwing my shoulders and my back into tipping one of the carts over, grabbing the rough timbers from beneath as Snocca and Cnebba each took a corner. It took the effort of all three of us with Serlo as well, but eventually I felt it slipping from my fingers, falling away from me and coming down with a crash on to its side. The barrels it had been carrying spilled and rolled into the long grass that grew in the open ground between us and the enemy. I'd half hoped they might contain something that we could use, but luck wasn't with us, for they were all empty.

'Next one,' Serlo said. 'Next one!'

Two of the carts remained, but there they would have to stay, since at that moment Turold yelled out a warning.

The cry was passed through the ranks and down the line, and I looked up. The enemy had seen what we were doing and now were sending men to stop us. Already the first column of them had begun the long march down the hillside and across the valley floor, beating their shield-rims and raising the battle-thunder. My heart thumped in my chest, louder than I had ever known it, but now the din drowned it out.

'To arms,' I shouted to the men and boys. 'Find your lines!'

Most did not need telling twice, but a few of the boys weren't listening. Running out across the meadows, four of them took the pole with the yoke that usually sat across the oxen's necks while two others pushed from behind. The wheels bumped over the uneven ground, sending some of the barrels toppling over the sides.

'Leave it, you fools,' Serlo roared, but it was no use.

Those of the enemy with bows had stopped to nock arrows to their strings, and now were letting fly. Most of the shafts fell well short, but one sailed true and sunk itself into a barrel inches in front of the nose of one of the boys pushing. A delighted cheer went up from the rest of the enemy warriors as they closed on us, little more than a furlong now from our makeshift barricade.

'Bring your men forward,' I shouted to the barons, not for the first time. If the wall and the carts were to be of any use, I needed our shield-wall right behind it where their combined spearpoints and axe-blades could threaten the enemy as they tried to negotiate the obstacle.

Now that the enemy archers had found their range, steel was falling in showers all about the lads hauling the cart. A silver point struck one in the back; he fell to the ground and suddenly the rest were shouting to each other, fleeing back to our lines, leaving their fallen companion where he lay on his back, his eyes tight and his teeth clenched, as forlornly he cried out for help that would not come.

For the enemy were on their way, hundreds of them roaring with one voice. They did not march in even ranks but rather came at us in a disorganised rush, having divided themselves into two main groups: one approaching our left wing in front of which stood the wall and the overturned carts, the other across the boggy ground where Wace and the Welsh princes blocked their path, while the contingent of archers drew up in a line behind both. At least with the river at our backs the enemy could not outflank us, although they did not need to. All they had to do was throw more and more men at our shield-walls until our resolve broke, as eventually it must.

I took my place next to Eudo in the first line of the shield-wall, with Serlo to my left and Turold and Pons on the other side of him. Hurriedly I donned my helmet and tied the chin-strap, before someone from the rank behind passed a spear forward to me.

'How long do you think we can hold out?' Eudo asked as he overlapped the rim of his kite shield with that of mine.

I had no answer to that, and so said nothing.

'I never thought I'd meet my end like this,' he said. 'I always thought that it would be in the midst of the charge, not fighting like a cornered beast to hold some godforsaken scrap of land, in Wales of all places.'

'All of us die someday,' I replied. 'And if today is our time, then the least we can do is kill as many of them as possible first.'

The first of the enemy were less than a hundred paces away now. I fixed my gaze upon them as they ran through the tall grass towards us, so close now that I could almost see the visions of blood and slaughter in their eyes. One or two stumbled as they ran, falling over the hidden barrels, but not nearly as many as I had hoped.

'Stand firm and hold the wall!' I yelled to those around and behind me, my voice already growing hoarse. 'Keep your shields up; don't let them through. Remember the faces of the men either side of you. The enemy may be strong but we are stronger! We will defend our banners; we will hold our ground whatever it takes, we will grind them into the mud and we will kill them!'

The words came tumbling out in a rush. It was not much of a rallying call, but it would have to do.

'Kill them!' Eudo echoed, and the cry was repeated through the ranks, the words coming in time with the beating of their weapons, until with one voice they were shouting: 'Kill them!'

Had we had more time I might have tried to offer further encouragement, to rouse their spirits and inspire them to even greater fury. Still, words could only do so much, and valour alone never won a battle. Will, wits and the strength of one's sword-arm were what really mattered, and I could only hope that our small host possessed enough of those things. Enough, at any rate, to overcome their fear. For no matter how many years a man had been fighting, no matter how proficient he was with spear or sword or axe, he would have been lying if at that moment he said that he was not scared.

I inhaled deeply, steeling myself as best as I could, grasping my spear-haft tightly, feeling the grain of the wood against my palm.

And then they were upon us. Some worked together to try to pull the carts aside and make gaps through which the rest could charge, while others stood next to them, protecting them with shields from the javelins that those in the ranks behind me were hurling at them. Most glanced off their bosses or else lodged in the wood, but one at least found its target, plunging into a gangly Welshman's breast right where his heart was. His eyes glazed over, his mouth gaped wide and his knees gave way beneath him. No sooner had he hit the ground, however, than another came to take his place, stepping over his blood-stained body.

My ears were filled with the sound of men yelling, cursing, screaming, dying. We pressed forward, thrusting our spears over the top of the stonework and through the gaps between the carts, aiming for the enemy's heads, since only a few possessed helmets. That was when I realised that most of this rabble were no more than peasants: sent, no doubt, to test our fighting spirit, to soften us up and tire us out before the more hardened warriors were given their chance to finish us. Yet for all their enthusiasm, mere farmers and labourers such as these usually lacked the stomach for a long struggle; they could hold a spear but little else. It would not take much to break them, or so I hoped.

My blade found a man's neck, tearing a gash between the bottom of his ear and his collarbone, and he reeled back, clutching as blood bubbled from the wound. Some way to the right, his countrymen had managed to partly shift one of the carts, exposing a gap in the wall wide enough for a couple of men to stand shoulder to shoulder, but none of them wanted to be first to try their luck against our stout shield-wall. The two at the front hesitated, uncertain what to do, until eventually the weight of bodies behind them forced them forward on to Norman spears.

'Ut!' the enemy bayed, a deep-throated call that put me in mind of wolves on the hunt. 'Ut, ut, ut!'

It was a battle-cry I knew well. I remembered first hearing it that October morning at Hæstinges, when with the glimmer of sun rising over the trees and breaking through the clouds, we had stared up the slope at the ridge they called Senlac, and shivered at the sight of so many hundreds of the usurper's vassals and their retainers, their pennons flying defiantly in the breeze, their mail and their spearpoints flashing in the autumn sun.

Which meant that these men standing before us were not Welsh but English: some of those who had taken up arms under Eadric's standard, I didn't wonder.

Across the top of the wall, their shields met ours. The sound of steel upon limewood rang out as all along the line blades and bosses clashed. My feet were braced, ready for the impact, but even so it jarred through my entire body and I was forced to take half a pace back to steady myself. The man who faced me was a giant; easily more than six feet tall, he towered the better part of a head above me. The bloodlust was in his eyes; wordlessly he yelled as he tried to thrust his spear down towards my groin, but I saw it coming and used the face of my shield to trap it against the wall, before smashing the upper edge into the base of his chin. His jaw streaming with crimson, he reeled back, stunned. Before he had a chance to recover I lunged forward, aiming for his groin, gritting my teeth as I tore upwards into his bowels and then quickly wrenched my weapon free. Like a great oak uprooted in a storm, he toppled backwards, almost falling on top of one of his comrades, who just managed to dodge aside as he crashed to the ground.

Blood and shit pooled around his limp body. The stench of fresh-spilt guts filled the air, so thickly that I could almost taste it. Burning bile rose in my throat but I held it back. Dimly I was aware of others around me, of shouts and screams and men falling on either side; my world had narrowed and I saw only myself, my spear and my shield, and the next Englishman who had come to meet his fate. This was the moment that the poets and the troubadours often told of. As the killing began, so they sang, at the same time came the battle-calm, and they were right, for I could feel it happening then. Blood surged through my veins, filling my limbs with renewed vigour. No longer did I need to think as I became lost to the dance of blades, to the clash of shields, to the rhythm of thrust and parry and cut, each movement ingrained in me through years of training so that it came as if by instinct, until suddenly the English were falling back.

Blinded by the bloodlust and deaf to the warnings of their lords and comrades, a few of our men followed them, breaking from their lines, clambering over the wall and rushing forward after the enemy, either alone or in groups of two, three and four. They started to cut down those who were limping or injured or otherwise straggling behind, but in doing so they were making themselves vulnerable.

'Hold back!' I bellowed, hoping that the other barons would hear me and prevent their men from committing similar folly. If the enemy had been in full flight then I might have allowed them to free their sword-arms and inflict some slaughter. But they were not; this was merely a lull while the enemy gathered their wits and their numbers for the next assault.

When people who have not known the sword-path hear tales of what happens in battle, they sometimes imagine endless clashes of steel upon steel, men standing toe to toe, trading blows, hacking at each other for hours at a time in fearsome duels of strength. Of course there are times when the lines will meet and there are such flurries of swordplay, but always there are moments of respite in between, when the lines fall back and all feels strangely still. Moments like this. They can be the hardest, for it is then, when his thoughts are no longer solely on keeping himself alive and he sees the corpses strewn across the field, that a man's senses and confidence are most likely to desert him. In the final reckoning battles are more usually won not by the most experienced warriors or those with the best sword- or spear-arms but by those with the staunchest wills, the strongest heads.

'Come and die, you bastards,' Eudo called out, partly to taunt the enemy but also partly, I thought, to inspire our own host. 'You goat-turds, you sons of whores, you worthless Devil-spawn! Fight us!'

Whether any of the enemy heard him above the din, I could not say, and I doubted they would have understood in any case, for few among their kind knew anything of the French tongue. But they came nonetheless, led by their thegns, who in times of peace were their lords and in war their leaders. I recognised them not just by the flags nailed to their spears, but also because they had the means to possess mail and helmets, to decorate their scabbards with bands of copper inlaid with gold and silver and precious stones. I searched about for Wild Eadric, hoping to identify him by some such embellishment or else by the size of his retinue, since I'd never seen his face and did not know his device. Perhaps he was among them, but I failed to spot him.

The English came a second time and a third, and with each assault the crude barricade was gradually weakened further, the carts either dragged to one side or else hacked to pieces by men armed with axes, while the wall, which was not mortared, crumbled and in some places fell down altogether. It had done its purpose and broken the first few onslaughts, allowing us to kill more than we might have managed otherwise. As they fell back again I saw that all that remained were loose stones, broken timbers and splintered fragments, like the detritus that the tide washes up on to the shore, strewn across the field together with the bodies of their countrymen and no doubt more than a few of our own. It was hard to tell amidst the blood and the long grass, although as I glanced down our front line, I saw several faces that had not been there before.

On our right wing, where Wace, Maredudd and Ithel were commanding, we seemed to have lost fewer men, but then the ground was trickier there and the enemy seemed to have found it difficult crossing the bogs. Several score had fallen to Maredudd's archers before they had even reached the shield-wall. Their corpses lay in the mud; from their chests and their sides protruded long goose-feathered shafts, which the bowmen were now rushing to recover before the enemy returned.

I felt down the front of my shirt for the little silver cross that hung there, which for years had protected me, and also for the pendant that contained St Ignatius' toe-bone, grasping both tightly in my fist as I closed my eyes and silently said a prayer to God.

'Christ be my shield,' I murmured when I had finished, and briefly put the cross to my lips before tucking it back underneath my mail.

Again the English rushed forwards, marching now in ordered lines, with their thegns once more leading the assault, and it seemed that they were throwing the greater part of their force against our wing: against myself and my knights and Eudo. They knew that if they could breach our line in one place then it would not be long before the rest of our ranks broke. Not that that meant there would be any respite for Wace and the princes fighting to our right, since I saw one of the two lion banners making its way down from the ridge. Beneath it marched a horde of Welshmen, and at their head rode one of their kings: either Bleddyn or Rhiwallon, though I had no way of knowing which.

Obviously they'd decided that they had played with us for long enough. They were throwing their full force against us and now the real fight would begin. Sweat rolled off my brow, stinging my eyes, and I did my best to blink it away, breathing deeply, knowing that if we could not hold the line we would all be dead men very soon.

'Stay close,' I called out. 'Keep your shields together! For Normandy—'

It was all that I had time to say before our lines clashed once more.

The shield-wall is a brutal place to be. In all my years I have known nothing else like it, and to those who have not experienced it, it is a hard thing to describe. For until a man has stood shoulder to shoulder with his fellow warriors and stared death in the face – until he has stood so close to the man trying to kill him that he can gaze into his eyes, that he has smelt his putrid ale-stinking breath, his shit-filled braies and the sweat running from his armpits; until he has buried his blade in that enemy's belly and watched his guts spill forth and his lifeblood slip away – until he has done all that and survived to tell the tale, he has not truly lived.

How long we held them there I could not say. It felt like hours, and perhaps it was, for the next I could recall the skies had grown black with cloud and the rain was lashing down upon us, bouncing off my helmet and ringing in my skull, running down my face and dripping from my chin, soaking through my mail and plastering my tunic against my skin. Men fell to my blade, and more than once I had to let someone in the rank behind take my place while someone passed me a fresh spear when the one I'd been holding had had its head snapped off or its shaft sheared through. I lost track of the number I had killed, and yet however many it was, it was not enough. Still the enemy came, and gradually we were being pushed back from what remained of the wall towards the river. Not by much, but with every step I knew we were losing ground, losing the fight.

To my left Turold gave a yelp of pain as he staggered back. The young knight's shield had splintered and he was clutching his bleeding side as a lank-haired foeman swung wildly with his seax, trying to finish him. Except that in doing so, he had abandoned the safety of his own wall. Even as he pressed his advantage he found himself in the midst of more Frenchmen than he could probably count, and before he could get close enough to Turold to finish him, Serlo had driven him through, burying a wide spearhead in his lungs and gouging a deep wound in his breast.

Turold lay on the ground, wide-eyed as crimson dribbled thickly from under his mail shirt.

'Stand up!' I shouted to him desperately. 'Stand up!'

No sooner had the words left my lips than I realised how futile they were. He could not stand, let alone fight. The next man stepped over him, taking his place in the front rank, and then other hands were dragging Turold back out of reach of the enemy's weapons, and that was the last I saw of him.

I had my own worries, though. An axe bore down upon me: a weak blow that I fended away easily; or so I thought until my opponent managed to hook the curved part of his blade behind the top edge of my shield. Too late I understood what he meant to do. With one heave he forced my shield-arm down and out of position, at the same time tugging me off balance and bringing me stumbling out of the wall. The ground was slick with mud and guts from the foemen I had dispatched, and I slipped, falling at his feet as he raised his weapon for the telling blow.

In the distance war-horns bellowed out their doleful cry. Close by, voices cried out, but the blood was thundering in my head and I could not make out what they said or even if it was meant for me. Rolling on to my back, I managed to lift my shield just in time to meet the Englishman's strike. The impact shuddered through my arm as the blade rang off the boss, hewing chunks of leather from the face and shattering the rim. How it missed my neck I will never know. Again he hefted his weapon above his head, and at the same time a satisfied, gap-toothed grin spread across his face as he glimpsed my helmet-tails and sensed that glory would shortly be his.

'*Godemite!*' he yelled, his pox-scarred face red with anger.

My spear lay on the ground just beyond arm's length and I reached to my sword-hilt instead, freeing the blade with a flourish. Before he could bring his axe to bear for a second time I swung it around, aiming for his legs. It was a wild, brutish strike, lacking in finesse, but none of that mattered, for he did not see it coming. The edge bit into his ankle, ripping through sinew, smashing bone, cutting clean through so that he was left with a crimson mess of a stump where his foot had once been. With a scream he fell backwards, limbs flailing as he crashed through the shields of the men standing behind him, the axe falling from his grasp.

Hardly believing I had survived, I scrambled to my feet, taking my place again in the wall, all the while expecting to find more spears thrust at me than I could count. But Eudo and Serlo were protecting my flanks, holding the enemy off, and for some reason the English seemed to be wavering, unsure whether or not to press their advantage, even though they must have seen that our numbers were dwindling. In battle even the slightest hesitation can prove fatal, as I had often seen, and I knew we had to seize this chance.

'Forwards!' I shouted, in spite of my splintered shield. My voice was hoarse as I raised my sword to the sky. 'Forwards!'

The strength of the shield-wall lies in its numbers and its close-packed ranks, and yet for all that it is a fragile thing, for if those ranks are ever broken it can quickly collapse. And so it did then as we rushed forward, driving a wedge into the gap where the man whose foot I had severed had stood, and which the English had not yet filled. My sword had a life of its own as it struck out left and right, dancing from one foe to the next: parrying, carving, thrusting, cleaving a way through the enemy's midst. This was the mêlée, the truest test of a warrior's footwork and sword-skill, and we were winning: sending the English to their deaths, or else fleeing back towards their Welsh allies. We might have succeeded in fighting off the first few attacks, but as I surveyed our host, I saw what the cost had been. Dozens had been wounded and scores more lay dead. Their broken bodies lay sprawled in the mud, spears lodged in their bellies with pennons drooping limply from their hafts, their clothes and their faces plastered with a sticky red-brown mess. Some of those faces were ones that I recognised, men I had made conversation with over the last few days, spearmen and knights and other barons. We could not withstand another assault like that.

Except it seemed that the two lion banners were on the move. Rather than making their way down the hill to try to finish us, to my surprise the Welshmen were marching along the valley to the north, beyond the mill. Again the horns blew, and this time I realised where the sound was coming from, and what it meant.

Riding from out of the rain and the gloom to the north came conrois upon conrois of mailed horsemen, too many to count, kicking up mud and stones as they came. Held high above them, streaming in the wind, were black pennons and flags, and emblazoned in white upon each of them was a device that I recognised, in the shape of a wolf.

Earl Hugues had arrived.

Sixteen

T here he was, surrounded by his knights, riding up the valley through the driving rain, between the copses and the briar patches and across the fields and the meadows towards us. 'The Wolf!' Eudo cried out, laughing and whooping with joy at the same time. 'It's him!'

Word must have reached him, and now he had come to give battle in person, together with his army of fifteen hundred men. In an instant our fortunes had turned, and now it was the Welsh who were shouting rallying cries, bellowing orders and trying desperately to encourage their men. Under the twin banners of the blue-tongued lion, they rallied against the greater threat coming from the north, and this time I could make out both their kings, Bleddyn and Rhiwallon, each on horseback and each surrounded by his teulu. Meanwhile the Englishmen who not so long ago had been throwing themselves in their scores against our shield-wall were now falling back, leaving their Welsh comrades to stand alone against the onrushing wave of Norman horsemen sweeping across the flood plain of the valley floor. Clods of turf and mud were thrown up by their passage, and their hundreds upon hundreds of hooves raised a thunder that resounded off the hills.

Above that din came a repeated cry, one that was taken up all along the line, until they were shouting with one voice: 'Normandy!'

And then they were upon the enemy. Often horses will refuse to go up against a properly formed line bristling with spears firmly set against them, but equally a mounted charge is a terrifying thing to face, and any shield-wall lacking in either discipline or nerve will quickly crumble. So it was then, as the Wolf's knights drove wedges into the massed shields of the Welsh lines. Like nails being hammered into timber they smashed through their ranks, skewering foemen on their lances and trampling their corpses into the dirt. The tide of battle was turning; suddenly the enemy were being pushed back towards the ridge, and all that lay between us and Earl Hugues was open ground, albeit open ground that was strewn with loose stones from the destroyed wall, with what remained of the carts, with broken bodies, snapped spears and splintered shields.

'To horse,' I said to Serlo and Eudo beside me, then called out for all to hear: 'To horse!'

I did not so much as bother to wipe my blade clean as I sheathed it, then made for the field by the river behind our lines, where the beasts had been corralled. My arms felt heavy, weary from so much killing and weighed down by mail and shield, and my legs protested, but I knew this fight was far from over yet. Snocca and Cnebba brought me Nihtfeax and I mounted up, though not before untangling my forearm from the straps attached to the ruined piece of wood and leather, and casting the thing aside. A broken shield was about as much use as none at all, or perhaps even worse, for it was a burden that offered no protection.

'Sceld,' I said to the boys. 'Bringath me sceld.'

Cnebba hurried away while Snocca passed me a wooden bottle filled with water. I took it and drank as quickly as I could manage; the liquid spilled down my chin and the front of my hauberk, and when I'd finished I tossed the empty vessel aside.

Knights flocked to their lords' banners, their horses snorting impatiently. Among them were men of all ages: some so young they must have only recently taken their oaths, their eyes eager and filled with the battle-hunger; a few much older than myself, many of whom were missing ears or fingers and whose faces were lined with the scars of campaigns past.

'What's your plan now?' a familiar voice growled. I turned; it was Berengar. His face was flushed and he was nursing a fresh cut, bright and glistening, that ran across his cheek just above the line of his jaw. At least that showed he had been making himself useful, rather than hiding behind the spear-arms of other men.

'Now we take the fight to them.' Waving to those men who had been with me in the charge earlier, or as many of them as were left, I shouted with hoarse voice: 'Conroi to me!'

As they were driven back to the slopes beneath the ridge, however, the Welshmen began to rally. The strength of the charge lies mainly in its speed and the sudden force it can bring to bear, but against a tightly packed formation it can quickly fail. Having recovered from the shock of the opening collision, the enemy now closed ranks and locked shields against Earl Hugues's knights, forcing them to abandon the attack lest they became surrounded. The Normans peeled off, back down to the level ground on the valley floor, to where the Wolf was marshalling the rest of his host: his five hundred knights, to which we could now add the fewer than three hundred that at a glance I reckoned I had left to me. Eight hundred at most, then, against an enemy numbering probably twice as many. Somewhere amongst them had to be Lord Robert. I wondered where all the Wolf's foot-warriors were, and then glanced to the north and saw ranks upon ranks of shield-bosses and spears coming to join us, albeit still more than a mile off. The enemy must have seen them too, and realised that they had to make use of their advantage now if they were to stand a chance of defeating us. Once more they came, this time hurling their entire force into the fray, spilling down the hill in pursuit of Hugues's knights as they broke off from their charge.

'Defend the wolf banner,' I cried. 'Go, go, go!'

What remained of our raiding-party had marshalled by then, and I waved to them, urging them on, directing them towards the left wing of the Wolf's army where the lines looked thinnest and in desperate need of reinforcement.

I was about to spur Nihtfeax on and follow them when out of the corner of my eye I saw Maredudd and Ithel riding towards me, having gathered together those of their hearth-troops that were left. Both looked weary; their faces and hair were streaked with dirt and spattered with the blood of their foes and some that might have been their own, but there was a determination in their eyes that I had not seen before.

'Stay together,' I said. Men raced past us on both sides and I had to raise my voice to make myself heard above their shouts and the hammering of hooves. 'As long as we manage that, we stand a chance of making it through this day with our heads still attached to our necks.'

Ithel shook his head fiercely. 'We will not get a better chance than this to slay the usurpers, those defilers of law and of the Church, those stealers of kingdoms. They have denied us our birth-right for too long!'

'No,' I said. 'If you and your retainers break away to go after Rhiwallon and Bleddyn, you'll not only be riding to your own deaths but risking our skins too. All we need to do is hold off the enemy until Earl Hugues's spearmen arrive to bolster our ranks.'

'We came seeking the help of your earl, Fitz Osbern, to drive them out of our lands, out of Wales,' Maredudd put in, his tone less impassioned than his brother's, though he sounded no less determined. 'This is the day for which we have been praying for seven long years. We will not be denied.'

'We will drive our swords into their bellies and rip the hearts from their chests,' Ithel added before I could so much as get a word in. 'We will throw their corpses to the dogs to feed on and carry their heads as trophies to show to their vassals in Mathrafal. We have vowed to kill them and we will do it today, in this valley, here in Mechain!' He turned to his retainers. '*Ni ae lad wynt!*'

The Welsh horsemen, of which there were perhaps two dozen, roared as one. Perhaps some of them had been drinking in the lulls between the fighting, or perhaps their blood was already up after the killing of their fellow warriors, but whatever he had said, it was enough to stir the battle-rage within them.

'No,' I said sharply, grabbing Ithel's shoulder and forcing him to turn and face me. 'Listen to me.'

In an instant he had twisted free. 'Take your hands—'

'Shut up and listen,' I interrupted him. 'If we're to succeed and see this day through, I need you and your men to stay with me.' Desperately I met Maredudd's eyes. Being the older of the two, I thought he would be more likely to see reason. 'Surely you under-stand this?'

'Lord,' said Serlo. He was pointing upriver to the south, from where the party of foot-warriors that the enemy had sent to cut off our escape was beginning to march, looking to bring their weapons to bear. And then I glimpsed cloth flying, with what looked like a crude depiction of a boar being speared embroidered upon it.

'That's Wild Eadric's flag,' said Maredudd. 'I have seen it before.'

To whom it belonged to hardly mattered, although I confess that upon hearing those words a shiver ran through me. If we did not ride soon, Earl Hugues and his men would quickly find themselves overwhelmed and all would be lost.

'I want your oaths that you'll stay with the rest of us,' I said to the two princes.

His expression a mixture of anger and disbelief, Ithel stared at me. 'You want us, the sons of Gruffydd, the rightful kings of Wales, to give *you* our oaths?'

'I want you both to swear it.'

They exchanged words in their own tongue that I could not understand. Maredudd placed his hands on his brother's shoulders, trying to calm him down, but Ithel shook him off, pointing a finger angrily at me. His cheeks even redder than usual, he uttered a series of short words that I could only guess were curses, but then the elder one's tone grew sharper and Ithel, shaking his head, backed down.

'We swear it,' Maredudd said solemnly, and Ithel shrugged. Whether that was meant as defiance or as grudging agreement I couldn't be sure, though it seemed that was the best I was likely to get from him. I only hoped he would not do anything foolish. He seemed a dependable enough warrior, a better swordsman than most from what I'd seen, and certainly he was eager. Still, all that would count for nothing if he lacked the temperament to match: if he allowed his desire for revenge to get the better of him.

'Remember who's beside you,' I added, calling this time to my knights as well as to Maredudd and Ithel, who in their own tongue repeated what I hoped were the same orders to the mounted men of their teulu. 'Don't lose sight of them. They will protect your flanks as you protect theirs. Keep formation and above all stay together!'

I exchanged a final look with Serlo and Pons, then glanced further down the line to Eudo and Wace. Their eyes were fixed, unwavering, on the enemy masses gathered under the twin lion banners, possibly picturing what they would do when we met their lines, rehearsing in their minds the slash and drive and cut of their sword-arms. Then Eudo crossed himself, something I rarely saw him do before battle, and suddenly knowing his fear made me more nervous too.

Trying to rid myself of such doubts, I wheeled about, freeing my sword from its sheath and pointing it towards the heavens. 'For St Ouen and for God; on, on, on!'

'Cymry,' I heard the princes shout, and the cry was taken up by their retainers: 'Cymry, Cymry!'

With that I dug my heels into Nihtfeax's flanks and drove him into a canter. Our fates were no longer in our hands but those of God, and I prayed that He would see us safely through.

Often in battle there are times when instinct takes over and it is a struggle afterwards to recall exactly what happened, and this was one of those times. I remember the foul smell of the fresh-spilt guts rising from the bodies strewn across the meadows, the burning in my chest as I took each breath, the cold wind piercing my mail and my tunic, the feel of the rain, iron-hard, striking my cheek, the stinging as the water mixed with the sweat upon my brow and ran into my eyes, the thunder of hooves, the blood-stained grass flying beneath us as we broke into a gallop. Not far off to our right hand I glimpsed the black-and-gold banner belonging to Lord Robert, and for some reason that sight filled me with renewed confidence.

Swarming down the slopes before us were a horde of Welsh and English, so many that I could not count them, throwing themselves against the Wolf's knights. The lion banners of Rhiwallon and Bleddyn held the centre, leading their mounted hearth-troops into the heart of the mêlée, while the rest – the more lightly armed spearmen, lacking even helmets or leather corselets to defend themselves – came around Hugues's flanks in an effort to hem him in.

Into that tumult we rode. Like a wave breaking upon the shore we crashed into their ranks, sweeping foemen before us. Hooves battered upon limewood, sending Welshmen sprawling, smashing ribs and limbs and skulls, and my blade flashed silver as I heaved the edge across shoulders and necks, buried its point in faces and chests. And still we drove on, further and further, until we were amongst them, spreading out to wreak our fury more widely, our swords ringing with the sound of slaughter. Some stood against us with spears or wood-axes; others launched javelins; while the few who were armed with bows held their lines further up the slope towards the ridge, raining barbed arrows down upon us. So scattered were we that most of those missiles failed to strike, lodging harmlessly in the turf, but more than once I had to duck suddenly and raise my shield to prevent sharpened steel finding my neck.

'They're coming!' Wace bellowed from close by my flank, and I turned to see one of the two lion banners making its way in our direction. Their king and his teulu, some fifty or sixty strong, were riding in our direction to bolster the failing ranks of foot-warriors, to rouse their spirits, to bring the fight to us and cut us off.

'*Riwallawn Urenhin,*' they chanted. Above the crash of steel and the screams of the dying I could only just hear their voices and those two words: '*Riwallawn Urenhin!*'

The name I recognised, and I had heard enough of the Welsh tongue to know what that meant. King Rhiwallon. This, then, was the man who was responsible for the raids on Earnford. For despoiling my manor and killing my people. For killing Lyfing. I could barely make him out amidst his retainers, so tight was their formation. Shorter and slighter of stature than I might have expected, he did not look the most formidable of men, but then appearances could easily deceive. A red moustache adorned his face, and across the top of his helmet ran a crest of black feathers, no doubt to mark him out to his men.

It seemed to work, for as they caught sight of their king riding to their aid, throwing himself into the fray, the enemy began to recover their confidence. They stiffened their ranks in the face of our attack and rallied their shield-wall. With every moment the noose was closing around our necks. Again I glanced to the north, where our foot-warriors were closer than before but not yet close enough, being still half a mile away and more. At this rate they would never reach us in time. Unless we did something soon, we would find ourselves trapped once more, with death the only way out. Earl Hugues and Lord Robert were struggling to hold back the flood of foemen, and I knew that the only way we could hope to stand fast until those spearmen reached us was if we all kept together, kept formation.

'With me!' I called to the thinly spread men of my raiding-band, trying to rally them around me. 'Conroi with me!'

Quickly the message was passed on, to Wace and Eudo and Berengar and the other barons, to our Welsh allies under the princes Maredudd and Ithel—

Who were not there. It took me but a heartbeat to spot the serpent banner across the field of corpses, and in that heartbeat my gut twisted. They had ignored my instruction, broken their oaths, and instead of following us they were charging, in spite of their meagre numbers, towards Rhiwallon and his bodyguard, roaring to the heavens as they drew their swords, their expressions twisted in hatred of their enemy.

'Cymry!' they called as one. The cry was echoed by their archers, who having spent their arrows now lent their support and the weight of their massed bodies to their princes' charge. 'Cymry, Cymry, Cymry!'

'Back!' I shouted after them, but it was in vain. Either they could not hear me, or they chose not to, for they did not stop.

Swearing aloud, I brought Nihtfeax to a halt. The princes' retinue was too small to challenge the fresh troops headed by their foe and rival. Together we could hold our own, but divided as we were, defeat beckoned. All this because of their selfishness, their stupidity and recklessness.

'Sons of whores,' Pons said as he checked his destrier beside me.

On my other flank, Serlo's expression was grim. 'What now?'

In such moments did the fate of battles lie. Whatever decision we made now, it had to be made quickly, and there would be little chance of turning back from it.

'We follow them,' I said grimly as I dug my heels into Nihtfeax's flanks. Ahead, the enemy were taunting us to come and die on their spears, but I turned Nihtfeax away to the right, towards the lion banner and the black-crested helmet bobbing beneath it. 'We'll take the battle to the enemy's king!'

I fixed my eyes upon Rhiwallon ap Cynfyn as he and his men met the sons of Gruffydd, each side aiming their spearpoints towards the chests and helmets of their opponents to try to knock them from the saddle, or else cutting with the edges of their swords across the flanks of their mounts. Men on both sides fell on to the churned earth; splinters of wood flew as hafts snapped and shields were fractured. Those less badly injured rose to carry on fighting, joining their side's foot-warriors who were throwing themselves into the struggle, while others less fortunate were ridden down or run through even as they tried to get to their feet or crawl out of danger.

Knee to knee we rode into the heart of that mêlée: through the rain, across a field strewn with corpses, through puddles made red where blood had run into the rainwater, up the hill. I no longer knew how many we numbered altogether; all I cared about was keeping that black crest and that scarlet lion in sight. All was chaos as the two groups of Welshmen rode amongst each other until I could barely tell ally from adversary. Neither side held its formations but instead struck out at whoever crossed their path, their patience spent and discipline forgotten as rage and years-old rivalries took hold.

'Stay close,' Wace called out to some of the knights on our left who were drawing ahead of the rest of us, fanning out in pursuit of the kill. 'Stay with Lord Tancred!'

Then I saw them: the brothers Ithel and Maredudd with their nasal-pieces and cheek-guards inlaid with shining gold, riding along-side each other with swords raised high, making straight for the red-moustached King Rhiwallon, who somehow in the midst of all that butchery had found himself almost alone with only four of his retainers for protection. The two sides met and their blades shrieked as steel scraped against steel.

After that everything happened quickly; so quickly, indeed, that there was nothing any of us could have done. For one so slight, Rhiwallon was a more than able warrior, a good horseman and fast with his blade too. Ithel was the first of the princes to test his sword-arm against him, backhanding a wild swing at his head, but the king jerked his mount sharply to the left, at the same time leaning out of the way. The point missed his cheek by a hair's breath, and as Ithel was recovering, raising his blade ready for another strike, Rhiwallon was already turning, slashing across the young man's forearm, in one blow severing his hand with the fingers still clasped around the sword-hilt. Ithel yelled in agony and in horror at the bloody stump that was left.

'Get back!' I shouted, but it was too late; one of Rhiwallon's men finished what the king had begun, thrusting the point of his blade under Ithel's hauberk into his gut. The prince clutched at the wound with his one remaining hand, and as his mount reared up he tumbled backwards over the cantle of his saddle. His neck snapped back as he struck the earth.

'Ithel!' Maredudd screamed despairingly.

He wheeled around to face Rhiwallon, dug his spurs into his mount's flanks and charged, followed by what was left of his teulu and his contingent of spearmen, with myself and my conroi trailing behind. Faced with so many adversaries, this time the King of Powys hesitated, just for a fraction of a heartbeat, but it was a fraction too long. Uncertain whether to meet the prince's charge or to seek safety behind the lines of his foot-warriors, in the end he did neither. Maredudd was upon him in an instant, battering down with his sword so hard that the yellow and scarlet painted hide fell away from Rhiwallon's shield. But still the king did not retreat, even while his retainers on both flanks were being cut down and beaten back, and when Maredudd's next strike missed and he left himself exposed, the king seized the opportunity, slashing across the prince's unprotected thigh.

It was the last blow that Rhiwallon would have the chance to land. Howling in pain and rage, Maredudd flung himself from the saddle at his foe, seizing him around his mailed chest and pitching them both flailing to the ground.

I didn't get the chance to see what happened next. The king's retainers were swarming forward again and the banner of the house of Cynfyn still soared, though not for long.

'The lion banner,' I yelled. 'His weight in silver for the man who takes it!'

Such wealth was not mine to give, but that hardly mattered, for it was enough to encourage the men who were with me. Those who not much earlier had seen only defeat ahead of them suddenly glimpsed victory and glory. With renewed spirits they spurred their mounts onwards, riding harder and faster, and in the face of our charge the enemy crumbled. Perhaps having seen their king fall they no longer had any stomach for the fight, for suddenly we were scything our way through them as easily as a farmer cuts the wheat at harvest-time, losing ourselves to the wills of our blades, to the sword-joy. The hard struggle that we had experienced in the shield-wall seemed a lifetime ago. Then a cheer rose up and I saw one of our knights slice across the throat of the young man who had been carrying the enemy's banner.

'For Normandy,' the knight cried as he leapt down from the saddle. With his knife he cut a long slash across the belly of the scarlet lion before raising it aloft and waving it for all to see. The rest of the enemy were running now and none dared challenge him. 'For Fitz Osbern and for King Guillaume!'

That was when I recognised his pudgy face and his stout build. Berengar. It shouldn't have mattered to me who had taken the flag, but somehow, even amidst everything else that was happening, it did. I only hoped he did not expect me to make good on my offer.

Having seen their banner and their king fall, Rhiwallon's men were turning tail now, but they were not the only ones. Bleddyn and his retainers had driven deep into Earl Hugues's ranks, and on all sides were cutting Normans down in their dozens. Blood sprayed and mailed knights toppled from their saddles, and suddenly those conrois were breaking. A horn blasted out: a single long note that was the signal to withdraw. The white wolf and the black and gold were turning, and suddenly along the whole battle-line knights were peeling off, taking to flight. Nor was this the feigned flight that we often practised, that had worked at Hæstinges to draw the enemy out from their positions and help divide their forces. I had campaigned long enough to recognise panic, and theirs was real enough.

The Welshmen pursued them in their hordes, running through those who were too tired or injured to flee, with Bleddyn and his mounted bodyguard leading the massacre.

The battle was lost. After everything, we had failed, and now the field belonged to the enemy. Anger boiled within my veins.

Even as I sat there, my feet rooted to the stirrups, a red-faced Wace was shouting, not just to his men, but to everyone: 'Retreat! Go north; follow the river!'

Similar cries were raised by the other barons, weary horses were spurred on again, and I had no choice but to follow. Around me men were running, abandoning their pursuit of the enemy, abandoning the fight as fear took hold of them.

Maredudd's retainers helped him to his feet and on to his horse. His eyes were tight shut, his face contorted in agony, the thigh of his trews dark with blood. His men were gathering one by one, standing by their horses and watching, seemingly oblivious to what was going on around them, to the sound of the war-horns and sight of the men fleeing. I had seen men take worse injuries and live, but not often. And yet one thing was for certain: he would die if we did not get him away from there.

Not ten paces away lay Rhiwallon's body, his eyes wide in death, his mouth hanging open as if gasping for breath. The black-crested helmet was still attached to his head, but even were it not, I would still have recognised him by his red moustache. His throat had been slit and Maredudd's dagger with its gold-worked hilt left in his groin for good measure.

'It is done,' Maredudd said when I rode alongside him. 'His life for my brother's.'

His breath came in stutters and I could see it was hard for him to speak, let alone find the French words.

'Come on,' I said. 'We have to get away from here while we can.'

Only too well did I understand his grief. And for all his arrogance, I had liked Ithel too. But there would be time enough for that later. Serlo was shouting at me, telling me to leave the Welsh whoresons behind; that if they wanted to stay and get themselves killed, that was their choice and not mine.

The chants of the enemy were growing ever louder, ever closer. I glanced once more across the muddied field towards those lines of brightly painted shields and shining bosses marching towards us, then I turned and spurred Nihtfeax on, following my conroi, thinking of nothing save pushing harder, riding faster. Hooves churned what was left of the turf into a quagmire as, with the enemy's cries of victory lifting to the stone-grey heavens, we raced across the meadows, through the cold mist and the soaking rain, away from that place.

Seventeen

T he enemy did not pursue us. No doubt Rhiwallon's death had shaken them, and left them without the stomach for a long chase. It was small relief. Our raiding-army – the one that not much more than a week ago had ridden to war dreaming of blood and of glory – was all but shattered. Of the five hundred with which I'd begun that day, less than half now remained. Nor had Earl Hugues's host fared any better, as I saw when eventually we caught up with him. He'd left Scrobbesburh at the head of fifteen hundred fighting men, but whereas his spearnen were still for the most part fresh, having never had the chance to face the enemy, easily half his knights – his best fighters – now lay dead.

In all it was a sorry band of warriors that we were left with: spent, bruised and broken, in spirit if not in body; limping, leaning on the hafts of their spears and shoulders of their friends for support; their faces smeared with dirt, their tunics soaked in vomit and their trews reeking of piss and shit. Many were grievously wounded, soon to leave this world for whatever fate awaited them beyond, comforted in their final moments by their companions.

Among those left behind was Turold. He had clung to life as long as he could, they said, but the spear that had pierced his side had been driven deep, and the wound was too severe. His final breath had left his lips moments after he had been dragged from the fray.

'He was a good fighter,' Serlo said once the priest had left us. The big man was not usually one to show his emotion, but I saw the lump in his throat as he swallowed.

Pons's head was bowed towards the ground. 'A good fighter,'

he echoed, more solemnly than I had ever heard him speak. 'And a good friend.'

I nodded silently; there was nothing more I could add. Turold had been the first of my knights to enter my service, mere days after Lord Robert had granted me Earnford. The only son of a wine merchant from Rudum, when I met him he had been begging outside the alehouses of Lundene, having been cast out by his drunkard of a father not long before. Three boys his age had taken a dislike to him for whatever reason: perhaps he had insulted them, or else they were simply looking for a fight, for they had set upon him. For a while he held them off, wrestling one to the ground, biting the arm of another and kneeing him in the groin, and bloodying the nose of the third. Eventually, however, they got the better of him, and he was pinned against the wall. Had I not frightened them away then he would probably have ended up with broken bones, or worse. Still, for one who had never had any training he had proven himself a ferocious fighter, and I saw that his youthful appearance belied a quick temper and a stout heart.

Perhaps it was because I was sorry for him, or because he reminded me in some small way of myself at that age, but I took him in. It was often said among men of noble birth that if a boy had never ridden a horse or begun to practise sword- and spearcraft by the age of twelve, then he was fit only to be a priest. That said, I was into my fourteenth summer when I started on that path, and things had not turned out badly for me. Turold was seventeen, he reckoned, though he did not know exactly. Despite that he was a sturdier lad than I had been, and already a talented horseman, with a natural affinity for the animals: a more accomplished rider, in fact, than many men twice his age. Eager to learn and to please, he spent hours each day in the training yard, practising his cuts and strokes at the pell. Within months he was using the skills he had learnt on the Welsh bands who came raiding across the dyke.

It all seemed so long ago. In fact I had known Turold little more than a year, hard though that was to believe; it felt like much longer.

But while Pons and Serlo both seemed to take his death hard, I could feel only numbness.

Our host finally halted some hours later. Thankfully there had been no sign of enemy scouts following us, and so we had some respite while we decided what to do next. Still, we were in a low-lying position in open farmland that afforded little protection; the only reason we had stopped was because so many were collapsing from exhaustion. The sooner we could move from here, the better.

I went to seek out the black-and-gold banner. Lord Robert and his knights had survived for the most part with little more than cuts and grazes, together with a few broken teeth. Nonetheless, they were decidedly fewer than when I had last seen them in Scrobbesburh.

Several of the men fixed me with cold stares and spat on the ground when I approached.

'You,' one said, rising to block my way. Broad-shouldered and brusque in manner, I recognised him for Ansculf, the captain of Robert's household. 'What do you want, Tancred?'

We had met several times, the first of those being a year earlier. I had not liked him much then, and I liked him even less now. As always a thick smell of cattle dung clung to him, though I had never worked out why that was. He was some years older than myself, and he resented me, as he resented Eudo and Wace, for having been rewarded so generously after Eoferwic while he still remained landless, without the honour that a manor of his own would give him. This I knew because he had told me as much on more than one occasion.

'I want to speak with Robert,' I said. 'Let me pass.'

'You're not welcome here. It's because of you that Urse, Adso, Tescelin and the others lie dead.'

I bridled at his tone. Of those three names only the first was familiar, and I tried to remember which one Urse was; after a moment his round, piggish face rose to mind.

'Because of me? What do you mean?'

'Leave him, Ansculf,' called Lord Robert. He strode towards me, his expression tired and hollow. 'I will speak with him myself.'

But Ansculf was not going to back down readily. 'Lord, this man—'

'Enough,' Robert said sharply. 'Tancred, come with me.'

I followed him until we were out of easy earshot of his knights, although they kept casting sneering glances in my direction and I could still catch parts of their conversation. They spoke loudly of how my mother was a whore and the daughter of a whore besides, and how they had heard that I preferred the company of men to women: all of it doubtless meant for my ears, to provoke me.

'They are angry,' Robert said dismissively. 'Their sword-brothers are dead and they need someone they can blame.'

'Then they should blame the men who struck the blows that sent them to their graves,' I said. 'What do their deaths have to do with me?'

The words came out more petulantly than I had meant them, and I saw that they had stung Robert. For a moment he looked as though he were about to turn on me, but after a moment's hesitation he simply shook his head.

We kept walking until we had come to the wolf banner, which had been planted in the ground at the edge of one of the pasture fields. An audience had gathered around Hugues d'Avranches by the time we arrived, and among them I recognised many of the barons who had been there in the hall at Scrobbesburh, their faces red with anger as the young earl tried to shout them down, demanding order.

They fell silent as I approached, and one by one turned to fix their gazes upon me.

'At last he decides to show his face,' one of them called. 'The Breton for whom so much Norman blood has been spilt.'

I felt as though I were on trial, accused of some misdemeanour of which I remained ignorant.

'What?' I asked, but no one seemed willing to answer. The Wolf gazed back at me, stony-faced and stern despite his youth, as if somehow I ought to understand already. As if I were stupid for not being able to see it.

'He is no less a Norman than any of you,' Robert said. 'So unless you have anything useful to say, you would be wise to keep those tongues inside your heads.'

One of the barons shoved me in the shoulder as we made our way through the crowd. Even so many hours after the battle my blood was running hot. The pain of defeat was still fresh, and that small slight was enough to bring my anger to the surface once more. Without pausing to think I shoved him back. In an instant he had drawn his knife and I mine as we faced each other.

'Put away your weapons,' the Wolf barked. 'This is not the time for squabbling.'

'I'll sheathe mine as soon as he apologises,' I said, staring into the cold blue eyes of the one who had laid his hands upon me.

'Apologise?' he snorted. 'To the man on whose account some of my best knights lost their lives? It was your own foolhardiness that led you into the enemy trap. It would have been far better if we had left you and your Welsh friends to your fates.'

'If you had left us?' I asked, frowning. 'What do you mean by that?'

I glanced at Robert, but he would not meet my eyes.

'I didn't have to come and rescue your wretched hide,' Earl Hugues said. His voice was hoarse, but there was no mistaking his frustration. 'You weren't supposed to meet the enemy host at all. If you hadn't blundered into their ambush, we could have forced them to meet us on ground that suited us.'

'Why did you come, then?' I demanded. 'Tell me that. If there was no advantage to be had, why did you commit your men at all?'

'Because of your lord.' He gestured at Robert. 'He convinced me to meet the enemy in battle, to take the fight to the brothers Rhiwallon and Bleddyn. You would not be standing here now were it not for him, so have some respect and be thankful that you and your companions still live while so many do not.'

His fiery gaze burnt into me, but I held it. Eventually he turned away, shaking his head. A hush fell; no one dared to speak.

Lord Robert was the one to break the silence as he said: 'What do we do now?'

'We return to Scrobbesburh and make ready to face the enemy there,' the Wolf replied.

'You'd have us retreat?' I asked.

'We haven't the strength to fight another battle,' the Wolf replied. 'On the other hand the enemy's confidence will have grown in the wake of their victory. As the news spreads, even more men will flock to their banners. Soon they will march again.'

'One of their kings lies dead, struck down on the field,' I said. 'If ever there was a time to strike, it is now, before they have the chance to rally and bolster their numbers.'

'Look around you, Tancred,' said Hugues, an exasperated glint in his eyes. 'Look at the faces of the men. How many of them do you think have the heart for another clash with the enemy? Many have lost friends and brothers and most are half-starved besides. How well do you think that they'll fight on empty stomachs?'

To escape the battle we'd had to abandon most of the heavily laden sumpter ponies that carried our packs, in which had lain the bulk of our provisions. Only by cutting loose the straps to relieve them of their burden had we managed to save even a few of the animals. My own horses were among them, I was relieved to see, rescued by the ever-dependable Cnebba and Snocca, both of whom had been fortunate to escape with little more than scratches and bruises, torn tunics and dirt-streaked faces.

'We raid, just as we did before,' I said, growing more desperate. 'Send bands out to forage. As soon as the men are rested and their bellies are full we can ride once more. We still have most of our spearmen left, all of them fit to fight.'

I glanced about, hoping to rouse the enthusiasm of the other barons, trying to meet the eyes of those who had supported me back in the castle hall not so long ago. It was in vain. In silence they stared at me, arms folded in front of their chests. A few began to walk away, though whether in disgust or out of embarrassment for me, it was hard to tell. I sensed that my cause was a losing one, yet for some reason I could not stop myself.

'Yes,' I said, raising my voice, 'we can ride once more, surprise the enemy within their own camp—'

I broke off when I saw Robert shaking his head as if in warning. Defeated, my spirits sank. For the first time since the battle I felt empty, my limbs devoid of all vigour.

'Return to your men,' the Wolf called as the barons dispersed. 'Eat what food you have, rest while you can. We march within the hour.'

I was making my way back when the Welsh princes' chaplain, a man by the name of Ionafal, saw me and called me over to where his countrymen were gathered. The priest had just finished hearing Maredudd's confession and had given him the sacrament from a flask he carried inside his robes. His lord was not long for this life, he told me; if I wanted to speak with him then now was the time.

Amidst the confusion of our flight from the battle and everything that had followed, I had all but forgotten him. When I arrived, his pallor was worse than any I had ever seen, as if all the blood had drained from his face. He could not stop shivering, though the day was far from cold. His men had offered up their own cloaks, wrapping the furs around him. He was of an age with myself, but at that moment he looked much older.

'Tancred,' he said when he saw me. His voice came out at no more than a whisper, and he could barely keep his eyes open, but at least he recognised me.

Now that I was here, words deserted me. 'You fought well,' I said. 'You and your brother both.'

'Not well enough,' he said, and managed a smile, though it quickly faded as tears came into his eyes. 'If we had, then Ithel would still live, the usurpers would both lie dead and we would stand victorious.'

I gripped his hand in reassurance. His palm was moist with sweat, his skin burning with ague.

'You have been a steadfast ally, Tancred, and I thank you.' His face creased in pain and he began to cough: a dry, hacking sound that signalled he did not have much longer.

'Rest,' I said to him. 'Save your strength.'

His retainers were crowding close around us, and I made way

for them. Better that they were the ones with whom he spent his final moments: his loyal hearth-companions, the ones who had chosen to follow him into exile rather than bend their knee before the usurpers, who had been with him all these years. Besides, I had seen too much death that day, and had no wish to witness any more. Not since Hæstinges could I recall so many having fallen so quickly.

I'd not known the Welsh brothers long, and yet somehow I had come to feel a sort of kinship with them. Yes, they were ambitious and headstrong, as men of high birth often are, and forthright with their opinions. Nevertheless, in many ways it was because of those things, rather than for their fearlessness or prowess at arms, that I had come to respect them, not least because I recognised many of those same traits in myself.

Which was why, when the news eventually came that Maredudd had passed away, a deep-rooted chill came over me, a chill that made its way into my bones and gripped my very soul. For I knew that it could so easily have been me.

We travelled quickly in spite of the difficult terrain. For all that he had said about the men being too tired and hungry to fight, Earl Hugues pushed them hard.

More than once that day we saw bands of enemy advance riders trailing us, though they rarely came any closer than a couple of miles. They moved quickly, being lightly armed with only helmets for protection. The Wolf and Robert sent conrois out to pursue them, hoping that they would kill or capture a few, but they never did. The enemy were too quick, either disappearing into the cover provided by the dense woods, or else, if they found themselves in open country, splitting up into smaller groups and scattering in all directions so that our men could not follow them. But then those bands had no intention of meeting us directly. They meant only to harry us, to keep us always looking over our shoulders, and in both of those aims they succeeded. And so each time our conrois returned empty-handed.

In all that time the Wolf said nothing to me. In fact he spoke little to anyone, instead choosing to press on ahead in the vanguard, single-mindedly setting the pace. His face, when he did show it, was a picture of fury. No doubt he was wondering what he would say when eventually we reached Scrobbesburh. For he was the one who would have to give the tale of our defeat to Fitz Osbern, and I did not envy him that task.

Darkness still reigned by the time we rode through the town gates the next morning. We'd marched on through the night, despite the fact that many were close to exhaustion, almost dead on their feet and in their saddles, kept going only by the threats and curses of their lords. A messenger had been sent ahead to bear the news to Fitz Osbern, who was not there to meet us when we arrived but, we were told, was waiting in his chambers at the castle. Almost straightaway the Wolf and Lord Robert were summoned to see him, but there was no word whether he wanted to see me too.

'No doubt he will wish to hear from you in time,' said Robert, 'but for now it is best if you wait, and in the meantime try to get some rest. God only knows we need it.'

'You'd have me keep quiet while the Wolf blames me for what happened?'

'Naturally Earl Hugues will be allowed to present his story, but I know Fitz Osbern better than most; he will listen to me if he listens to anyone. He'll see that it was not your fault. You could not have known that the Welsh would be lying in wait.'

'The Wolf doesn't see it that way,' I said sourly. 'He is an arrogant, spoilt runt who only cares for himself. The only reason anyone listens to him is because his family has wealth to spare.'

Robert fixed me with a stern look. 'I understand that you're angry,' he said. 'None of us wishes things had happened this way. But you will do yourself no favours by making an enemy of Hugues.'

'I'm angry because many men were killed yesterday,' I said, speaking through gritted teeth. 'One of my own household knights was among them, and both Maredudd and Ithel too. Good warriors who did not deserve to die.'

With that I turned and walked away. There was nothing more to be discussed. Nor for that matter did I wish to speak to anyone else. I needed time alone, to gather my thoughts and work out what I would say when eventually Fitz Osbern called me to face him.

I managed to rest, though not for long, since dawn was only a few hours away. At sunrise I climbed a knoll looking out across the camp to the west and the distant hills that glowed as the first rays fell upon their slopes. Somewhere beyond them Bleddyn and Eadric were lurking; before long they would be marching, and what might happen then only God could know.

I was still sitting there, lost in thought, when Beatrice found me. She came alone, save for her maidservant Papia, who was waiting with her horse a short way off.

'I suppose your brother sent you,' I said without so much as offering a greeting.

She did not bridle at my rudeness, as I might have expected, or at least if she did she was careful not to show it. I had not slept well, and my ire from the previous night had hardly diminished.

'No, he didn't,' she said. 'When I heard what happened I thought you might wish to talk to someone. I found your men sharpening their swords but they didn't know where you had gone.'

'You came looking for me?'

'Would you prefer that I hadn't?'

I wasn't sure whether to be annoyed or thankful, but settled for the latter. For once I was glad to have some company. Had I been back in Earnford there would have been Leofrun to comfort me, or else I could have spoken with Father Erchembald. Here, though, surrounded by all these strange faces and by so many men who seemed to bear grudges against me, I felt alone in a way that I had not known before.

'No,' I said at last. 'I'm glad you came.'

She seated herself on the damp grass next to me, folding her skirts neatly beneath her. 'Earl Hugues has taken his leave of us, you'll be pleased to hear.'

'So I've been told.'

He had departed shortly before I had risen, so early in fact that few had seen him go. There was trouble in Ceastre, where the townspeople had risen against the Wolf's steward. The story was that his knights had beaten and imprisoned the city's port-reeve and cut off his right hand when they found he had been allowing merchants to use the old silver in the market: the coins that bore the name of Harold the usurper. Blood had been spilt on both sides as the townsmen fought the knights in the streets, and now the garrison was trapped in the castle, under siege and in desperate need of relief. Whether that was the whole reason for his leave-taking, or whether there had been some quarrel between the earl and Fitz Osbern during their meeting last night, no one knew.

'As Robert tells it, there was some disagreement between you and the earl,' Beatrice said.

I gave a laugh, though I did not feel much cheered. 'That's one word for it, I suppose.'

'You must be relieved to see him gone.'

In all honesty my feelings were mixed. In spite of my dislike of him, he'd brought men to our cause, and I was only too aware of the difficulties his sudden departure brought upon us. For with him he had taken more than half his knights, and nearly as many foot: a little less than four hundred spears in all. Four hundred that we could not afford to spare.

'I don't know,' I said, and it was the truth. 'I don't trust him, and yet without the men he commands, what chance do we have of defending Scrobbesburh?'

'There is talk that some of the other barons might desert. Having seen the Wolf ride away to defend his possessions and his home, many are now thinking of doing the same.'

I made a noise of disgust and shook my head. Nothing was going as it should do. This realm that we had fought so hard these last four years to forge was falling apart, breaking into splinters.

'Can you blame them?' she asked. 'Like you, they have lost some of their ablest and most faithful retainers, their best warriors. If they stay and fight, they stand to lose even more.'

'And yet if they don't, they simply make it easier for the enemy, who will overrun their manors anyway just as soon as they've defeated the rest of us here.'

The words, and the bitterness with which they came out, surprised even myself. After all, it wasn't so long ago that I had shared their fears, been reluctant to leave the people and the place I had come to know so well. What had changed? Was it that I had now seen with my own eyes the threat we faced? Or was it because I sought redemption for the deaths of Turold, Ithel, Maredudd and all the others?

'How can you be sure that the enemy will come, in any case?' asked Beatrice. 'By all accounts they suffered heavily too in the battle. One of their kings lies dead.'

'Which is exactly why they will come. Bleddyn will want revenge for his brother Rhiwallon and all the rest of his countrymen, and he won't rest until he's taken it.'

And then of course there was Eadric, together with the rest of the English rebels who had followed him across to the Welsh side. They still sought the lands that they had forfeited, and would stop at nothing to reclaim them.

For a while we sat in silence. I didn't know what else to say and neither, it seemed, did she. The sun was breaking over the roofs of the houses behind us and the river sparkled in its light. Even though the hour was early, I could feel its warmth upon my back as I picked at the grass beside me.

After some time Beatrice said, 'Tell me about Earnford.'

'What do you want to know?'

'Anything,' she said. 'Everything. The place, the people. What it's like to live out in these parts, so close to the dyke.'

This was the first she had ever asked me about my manor. I glanced sidelong at her, trying to work out the reason behind her sudden interest.

I sighed and closed my eyes. 'It's a special place,' I said. 'I've never known anywhere like it. The hall stands on a mound over-looking the river; around it the fields are golden with wheat and barley; on either side of the valley sheep graze the pastures. We catch fish in the stream, trap hares in the woods. There is everything there.'

'I would very much like to see it sometime.'

'If you did you would never want to leave. Even in the winter when the ground is frozen, the wind is tearing at the thatch, and mud and snow make the tracks impassable.' I smiled for what seemed like the first time in a long while. 'At Christmas the swineherd Garwulf brought me one of his fattest boars as a gift. We slaughtered it in the yard and roasted it over the hearth in my hall. The whole village came and we feasted like kings on its meat for three whole days, until there was nothing left but bone. There was drinking and there was dancing; the hall was hung with holly branches and the fire burnt brightly through those long nights.'

'You are happy there.' The way she said it made it sound almost like a question.

I shrugged. 'It is home. If you'd asked me when we first met last year whether I could ever be content somewhere like that, I'd probably have laughed. I know it's not much, not really, but yes, I am happy. I have Leofrun, and all being well soon I will have a child too.'

In only another month, in fact. I only hoped that I would be back when her time came, though with every day that passed that seemed less and less likely.

'Leofrun?' Beatrice asked, frowning.

I'd forgotten that she didn't yet know. I supposed there was no better time than now to break it to her.

'My woman. She's been with me for the better part of a year.'

Beatrice cast her gaze down, and I noticed her cheeks reddening. Suddenly she looked younger than her twenty-one years. 'I didn't know,' she mumbled.

'I ought to have told you sooner. I'm sorry—'

She waved a hand, cutting me off. I wasn't sure what else to say, and neither it seemed was she, for without a further word she got to her feet and left me there alone.

Eighteen

When word eventually arrived from Fitz Osbern towards noon I was bathing in the river: rinsing several days' worth of dirt and sweat and blood from my clothes and my skin, and with it the memory of the battle, the stain of Turold's death.

I spotted the messenger while he was still some way off, being pointed in my direction by a group of boys who were training with wooden rods by the riverbank. He was little younger than myself, with a humourless countenance and a stiff bearing.

'Tancred of Earnford?' he asked as he halted and looked down from his horse.

I shielded my eyes against the sun as I looked up at him. 'That's my name,' I answered. 'What do you want?'

'Lord Guillaume would speak with you now.'

Not before time, I thought, although I did not say it. Instead I nodded and turned my back, splashing cool water into my face.

'Without delay,' the messenger added, perhaps thinking that I hadn't heard him properly. 'He's waiting for you in his hall at the castle.'

He was the sort of man, I decided, who enjoyed the sound of his own voice; one who was accustomed to being listened to, and who did not take kindly to being ignored.

'I heard you,' I replied, rubbing my armpits with a wet scrap of cloth. 'You can tell your lord I will be there as soon as I can.'

He gave me a disapproving look, although if he thought that would hasten me he was disappointed. Shortly he rode off, probably to inform his master of my insolence.

If Fitz Osbern wanted to speak with me then he would have to be patient. He had kept me waiting this long; now he in his turn would have to wait a little longer. In any case, it wouldn't do for me to meet with the second most powerful man in the kingdom soaked to the skin and with hair drenched like a water vole's. Fortunately the morning was warm, the sky cloudless and the sun bright, and I soon dried. Hanging my still-wet clothes to dry over the canvas of my tent, I dressed in my spare tunic and trews, and, as always, buckled my sword-belt upon my waist.

Not much later I was riding through the castle gates. Above them flew streamers of cloth decorated in Fitz Osbern's colours of white and crimson, signifying that he had formally taken over command of the castle from its appointed guardian Roger de Montgommeri.

I left Nihtfeax in the care of one of the castle's stable-hands and made my way around the training yard to the far side of the bailey, where the great hall stood. Servants were rolling barrels from one of the storehouses to the kitchens; others had been less lucky in the tasks given them and were shovelling heaps of horse shit on to the back of a cart while clouds of flies swarmed about them. The steady hammering of iron upon iron rang out from the farrier's workshop; in the yard oak cudgels clashed against limewood shields; from beyond the walls oxen bellowed and snorted as they were driven through the streets.

'Lord Guillaume is in his solar,' said the door-ward when I arrived at the hall and gave him my name. 'He is not accustomed to being made to wait. He was expecting you a half-hour ago, and I should tell you that he is in a foul temper.'

I thanked the man for his kind warning as he led me to the stairs, where he left me. Along the length of the up-floor ran a hallway, at the end of which the door to the solar lay ajar. I knocked and entered.

The shutters lay open but even so the chamber was stifling. Thick rugs covered the floorboards, while richly coloured embroideries decorated the walls, displaying scenes from what I could only assume was a marriage feast. Within a long hall stood a long table replete with all manner of dishes, behind which were seated the lord, his arms outstretched as if in greeting, and beside him his bride, dressed in a blue gown. Around them servants bore bowls of soup, platters of wildfowl and gilded wine-cups, while a fool danced and a minstrel played upon a harp.

Fitz Osbern stood at the far end of the room, gazing out of the open window, his hands clasped behind him. Beside him was a round table and upon it stood an earthenware pitcher together with a goblet of green glass, elaborately decorated with a golden lattice pattern and half filled with what I presumed was wine. He showed no sign of having heard me come in.

'My lord,' I said. 'You wished to see me.'

'You're late.' His tone as usual was curt.

'I came as soon as I was able,' I replied just as flatly.

He did not turn from the window. 'When I summon you to my presence, you do not hesitate but simply do as you are bid. Do you understand?'

I kept my mouth shut, knowing that if I opened it then all the frustration and ill feeling that had been building within me would let itself out. Fitz Osbern did not repeat himself; instead he waited for my answer. When it was clear that none was forthcoming, he turned to face me.

'I wonder if Malet's son has indulged you rather too much. A better lord would see that his vassals learnt the meaning of obedience. A true leader would make sure that they knew their place. But then the Malets have always struggled to win the respect of their followers. Or, for that matter, of anyone else.'

This last he muttered almost under his breath. What did he mean by it?

'Lord—' I began.

'Let me warn you, Tancred a Dinant,' he said, cutting me off. 'You do not want to make an enemy of me. I have King Guillaume's ear. If I so wished, I could have you stripped of your lands, expelled from the realm, or worse. So whatever you mean to say, you would be wise to think first, and choose your words with care.'

He held my gaze, his expression fixed in contempt, as if I were nothing more than a louse to him: an irritant, but one that could be easily crushed. There was a slight slur to his words, and I smelt wine on his breath: sour and pungent, faint but enough to be noticeable. How long had he been drinking before I arrived?

'No?' he said, raising his eyebrows in mock-surprise. 'Very well.' He began to pace around the room. 'I am a patient man, Tancred, but not so patient that I readily forgive those who cross me. Consider yourself fortunate on this occasion, but do not presume that I will be nearly so lenient next time.'

'No, lord.'

He nodded, seemingly satisfied, and when he spoke again it was in a milder tone: 'Do not think, either, that I hold you responsible for what happened in Wales, or that I believe Hugues to be blameless in this matter either.'

'Thank you,' I said. That at least was some relief.

'I am not looking for gratitude. I only tell you this for your own peace of mind.' He sighed. 'In any case, all that is behind us, and we have more pressing matters at hand. We must reserve our hatred for the enemy, not waste it on each other. It will do us no good to spread discord amongst our own ranks as long as the enemy is afield.'

'Has there been any word of their movements?'

'Not yet,' Fitz Osbern said. 'I have sent my fastest riders to keep watch along the valley of the Saverna, and had beacons erected between here and the dyke, the fires to be lit as soon as the enemy show themselves. Thus far, however, there has been no sign of them.'

Some of those beacons we'd seen as we had withdrawn back down the Saverna valley to Scrobbesburh. At best they might give us a couple of days' warning of any approaching army: a few more hours, then, for us to spend waiting for the inevitable, for those banners and spearpoints to appear over the distant horizon.

'They will come sooner rather than later,' I said. 'They know that we are weakened. They'll want to press their advantage while they still can, before any reinforcements reach us from Lundene.'

Fitz Osbern shook his head and turned back towards the window. 'There will be no reinforcements,' he said quietly.

'What do you mean?'

'Word reached us from the southern shires yesterday morning

with the news that the people of Defnascir and Sumorsæte are rising, and not only that, but sending messengers to foment rebellion throughout the rest of Wessex. Meanwhile across the sea our enemies in Maine and Brittany are said to be conspiring with the French king against us.'

He almost spat the name of the land of my birth. For longer than most could remember Normandy and Brittany had been warring, and while those wars had for the moment ceased, the enmity they had spawned between the two peoples had not entirely died. Perhaps Fitz Osbern had forgotten to whom he was speaking, or perhaps the slight was intentional, to remind me of my place. If I were to speak honestly, it was a long time since I had truly thought of myself as Breton, so many years had I spent fleeing the place of my youth, serving under lords who swore their fealty to the Norman duke. Not that that had ever stopped others from holding my parentage against me. I was well used to hearing such base insults upon my person, so much so that I no longer felt their force, though it was rare that they came from men as highborn and as learned as Guillaume fitz Osbern.

'The Bretons and the Manceaux are always stirring up trouble, lord,' I said. 'That means nothing.'

'Perhaps not,' he replied. 'But that is not all. As we speak the Danes are setting sail with a fleet of more than three hundred ships.'

'Three hundred?' I repeated. That was as large as our own fleet of four years ago.

'So the traders who bring us this knowledge say, or at any rate the ones that we pay, since they are usually more trustworthy than the rest.'

Three hundred ships. The number seemed so large as to be scarcely believable. That could mean anywhere up to fifteen thousand men, at least half of whom we could expect to be warriors. It made our own force here in Scrobbesburh seem paltry by comparison. Nor was that the worst part, for in my experience every Dane was worth two Englishmen, hailing as they did from the cold and wind-battered lands across the German Sea, where food was scarce and men had to fight their neighbours for every crumb if they did not want to starve. They were renowned for their savagery in battle, feared throughout Christendom from the frozen isles that lay beyond Britain's northernmost shores to the distant sun-parched lands of the eastern emperor, where some of their best warriors were reputed to serve as his personal guard. They had conquered this kingdom themselves more than once before. Now they were coming again: the invasion for which we had been waiting a year and more. Few had expected it would ever happen. All through the winter men had joked about the Danes and their king, Sweyn, and about his threats that always came to naught.

Now that it was happening, though, I found that doubts were creeping into my mind as to whether we could fight them off. Not while we had our own troubles to face here on the March. Nor was I forgetting that somewhere in the north there was also the ætheling, whose plans could only be guessed, so little had been heard of him.

'They will most probably land in the south and try to take Lundene, just as we did,' Fitz Osbern went on. 'King Guillaume himself has hastened back from Normandy and is now encamped at Westmynstre. He cannot allow the city to fall. He will need every able-bodied man of fighting age that he can marshal from the southern shires – every hauberk and helmet, every axe and pitchfork – if he is to prevent them taking it.'

'Then we must do the same,' I said. 'We have to raise the *fyrd* not just from along the borderlands but from across the rest of Mercia too.'

The fyrd was the English peasant levy, raised by the reeves and the earls, organised according to the various shires and hundreds into which the kingdom was divided. The men who made it up were not warriors but farmers, most of whom could barely tell one end of a spear from the other, and it was foolish to rely upon them holding firm in the shield-wall. I was not suggesting calling upon the fyrd for their skill at arms, however, but simply for their numbers, for that was what we lacked.

'We might call upon them, but that does not mean that they will come,' Fitz Osbern said. 'Nor do we have so many men that I can readily afford to send them out into the shires to enforce the summons, not when the enemy could march upon us any day now. In Wessex it is different, for the people there hate and fear the Danes. The Mercians will not fight their own kind. If they deign to lift their spears at all it will be under Eadric's banner, alongside those of their countrymen who have already joined him.'

'What then? If the king won't send us men, how are we to defend Scrobbesburh, let alone the rest of the March?'

He did not answer. Of course he was known to be a close friend of the king, and one of his most trusted advisers, the two having known each other since they had grown up together at the ducal court in Normandy. That the king could not spare even his most loyal servant the forces he needed was a sign of how serious he considered the Danish threat to be.

There was a stool by the table and Fitz Osbern sat down upon it, burying his face in his palms and making a sound of frustration halfway between a sigh and a groan.

'Are you unwell, lord?' I asked.

'The enemy are coming, and meanwhile all we do is quarrel and tear at each other's throats in the manner of wild beasts.' He shook his head and a grimace spread across his face. 'Like packs of wolves,' he muttered.

To my mind that last remark could refer to only one thing. Perhaps that was why he was in such a foul mood.

'What of Earl Hugues?' I asked. 'I hear that he took himself back to Ceastre earlier this morning.'

He looked up sharply, as if I had been eavesdropping upon his thoughts. In truth the connection was not hard to make.

'Hugues,' he said as his expression grew hard. 'He has his own battles to fight. All his arrogance and belief in his own self-importance do not disguise the fact that, at only twenty years, he is little more than a child, with a temper to match. He must always do his own thing; he takes neither instruction nor advice from anyone. And always it is to the detriment of others, just as now as he leaves us short of four hundred spears that we might other-wise have usefully employed.'

'They say that some of the other barons are looking to follow the Wolf's example,' I said, remembering the rumours Beatrice had spoken of. 'They plan to desert and return to their own manors.'

'Do you think I don't know that? Do you think that I don't have my own people within the camp, that I must rely on whatever scraps of news you choose to bring me?'

'I didn't mean to presume—'

'No, of course you didn't,' he said, with more than a hint of sarcasm. 'Fortunately I am well aware who those barons are, and they will know it soon enough, too.'

'Surely, lord,' I said, trying to restrain my frustration, 'punishing them will only give them further cause to abandon us. Instead wouldn't it be better to assuage them with promises of gold and silver and whatever else is necessary to keep them happy?'

'I will deal with them how I choose,' he snapped. 'I do not need advice from one such as you!'

Why, then, had he called me here, if not to chastise me or ask what I thought? I wondered whether he himself had forgotten.

'All this could so easily have been avoided,' he said bitterly. His fingers clenched into a fist, his knuckles turning white. 'I thought that by sending a raiding-army across the dyke Eadric and the Welsh might be quelled before they could bring their might to bear. Instead we can only wait for them to come to us, and pray to God that when they do we have the strength to fight them off.'

'We will find a way,' I said, doing my best to sound confident. 'When the time comes we will send them running back across the dyke with their tails between their legs. We will show them slaughter such as they have never before seen.'

I might as well have been speaking to myself, since Fitz Osbern wasn't listening. Instead he seemed lost in his own world as he went on: 'Our enemies circle around us, taunting us, preparing themselves to descend and strike, and meanwhile we are powerless to do anything at all!'

His eyes were filled with fury as he brought his fist down upon the table beside him with such vehemence that the glass goblet toppled. His jaw clenched, with the back of his hand he swept the drinking vessel and jug from the surface, sending them flying against the wall, where they smashed, scattering shards across the floor, spraying scarlet droplets everywhere.

None of which was enough to satisfy him. He rose sharply, grabbing the edge of the table and upending it with a crash before, swearing, he turned to face once more out the window.

Over the years I'd had dealings with many powerful barons, but never had I known any of them lose control so completely in front of men of lower rank than themselves. And while I'd heard tales of Fitz Osbern's fierce temper before, this was the first time I had witnessed it. For the second time I found myself wondering how much wine had passed his lips that morning. Naturally he was angry at the situation in which we found ourselves, but I wondered if some of that anger he reserved for himself too, for having misjudged the enemy's strength so gravely, for having sent us on the expedition in the first place. And yet I couldn't help but feel that on a different day, that battle in Mechain could so easily have turned the other way. If Ithel had not let his desire for vengeance get the better of him, and if his brother had not gone after him, then their lives and those of their men need not have been wasted in a hopeless cause. That in itself might have been enough to save us from the rout that had ensued. In such moments of folly, courage and desperation rested the fate of entire kingdoms, difficult though it was to see it at the time.

All this I kept to myself as I waited for Fitz Osbern to break the silence. When eventually he did speak, it was in more muted tones, and I wondered whether that meant the storm had passed.

'Everything is falling into ruin,' he said. 'Everything we have toiled these last four years to build is collapsing: the kingdom like a house whose posts are rotten, whose thatch is being torn from the roof-timbers. We strive to repair it, but it is all in vain. The winds only howl more fiercely and the rains lash down more heavily, and there is nothing we can do to keep them out.'

Not for the first time I was unsure what to reply, if indeed he expected me to say anything at all. His back was turned and I wasn't entirely convinced that he knew I was still there.

Outside I heard knights training in the yard as well as the sounds of sawing and hammering as builders and labourers worked to strengthen the castle's defences. On my way here I had seen them driving pointed stakes into the ditch to deter any attackers who might try to assault the walls. Nothing was being left to chance. Of course Fitz Osbern would recall what had happened at Eoferwic last year, when Malet had thought the city's walls sufficient to keep out the besiegers, only for the Northumbrians to storm the gates with the townsmen's aid and force him back to the castle, in the process killing a large number of the Norman garrison. We could not afford to make the same mistake this time, nor allow ourselves to feel too secure, which was why so much effort was being expended to further fortify the town.

And yet if Fitz Osbern was right, even that might not be enough to stop Eadric and the Welsh, and all the others who threatened the kingdom. In times of crisis men always look to those above them to give them confidence, but I had not gained any from him. Rather, it seemed that he had all but given up hope, not just of defending the March but of holding England altogether. Unlike some other lords I had known over the years, I had always considered him a formidable man, a rival even to the foremost princes of Christendom. A staunch and uncompromising leader, he inspired respect in everyone: from the lowliest knight to King Guillaume himself, who was said to hold his counsel in higher regard than that of any other man. Today, however, I had seen a very different side of him, and all at once I found the admiration that I'd held for him slipping away, as if a veil had fallen from my eyes. I felt strangely embarrassed to be standing there, as if I had witnessed something that I had not been supposed to.

I cleared my throat. 'My lord, if you have no further need of me, then I ought to return to my men, and see what needs to be done.'

He didn't deign to offer a reply, but waved a hand absently, and I took that to mean that I was dismissed. Without a further word I left him to gaze despondently out across the yard by himself, closing the door softly behind me. Even as I did so, however, a small voice of doubt rose at the back of my mind, and the thought occurred to me: what if he was right?

Nineteen

Scrobbesburh's market square was a quieter place now. Probably the merchants who usually came had made instead for safer ports where they could sell their wares without the threat of Welsh steel slicing open their bellies. Still, as I made my way back past the stalls of the wool-sellers and the stacked cages of chickens and wildfowl destined for the spit, my mood lifted when I glimpsed a familiar face amongst the traders.

'Byrhtwald!'

With his familiar tired grey mule and cart with its green and scarlet streamers, it could be no other. At the sound of his name he looked up. He did not spot me at first, but as I led Nihtfeax around the side of a pair of haywains towards him, a grin spread across his face.

'Lord Tancred,' he said, clasping my hand in greeting when I reached him. 'You've been having many adventures, or so I hear. The Welsh haven't managed to kill you yet, then.'

'Not yet.' I returned his smile. 'And I'm hoping that they don't for a while longer, too. What are you doing here?'

'Buying and selling,' he said. 'What else do you think? There's no better place to make money than a marketplace when there's an army encamped not an arrow's flight away.'

'And no better place to hear news that you can later sell to those who'll pay.'

'You know me too well,' he said. 'If I'm honest, though, I've learnt little that isn't already common knowledge. Still, I was right about Wild Eadric and the Welsh, wasn't I?'

'You were,' I conceded. Not that it had helped me much.

'I see you carry the reliquary with you,' he said, nodding at the bronze pendant that hung around my neck. 'I thought that was bound for the altar in your church. The priest seemed rather taken with it, as I remember.'

'He wanted me to wear it, so that the saint would protect me in battle,' I said. 'Since I'm still alive, I suppose he must be looking after me.'

'I'll confess that's one sale I regret making. My wife was not best pleased when I told her I'd let you buy it off me, and for less than a pound of silver at that. I should never have agreed to such a price. Clouted me around the head for that, she did.' He rubbed his temple. 'I had a lump right here for days afterwards.'

'Your wife is well, then?'

'Well enough, thank you kindly for asking. She's a tough woman, as strong as an ox, and don't I know it.'

'No sign of her illness returning, I hope.'

'Illness, lord?' He frowned for a moment, before he seemed to remember. 'Oh yes,' he said hurriedly. 'Terrible days those were, but God be praised she still lives. To tell the truth, I've never known her in such good health as she is now.' He pointed to the relic-pendant. 'And to think that she might not be with us at all, were it not for the intervention of blessed St Mathurin—'

'Mathurin?' I interrupted him. 'You said this belonged to St Ignatius.'

'St Ignatius, of course,' he answered, red-faced all of a sudden. 'That's what I meant to say. The hair of St Ignatius.'

'Toe-bone.'

'What?'

'It was his toe-bone, or so you told me.'

'And so it is,' he said, beaming as if he had just been proven right. 'His toe-bone, indeed.'

Frustrated, I gave up. I suspected Byrhtwald was merely having a jest at my expense, but I couldn't be sure. Sometimes it was useless trying to talk with him. For all that I liked him, I always had the sense when we spoke that I was playing some manner of game, the rules of which I did not quite understand. Worse, it was a game

I always seemed to end up losing. Quick with his words and confident in his manner, Byrhtwald was the kind of man who would try to sell me the shirt off my own back if he thought he could get away with it. Even then I would probably end up convinced that I'd made a good trade.

'The enemy are coming,' I said. 'They know that we are weakened, and no doubt Bleddyn will be wanting to avenge his brother's death too. I don't know how long it'll be before they march, but you probably don't want to still be here when they do. Otherwise you might find Fitz Osbern forcing a spear into your hands and putting you on the ramparts to help defend the town.'

'Have no fear on my account,' said Byrhtwald. 'I promise you that Cwylmend' – he patted the mule's flank – 'and I will be gone long before the enemy get here.'

'*Cwylmend?*' My understanding of the English tongue was far from perfect, but I knew enough to be able to translate that. 'You name that wretched excuse for an animal Tormenter?'

'Watch what you say in her company,' he said indignantly, covering the mule's ears with his hands as he glared at me. 'She's a loyal friend to me, and fierce in her own way. She doesn't like to show it, that's all. Last week a man tried to hit her and she savaged his right hand, bit off all his fingers and left him with only the thumb. If she wanted, I reckon she could probably have your head off.'

Ignorant of what we were saying about her, Cwylmend continued to munch upon a pile of hay. Flies buzzed around her and once in a while she would swing her tail lazily to fend them off.

'Make sure that you don't tell Fitz Osbern about her,' I said. 'If he finds out that she's good for killing Welshmen, he'll have her in the first rank of the shield-wall when the enemy come.'

'I never said she'd killed anyone, lord. Truth be told, I don't think the old girl has it in her to take a man's life, but that doesn't mean she isn't willing to cause some pain where it's warranted.'

He left me for a moment to deal with one of his countrymen, a grey-bearded fellow with a large wart upon his nose, who was looking to exchange a blackened chicken on a stick for one of the ointment-jars that the pedlar had laid out on a bench in front of his cart.

The deal having been struck, Byrhtwald turned back to me, already tearing into the charred meat. 'Forgive me,' he said between mouthfuls. 'I haven't eaten in hours. Do you want some?'

I thanked him but declined, and was about to ask him where his travels had taken him since last I saw him, when he waved the carcass in the direction of St Ealhmund's church across the market square.

'Friends of yours?' he asked.

A group of five knights were riding towards us, and at their head was Berengar. I had avoided him as best as I could since arriving back from the expedition, for I had no desire to see his face.

'Not exactly,' I replied.

The tale of how Berengar had captured the Welsh banner in the battle had begun to spread, and everywhere now men were singing his praises, hailing him as a hero for his feats of courage and the number of foemen he had slain. Some were even beginning to say that it was he who had killed Rhiwallon, and though he knew as well as I did that that was not true, he hadn't made any attempt to deny it.

The crowd parted to make way for him and his retinue. Their faces I recognised, for they had all ridden in my raiding-host, always at Berengar's side, unwavering in their loyalty to him. As usual Berengar had a scowl upon his face: the only expression that to my recollection he had ever worn.

'Consorting with the enemy are we now, Tancred?' he said as they halted before us. 'Or are you going to tell me you didn't know?'

'Know what?' I asked.

'We're arresting all the travelling merchants and pedlars who are still in the town, and seizing their goods forthwith. The order was given earlier this morning.'

I frowned. 'For what reason?'

'To prevent them selling news of our numbers and disposition to those across the dyke. Already three men have confessed to being spies in the enemy's pay. No doubt the rest will do so in their turn just as soon as we can question them properly.'

'Why haven't I heard of this?'

Berengar shrugged. 'How should I know?' He fixed Byrhtwald with a stern gaze, although if the Englishman was at all perturbed he did not show it. 'Now, if you'll make way, I intend to apprehend this man and take him to the castle.'

I did not move. 'Who gave this order?'

'Fitz Osbern himself placed me in charge of the task.'

'He didn't mention any of this to me,' I said. 'I was speaking with him not half an hour ago.'

'And because of that you assume that I'm lying?' Berengar sneered. 'You think he considers you so worthy of his attention that he must keep you informed of his every decision? After what happened, you're lucky he hasn't put you in chains and cast you into the deepest, dankest pit he can find. At the very least he must realise how misplaced was his faith in you. It took him long enough. We all saw it long ago.'

He glanced at his five companions, who were all sniggering. By now I had grown used to such childish scorn, and this time I refused to rise to it. Berengar swung down from his horse and marched in front of me, drawing himself up to his full height.

'Unless you want to join your English friend, I suggest you get out of my way,' he said.

We stood eye to eye. He was slightly the taller of the two of us, with, I reckoned, a longer reach that would give him an advantage if it came to a fight, but his greater girth would surely slow him down and make him clumsier on his feet.

'If you want me to move, you'll have to make me,' I said.

He gave me a questioning look, as if he had expected that his words alone would be enough to make me stand aside. As if I cared for any instruction that came out of his mouth. Uncertain what to do, he held my stare for a few moments, before slowly a smile broke out across his face and, forcing a laugh, he turned to his friends.

'He thinks he can stop us.' He raised his tone for all to hear, throwing his hands wide as if beseeching the crowd to witness my obstinacy. 'He thinks he can defy Fitz Osbern's bidding!'

A few of the market-goers were turning their heads to watch, but most were staying well back. Even if they didn't know enough French to understand what was being said, they surely sensed that this was something they wanted no part of. A woman hustled her children away down the street, glancing over her shoulder nervously as she went. A farmer and his son who were driving a herd of pigs towards the pens on the other side of the square decided not to try to pass us but rather to take the longer route through the side streets.

'This has nothing to do with Fitz Osbern,' I said to Berengar. 'This is about your pathetic feud with me.'

He spat on the floor, narrowly missing my foot. 'I have no feud with you,' he said, not entirely convincingly. 'You're worth about as much as a sheep's turd as far as I'm concerned. Now either go from here back to the ewe's arse that shitted you out or I'll spill your guts on to the street for all these people to see.'

'You could never kill me,' I said. 'You draw your blade and I'll run you through before you can so much as let out a scream.'

He drew closer, so that I could feel his warm, reeking breath upon my cheeks and see the pockmarks covering his face. 'I'm not afraid of you, Tancred. Others might stand in awe of your reputation, but I see you for what you are. You're no different to the rest of us, nor, when it comes to it, any less mortal. If you stand aside then I will stay my hand. Otherwise I cannot promise you anything. It is your choice.'

Laying one hand upon the round disc of his sword-pommel, with the other he gave a flick of his fingers as a signal to his friends. They dismounted, drawing their blades as they formed a half-ring around me and Byrhtwald. Behind us lay the trader's cart together with Cwylmend, who was still chewing contentedly, oblivious to everything that was going on.

'This wasn't wise, lord,' Byrhtwald said.

I hardly needed him to tell me that. 'What would you rather I'd done?'

To that he had no answer. From his belt hung a long hunting knife. I'd never seen the Englishman fight and so I had no idea how skilled with a blade he was, but he would have to be exceptional indeed if the two of us were to win out over the five of them. The way the colour had all but drained from his face did not inspire much confidence. If Berengar truly wanted to kill me, then he would not get a better chance than this. Yet I could hardly back down and leave the pedlar to his fate, and even if I did I wasn't convinced that Berengar would hold true to his word and spare me. Not after everything that had passed between us of late.

'Have your men put away their weapons,' I said to him, hoping that he didn't sense my anxiety. 'We can settle this between ourselves.'

His fingers curled around his hilt. 'It's too late for that. Perhaps if you hadn't set about trying to disgrace me in front of my men, it need not have come to this.'

'Disgrace you?' I repeated. 'You were the one who started this quarrel. You're the one to blame for—'

I never got the chance to finish. His sword was free of its sheath in a heartbeat. Barely had I time to work out what was going on than he was rushing at me, swinging the blade wildly across my path, roaring with unrestrained fury. I threw myself to the side just in time as sharpened steel cleaved the air where I had been standing, before lodging itself firmly in the frame of Byrhtwald's cart. As Berengar struggled to free its edge from the timbers, I staggered to my feet, drawing my own weapon in time to meet the challenge from one of his men. With a scrape of steel on steel I parried his blow, forcing his weapon down and out of position while I stepped forward and slammed my free fist into his jaw. Bright blood dribbled down his chin as, thrown off balance, he staggered sideways, tripping over the bench with the ointment jars and ending up sprawled on his back in the dirt.

I didn't wait for him to rise or for any of Berengar's other friends to bring their blades to bear. Instead I rushed behind the cart. A collection of copper cooking pots sat on top of the canvas; I lifted one of them and hurled it at Berengar's head, as, red-faced and with gritted teeth, he tried to work his sword free from the timbers into which it had become stuck. He saw it coming, ducked, and the pot sailed over his head, missing him by a hair's breadth and clattering upon the ground. Abandoning his sword and drawing his knife instead, he approached around one side of the cart while two of his companions came around the other.

Knowing that I couldn't fight all of them at once, I ran. A number of side streets and alleyways led away from the marketplace and I made for one of those, pushing past those who were in my way, doing my best not to fall over the crates and barrels stacked upon the ground. Chickens flapped wildly, shedding feathers as they strayed across my path. Everywhere men were shouting; behind me came a scream and I glanced over my shoulder to see Berengar and his men shoving a young woman out of their way. Some of the market-goers took refuge behind their carts and their stalls, while others were running, abandoning their wares and their animals at the sight of naked steel.

Berengar shouted at them to stop me, but they knew better than to risk their lives in something that was none of their concern. I rounded the end of the row of stalls, pausing for the barest heart-beart to kick over a low table stacked with baskets of wet-glistening eels and other fish.

I was wondering where Byrhtwald had gone when I heard the Englishman shouting to me from further up the street. Leaving Berengar and the others to negotiate the fallen table and baskets, I rushed after him. He was nimbler than his years and his squat stature suggested, diving in between the stalls, fighting his way through the throng. Ahead lay the farrier's workshop, from which clouds of white charcoal-smoke were billowing out across the street.

'This way!' Byrhtwald said before darting through the smoke and down an alley that led between the forge and the tanner's place.

I charged after him through the clouds, shielding my face, for all the good that seemed to do. My eyes stung with the smoke and the heat, but I was quickly through it—

And straight into the flank of an ox, one of a pair hauling a wagon loaded with timbers up the alley. The beast snorted indignantly and its owner yelled at me in words I didn't understand, but I had no time to stop and apologise, even if I could remember the right English phrase. No sooner had I recovered my senses than I was turning, breaking once more into a run, only for my forehead to meet the end of one of the planks, which was jutting out across the side of the wagon. Stunned by the blow and cursing in pain, I lost my footing on the soft ground, and found myself lying amidst the mud and the cattle dung. Blood, warm and sticky, trickled across my brow and down between my eyes. Dazed and not entirely sure what had happened, I put a hand to it and my palm came away smeared with crimson streaks.

Somewhere in the smoke shadows moved about. The man with the cart and oxen had stopped but now there were voices and he was being hurried on. One of the shadows resolved itself into the shape of a man. At first I thought that the pedlar had come back for me, but then the figure stepped closer and as I blinked to clear my sight I saw his face, fixed as it always was in an expression of hatred and spite.

Berengar. He stood over me, sword in hand. The tip of the blade he pointed towards my chest in warning, lest I had any thoughts about trying to get up. I hadn't; my head was pounding and already I thought I could feel a lump forming. My own blade had fallen from my grasp when I fell, and lay easily more than an arm's length away, in one of the puddles that had formed in the wheel-ruts. Too far for me to be able to reach in the time it would take for Berengar's sword-point to come down.

'At last the great Tancred a Dinant finds himself at someone else's mercy.' He spat in my face; I blinked and turned my head in time but that only meant his phlegm struck my cheek rather than my eye. 'Have you anything to say?'

'Only that if you kill me you'll have my men to answer to,' I said, with more confidence than I had any right to, given the situation. 'As soon as they find out what you've done, they'll hunt you down like the worthless dog you are. When they catch you, they'll string you up from the nearest tree, tear out your guts and enjoy watching you squirm as they roast them in front of you. They will—'

'Quiet!' He moved the tip of his blade a fraction closer to my neck; I felt the cold steel touch lightly upon my skin. 'I do not fear your men, any more than I fear you.' But a tremble in his voice betrayed his uncertainty.

'What about Fitz Osbern?' I asked, changing tack, doing my best to hold my nerve. I couldn't afford to show any weakness. 'He won't take kindly to blood being spilt in his streets.'

With every moment that passed I was growing more desperate. I hoped at least that Byrhtwald had managed to get away, that he was bringing help, until I noticed him being held by one of Berengar's knights – Frederic by name, as I recalled – with a knife at his throat. He met my gaze, an apologetic look in his eyes.

'Fitz Osbern is too far gone in his cups to care,' Berengar was saying. 'He has more things to worry about than the death of one man who defied his word.'

I was not convinced that Fitz Osbern would be so callous; one way or another justice would be dealt. Unless Berengar planned to flee the town altogether, he would struggle to avoid it. Even if he managed to evade those who would avenge me, he would still have God to answer to eventually. Perhaps those same thoughts were what was causing him to stay his hand now, or at the very least to doubt himself. He stood unspeaking with clenched jaw, his gaze fixed upon me. I counted each breath I took, wondering if it would be my last, waiting for the finishing blow that never came, until eventually I could hold my silence no longer.

'Are you going to kill me, then? Or are you simply going to stand there?'

I meant it as a challenge, but the words came out less strongly than I would have liked.

'Don't think I won't do it,' said Berengar. 'I only want to enjoy this moment so that I remember it for a long time to come.'

As he spoke these words, behind him through the smoke appeared the form of a horseman. Berengar had no time even to turn around before he found a spear levelled beneath his chin, the flat of the head brushing against the underside of his jaw.

'Put away your sword, Berengar fitz Warin,' the horseman said, and never had I been more glad to hear that voice, for it belonged to Lord Robert. 'Do it carefully, too. I wouldn't want my blade to accidently slip and bury itself in your throat.'

Berengar hesitated. He had a wild, cornered look in his eyes. For a terrifying instant I thought he might decide to take his chances, and kill me even if it meant meeting his own end.

'Do it,' Robert repeated, and then to the others said: 'Unhand the Englishman.'

Thankfully the moment passed. Not once taking his eyes from me, Berengar grudgingly withdrew the blade, tossing it to one side, where it fell in a puddle. It was not quite what had been asked of him, but it sufficed nonetheless. The captain of Robert's household, Ansculf, picked it up.

Relieved, I breathed deeply for the first time in what seemed like an age, letting the air fill my chest.

'Get up,' Robert barked at me, a little harshly I thought, given that I was the injured party. 'And you,' he said to Berengar, 'get yourself and your men gone from here, and be thankful that I'm letting you leave with your head still attached to your neck.'

Berengar didn't seem to hear. 'This isn't over,' he said to me as I rose to my feet. 'You'll suffer for all your insults – I will make sure of it!'

'Not before I've driven my blade through your bowels and left you to drown in your own shit,' I retorted, rubbing my forehead.

'Enough,' Robert said. 'Both of you. Now go, Berengar, unless you want me to give Tancred a chance to make good on his promise.'

Berengar shot me one final, vicious look before turning and signalling to his men, and together they stalked off. No doubt he would take word of what had taken place and the many injustices he had borne back to Fitz Osbern. As well he might, though whether the latter cared enough to listen to what he had to say was another matter altogether.

I turned to Robert. With him was half his conroi, armed and

mailed, their horses' coats glistening with sweat, and I guessed they must have recently returned from a scouting expedition.

'Thank you,' I said. 'If you hadn't arrived when you did—'

'Spare me.' He shook his head in a manner that spoke of frustration and disappointment. 'You were fortunate. As I recall, this isn't the first time I've had to rescue your hide. How is it that whenever a fight is taking place, I always seem to find you in the middle of it?'

'It was hardly my fault, lord.'

'It never is, is it?' His tone was cold and lacking in humour. If anything he seemed angry, but what he had to be angry about I wasn't sure. No blood had been spilt nor any injury done, save perhaps to Berengar's pride, although that seemed to me battered enough as it was.

'What do you mean by that?' I asked, feeling suddenly defensive.

He didn't answer directly but said instead, 'Nothing good will come of this feud. It has to end, and not by one of you having a knife driven into his back. If you don't mend this, it will only grow worse, believe me. I have seen it happen.'

'Perhaps.' Even were it possible, I was not enamoured with the idea of coming to terms with Berengar, especially given that this quarrel was all his making. Over the years I'd made many foes and rivals, but none as openly hostile as him.

'If you're looking for enemies you'd do better choosing one who is at least predictable. The last thing you want is someone as capricious as he is, whose heart is ruled by hate, who will stop at nothing to get what he wants.'

'I'll deal with him if he comes for me,' I said.

'As you dealt with him today, you mean?'

I didn't dignify that question with an answer. Berengar had merely been lucky. If those oxen and wagon hadn't been there when they were, or if I had only seen them, then I wouldn't have struck my head and he would never have found himself in a position where he had a chance of finishing me.

'Whatever he tries, I will be ready for him,' I said.

Robert sighed. 'Of course you must do what you think right, Tancred. I'll warn you, though, that if you do not mend this by whatever means it takes, it will be your undoing one way or another, if not straightaway, then sometime.'

Sometime was good enough, as far as I was concerned. Sometime stretched a long way into the future: weeks or months or years, in which time I could easily meet a thousand other worse fates than Berengar's sword. Besides, I doubted he would be so patient; more probably he would grow tired of me and find someone else to harass rather than wait that long.

Robert turned to Byrhtwald, who was nursing his shoulder where one of Berengar's men had held him. He looked shaken but otherwise unharmed.

'Who is this?' Robert asked.

I gave him the Englishman's name. 'A friend of mine,' I added. 'He comes to Earnford every few months with his wares and his stories.'

'And he pays well for them, too,' Byrhtwald said, smiling. 'You must be Tancred's lord, son of the noble and illustrious Guillaume Malet.'

'That's right,' Robert said. He didn't offer his hand in greeting, perhaps trying to work out whether the Englishman was being sincere in his praise, or whether it was some kind of jest at his expense. Byrhtwald had an odd sense of humour that even I, despite having come to know him reasonably well, did not always understand.

'Are you all right?' I asked, changing the subject quickly. I did not want another confrontation.

'I'm still in one piece, if that's what you mean,' the pedlar replied. 'Nothing more than a few bruises, though that'll be enough to get me a scolding from my wife when she sees them. It won't be the first time, either. She always gets frightened for my sake when she hears I've been in a fight. Says I'm too old for them.'

'And she's probably right,' I said. 'Still, at least you're taking her advice. You ran from that one quickly enough.'

'It looked like you were doing well enough on your own. I didn't want to get in the way and spoil your fun.'

'If you want my advice, Englishman,' Robert said, interrupting, 'you'd be wise to leave this town as soon as you can – if you value your life, at any rate. Most traders left days ago from what I hear, and you won't want to be here when the Welsh come.'

'If you live even that long,' I said. 'If you remain in Scrobbesburh, Berengar will take it as a personal insult and he'll do everything he can to see you in chains, especially after this.'

Robert frowned. 'In chains? What has he done?'

I repeated what Berengar had told me of Fitz Osbern's decree that all merchants still in the town were to be arrested forthwith on suspicion of acting as spies.

'It's the first I've heard of this,' Robert muttered. 'If it's true then Fitz Osbern has taken leave of his senses altogether. After all, if it weren't for the traders bringing news from their travels, we would know even less about the enemy and their movements than we do now.' He turned again to Byrhtwald. 'I'd worry less about the chains and more about Berengar's sword-edge if he ever sees you again. Leave and get back to your wife and family. Otherwise, if he doesn't kill you, the Welsh probably will.'

'Have no fear on my account, lord,' the Englishman replied with his usual roguish grin. 'I'll survive. I always have.'

I didn't doubt that he would. In some ways he put me in mind of a rat, except twice as crafty and only half as dirty: quick enough to scurry away when he sensed danger approaching, happy enough to live off the scraps that others cast aside but careful, too, never to miss a chance to fill his stomach. Or his coin-purse, for that matter.

We made our way back to the marketplace, where a group of youths were taking advantage of Byrhtwald's absence to search for things that they could easily steal. While one was busy stuffing his pockets with the ointment jars that lay on the ground, a tall, fair-haired girl in a tattered dress had climbed on top of the pedlar's cart and begun passing down to her friends bundles of firewood, handfuls of candles and a brass lantern, among other things, all of which they were piling into a large sack. As soon as they saw Byrhtwald coming they fled, with the girl trying to drag the sack behind her, except they had filled it too high and it was too heavy. Before long she broke into a sprint, abandoning it as she ducked in and out amongst the animals and people, narrowly avoiding one of the other stallholders who tried to stop her. Soon I lost sight of her.

One of Robert's men had fetched Nihtfeax; with thanks I took the reins. Byrhtwald had righted the bench that had been knocked over and was busy recovering those goods that had been purloined, loading them back on to his cart. I offered to help but he declined.

'In that case, take care on the road,' I said. 'The enemy could be marching any day now.'

'I will.' He extended his hand, and I clasped it.

'With any luck our paths will cross again soon.' Though if the enemy succeeded in taking Scrobbesburh, my path might be very short indeed. Nonetheless, a small part of me sensed I would see the Englishman again before too long. He had a habit of appearing when I least expected him.

'I'm sure of it, lord,' Byrhtwald said.

'Keep your wits about you,' I said. 'I wish you safe travels.'

'And to you the same,' he said. 'Whatever happens and wherever events take you from here.'

A strange thing to say, I thought, but Lord Robert was waiting, so I bade the pedlar farewell. We led our mounts through the narrow, piss-stinking streets in the direction of the camp. This was the height of summer and the heat of the day was upon us, so intense as to be oppressive, reminding me of those long campaigns I had fought under the scorching Sicilian sun in the years before the invasion. Flies swarmed around mounds of steaming ox dung, buzzing in my face as we led our horses past. One flew into Robert's mouth and he spat it out, his face screwed up in disgust.

After we had walked a little further, he said, 'We're leaving this place.'

I was taken aback, not just by the announcement but by the suddenness of it too. 'We're leaving?'

I wondered if that was what Byrhtwald had meant. Yet how could he possibly have known?

'Don't say it too loudly.' Robert glanced about. The rest of the conroi was lagging some way behind us, laughing at some joke that one of them had heard, and save for a lone beggar sitting cross-legged by the side of the street, there was no one else close by who might have heard. 'After I heard of Hugues's leave-taking this morning, I made my decision. I've had enough of this town. All is falling apart, and Fitz Osbern seems to be doing little to repair the rot. The barons are deserting in ever greater numbers; those who remain do nothing but argue all day and fight between themselves.'

Most likely that censure was directed at me. If it was, though, he didn't press it.

'If we leave, lord, surely we only make things worse for those who remain. Our army is desperately short of men as it is.'

'I didn't come to these parts prepared for war. If I had, I'd have brought with me two hundred men at least. Instead I now have barely forty knights left under my banner, including your retinue and those of Wace and Eudo. Fitz Osbern will not trouble himself over so few, nor are they likely to make much difference when the enemy come.'

'I suppose the Wolf took many more than that with him.'

'Indeed,' Robert said with a sigh. 'In any case I'll be damned if I'm going to risk my life and those of my men fighting in a hopeless cause. That's why tomorrow morning before dawn we ride from here, and Beatrice as well.'

If the worst happened and the enemy captured Scrobbesburh, the town would be no safe place for a woman, even for one of high birth as she was.

'What about her betrothal?' I asked. 'Fitz Osbern will not be pleased.'

'Whether he still wishes the marriage to happen or not is for him to decide. For now, all I'm concerned about is seeing her somewhere safe.'

'Where, lord? The Danish fleet will soon be raiding the coast along the German Sea. You can't take her back to Suthfolc, or to your father's house in Lundene either. If King Sweyn lands in the south and lays siege to the city she'll be in even more danger there than she is here.'

'I know. There's only one place we can go where I can count on her being safe.'

He looked at me, as if expecting me to guess what he was thinking. I was not in the mood for games. 'Tell me,' I said.

'Eoferwic.'

Twenty

My heart sank. Robert would take me even further away from Earnford and the Marches that were my home. From Leofrun and my firstborn child, who all too soon would be entering this world. I would not be there when it happened.

'Eoferwic?' I asked.

'There's nowhere better,' Robert said. 'It lies far enough from the Marches and from the Danes to be in any danger, and it's where my father is too.'

'What about the ætheling?' I countered. 'If the news coming out of the north is right, he'll be marching sooner rather than later. When he does, his mind will be set on Eoferwic.'

'Don't forget he was ousted from there once before, and his entire army routed too. If he has any sense in him – if he's learnt anything – he won't want to suffer the same reversal twice. He has spent the months since then trying to convince the Northumbrian nobles to give him their support again. Now that he has it, he won't want to squander it.'

'Unless his overweening pride demands that he achieves what he failed to last year,' I said. 'He is that kind of man: determined and ambitious.'

Robert shrugged. 'He can try as much as he likes but he will not succeed. He won't take the city a second time. Its walls have been rebuilt, and with two castles now defending the riverbanks, any fleet or land army would be foolish to attempt an assault.'

I wasn't convinced of that. I had lived long enough to know it was ever dangerous to underestimate an opponent, especially when it came to ambition and resourcefulness: two qualities I knew Eadgar did not lack.

'You can't assume that the ætheling will abandon his journey simply because the road is difficult,' I said. 'He might be young but he is arrogant. He'd rather take the riskier route if the prize on offer is great enough. You haven't met him, but I have, and I know.'

Indeed Eoferwic was a jewel to be prized: the greatest and most prosperous of all the towns in the north of the kingdom, second only to Lundene in the whole of England. With that in mind, it seemed to me unlikely that Eadgar would be deterred by the fact of the ditches having been dug a little deeper and the ramparts built another few feet higher. He had come close to succeeding before, and now that the king's forces were spread even more thinly, the time was ripe for him to try again.

'If you have somewhere better in mind, name it now,' Robert said, clearly growing frustrated.

His tone took me aback, but I had nothing more to add or any other refuges to suggest. And so Eoferwic it would be. As a place where Beatrice might safely weather the storm to come, it was certainly no worse than Scrobbesburh. When last I was there the second castle was still being completed, under the eye of Guillaume fitz Osbern, no less. That was over a year ago: not since Wace, Eudo and I had given our oaths to Robert in the weeks following the great battle had I walked its streets. Only a month or so before that, we had been escorting his sister and their mother from Eoferwic to the safety of Lundene. Thus it was ironic that for the same reason, our paths now led us back there.

It is strange how sometimes we find our lives unfolding in circles, each step taking us not forward but merely around and around, until at last we end up where we began.

Eoferwic was where I had first sworn my allegiance to the Malet house and the banner of the black and gold. It was where this reputation I had unwittingly won for myself had been forged. If God were a poet and my life a song, then Eoferwic would be the refrain.

* * *

That night I slept better than I had done in some while. The wind was changing direction, turning to the east, and the air felt cooler, less stifling than it had been of late. I was long due some proper rest after days on campaign, bedding down on stony ground that dug into my back and my side. Indeed the first time I woke was when the tent-flap was pulled aside and I heard Robert's voice telling me to wake.

Bleary-eyed, my mind still clouded with sleep, I raised myself from the blankets and crawled out. He and his conroi were already waiting. One of his knights carried the familiar black-and-gold banner, furled around the staff so as to attract less attention, while another carried a torch that hurt my eyes to look at.

'I'm going to meet Beatrice,' Robert said. 'Join us by the town's northern gates as soon as you can.'

He left some of his manservants to help us; I sent them to fetch our destriers and rounceys. Our saddlebags were already packed, and we had filled our wineskins the night before in readiness. While Snocca and Cnebba loaded them on to the sumpter ponies that we shared, the rest of us set about striking camp. The quicker we could be gone, the less attention we would draw. And the fewer people knew we were leaving, the fewer questions there would be.

We were tying our bedrolls to the ponies' harnesses when Pons gave a shout. I turned quickly, thinking that something was wrong. Swearing violently, he dragged his foot out from one of the latrine pits; in the dark they weren't easy to spot and he must have lost his footing. His shoe and the hem of his trews were soaked in piss.

'Quiet!' I told him as I buckled my sword-belt on to my waist. The last thing I wanted was too much noise. 'Be more careful.'

He glared at me but thankfully after that he kept his curses quiet, muttering under his breath.

Mailed and mounted, we rode out. There was neither honour nor pride to be had in running from a battle, and even though I knew it was for the right reasons, still the thought made me feel uneasy, as if somehow I were a traitor to my countrymen. I tried to put it from my mind. My allegiance was to my lord and his kin, and to their protection; nothing else ought to matter.

By then a few men, probably woken by Pons's curses, had emerged from their tents. They called to us, asking who we were and what we were doing about so early.

'Ignore them,' I muttered. 'Don't say a word to anyone.'

From the amount of baggage we carried they would soon realise that we weren't headed out on any scouting expedition, and it was but a short leap from there for them to guess we were deserting. Even so, I preferred to let them work that out for themselves. By the time word got around the camp and made its way to Fitz Osbern that the son of Malet and his followers had gone, I hoped the town would be many miles behind us.

Robert was waiting for us at the town's north gates when we reached them. Beatrice was with him, huddled in her cloak so that she seemed somehow smaller, her face pale in the moonlight. She would not meet my eyes. Her brother gave a nod to the sentries posted at the gate; I wondered how much he had paid them to let us through at this hour, and to hold their tongues too. The gates swung open with a great grinding noise, loud enough to wake the whole town. I winced at the sound as I took up position at the rear of the column alongside Pons and Serlo. In silence we filed through the gates under the watchful eyes of the sentries. Open country lay before us, the hills and woods lit dimly by the cloud-veiled moon. There was no sign yet of the approaching dawn.

Eudo and Wace weren't to be found among Robert's retinue. They and their knights had left the afternoon before, Robert having sent them back to his manor at Heia to help defend it against the Danes in case they landed in Suthfolc. Since the battle both had tried to avoid me whenever possible – as if they, like the Wolf and so many others, held me responsible for the deaths of their men – and at the very least I should have liked to wish them well before they went.

We had ridden perhaps a hundred paces along the track out of Scrobbesburh when behind us I heard the sounds of hooves and a man's voice, calling out what sounded like my name. Over the jangle of harnesses and the wind rustling the stalks in the nearby wheatfields it was hard to make out, and at first I thought myself mistaken. But as I glanced at Serlo and Pons I saw that they had heard too. We hadn't left anyone behind so far as I could tell, and so it couldn't be a straggler. And apart perhaps from Byrhtwald, who had already fled the town, who knew that we were leaving?

'Tancred,' the cry came again. 'Tancred a Dinant!'

Wondering who this could be, I turned to see a lone horseman waiting beneath the arch of the gatehouse, silhouetted by the flickering light of the sentries' torches. As soon as he saw that he had my attention, his shouts ended.

'Who are you?' I called back. 'What business do you have with me?'

He did not answer. Instead he seemed to be conversing with the sentries, although what they were saying I had no hope of telling from such a distance. It was hard to make out his features, though if I had to describe him I would have said that he was stouter of build than most men.

'Is that you, Berengar?'

He looked up once more. If indeed it was him and he wished to say something, he would do so to my face, not like a coward from one hundred paces. I spurred Nihtfeax into a gallop, back towards the gates. No sooner had I done so, however, than he turned tail and was gone, leaving the sentries and slipping beyond the torch-lit gatehouse into the shadows of the town.

'Get back here, Berengar,' I shouted. 'Don't run from me, you worthless Devil-turd!'

I had no way of knowing whether he had heard me or not, but I hoped that he had. This feud that he had begun was one thing I wouldn't miss. Even so, I would have preferred to have settled things one way or another. Instead he'd had the satisfaction of watching me ride away, which he would turn to his own gain. Among his comrades he would call me a coward and worse; he would brag about how, too frightened to face him properly, I had slunk away under the cover of darkness, in so doing admitting defeat. He would spread his lies and I could do nothing to refute them. I clenched my teeth. I was no coward, as anyone who knew me would testify. In time I would return and prove it, at the same time making sure that everyone saw him truly for the cur he was. But not now.

I returned to join the others, who had not waited. Robert did not hide his fury when he saw me.

'If word wasn't already out about our leave-taking, it surely will be now,' he said. 'Whoever that was—'

'It was Berengar,' I said.

'Enough of you and him,' Robert snapped. 'Do you think I care? Whoever that was, he knows now that you're with us. It won't be long before he makes the connection with myself and takes that knowledge to the castle. If Fitz Osbern hasn't sent someone after us within the hour I'll be surprised.'

We pushed our horses hard until daybreak, trying to put as much distance between us and the town while the blanket of night still wrapped itself around us. All too soon, though, the eastern skies were growing light and then suddenly the new day was upon us. I kept glancing over my shoulder to see if there was anyone behind us on the road, perhaps a glint of steel helmets and spearpoints in the early light. There never was, however, and so as the sun began to climb we dismounted from our destriers, our beasts of war, leaving them in the care of the grooms and stable-hands who travelled with us, and exchanged them for our rounceys, which were our riding horses, less fleet of foot but more suited for enduring the long miles that lay ahead of us.

Rather than taking the better-known tracks by way of Deorbi and Snotingeham and thus skirting the southernmost of the high peaks, we headed north. It would be the shortest route, Robert told us, a little more than one hundred miles according to his reckoning. I could not dispute that but I knew that it would take us across the most unforgiving of country, over wet and windswept fells, through steep and stony vales and high and desolate passes: hard going for even the toughest of men and animals. To tell the truth I was not looking forward to it, and neither were most of Robert's men. The pall of the battle in Mechain still hung over us; even after a day's rest in Scrobbesburh we were all still saddle-sore from the march into Wales and the forced retreat.

The sun climbed higher; the day grew warmer. As midday approached and there was still no sign of any message from Fitz Osbern, slowly we began to relax our pace. If Robert was relieved, he did not show it, but among the rest of the men spirits seemed to be lifting, for the first time in several days. We paused for a while by a brook to fill our wineskins and give our animals drink, and to give our backs and arses a rest for the first time since we had woken.

At one time there appeared a faint cloud of dust as might be kicked up by passing hooves, about a mile to our rear. They were too far off for any of us to make out any figures, but whoever it was always seemed to keep their distance, never growing any closer, and so it seemed unlikely that they were riders sent to pursue us. More probably that dust-cloud belonged to mere travellers, although these were dangerous times to be upon the roads. Indeed that day we had come across very few of the kind of folk one might usually expect to find: cowherds and gosherds driving their animals to market; monks on their way from one convent to another; or merchants and pedlars such as Byrhtwald. I wondered where he was by now, and when and if I would next see him.

Not much later we found ourselves riding through dense woods of oak and hornbeam, elm and birch. Whoever held these lands had been neglecting his responsibilities, for the track looked as though it had not been cleared in many months. In some places it was so boggy and thick with mud that no cart stood a chance of making it through; in others it was overhung by so many boughs or choked with such dense clusters of nettles that it was almost impossible to see in which direction it was supposed to lead.

'We'll have to find another way,' I said. We had spent the better part of half an hour hacking with our knives at the undergrowth, taking saws and axes to fallen branches, to little avail. The path had grown steadily narrower as it delved deeper in the woods until I began to suspect that it was nothing more than a deer track.

'We must have lost the road some time ago,' said Robert, red-faced from exertion and frustration. We had been following one of the old Roman roads, which were usually well frequented, so that it was never hard to find someone who knew the way to wherever one was going. Except that this day they had been particularly quiet, and those we occasionally spotted in the distance took flight at the very sight of so many armed men. Thus when the road appeared to fork unexpectedly we had nothing but our own judgement to rely upon. Or rather Robert's, since he had decided he knew better than the rest of us. And it was his pig-headedness that had brought us here.

'I saw a manor upon the hill before we entered these woods,' Beatrice spoke up. 'We could ride back and ask if anyone knows the way.'

'And while we're there, we can give their lord some advice on how to manage his lands and keep the ways clear,' Pons muttered.

That got a murmur of approval, and in truth Beatrice's was as good an idea as anyone had thus far suggested. Grudgingly Robert agreed. Following our own trail of hewn nettles and horse dung, we wound our way back along the path, leading our animals in single file, until I felt I was beginning to recognise where we were. We had wasted a good hour or more, but if we could find the road again, it would not matter.

Serlo was telling some long-winded joke involving a washer-woman, a nun and an alewife, though it was hard to follow what he was saying for he was some way behind me. From the tone of his voice I guessed he was nearing the end, when suddenly Robert gave a shout from the head of the column. I craned my neck to see what was happening.

He stood by the edge of the path, holding aloft a leather bottle. 'Did one of you drop this earlier?'

All my provisions were safely stowed in the panniers on our packhorse. I had taken care to check that the harness was securely fastened when last we stopped. There was little chance that anything could have dropped while we were riding. I glanced over my shoulder at my two knights; they both shrugged.

'Any of you?' Robert asked, clearly growing frustrated. 'Ansculf? Tancred?'

We had all halted by then, but we were so strung out along the track that not all of those in the rear knew what was going on.

Handing the reins of my horse to Cnebba, who was walking ahead of me in the column, I trudged through the mud towards him. 'Where did you see it?'

'Lying beside that clump of bracken,' he said as he tossed it to me, pointing to a spot about five paces off the path.

I turned the bottle over in my hands. It felt light and when I shook it I could hear the barest splash of liquid inside, whereas we had filled ours not long ago. Unless someone had been especially thirsty – clearing the path had not been easy work, after all . . . yet no one wanted to claim it.

The air was still. Everyone had fallen quiet, and there was only the faint sound of wasps buzzing and birds chirping. I glanced around at the trees, searching deep into the heart of the wood, for what I did not know, but for some reason suddenly I felt cold.

'I don't like this,' I said. 'We should keep moving. We need to get out of these woods as soon as we can.'

Robert nodded and gave the order. Heart thumping, I hurried back to Cnebba.

'What is it?' Serlo asked as I took the reins.

'Keep a lookout,' I said as I kicked on. 'Tell me if you see—'

Even before I could finish, it happened. A flash of gleaming steel, it flew from out of the trees to my flank and it flew true, burying itself in Cnebba's chest, transfixing him where he stood in front of me. He was dead before he hit the ground. Where only a moment ago there had been silence, now the air was filled with whistling shafts, the shouts of men and the whinnying of horses. Spooked, my rouncey reared up.

'Ride,' I yelled, and up ahead I could hear Robert doing the same: 'Ride, ride!'

My steed's hooves came crashing down, and I swung up into the saddle, digging my heels in, wishing that it was even-tempered Nihtfeax beneath me instead, but one of Robert's stable-hands had him. Another cluster of silver points shot overhead and I ducked low, trying to avoid them. Whether the others were behind me I did not know, but there was no time to check.

Up ahead, Beatrice was shrieking, desperately trying to control her palfrey. A feathered shaft protruded from the animal's hindquarters; blood, thick and dark, was gushing down its coat. All of a sudden its legs gave way and she was pitched forward with a cry, landing in the mud amidst the ferns. The men around her clearly cared more for their own lives, however, since they did not stop, but rode and ran past her as if she were not there.

'Beatrice!' Robert said, pulling hard on the reins and turning, drawing to a stop. But at least four of his knights lay dead already, their corpses strewn across the path, and we would lose many more if we did not keep moving.

'Go,' I shouted, waving to him as I jumped down from my mount and sprinted to his sister's side. She had fallen badly; by the looks of it she had twisted her ankle and also hurt her wrist, but somehow I had to get her away from there. Above all the noise, I began to make out the beating of weapon-hafts upon shields.

'Take my hand,' I said to her. 'Take it now.'

Her eyes were filled with fear and shock, but she had enough presence of mind to do as I said. I helped her to her feet, at the same time unslinging my shield from where it hung across my back, working my arm through the straps and raising it high to fend off any shafts that might come our way. It was not much protection, especially for two people, but it would have to do.

'Come on,' I said as I put my arm around her waist to hurry her along.

Within a few steps I saw that it was no use. She had hurt her foot too badly and could barely walk; all she could manage was a half-hobble, half-stumble, and we were in danger of being left behind to the mercy of whoever was attacking us.

'Beatrice!' Robert was fighting the tide of men, though the path was not really wide enough to allow it, riding back towards us even as his knights tried to make for safety. But he was still some way off, and I couldn't wait for him to reach us.

Hearing hooves behind me, I glanced up and saw Pons riding past. I called his name; he halted and looked down.

'Lord?'

'Take her and make sure she's safe,' I told him. Abandoning my shield, I linked my palms. 'Quickly,' I said to her. Still wincing in pain, she raised her unhurt foot and stepped into the foothold I had made. Despite her height she was light and it was easy to lift her up to Pons, who extended his arms and helped her clamber ungracefully on to the back of his horse behind him.

'Hold tight to Pons and swing your leg around,' I said, which thankfully she managed to do. No sooner was she settled, with her arms around his chest, than I slapped Pons's horse on the rump. 'Now go,' I told him. 'Ride!'

He didn't need telling twice. Around us all was confusion. Corpses lay sprawled in the dirt; riderless horses fled in all directions, and I saw my own rouncey trying to make for the cover of the trees, crashing through the undergrowth. Panniers had come unhitched from the saddles and their contents spilt across the path: provisions wrapped in cloth, silver coins, bundles of kindling, tent-pegs and canvas. I had lost sight of Serlo and Pons and any other familiar faces; my mind was whirling and it was all I could do to keep running. The arrows had all but ceased and now from out of a ditch some way inside the trees men charged with gleaming shield-bosses and blades, roaring and swearing death upon us all.

'To arms,' I yelled. 'To arms!'

Up the path I glimpsed Pons and Beatrice, with Robert alongside them and some dozen knights. Beyond them, forming a line across the path and blocking their escape, stood a wall of overlapping shield-rims with bristling spears held out. Between those men, and the ones rushing out of the woods on either side, we were trapped.

I had enough time to lift my shield from where I had cast it down and brandish my sword. And then they were upon us, whooping with delight at the impending slaughter, their eyes filled with blood-lust, and they thrust and hacked wildly with spears and knives: a flood of Welshmen, to judge by their appearance. I called to those of Robert's men who were nearby, trying to rally them, but it was in vain. A few drew their weapons and joined me, but many more were running, not yet understanding that they had nowhere to go. Yet even had they all stood their ground, I could see that we were hopelessly outnumbered.

'Stay close to me!' I called to those who had drawn arms, but it was no use. They could not stand against such a tide and were falling all around me, spearpoints buried in their breasts and in their throats, their blood spilling across the path.

I heaved my sword up and into the unprotected brow of one of the enemy. It bit into his skull, penetrating the bone. The fuller was running with crimson as I tore it free and he staggered forward, collapsing across my shield. With a grunt I threw his limp corpse to one side; he slid off its face just in time for me to fend off the axe blows rained upon me by one of his companions, a towering, broad-chested man in his middle years. For all his size and reach, however, he could not block the low blow at his legs. As he pressed forward, using the weight of his body to push against my shield, I struck, thrusting my sword-point down into his shoe, through the leather and into his foot, pinning it to the ground. Howling, he bent double. As he did so I slammed the face of my shield into his head before jerking my blade free and smashing it into his mailed arm with enough force that I heard bone crack.

'Ymauaelwch ef!' yelled one that I took for their leader. Short of stature, he had a red moustache and wore a helmet with silver-inlaid cheek-plates and a crest of black feathers, much the same as I remembered Rhiwallon had worn in the battle at Mechain.

And then I realised. This was his brother, Bleddyn, the King of Gwynedd, who had put the Wolf to flight in the battle.

'Ymauaelwch ef!' he repeated, pointing at me.

Slashing, parrying, thrusting, I tried to hold them off. The enemy were so many and we so few, and growing fewer with every moment that passed. Snocca fell, his chest carved open by Welsh steel. All too quickly we found ourselves surrounded: myself and seven others, forming a close ring as we protected each other's backs.

'Tancred!'

Between blocking one man's blow with my shield-boss and ducking beneath the axe swing of another, I glanced up the path where the shout had come from. It was Robert. Together with Ansculf and three other knights, he scythed a path through the enemy towards us, beating them down and trampling their corpses beneath his mount's hooves, using the full weight of his blade to splinter their shield-rims. As more foemen rushed from the shadows of the trees to block their path, I saw that his efforts would be in vain. Even if he and his men did manage to reach me, they would soon be cut off without hope of retreat, and I couldn't let them sacrifice themselves in that way. Not when they could still save their own skins.

'Go,' I called to them, my voice growing hoarse. 'See yourselves to safety; that's the only thing that matters!'

Above the clash of steel and the screams of the dying I wasn't sure if he heard me. The enemy began to rally, forming ranks and presenting their spearpoints, crowding Robert. In that moment I knew that all was lost and that they would not get to me; they were only a handful of swords against countless spears.

'Go!' I shouted out as I wiped the sweat from my eyes. The Frenchman to my right screamed as he was skewered on a Welsh spear. The ring broken, the enemy surged forward. They were among us now, unstoppable, cutting down those who remained.

Roaring wordlessly, I summoned all the vigour left to me, heaving my blade around, striking out on all sides. If this was my time, I would face it not as a coward but with the sword-joy coursing through me.

'Die, you bastards,' I found myself shouting. 'For Earnford and Lord Robert!'

Their cries and their laughter filled my ears as I lashed out, but my blade-edge found only air. Panic gripped my chest; my heart was pounding as I looked for a way through, but they had me surrounded and there was none. I glimpsed the feather-crested helmet, and for the briefest moment thought of spending my final breaths taking his life, but he was well protected by his teulu and I had no hope of reaching him.

And then without warning they were upon me. Even as I fended off one heavyset warrior, another was clutching at my sword-arm, and another still grabbing at the top edge of my shield, trying to pull me off balance. But I would not surrender, and kept on struggling, determined to take as many of them as possible with me to my grave.

A heavy blow connected with the back of my head, near the base of my skull, and suddenly the world turned hazy. My legs seemed not to support me and I staggered forward, my sword-hilt slipping from my numb fingers. I was dimly aware of men crowding about me as I struck the ground. The last thing I remembered was the wide, white grin spreading across Bleddyn's face as he stood gazing down upon me, before my mind clouded and darkness claimed me.

Twenty-one

I awoke with the sharp taste of blood in my mouth. My lips were parched and a dull ache pounded inside my skull. I was on the ground, lying on my side; my mail, helmet and shield were all gone, and even my shirt and shoes had been taken from me, so that I was dressed in only my braies. Stones dug into my side and I tried to raise myself up, but my hands and feet were bound tightly with rough rope that chafed and dug into my wrists and ankles, and I could not move them.

For a moment I lay confused, trying to take in my surroundings, or as much as I could see of them at least. Horses, some dozen or more, saddled for riding but hobbled to keep them from wandering far, by the edge of a copse or wood. A banner in pale yellow, with a blue lion emblem that I dimly recognised, though recalling to whom it belonged was like wading through mud, for my mind was still hazy.

Voices, speaking in what sounded like both English and Welsh, drifted on the faint breeze. I rolled over on to my other side and straightaway found myself staring into cold blue eyes. A man crouched beside me, watching me. His hair, like his moustache, was red and his face was pock-ridden and marked with scars where the flesh had not properly healed. His black-crested helm lay on the ground beside him.

And then I remembered.

'You are awake.' He spoke in French, with a heavy accent, though not so heavy as to be unintelligible.

My throat was dry and no words would come.

'Do you know who I am?' he asked.

'Bleddyn,' I managed to utter. A violent cough gripped my chest. 'Bleddyn ap Cynfyn. The one they call King of Gwynedd.'

In his hand he clutched a leather thong on which was attached a bronze pendant that I recognised in an instant. Only then did I realise that my neck was bare. As well as the toe-bone of St Ignatius he had also taken my silver cross: the same one that had hung there for more years than I could remember, that I often kissed before battle, that had helped see me safely through countless struggles.

'A fine object,' Bleddyn said as he examined the pendant, opening it up and squinting at the writing on the strip of parchment within. Either his eyesight was not the best or else the elaborate script defeated him; he quickly shut it again and fastened the thong around his neck. 'Alas your blessed saint seems to have forsaken you, Tancred.'

I swallowed to try to ease my throat. 'How do you know my name?'

He smiled, allowing me a glimpse of his ivory-white teeth. 'Who hasn't heard of the great Tancred a Dinant, he of the hawk banner? I know many things about you, not least that you were there in the battle when my brother was murdered.'

Once more it seemed my reputation went before me. Gradually everything was returning to me. The path through the woods; how we'd had to turn back. The attack. If only we hadn't strayed from the road, or instead had taken the longer route east by way of Deorbi. If only Robert hadn't been so pig-headed, then perhaps I wouldn't be here.

'What about the others?' I asked, at the same time wanting and not wanting to know the answer. 'Are they dead?'

He hesitated as if unsure what to say, and I took that to mean that they had got away. If there was any relief to be had, I supposed that was it, so long as they were unharmed and they managed to reach Eoferwic safely.

'We have what we came seeking, and that is all that matters,' Bleddyn said. 'Indeed I should thank you for making it so easy for us.'

'Easy?'

'We'd been following you since you left Amwythic, the place you call Scrobbesburh. When you pursued that trail into those woods, we knew God was with us.'

This had been no mere ill fortune, then, no chance encounter. That dust-cloud we had spotted must have belonged to their scouts. And we had gifted them the perfect opportunity to way-lay us.

'You were following us?' I asked. They must have been informed that we would be passing this way. And I knew who was responsible. 'This was Berengar's doing, wasn't it? Somehow he got word to you. He betrayed us.'

'I do not know the man's name,' said Bleddyn.

To my ears that was as good as an admission. In the space of two days Berengar had first tried to kill me, and having failed at that he had then sold me to the enemy, probably for a handsome amount of silver. And not just me either, but Lord Robert and Beatrice too. I'd known he could be cold-hearted and vindictive, but never had I thought he would turn traitor. But if he'd hoped the enemy would do what he had been unable to, he had reckoned wrongly. For here I was still. Alive.

'You could have killed me,' I said. 'Why didn't you?'

Bleddyn laughed. 'A corpse is worth nothing to us. Eadric wishes you alive so that he can take you north to the one he calls king. The ætheling will not pay otherwise.'

'The ætheling?' And then I remembered the reward of gold and silver he had offered for the man who brought me to him. Byrhtwald had told me when he last came to the manor; it could only have been a few weeks ago and yet with everything that had taken place since, it seemed like a distant dream. As did Earnford itself: a dream that was receding further and further with every passing day.

'He has sent word to say that already he is marching,' Bleddyn said as he rose. 'He will look forward to meeting you, I'm sure. I know that Eadric is.'

With that he left me, barking orders to his countrymen. Someone came to unbind my ankles, but I had no time to enjoy my legs' newfound freedom as a spear-haft was jabbed hard into my ribs.

'*Kyuoda ti,*' said a burly Welshman reeking of piss, and I guessed that he wanted me to get up.

Still dazed and not feeling entirely steady, I rose to my knees, where I paused. The bonds around my ankles had been tied tightly; my feet were still tingling and stabbing with what felt like tiny pinpricks as the blood returned to them, and I wasn't sure that they would support me if I put any weight on them.

'*Kyuoda ti,*' the man repeated, landing a sharp strike across my back. I winced and stifled a grunt. Deciding that it was better to show willing than to resist, I tried to get to my feet, stumbling at first but eventually managing.

No sooner had I done so than the spear-haft was once more thrust in my back. I took that as a sign to start walking, to God alone knew what fate.

We marched throughout the rest of that day, heading towards the west. From time to time Bleddyn's men would goad me, hurling pebbles at my exposed back, while a few attempted curses in what smattering of French they possessed. I did my best to bear it all, gritting my teeth at every sting of pain, concentrating only on putting one foot before the other. My shoulders were burning beneath the sun, my brow was running with sweat and the back of my head still ached where I'd been struck.

It was long past dark by the time our journey came to an end at a small village with crumbling houses and a great hall that to my eyes more resembled a barn, and one that had seen better years at that. Others had arrived before us; to judge by the number of fires and tents, this was a sizeable marching-camp. How many miles we had travelled I couldn't tell, but we were probably not too far from the dyke. For a while I'd held out the slender hope that Robert and the others would return for me: a hope that was steadily dwindling. Not that I blamed him if he didn't. Whereas there had to be several hundred men here, we had ridden from Scrobbesburh's gates with fewer than fifty, of whom half now lay dead, their bodies stripped of everything that was of value and forgotten by all but the carrion beasts. If Robert had any sense, then, he wouldn't try to come after me. Whatever responsibility he had to me as his vassal, the duty of protection he had towards Beatrice was greater.

One guard on each flank, I was led through the camp. Welshmen and Englishmen alike jeered as I passed, recognising me for a hostage. Some spat at me and others threw clods of earth, though any who tried to come too close were driven away. While he had let his household warriors have their fun earlier, Bleddyn obviously did not want to see me too badly injured before I was delivered to Wild Eadric.

They took me to the hall, halting outside by the entrance to what at one time must have been a wine cellar. While one of my guards forced me to my knees on the damp ground, the other produced a key from a ring at his belt and opened up the trapdoor. Then, hauling me up by the arms, they threw me in. My hands were still tied behind my back, preventing me from breaking my fall. Their laughter rang in my ears as I tumbled down the hard stone steps, eventually landing with a splash in a cold puddle at the bottom. Swearing loudly, I tried to stand, but after so many hours of marching without food or water my feet were clumsy, and before I could do anything the trapdoor came down, shutting out what little light there had been, leaving me in darkness. Outside I could still hear the guards muttering to one another, their voices growing ever fainter as they moved away, until eventually I could hear them no more. I was alone.

Or so I thought. But then I heard what sounded like a low groan, coming from behind me.

'Is there someone there?' I called into the darkness. It was as black as pitch down here and I could see nothing, not even the walls or the ceiling or the floor beneath me. For all I knew this chamber could have been five paces across or five hundred. Somewhere, water fell in a steady drip-drip, but otherwise all I could hear was my own heart beating. As I listened more closely, however, I began to make out what sounded like breathing, faint but laboured, like a rasp being drawn slowly over coarse timber. A man rather than a woman, I thought, and plainly in some discomfort.

'Are you all right?' I called into the darkness.

He groaned again and then gave a great hacking cough. 'Who's there?'

Clearly his captors hadn't shown him the same level of kindness that mine had. Deciding it could do no harm, I gave him my name.

'Tancred? Is that truly you, lord?'

That was when I recognised his voice. 'Byrhtwald?'

'Yes, lord,' he said weakly. 'It's me.'

'What are you doing here?'

The Englishman did not answer at first, for at that moment he began to whimper. Not great heaving wails of agony but muffled, wretched sobs. Raising myself to my knees, I made my way in his direction, edging my way across the sodden floor towards him, wishing that my guards had freed my wrists or at least bound them in front of me rather than behind, so that I could feel where I was going. The air was filled with an overbearing putrid odour that made me think an animal had died down here, or possibly more than one.

'They caught you,' he said between sobs. His breath came in stutters. 'Forgive me, lord. I did not mean for this to happen, for you to end up here. I would never of my own will betray you, I swear—'

'Betray me?' I asked. 'What do you mean? What happened, Byrhtwald?'

It took a while before he could recover his composure enough to tell me, and even then events did not come out in their proper order, but gradually from what he said I was able to piece together the story of what had happened. A Welsh scouting-party had intercepted him soon after he'd left Scrobbesburh. Recognising him for a pedlar and one who dealt in secrets, they'd taken him captive, brought him to Bleddyn and forced him to tell everything he knew: the condition of the walls and the gatehouses; how well provisioned was the castle; what the mood was within our camp; how many men we had to defend the town; how many Earl Hugues had taken with him; the names of all the nobles who were left and who still supported Fitz Osbern. How long they had questioned him he could not say, but at some point he had let it slip that Robert Malet and

I were planning to leave for Eoferwic the following day. Which was how Bleddyn came to be following us, and how I had ended up here.

'Forgive me, lord,' the Englishman said again. 'They kept beating me until I had nothing more to give. I never meant for this to happen. It is all my fault, all my fault . . .'

While he wept I sat in silence, cold and still, my eyes closed as a numb feeling spread through my body, working its way through my limbs and into my very bones. In a way I would have preferred it had my first suspicions been right and Berengar were the one responsible. To be betrayed by a hated rival was one thing, but to be given away by one I considered my friend was a far harder thing to swallow. Still, it would have been easy to lose my temper, to curse the Englishman and say that he shouldn't have let himself fall into their hands. But what was the use in that? Nothing could undo what had already been done. We were here in this dank shit-hole, and somehow I had to think of a way that we might escape. That was all that mattered. Otherwise I would soon meet my fate at the hands of the man I had once sworn to kill. The same man who had murdered my lord and whose face had haunted my dreams for a year and more. I had no desire to see that happen.

Nor, if I were being truthful, could I lay any blame upon Byrhtwald for talking. A man will say and do anything if it means he might keep his life, and what he had suffered at their hands I couldn't begin to imagine. Never in the short while I'd known him had he given anything away cheaply, whether goods or knowledge. To have got so much from him they must have worked him hard.

How long it was before either of us spoke again, I had no way of knowing. It might have been as much as an hour, and possibly more.

In the end it was Byrhtwald who broke the silence. 'If only I hadn't sold you that pendant. Perhaps if I hadn't done that, the saint's favour would still shine upon me and none of this would have happened.' He gave a hollow laugh that quickly descended into a choke. 'Do you still have it, lord?'

'They took it from me,' I said bitterly. 'Bleddyn has it now, for all the good it will do him. St Ignatius never helped me.'

When I most needed his protection, where had he been?

The pedlar was quiet for a moment before saying, 'I might as well tell you now, lord. Perhaps I should have spoken of it earlier, but I was ashamed . . .'

'Tell me what?'

'My other sin. Those were never any sacred relics. What I sold you was nothing more than pig's bone, the protection not of a saint but of an old sow. For that misdeed God now punishes me, by delivering me to my enemies.'

Pig's bone. I'd long suspected the truth would be something like that, and still I'd fallen for the lie. Such a fool I had been. Yet even in the darkness, in the cold and the damp and the putrid stink that surrounded us, I laughed.

After a while spent feeling my way on my knees I found a patch of floor next to one of the walls that was a little firmer and drier, wide enough that a man could lie down. There I rested, or tried to at least. Every so often Byrhtwald would erupt into a series of coughs, waking me, and each time he sounded worse.

Eventually tiredness must have caught up with me, for I fell into a deep and dreamful sleep, finding myself back in the monastery at Dinant where I had spent so much of my youth, although somehow it was a different place to the one I had fled. A thick fog had settled everywhere, lending everything a grey and ghostly appearance. The ancient oak tree had gone and the walls were higher and somehow more forbidding, the cloister filled with looming shadows that, when I got closer, turned into the dark habits of monks, who gathered around, their cold gazes passing judgment upon me as if I were guilty of something, though what that might be I struggled to recall. I turned, hoping to escape, only to find the prior standing over me. In his hands he held a rod of birch.

'For leaving us,' he said. 'For shirking your duties and turning your back upon the Lord our God.'

I wanted to protest, to tell him I had shirked no duties, that although the contemplative life was not for me, I had always remained a loyal servant of God. For some reason the words would not form and my tongue lay as if frozen in my head. The prior's face was dark and drawn, lined with the marks of old age. From thin lips were issued two words, which he repeated over and over like an incantation while he lifted the rod: *Deus vult. God wills it.* Gradually the same chant was taken up by the rest of the brothers, whispered at first but steadily growing louder as they pressed so close that I could not move, until the words were ringing in my ears—

I woke to the sound of voices and the creak of hinges as the trapdoor opened. Daylight flooded in, so bright after hours spent in full darkness that I had to squint until they adjusted. I was still trying to remember where this place was and how I had come to be here when men descended the steps. I was hauled to my feet once more and dragged, blinking, out into the open. Behind me I could hear Byrhtwald spluttering as they struggled to lift his limp form up the steps.

'He needs water,' I said to the guards flanking me. 'Have some mercy; let him drink.'

Either they didn't understand me, or they chose to ignore me. The pedlar looked worse than I had ever seen him. They had taken everything from him save for his braies, which were soaked through and marked with brown stains that were either mud or his own shit. Countless bruises and weals decorated his back and chest. He could barely stand without aid, but hunched forward like a man many years older, in danger it seemed of collapsing at any moment.

They led us to what I supposed had once been the stable-yard behind the hall, except that the buildings had long since fallen into disrepair and everything was overgrown with nettles and thistles. Half a dozen horsemen awaited us, with spears that carried pennons in the pale yellow and blue of the house of Cynfyn. There the guards made Byrhtwald get down on his knees, while one of the horsemen, a bald-headed man of solid build, dismounted. Handing his spear to a retainer, he drew a long sword with polished blade and gleaming edge.

And suddenly I understood why we were here.

'No,' I said, struggling against my captors, but their hands were firm upon my shoulders, holding me back. Hunger and thirst had weakened me and I was helpless to act. 'You can't do this!'

'He is of no more use to us,' said the one with the sword. 'Now his life is forfeit.'

Byrhtwald looked up at me. His eyes were red-rimmed and bloodshot, and I saw the great sadness that lay behind them. Like the bravest of warriors he was doing his best to hold his nerve and show courage in the face of death, but he trembled nonetheless.

'Remember me, lord,' he said.

The tears were in my eyes as they were in his. I had witnessed the blow that killed Turold and seen the twins Snocca and Cnebba cut down before my eyes. All three I had known well, far better than the pedlar, and yet for some reason the knowledge of what was about to happen troubled me much more than had any of their deaths.

They forced him to bow his head, exposing the back of his neck. The bald man stepped forward, laying the flat of the steel upon it before raising the weapon high. Eyes closed and taking deep breaths, Byrhtwald first muttered a prayer in his own tongue that I could not make out, before reciting the familiar words of the Paternoster.

'*Et ne nos inducas in tentationem*,' he said, drawing the words out as he realised that with each one he spoke his end grew nearer, '*sed libera nos a malo.*' Behind his back his fists clenched and he let out one final sigh. '*Amen.*'

No sooner had he finished speaking than the blade came down.

It took three blows to remove Byrhtwald's head from his shoulders. Either the man who did it was unused to wielding a sword or else he was unskilled in such killings. The first stroke missed and sliced into the Englishman's shoulder instead, causing him to pitch forward, screaming in agony. As he writhed on the ground, his hands clutching the place where he had been wounded, the blade struck again. This time it did find his neck, in an instant slicing through his throat and his spine. That was the stroke that killed him, though it needed one more to sever the head entirely.

Thus it was done, and Byrhtwald my friend was gone.

'He was nothing to you,' I yelled at the Welshmen, spitting in the direction of the one who had killed him. 'He was nothing to you. He didn't have to die!'

But dead he was. With bloody fingers, the swordsman held Byrhtwald's head up by the hair, displaying it proudly for all to see, before with a roar and a chorus of laughter and cheers from his comrades he hurled it over the walls of the yard.

And as he wiped the sword on a patch of grass, I recognised the smoke-like pattern of the steel and the two blood-red stones embedded in the hilt, and saw that it was my own blade that had spilt his blood, that had taken his life.

From the position of the sun I reckoned our route took us once more west and south, and that reckoning was proven right when later that day we crossed the dyke. Back into Wales, as if I hadn't already seen enough of this godforsaken country.

Bleddyn and his raiding-band did not ride with us. Where they were headed I was not sure, though I could make a guess: Scrobbesburh. Instead I was escorted by the same six horsemen who had been at Byrhtwald's killing.

'Are you taking me to Eadric?' I asked them some time later, when that place was long behind us.

'Eadric?' snorted the bald-headed one, whose name I had learnt was Dyfnwal. From the way he had assumed charge I guessed he must be their leader. 'If he wants you, he'll have to come and fetch you. And when he does he'd better bring with him a cart full of silver. He's a fool if he thinks he's getting you for nothing.'

This raised a snigger amongst the others.

'Where are we going, then?'

But Dyfnwal had grown tired of my questions, and the only answer I got was the customary nudge between the shoulder-blades: the sign to shut up and keep moving. I was confused, since from what I had heard Eadric and the Welsh were firmly aligned, their alliance founded upon a common cause and cemented with mutual oaths. Perhaps their ties were looser than any of us had suspected. Certainly the way that these men spoke of Eadric suggested they had little liking for him.

Nor did Dyfnwal provide any more answers over the hours that followed. They did at least give me a small amount of bread and ale. In truth it did little to sate my hunger but it was better than nothing at all, and I accepted what was offered without complaint.

We marched on for the better part of two days, across valleys and over thickly wooded hills, never seeing another soul. They had not returned my shoes, which were probably on the feet of some other man by now. My ankles were nettle-stung, my bare soles swollen, in places cut and beginning to bleed, so that with every step came a fresh jolt of pain. I was beginning to wonder how much further we had to travel when I realised that I recognised the shape of these gently sloping hills, that I knew where we were.

And then as we crested one of those hills, in the distance I saw the place they were taking me to: a powerful stronghold ringed with high ramparts, along the top of which ran a sturdy stockade. The river lay on one side and it was girded on its other three flanks by a wide moat. As we grew closer I saw heads mounted on spears above the gatehouse: heads of what from their short hair and clean-shaven faces could only be Frenchmen. Nailed to the timbers were the tattered, blood-stained remains of the serpent flag that had once belonged to the brothers Maredudd and Ithel. Not so long ago they had dreamed of assaulting this fort, the ancient home of the men who had stolen their birthright, of claiming it for themselves and seeing that banner soar proudly in this valley. But no longer. And now I had returned, not at the head of an army but as a prisoner.

To Mathrafal.

Twenty-two

They led me through a wide yard ringed with wattle and cob huts to an empty storehouse close by what I guessed from the smoke and the pungent smell of fish were the kitchens. There they left me, though not before manacling my wrists and shackling my ankles by means of a gyve and chain to an iron rung set into the stonework so that I could not escape.

By now Robert and the others would be somewhere up in the high hills, I reckoned, with several days' hard going ahead of them before they reached Eoferwic, unless they'd heard that the Northumbrians were marching and had decided to make for elsewhere. They must have thought me dead, and I supposed I might as well have been, since it would not be long before Eadric came for me and I was delivered to the ætheling.

Nor were Robert and the others the only people who came to mind over the dark days that followed. With not a little guilt I thought of Leofrun back in Earnford, and dreamt of holding her, of lying with her in our chamber upon our feather-filled mattress. I pictured her face in my mind: her soft pinkish cheeks that dimpled when she laughed, her ears that she thought too big, her auburn hair that tumbled in great waves across her shoulders when she unbound it from her braids. Already at only seventeen summers old she was as good and gentle a woman as I had ever known, devoted to me from the moment I had laid eyes upon her and purchased her freedom from the slave-seller who had previously owned her, and taken her away with me to Earnford.

Earnford, my home. It wasn't just the manor itself that I'd grown fond of but the folk who lived there too: wise Father Erchembald, who together with Leofrun had taught me the little English I knew; Ædda, who despite his initial distrust of me had grown to become one of my staunchest allies and closest friends among the English. With each day that went by it looked ever more unlikely that I would see any of them again.

My biggest regret was that I would not live to hold my child in my arms. Often over the past few months I had wondered what he or she might look like, how much of myself I would recognise in that face. Were it a boy, I would have looked forward to watching him grow up, until he was old enough that I might begin to train him in the skills of swordcraft, the art of horsemanship and the pleasures of the hunt. Indeed, were it a girl, I might well have done much the same, except that Leofrun would never have allowed me to teach her the sword. Instead I'd have found someone teach her how to use the bow, and enjoyed watching her practise at the butts until she was as good a shot as any man.

These delights I would never know. All my hopes, my ambitions and my desires – everything I had striven for – had come to naught.

Once in a while my captors would bring me something to eat and drink. Sometimes it would be a bowl of half-warm beans mixed with some kind of smoked fish, but on the whole I considered myself lucky to receive anything more than a miserly half-cup of ale and a scrap of mouldy bread. A pair of guards would release my hands so I could eat, and they would stand over me as I did so, waiting until I'd finished before snapping the manacles back around my wrists and leaving me alone once more. Occasionally I was asleep when they came, whereupon they would kick me hard in the ribs or spit in my face to rouse me, and when they found me awake they would often taunt me by passing the dishes beneath my nose repeatedly, torturing me with the smell and the promise of food until, after what seemed like hours, they would at last unchain my hands. Such were the games that they played.

By night I bedded down upon piles of damp straw and huddled beneath the rough linen blanket they had given me. Clearly they had no wish for me to perish through cold any more than they wanted me to starve, although at the same time they weren't going to make it comfortable for me either. The only time they freed me from my chains was when I needed to relieve myself, when they took me to the privy across the yard. Even then they kept me closely guarded, with an escort of two or sometimes three guards. Once I managed to evade them, making it as far as the stables before a pair of well-set men wrestled me to the ground. And in truth there was nowhere I could have gone. Most of the time the gates were kept closed and, so far as I could see, there was no other way in or out of the fort. Perhaps they were being over-cautious, since they did not take me to the privy after that. Instead they made me relieve myself in my small prison, so that when I lay down to sleep it was with the stench of my own piss and shit around me.

Days slipped by, each one the same, so that I quickly lost count of them. Weeks must have passed since I'd first arrived, I thought, although how many I could no longer say. I wondered if the enemy had begun their siege of Scrobbesburh, whether Fitz Osbern still held out in the castle, whether the Danish fleet had yet arrived upon these shores. From time to time I prayed, hoping that God had not forsaken me altogether, that He would still hear me and bring me some hope. In all that time, however, I never received an answer.

And so I sought refuge in my dreams, where the faces of my friends and companions could return to me and for a while at least I could believe that I was elsewhere.

I woke to the sound of raised voices outside. Men called to one another in urgent tones, though I had no way of knowing what they were saying. Mail chinked as heavy footsteps made their way around the side of the storehouse. Through the crack between the door and the frame shone the orange glow of a torch or lantern. I must have been asleep for some while, for the last I could remember it had still been day, but now it was full dark. What hour was it?

I sat up, too fast as it turned out, since straightaway I felt light-headed. Until now Mathrafal had remained quiet. This was the first time that there had been any sign of anything happening. Had

Bleddyn returned from Scrobbesburh, and if he had, did that mean he was victorious or defeated?

These thoughts were running through my head when the door was flung open and a cold breeze flooded into the room. Dyfnwal stood in the doorway, his bald pate flickering with reflected torch-light. Buckled upon his waist as before was my sword-belt.

'Time for you to go,' he said. 'Eadric has arrived.'

'He's here?'

The Welshman grunted. 'Sooner than expected, too. He's waiting for you.'

Wild Eadric. The man I had heard so much about in recent weeks.

Dyfnwal made way for two other men. The taller of them had in his hand a ring of keys, from which he selected one and used it to release me from my chains. For the first time in what seemed like an age both my wrists and ankles were free, though they no longer had to worry about me struggling or being able to escape. My feet had by then recovered from their march across the dyke but were not nearly as steady as they should have been. A sharp ache ran through my neck, which felt barely able to support my head.

Out in the yard were gathered close to two dozen warriors, I reckoned, each with a spear in one hand and a round painted shield in the other. At their head were the men of Bleddyn's teulu – the ones who had brought me here – mounted and armed as if ready for war. Dogs were barking; somewhere a cockerel had been woken by the commotion and was crowing, though there was no sign yet of the approaching dawn. Nor was there any sign of Eadric, though the gates to the fort lay open. Blackness lay beyond; cloud veiled the stars and the moon so that not even the river could be seen.

Dyfnwal called to one of the watchmen upon the walls, who replied in what I took for a negative tone.

'He waits for us outside,' he told me in halting French. 'He is afraid, you see. For all his posturing the Wild One knows that if he sets foot within Mathrafal he is relying on our kindness and placing himself at our mercy.' His expression twisted in distaste, he gazed out beyond the gates into the country beyond, where tiny pinpricks of lantern-light now shone, glinting off spearpoints and mail hauberks. 'King Bleddyn might have forgotten his past misdeeds, but many of us have not, nor have we forgiven him for the blood that he shed.'

That was the most that I had ever heard the sour-faced Welshman speak; the most, indeed, that anyone had said to me in many days. I wondered what he meant by it. Of course if Eadric had held land out on the Marches under the old king then probably he had once fought many of the men with whom he was now allied. That was some years ago now, but clearly there were some among the Welsh who still bore a grudge against him.

'*Dilynwch fi*,' Dyfnwal shouted to his men, and to me said simply: 'Move.'

We passed beneath the gates, along the rutted track that followed the river to a marker stone perhaps two hundred paces from the fort. The furthest that an arrow-shot from the top of the gatehouse could reliably find its target, I supposed: there as a warning to any who approached that they were within the killing range. Eadric and his retinue had drawn to a halt a little way beyond it, although whether that was by mere happenstance or whether that was borne out of fear, as Dyfnwal had insinuated, I was not sure. With him were some thirty or more warriors, all with horses, together with a single cart drawn by a team of oxen, a man in dark robes who could have been a priest or a monk, and a huntsman with a pack of dogs. A sizeable company, all told: less a war-party than a noble entourage, but then perhaps that was the point, since Eadric had come here not looking to fight but to bargain.

Though he had been there at Mechain, I had never seen the man at close hand before, and so at first I was taken by surprise. He was not as men had described him to me, nor how I had imagined him either. Despite his byname he seemed to me far from wild, either in appearance or in manner. In my mind he had been a hulking brute of impulsive nature, built like a blacksmith, stinking and unkempt, with a long, straggling beard and hair growing out of his nostrils. A young man, indeed, whereas the one stood here was in his middle years, well groomed, with a stiff bearing and small, hard eyes that possessed a gaze sharp enough to pierce the best mail. Surrounding him were his armed retainers, his hearth-troops, his *huscarls*: stout fighters with whom I would have thought twice before crossing swords, even were I fully awake and fit.

The Welshmen dismounted, leaving their ponies by the marker stone and approaching on foot so as to meet the Englishmen on equal terms. The hunting dogs growled and strained at their leashes, but Dyfnwal ignored them.

'Lord Eadric,' he said. He spoke in the English tongue, presumably in mock deference, for his words were not respectful. 'It is a while since I last laid eyes upon your ugly face. Should I assume that—'

'Assume nothing,' Eadric cut him off cleanly and sharply, like a butcher's knife cleaving through a haunch of meat. He nodded towards me. 'Is this him?'

'It is.'

He strode towards me, eyeing me closely, as if suspicious that I were not who Dyfnwal claimed. 'Tancred a Dinant?'

'So they call me,' I answered, doing my best to sound defiant, though I wasn't sure that I succeeded.

'You're shorter than I expected,' he said to me in French, though he was only slightly the taller of the two of us. 'And thinner too. Hardly the famed warrior whose feats and prowess I have heard so much about.' He turned to Dyfnwal. 'I sincerely hope you have been feeding him, Welshman. If he dies of starvation or ill health before the ætheling sees him, I shall hold you to account and he will have your head.'

'We have kept him fed.'

Not very well, I would have added, but decided it was probably better that I kept my mouth shut, for now at least.

'As for the price,' Dyfnwal went on, 'it has now increased. Twenty pounds in silver, or goods to the same worth.'

'Twenty pounds?' Eadric snorted with some indignation. 'You think I carry twenty pounds of silver with me? No, the price remains as I agreed with your king. Twelve pounds is what I bring, and that is what you will receive.'

The Welshman considered for a moment, and exchanged some words with his comrades. Either way it was a large sum. I supposed it was a tribute of sorts to the regard in which the enemy clearly held me, and perhaps in other circumstances I might have taken it as a compliment.

Dyfnwal shrugged. 'If that is all you offer, then you will not have him.'

'Do not test my patience, Welshman. Believe me when I say it would be better if you took advantage of my beneficence, lest my humour should blacken further.'

'You will not intimidate me, Eadric. I fear neither you nor your master the ætheling.'

Eadric stood in front of him, so close that I thought he was about to strike him. 'I don't ask that you fear me,' he said slowly, as one might if trying to explain something to a child. 'I ask only that you give me what was promised to me by your king. Now hand him over.'

'And if I refuse, then what?' asked Dyfnwal, smirking.

'Then this.' As if from nowhere Eadric's knife was in his hand. Without warning he plunged it into the other man's unprotected thigh, driving it deep and leaving it there while he flourished his sword. 'You will not stop me from taking what is rightfully mine!'

Dyfnwal fell backwards, clutching at the wound and yelling out in agony as blood spurted forth. All at once Eadric and his huscarls were amongst the Welshmen: slashing, swinging, thrusting, driving shining steel into their bellies. For a moment I stood rooted to the ground in surprise, but as the ones guarding me bared their steel and threw themselves into the fray my senses returned. One of the huscarls, more alert than the rest, made a grab for me, but the weight of his mail made him slow. I ducked low and twisted away before he could lay hands upon me. Even as the Wild One bellowed the order to seize me, I was turning, running as I never had before, my bare soles pounding the damp grass as I summoned every last ounce of strength in my legs. Once or twice I stumbled upon the turf, nearly tripping, but somehow managed to stay on my feet and to keep moving. If I fell they would catch me and all would be lost. This was my one chance and I could not let it slip.

Steel clashed against steel, ringing out through the darkness; the silence of the night was broken by shouts and screams as I rushed to the nearest of the Welshmen's ponies and clambered ungainly up on to its back, kicking my bare heels into the animal's flank almost before my arse had found the saddle. The wind buffeted my shoulders and my face as I clung to the reins and raced across the fields that surrounded the fort, following the course of the river as it wound up the valley away from Mathrafal. Before long, however, I heard Eadric's men riding in pursuit, hooves pounding in rapid rhythm. I dared not look back to see how many they were, but with every stride that my pony made I could hear their cries growing louder and knew they were getting nearer. Their mounts were stronger and faster than mine and in open country they would soon be upon me if I did not do something.

Leaving the main track and the river plain, I climbed the slope towards the woods, hoping to lose my pursuers in the trees, the undergrowth and the night. Relying on the nimbleness and sure-footedness of the Welsh horseflesh beneath me, I darted in and out of the trees, ducking to avoid the larger branches and crashing through some of the smaller ones, wincing as they made great scratches across my face and chest. I knew not where I was going, only that I could not stop. I climbed ever higher, pushing on until the shouts behind me had faded to nothing and my heart was no longer beating quite so hard, and even then I kept going, forcing myself to stay awake as I traversed ditches and streams and crossed grassy clearings where the ashes of old charcoal fires lay, venturing deeper and deeper, until at last I came out on the other side. A river ran before me; whether it was the same one or not I had no way of telling. Although we must have marched not far from here only a few weeks ago, I did not recall this country. Of course the night had a strange way of making even well-known places look new and unfamiliar, but that was only another way of saying what deep down I knew: as well as being hungry and cold, sweating yet shivering, I was now lost.

The one thing that gave me some cheer was the thought that if I had no idea where I was or where I was going, neither probably would Eadric and his huscarls, since these lands beyond the dyke would be as new to them as they were to me. That was my hope, at least, and since it was only a hope and not anything I could be certain of, I rode on, following the valley upstream for want of any better direction to travel in, trying as much as possible to keep the river in sight.

All too soon, though, my mount began to tire. I had pushed him hard and now his steps were growing ever slower and less steady, until he could go no further and I had to leave him and carry on alone. Somewhere in the distance dogs barked, or perhaps it was only my imagination. Still, I decided it was better not to wait to find out which, and so I forced my legs to carry me just a little further. Shortly I came to another tumbling brook, but this time instead of simply crossing it I splashed on up the slope that it came from. If Eadric's hounds did have my scent, then I had to lose them somehow, and this was the only way that came to mind. Sharp pebbles dug into my soles as I splashed through the frothy, noisy waters; in some places the bed was so uneven that I had to use my hands to steady myself. To give up was to choose death at the hands of the English, and that thought kept me trudging onwards, one step at a time, gradually climbing, until eventually the stream grew too steep to follow and I left it, instead striking out across the hillside for another mile or more, hoping that I had done enough to evade them.

Certainly I heard no more barking, and for that I was thankful. All my vigour was long spent and I could barely keep my eyes open. A thin rain was beginning to fall and I took shelter beneath the thick drooping branches of an old hornbeam. No sooner had I laid my head down upon the earth than I was lost in sleep.

The next I knew the skies were grown light. My head was heavy and throbbing with pain, my throat dry and sore. Rain pattered upon the ground around me; my braies were wet and clinging to my skin and

I was chilled to the bone. Something was jabbing into my back, once, twice, and again, each time harder than the last. Groaning, still not quite sure how I'd come to be here, I rolled over, straining my neck to see what it was. A man and a woman stood looking down upon me: the former in his middle years with greying hair, holding a crooked branch; his companion probably of an age with Leofrun, thin and with an ill-fed look about her, and guarded eyes.

'*Byw yw ynteu*,' the man said, whatever that meant. He exchanged a glance with the woman, who might have been his daughter or possibly his wife; it was hard to tell.

I wanted to say something, but at the very moment I happened to open my mouth a burning sickness swelled in my stomach, rising up my throat, until in one great heave it all spilled out on to the damp ground. Exhausted, I closed my eyes and collapsed back, my neck no longer able to hold up my head.

Dimly I was aware of them speaking, before I felt myself being moved. One taking my shoulders and arms and the other my legs, together they managed to carry me a few paces at a time. I had barely enough strength to move my arms, let alone struggle; my whole body felt numb with cold and fatigue.

How long it was before I realised that we were no longer in the woods, I couldn't say. No longer when my eyes opened did I see branches swaying overhead; no longer could I hear the wind rustling the leaves and birds calling to one another. Instead I saw soot-blackened timbers and thatch with a hole through which smoke was quickly rising. Kindling crackled in the fire-pit in the centre of the room; above it on a spit hung a small iron pot, inside which something was bubbling.

A rough woollen blanket had been laid over me, but otherwise I was naked. I lay upon a mattress of dried ferns, which in turn was raised off the floor by planks of timber; close by my head stood a large ironbound chest while on the other side of the room, close by the doorway, was a stout bench, upon which sat the young woman, picking at her teeth with a twig while she watched me. Perhaps my eyes had been playing tricks on me before, for my first thought was that she seemed prettier now. Not as pretty as Leofrun, it had to be said, but attractive nonetheless. She smiled when I met her eyes, and rose from her stool to help me sit up.

My braies, I saw, were drying over a stool beside the fire. While the woman attended to whatever was cooking, I held the blanket close around me, partly because I was cold and partly to keep my nether regions from her sight, though if she had been the one who undressed me then I was probably too late for that.

She returned in short order with a wooden bowl into which she'd ladled some sort of broth. At the very smell of food I thought myself about to vomit again, but somehow I managed to hold it down.

'*Yf*,' she said, kneeling beside me and proffering it to me. I took it in shaky hands, clasping it firmly so as not to drop it or spill any over myself. In the thin mixture I saw cabbage and leek, and some other small vegetables chopped finely so that I could not say what they were.

I raised the bowl to my lips and sipped at it, tentatively at first for it was still hot. It was not exactly what I would have called flavoursome, although perhaps had my tongue not been so fuzzy I would have considered it as good as the most lavish of feasts, for it was the first proper food to pass my lips in days.

'Thank you,' I said, forgetting for a moment where I was and that the chance of her being able to speak any French was slight at best.

'*Annest wyf i*,' she said, pointing at her chest. '*Annest. Pa enw yssyd iti?*'

Annest. I supposed that was her name. I was about to give her mine in return when a thought occurred to me. If Eadric and his men were still out searching for me, they might well ask folk nearby if they had heard or seen of anyone calling himself Tancred. Better in that case to give her a false name, or better still none at all. I chose the latter.

'*Seis?*' she asked, her expression earnest. That word was familiar for it meant an Englishman; one of the few bits of Welsh that I had learnt in my time on the Marches.

I shook my head. How to say I was a Frenchman, a Norman or

a Breton, all of which I considered myself from time to time, was beyond my knowledge, but then that was probably just as well, for I was unlikely to have volunteered even that much anyway.

'*Estrawn,*' she said. '*Mi ath alwaf Estrawn.*'

Whatever she was trying to tell me was lost upon my ears. Certainly my inability to speak her tongue seemed to frustrate or disappoint her, or both. While I took another sip of the broth she stood abruptly and disappeared outside, calling presumably to the man who was her husband or father. The rain still fell, pooling in the rut that had been worn in the doorway. In all my travels I had never known a country as wet and as miserable as this.

Alone, I tried to summon the strength to get up. One thing was for certain: I could not stay here. Where I might go I didn't know, only that the further it was from Mathrafal and from Eadric and Bleddyn's men, the less likely they were to find me. Unfortunately my legs were reluctant to do as they were told, my feet uncertain of their grounding. At the same time a sudden dizziness overcame me and I staggered sideways, colliding with the chest and cursing loudly.

At once Annest came back in, with the greying man behind her. Together they helped me sit back down upon the bed, bringing me a second, tattered blanket that they wrapped around my shivering shoulders. My forehead still ached and I held my palm against it, rubbing the place where the pain seemed to be coming from to try to relieve it.

Annest fetched more wood from outside and added it to the fire-pit, building it up until I could feel the warmth of the flames upon my skin. While she did so, the man went to the chest and produced what looked like a strip of bark, grey in colour. With his knife he carved off a portion about the size of my thumb, which he pressed gently into my hand. When I looked at him questioningly, he cut another piece, which he placed in his mouth and began to chew upon, exaggerating the movements of his jaw so as to demonstrate what I was supposed to do. Finally understanding, I did as he had showed me, grimacing at the bitter taste and the rough feel of it against my teeth and tongue. Father Erchembald sometimes gave a concoction of dried willow-bark boiled in water to those who came seeking remedies for fevers, swellings and other ailments, and I supposed that this was much the same.

Having chewed upon the strip until my jaw was tired, I lay back down. Soon my headache receded, and my last thought before I drifted into sleep was that willow-bark must be good for treating that too.

They took good care of me over the couple of weeks that followed: Annest and her father, as I decided he must be, who it seemed went by the name of Cadell. To begin with I grew worse, with bouts of sickness coupled with a burning ague. In my few moments of wakefulness I struggled, and failed, to recall the last time I'd felt so ill. Within a few days, however, the sweating and the shivering had subsided and my appetite returned. The more I ate of their food and drank of their ale, the more my strength was restored to me, until after perhaps a week my fever had lifted and I was able to venture outside once more, to help gather and carry in wood for the fire and water for the pot. I was still not as fit as I would have liked, and prone to fits of coughing, but simply being on my feet did me some good.

As well as my dried braies they found me a linen shirt, frayed at the hems, and a tattered deerskin cloak that might well have belonged to the man's father, if not his grandfather too, so many times had it been patched and restitched. Neither Cadell nor Annest wore any shoes and so they had none spare to offer me, but I was content to go barefoot, my blisters and sores being close to healed by then.

And so I gathered my strength, until the morning came when I knew it was time for me to leave. To say that I was fully recovered would have been a lie, but I'd tarried in this place long enough already. As long as there were battles to be fought and the fate of the kingdom remained at stake, I could not rest. Somewhere my brothers in arms, my lord and my king needed me, and it was my duty to do what I could to help them. And so I had to return.

The Welshman and his daughter knew it too; they had seen me

growing restless over the days and they did not try to stop me – as if they could. At first I'd been hoping to leave without disturbing either of them, while they still dreamt, but the girl was a light sleeper and woke at the first sound of my rising. I'd hardly made it halfway to the door when she shook her father awake.

'Estrawn,' Cadell said as he rubbed his bleary eyes. That was the name by which they had come to know me.

'I must go,' I replied, feeling that I ought to say something even if they could not understand me. 'I need to get back to my people.'

'*Aros titheu*,' he said, pointing a finger sharply at me as he cast off the blanket covering him and climbed from his bed, making for the trestle table that stood against the wall. He gathered some of the crumbling cheese and a few ends of bread from the previous evening's meal into a scrap of cloth and tied it to the end of a sturdy stick that rested by the door.

'*Dos ragot a Duw ath gatwo.*' His face was solemn as he held it out to me.

A parting gift. As if he and Annest hadn't already shown me enough kindness. Lesser folk might have left me to die, but they had troubled to shelter, feed and clothe me, and it wasn't right that their compassion should go unrewarded. I wished I had silver or something more useful to give them in return, by which I could show my gratitude. Save for the clothes on my person, however, I had nothing. Guilt made my throat stick and I had to choke it back.

I accepted the stick with the food bundle. Both smiled warmly; Annest threw her arms around me; her father clasped my hand. In that way we bade each other farewell, and I stepped beyond their door into the breaking dawn. Their house stood alone, sheltered from the wind in a shallow cleft between two rises, overlooking a pasture where goats grazed. Of any other cottages, a church or a lord's hall nearby, there was no sign, and the same was true of any road or track that I might follow. The sun was rising so I knew at least which direction was east, which was good, since from what I recalled of my flight in that rough direction lay Mathrafal, and I had no intention of walking back into the lions' den if I could possibly avoid it. If Scrobbesburh had fallen or lay under siege then it was pointless trying to seek refuge there, while to the west was nothing but a bleak land of mountains upon mountains, or so I had heard from those who had ventured into those parts, with the sea beyond them. With that in mind I headed south, knowing that somewhere that way was Earnford.

I turned to gaze back just once. The house was by then nearly out of sight, a mere speck of brown upon the green hillside. Cadell and Annest still stood outside the door, and I waved to them, hoping they would see me. Whether they did and whether they waved in return, I was too far away to be sure, but I liked to imagine that they did before I turned and was on my way.

If Eadric's men had been looking for me this past fortnight, there had been no sign of them in the valley where Cadell and Annest lived. Unless they planned to scour the entire land this side of the dyke I reckoned they must surely have given up the hunt by now. With luck and with God's grace that meant I would find myself in no trouble on my travels.

And so it proved as I struck out across the country. Or rather there was no trouble of the hostile kind, although with only my instincts to guide me the going was slow and frustrating. Quickly I began to appreciate how much I had relied upon Ithel and Maredudd's knowledge of the country the last time I had been in these parts. Several times I was forced to turn back or change my course when faced with slopes too steep to climb or descend, streams that were too fast to swim or too deep to wade across: when that happened I often had to go several miles out of my way to find a ford or, on occasion, a bridge. But having lived through the battle at Mechain, having survived imprisonment by the Welsh, I was not prepared to risk my neck without good reason. I was determined to make it back home, to Earnford and to Leofrun, and to do so whole, not to die from my own recklessness in this empty and godforsaken land.

There was little forage to be found and so I was careful not to eat all my bread and cheese at once. Ædda had once taught me something of the various berries and mushrooms that grew in the woods, namely which ones a man could eat without killing himself or causing him to empty the contents of his stomach. Still, I did not trust my memory and so I preferred to go hungry rather than take a chance. Nor for the most part did I venture near the few villages and manors that I came across; I couldn't rely on those there being as friendly as Cadell and Annest had, to one who by his speech was clearly a foreigner.

On my travels I met few people: a shepherd with his flock upon the hills; a wandering priest with a wooden cross around his neck, riding on a donkey; peasants out gathering armfuls of firewood from the copses on their lords' lands. Most were understandably wary of a lone traveller approaching them, especially one of unkempt appearance such as myself, and tried to avoid me when they could.

'Hafren?' I would ask on the occasions that they did greet me, that being how they referred to the Saverna in the Welsh tongue. After a moment's thought they would sometimes point me in the direction they reckoned I needed to go, though just as often they seemed to have no idea, or else would reply in words I did not know. Thus, like a blind man I found my way: gradually and with not a small amount of guesswork.

Eventually, however, I came upon the Saverna, which was less wide here than at Scrobbesburh. The waters were unusually low for that time of year, too, and so I crossed it easily by means of a ford before making east for the dyke, which thankfully was not much further. Turning then, I followed the course of that great earthwork southwards. Gradually the rise and fall of the hills grew more familiar, and while still I could not say exactly where I was, home felt closer by the hour. With renewed vigour I spurred myself on, even though my legs were weary, until I found myself stumbling along the same valleys through which we had pursued the Welsh band that had raided my manor, so long ago that it might as well have been years.

I thought of seeing my hall again, of holding Leofrun close to me, of seeing all the others. What would they say? Had they heard anything of what had happened in these last couple of months? How could I begin to explain everything?

That final hour was the most painful. Although they were not yet bleeding as they had after the march to Mathrafal, my feet were blistered and every step was an ordeal. My cloak was ripped in several places from when I had fallen through a clump of brambles; bruises and scratches decorated my chest and my arms. I had not eaten in two days, the few crumbs of bread and cheese having lasted only so long. My legs could barely support my weight, but I forced myself onwards, knowing that soon I would be in my hall, with my woman to help soothe my aches and meat and ale to fill my stomach, and all would be well.

It seemed as if an eternity had passed before I glimpsed Read Dun in the distance, which marked the western bounds of my manor. Now at last I knew which paths to take. I rounded the hill's wooded slopes as the sun broke from the clouds, slanting down through the leaves and branches. My heart was pounding while joy and relief welled in my eyes. Finally I emerged from the trees to look upon the place that was my home—

Or had been. For where houses had once stood, now there were only fallen, fire-blackened roof-timbers and heaps of ash. The church, the mill, even the palisade upon the mound and my hall within: all reduced to dust and smoke and memory.

All at once my strength fled my limbs. Helpless, I sank to my knees. My breath came in stutters, catching in my throat. I could not tear my gaze away, refusing to believe it was true and yet at the same time unable to deny what lay before my eyes. My hands clutched at my face, tore at my hair; sounds of anguish escaped my lips, and it was anguish of a kind I had never before known, as if a spear had first been driven deep into my chest, then twisted so that it pierced my heart before at last being wrenched free. I could not move, could not do anything at all as tears of what would have been happiness at coming home spilt over into torrents of desperation and defeat. Of anger at the men who had done this, at myself for not having being here to prevent it.

Everything for which I had fought so hard was coming undone, the tapestry of my life unravelling into loose threads that by themselves held no meaning.

For I had returned, but Earnford was gone.

Twenty-three

I n desperation I stumbled through the charred wreckage of
my manor, calling: 'Leofrun!'

But there was no sign of her, nor indeed of anyone left
alive. Corpses lay by the banks of the river where, to judge by
the blood-stained grass, it looked as if a few of the villagers had
made a stand. Men and women alike had met their ends here,
their bodies stripped of their clothes and shoes and anything else
of worth, left in the open, under the rain and the scorching sun,
to rot and become food for the carrion beasts. Many of their faces
were so crumpled and bloodied that I no longer recognised them,
although had Leofrun's been among them I felt sure I would have
known.

Kites and crows picked at them, pecking at eye sockets, digging
their beaks into pallid skin, tearing away glistening red strings of
flesh, and I ran at them, screaming wordlessly to try to make them
go away. With a flap of wings and a chorus of calls the Devil-birds
rose up into the air, only to descend upon another corpse a short
way off, and no matter how much I chased and waved my arms at
them I could not make them leave. The stench of decay hung
everywhere, like a deathly mist that had settled over the valley. Flies
swarmed and crawled everywhere.

Among those corpses that were recognisable were the grey-haired
swineherd Garwulf, whose fingers had played so nimbly on the
strings of the crwth at every feast, and the girl Hild whom young
Lyfing had died trying to protect. Where before her hair had hung
as far as her waist, now it had been cut to her shoulders and in
places much shorter, savagely and raggedly, as if someone had taken

a knife to it, and what was left was matted with blood that ran from a deep gash across the back of her neck.

Neither of them had deserved to meet their ends in this way. None of this was supposed to have happened.

Fire had been taken to the wheatfields, blackening the earth and burning all of what would have been the harvest, while the pastures were strewn all about with the stricken carcasses of cattle, sheep and goats. Whoever had done this had not been interested in taking anything back with them, only in delivering death and letting the fullers of their blades run with the blood of my people. This had been no mere raid. This had been a massacre.

I came to the ruins of what had once been the priest's house. 'Father Erchembald,' I called. 'Ædda!'

There was no answer. The priest's herb-garden had been trampled, the small vegetables ripped from the earth. The roof had been torn off the house before they burnt it, for clumps of straw lay scattered about. Often men hid purses of silver and other objects of value within the layers of thatch, and no doubt that was what the raiders had been searching for. Not that they would have found much. Unlike some priests I had known, Father Erchembald hadn't been much given to hoarding. Whatever fortune came his way he was always careful to share, and in the same way it seemed he had shared the fate of his entire flock.

The church had suffered as badly as every other building in Earnford. All that remained were the stones that made up the lower courses; everything else, from the wall-hangings that kept out the draughts in winter to the embroidered altar-cloth, had either been taken or had suffered at the torch. There was no sign of the gilded cross and candlesticks, or the silver pyx, engraved and inlaid with images of wild beasts, that the priest used to contain the consecrated body of our Lord, all of which usually rested upon the altar.

These were not men who had done this but godless fiends, the children of Satan himself, risen from the burning, sulphurous wastes of hell to wreak their hateful destruction upon this land.

It was too much to take in. By the time I reached the bottom of the mound and gazed up at what remained of my hall, I had almost no tears left to give. Trudging onwards, forcing one foot before the other, I climbed up the path towards the gap in the palisade where the gates had been. An acrid and overpowering smell wafted on the breeze: one that was only too familiar and that turned my stomach at once. The stench of burnt flesh. A lone hen clucked as she pecked at the dirt in the yard, more in hope than expectation as she searched for grain or seed; there was no one to feed her. As I came closer I spied thin wisps of grey smoke, so faint as to be barely visible, still issuing from the smouldering timbers that marked where the hall had once stood. This could only have happened days ago. Had I only recovered faster in the care of the Welshman and his daughter, had I only found my way across the hills more easily and without so much backtracking, I might have been here to prevent this, to defend those for whom I was responsible. Even if I'd failed, it would have been better to have died trying than to witness this.

It wasn't the first hall-burning I had ever seen. But it is a different thing altogether when it is one's own home that has been destroyed. I tried not to think of the flames spreading through the thatch, or the panic as the roof began to collapse and blazing timbers surrounded those inside. I tried not to imagine the smell of hair and flesh being set alight, the heat overpowering those souls, thick black smoke filling the chamber from wall to wall until, choking and spluttering, they burst out through the great doors, only to meet and be cut down by the sharpened steel of the foemen waiting outside. By fire or the sword: that was how it was done by the folk of this island. That was how my first lord had been murdered, and with him so many others that once I had known.

But I had seen too many similar things in my life to be able to shut such images from my mind entirely. Even when I closed my eyes, I could not stop imagining those orange tongues licking at the sky, the plumes of smoke and glowing ash billowing into the sky, or the faces of the dying, people I had known, calling out for help that would not come. And I felt their pain.

* * *

I wandered.

One part of me wanted to put that place behind me as soon as possible, to go anywhere so long as it was away from here. The other could not leave the only home I'd ever truly known, and that was the part that won out. This was where I belonged. There was nowhere else for me to go.

Torn and defeated, I staggered aimlessly from cottage to burnt-out cottage, calling out in case anyone was left still alive amongst the ruins. There was always a chance, I supposed, that some might have escaped; at the last count of heads there had been more than forty souls in Earnford, and I had not seen that many bodies. Which meant it was possible that Leofrun was alive and well somewhere, though where to begin looking I knew not. Admittedly it was a slim hope. More likely the enemy had taken her off along with the rest of the women, that some other man had claimed her as his own, to do with as he desired. I did not even want to imagine that.

I no longer cared about food; even had there been anything left amidst the ruins it would have made no difference. Rather I wanted to give myself up to sleep, to flee this world even if only for a few hours, and hope that when I awakened all would be restored to the way it had been, the way it should be, the way in my mind it still was, even though in my heart I knew that such hope was in vain.

Hours passed. The wind rose and the skies grew dark with cloud; there would be rain soon, and I needed shelter. The long cattle barn by the river was the only building left even half standing, the fire having claimed the thatch and one corner of the walls but spared the rest, including some of the roof-beams. It was far from ideal, but it was the best I was going to find. I had begun to trudge towards it, past the fishpond and the sheepfold and the hives, when a flicker of movement caught my eye in the distance, close by the mill. A single figure, so far as I could tell, of sturdy build, leading a grey horse. One of the enemy, I supposed, come back to see if there was anything left worth plundering. He must have spotted me, for at that moment he stopped.

'Hey,' I shouted, my voice hoarse, waving my arms as I stumbled in his direction. 'You might have killed them, but you didn't kill me! Come and fight me, if you think yourself a warrior!'

It was foolishness, especially since I had no weapon of any kind, but I was beyond caring. Everything had been taken from me. I had nothing left, no reason to live. If he wished to take my life today it would be only fitting. I had failed the people I was sworn to protect, and for that failure this was my punishment. I only hoped he did not prolong my suffering, but instead made it quick.

'Your kind did this,' I yelled. 'You bastards, you sons of whores, you're no better than animals!'

Leaving his mount to drink at the edge of the millpond, he approached, striding confidently towards me. Whether it was because of hunger or tiredness or the burden of everything I had seen that day, I felt suddenly weak. Dark spots came across my eyes, blurring my sight, and no matter how much I tried to blink them away they would not disappear. My entire body felt cold and somehow numb, as if it were no longer my own. I inhaled deeply, trying to calm myself. With each step that the man took the moment of my death drew closer, but I was determined not to go to it a coward but with my head held high.

It was no use. Unable to support me any longer, my legs gave way. They had carried me from Mathrafal across hills and moors and fields and streams, across miles and miles of open, wind-blasted country, but no further.

He was within a spear's throw now, his cloak flapping in the wind as he laid a hand upon the sword-hilt at his waist. My heart thundered in my chest; my mind was spinning, my eyes throbbing with pain as white stars were added to the dark spots. It would not be long.

Make it swift, I prayed. Make it swift.

I bowed my head, not wishing to look upon the face of my killer, concentrating solely on keeping the tears from my eyes. A noble end was all I wanted now.

His footsteps grew louder, until he halted about five paces away. I waited for the scrape of steel being drawn; the last time I would ever hear that sound. For this was the moment.

It did not come.

'Do it,' I said, unable to bear this much longer. 'Do it quickly.' I swallowed, readying myself for the blow to come. Would it hurt? Or would it be so sudden that I wouldn't even feel it?

'Lord?'

That voice. I knew that voice. Weakly I managed to lift my head, enough to meet the man's eye and see the blotched white skin on the side of his face where many years ago he had been burnt.

Like a weir bursting under the weight of the winter flow, the tears came again, streaming down my cheeks, but instead of tears of sorrow, for the first time in what seemed like an eternity they were tears of relief and of joy.

It was Ædda.

He was alive and as well as I had ever known him, though the same could hardly be said for myself. Seeing how weak I was, the Englishman gave me a handful of nuts and berries that he produced from a pouch at his belt, as well as the small draught of ale that remained in his flask. And with that we left Earnford. He allowed me his horse while he walked alongside, leading the animal by the reins and making sure I didn't fall from the saddle.

'I came back to see if any others were left alive,' he explained. 'The Welshmen laid everything waste. I didn't think I'd find anyone, least of all you. How is it that you're here, lord?'

The tale was too long and too complicated, and I was too weary to answer. Thankfully he did not press me. He took me to the others who had survived, the few of them that there were. They had taken shelter deep in the woods across the valley and over the hill, so far from any path or cart-track that at first I thought the stableman must have made a mistake and we had become lost. I should have had more faith in him, for not half an hour later we came upon them. Father Erchembald was the first I saw, his stout frame hunched over a fire upon which he and the rest were cooking a hare on a makeshift spit.

'God be praised,' said Father Erchembald when he saw me. 'Is it really you?'

Next to the priest stood the miller Nothmund with his plump wife Gode, Beorn the brewer with his daughter and two young sons, as well as a handful of the field-labourers – Rædwulf, Ælred,

Ceawlin, Dægric and Odgar – some of them with their families and some without. Looks of surprise turned to delight as they got to their feet and rushed to greet me. For the briefest moment hope stirred within my breast as I thought Leofrun might be there too, but as they crowded me and Ædda helped me down from the saddle, that hope was quickly crushed. For her face was not among them.

'Where is she?' I asked, glancing wildly about, craning my neck to see over their heads in case she was somewhere behind them. 'Is Leofrun here?'

At first no one wanted to speak, nor even meet my gaze. Deep inside I knew what their answer would be, knew the reason for their silence, though I did not want to believe it. Not until someone spoke it plainly.

'Someone tell me,' I demanded in English so that they all could understand me. 'Where is she? Nothmund? Odgar?'

Neither of them replied. Nor did Ceawlin or Beorn or any of the others, their eyes downcast. Eventually Father Erchembald broke the silence, his eyes heavy with sadness and sympathy.

'I'm sorry, Tancred.' His voice was consolatory but to my ears his words sounded hollow. 'We all are.'

'No,' I said, shaking my head, not wanting to listen. 'You're lying. It's not true. It can't be—'

I broke off, not knowing what to say. My mind was reeling. This could not be happening. Had I not been here before, not so long ago? First Oswynn, and now, barely a year later, Leofrun: both taken from me, their lives cut short because of me.

'She is with God now,' said the priest, laying his hand upon my arm in comfort. 'Her soul is at peace.'

Leofrun had been my one precious thing in all the world, more precious than any number of sparkling rubies or silver pennies, gleaming swords or battle-trained horses. More precious than land or rank or reputation. Gladly would I have given everything I owned if it meant she might live, if I might hold her even once more, one final time. The thought that I would never again see her face, never caress those cheeks or gaze into her grey-blue eyes or run my hands through her auburn tresses was too much to bear.

'It was Bleddyn's men who did this, wasn't it?' I asked, my fists clenching. 'They killed her.'

Erchembald glanced at Ædda, who said quite simply, 'The Welsh razed Earnford, lord, but they did not kill Leofrun.'

I stared at him, uncomprehending. 'How, then?'

'It was but a couple of weeks after you and Lord Robert left,' Erchembald said with a sigh. 'The child came early, in the middle of the night. I rushed up to the hall where I did everything that I could for her, but she lost too much blood in her ordeal. She died not long afterwards, with your son in her arms.'

My son. I almost didn't want to say what I was thinking, in case that single glimmer of joy was stolen from me too. But I had to know. 'What about him?' I asked quietly. 'Did he survive?'

The priest shook his head. 'He was too small, too weak. He lived just long enough for me to baptise him before his soul left this world. We buried him with his mother in the churchyard.'

'What was he called?'

'Leofrun chose the name. She called him Baderon.'

'Baderon,' I repeated, barely able to raise a whisper. 'After my father.'

She could have chosen an English name, one that meant something to her, that would have given her contentment in her dying moments. Instead she had been thinking of me and what I would have wished for, even at the very end.

A kinder, more gentle woman I had never known. But now she joined Turold and Byrhtwald, Snocca and Cnebba, Garwulf and Hild and everyone else.

Leofrun was gone, and without her I was lost.

After that it was as if a dense fog had descended upon my mind. Blacker even than the longest, darkest night, no light or warmth could penetrate it, so that I was powerless to do anything but stumble onwards, hoping but not truly believing that eventually I might find a way out. A feeling of loneliness overcame me, more · intense even than that which I'd known whilst lying amidst my own piss and shit on the cold floors in my prison at Mathrafal, and no one, not even the priest or Ædda, could tear me from its grip.

I'd hoped that by leaving Leofrun behind in Earnford, rather than taking her with me on campaign, I would have prevented her from meeting the same end as Oswynn. And I had, except that a different fate had befallen her, one from which, even had I been there, I couldn't have protected her. This time there was no one to blame, no one to swear vengeance upon, whom I could pursue to the ends of this earth until they paid for the blood they had spilt. This was God's will, Erchembald reminded me, or, as the villagers called it in their tongue, *wyrd*. Destiny. He had taken her from me for a reason, even if none of us here on earth could understand what that reason might be. It was scant consolation, and I told the priest as much and worse besides. He was patient with me, however, as he always was, telling me that in the fullness of time the hurt would pass, and that when the end of days came and we passed as the Lord's elect into the glory of the eternal kingdom, I would be reunited with her.

As sincerely as he spoke, his words could do nothing to raise me from my sorrow. So many I had known had perished of late: men and women who might not have died had it not been for me. With every day that passed it seemed the list of their names grew longer and longer.

But as day turned to night and fresh wood was cast on to the campfire, a new resolve kindled within me. Even if Bleddyn and Eadric and their kind were not responsible for Leofrun's death, they had taken everything else from me. They had stripped me of my mail and sword and dignity, had slain my companions and torched my home. For those things I would not forgive them.

Under Ædda's direction the others had built rough shelters by leaning branches against the trunks of two wide-bellied oaks and laying armfuls of bracken over the top to keep out the rain and the wind. Beorn and Nothmund kept watch by the fire while everyone else bedded down upon the stony ground and tried to rest. Everyone, that was, except for me. My mind was racing as I thought about what we would do come the morning, how I would sow terror in the hearts of my enemies and how I would make them suffer for everything they had done.

*　*　*

We marched as soon as the birds began their chorus. Eight men, five women, six children, a priest, three horses and myself. We were all that was left of the proud manor that had once been Earnford.

On our way I told them of everything that had happened since I had left, from our expedition across the dyke to the battle at Mechain, our retreat and then our desertion from Scrobbesburh, my capture by Bleddyn and how I had managed to get away. There were parts that I left out: some of it seemed so long ago that it was already fading from my memory, but there was plenty, too, that I was less proud of and which they did not need to hear about, my quarrel with Berengar being one of those things. How petty did all that seem now, after everything that had happened?

When we were nearing Earnford I made the rest wait while Ædda and I rode ahead on two of the palfreys that, along with one of my stallions, he'd managed to save from the stables. The sight of the burnt houses and the smell of decay was no easier to bear than it had been the day before, but we skirted around the worst of it and I tried to keep my gaze fixed on the summit of the Read Dun ahead of us, and on the path that led there. Crows scattered from our path, cawing in chorus as they circled above us, their obsidian beads of eyes watching us.

'I don't like this,' said Ædda, making the sign of the cross upon his breast as we began to climb the hill. 'This is an evil place, lord. Why have we come here?'

'You know why,' I replied. 'We aren't leaving until we have what we came for.'

Despite the Englishman's mutterings, I spoke no more until we had climbed the steep stony paths that led through the trees to the ridge above, and from there along the ridge to the summit where the stones kept lookout over the valley. It took me a little while searching in the long grass, but eventually I found the smallest one, slid my palm into the gap beneath its flat underside, and with the Englishman's help lifted it and rolled it to one aside.

The enemy had not found my hoard, I was relieved to see. All was exactly as I had left it.

Ædda made a sound of astonishment when he saw it. He knew I

sometimes came here, but perhaps he had not quite guessed how much silver and gold I had managed to amass over the last few months.

'How much of this do you mean to take with us?' he asked.

'All of it,' I answered. 'We won't be coming back here.'

We lifted out the saddlebags filled with coin, the pagan arm-rings with the strange inscriptions – which I donned straightaway – and the two gilded brooches. I had no idea exactly how much it was all worth, but I reckoned there was sufficient for a dozen strong warhorses, with enough left over to buy spears and shields for every man, woman and child in our party. Of the three seaxes I gave one to the Englishman, kept one for myself and placed the third with the silver, thinking to give it to one of the other men later. Odgar, perhaps: he was the youngest and the strongest of them, and would be a useful man to have beside me in a fight.

That left the sword, the last of three I had once owned, and now my only one. It had been given me by Lord Robert's father, Guillaume Malet, when I had entered his service for a few months the year before. Though he had released me from my oath after the unpleasant business with his traitorous chaplain, he had never asked me to return the blade. In some ways I would rather he had, for in my eyes the steel was imbued with the memory of that time, with all the betrayal and deceit that had surrounded it. For that reason I'd never much liked using it and thus it had lain resting in the ground for all these months. That I had not sold it had proven a blessing. Perhaps I'd known there would be a time when it would be needed again.

I buckled the sword-belt around my waist as I looked down upon the valley and upon Earnford, at the same time praying silently that it was not for the last time. But even as we began the slow journey back down the hillside, a cold sensation came over me, as if I knew it would be. As if my words to Ædda had been somehow prophetic, though I had not meant them in that way. In my mind I'd been speaking about the hoard and the hiding place upon the hill, but perhaps there was a greater truth contained within them: a truth I did not want to admit but which deep down I knew.

The truth that we would not be coming back to Earnford at all.

Twenty-four

W e struck out across that burnt and wasted land, staying off the main tracks as much as possible, while also keeping a look out for any raiding-bands that might be roaming. Spires of smoke rose on the horizon where the torch had been taken to other manors, and we took care to avoid them in case some of the enemy still lurked. Even from a distance it was clear they had not spared a single house, animal or soul. All about wheatfields lay blackened, the pastures devoid of any sign of movement. Where I might have expected to hear the bleating of sheep and the lowing of cattle and oxen, there was only an unearthly stillness.

'Crungon walo wide,' Ædda muttered as we skirted the edge of one such manor. 'Cwoman woldagas, swylt eall fornom secgrofra wera.'

Something about those words was familiar. 'Far and wide men were slaughtered,' I said, trying to remember. 'Days of pestilence came, and death took all the brave men away.'

Surprised, he shot me a glance. 'You know it, lord?'

'No,' I replied. 'But you said the same thing when you were insensible with the poppy-juice after you were injured. Erchembald thought it might be Scripture, although he didn't know the passage.'

'Not Scripture,' he said, his voice solemn as he turned his gaze down. 'It comes from an old verse, one that was spoken to me when I was small by my mother, God rest her soul. She received it from her father, and he from his father in turn, and in that way it has been passed down through my family across several lifetimes. I know not who first laid down the words, but all my life I have never forgotten them. Sometimes I think of all those

I have known who have perished, and certain lines will spring to mind.'

Death took all the brave men away. I thought of Serlo and Pons and Lord Robert, and hoped that somewhere they still lived: that death had not also taken them, my own fellow brave men.

And yet I sensed there was something the Englishman was not telling me: something he had hinted at before but of which he had never spoken openly. For my part I had never pressed him, but it seemed more important than ever now, when I needed strong and reliable men around me.

'You used to be a warrior yourself, didn't you?' I asked. 'You're no stranger to the field of battle.'

He did not answer, not straightaway at least, and for a while we rode on in silence. I caught a glimpse of a dog, thin and wretched, wandering the ruins of its former home, plaintively barking for its master who would not come. Apart from birds and the occasional hare darting across the path, it was the only creature we had seen all day.

'Do you remember that day earlier this summer when the Welsh came, when we pursued them into the lands across the dyke?' Ædda asked.

He knew I did, and so I waited for him to go on.

'That was the first time I had killed a man in fourteen years.' Anger stirred in his eyes and in his knuckles, which had turned white as his hands balled into fists. 'I did not like doing it then, and I like it even less now. Yes, it is true that I have seen war, but I am no warrior.'

'What happened fourteen years ago?'

He snorted, as if the idea that I might be interested were somehow ridiculous, but when he saw my stern expression, he answered: 'This story I have told to very few others. If I am to tell you, lord, you must swear not to repeat it, not to the priest or anyone else either.'

The rest of the party was a little way behind us, not so far separated from us as to be vulnerable should any attack come, but far enough to be out of earshot.

'Of course,' I said. 'Go on.'

He regarded me for a moment, as if considering whether or not he could trust me, then sighed. 'Since the beginning of that year the Welsh had been raiding all along the borderlands: plundering, raping and burning much as they are now. In the summer my lord chose me and my two brothers, Brun and Tatel, to go with him when he was summoned to the war-band of Bishop Leofgar of Hereford, whose writ at the time held sway along this part of the March.'

'The bishop?' I asked. 'What would he know of war?'

'Very little, as we would come to learn,' Ædda said bitterly. 'He was an angry man as I remember, overly fond of his wine and with a high opinion of his own talents. For all his posturing he was no more a war leader than myself or my brothers. I was barely twenty summers old then, and they were some years younger, both of them strong-willed and eager lads. Of the three of us only I knew anything of horsemanship or had any sort of skill at arms, but even I had not seen battle before.'

He inhaled deeply, as if to calm himself. 'Not until that night at Clastburh. The Welsh came upon our camp while we slept and inflicted a slaughter such as I could never have imagined. I lost my eye when one of the bastards put it out with a spear, although I was among the luckier ones, for I survived. Tatel and Brun fell beside me in the shield-wall, both meeting their ends along with most of our host, my lord, and the bishop himself.' He shook his head, and there was the slightest moisture in his eye. 'I was the one who had to take the news back to my sick mother. I was the one who tried to console her, but the grief proved too much for her heart to bear and she too died soon afterwards. After that there was nothing left for me, and though it shames me, I ran away from my old manor, begging in the towns and by the roadsides until my wanderings brought me to Earnford. The steward at the time took pity on me and gave me work in the stables. Until these last few days, that has been my life.'

Ædda had ever been a solemn man, who kept to himself and rarely smiled, and I had long suspected that some sort of hardship

307

lay in his past. Unlike the rest of the villagers he had no kin anywhere on the manor or those neighbouring. Now I knew why.

'I'm sorry,' I said, knowing the words were trite but having no others to use in their stead.

He nodded, wiping a hand across his face to rid his one good eye of the tears that were forming. 'I am not like you, lord,' he said, his voice suddenly small. 'I do not seek adventure; I have no desire for riches or glory. Just as your sword determines your path, so the horses determine mine, and that is all I have ever wanted.'

'I understand.'

He did not seem to hear me, but went on: 'Then this year the Welsh came again, and I slew them because they had done the same to men I'd known. In the same way I ride with you now. When the time comes I will be content to fight alongside you and send our enemies to their graves, for it will be justice. But I will not enjoy it.'

He turned to face me, wearing a grim, troubled expression. That was the most the Englishman had ever spoken in my company, and it took me a few moments to take in everything he had said.

Like me he had set foot upon the sword-path. He had tasted battle, had wielded naked steel and sent men to their deaths. But that was as far as our stories could be compared, for he had only ever done so out of duty. Ever since my fourteenth year all I had ever dreamt of was taking up arms, of serving my lord well and seeing my fame spread. Even now, after everything that had happened in my life, after seeing so many of my friends fall and knowing that I might easily have been among them, still I dreamt of those things. Still I craved the bloodlust, the feel of my sword and shield in my hands, the thrill of the kill. I could neither deny nor restrain it, so deeply was that fighting instinct ingrained within my very bones. It was as much a part of myself as my heart or my head or my stomach. Cut it out and I would die.

In pursuing those desires these last few months, however, I had somehow lost myself and forgotten who I was. Exactly when it had happened I could not say, but at some point my reputation had overtaken me. I had grown proud, and deaf to the good advice of my friends and comrades: all the things I despised in others; all the things I'd promised myself I would never become. I had spent too long glorying in my newfound fame, listening to the tales that other men wove around my exploits, until I had started to believe them myself. Until the myth figured in my mind more clearly than the truth. All this I had allowed to happen, and in so doing had nearly lost everything. Leofrun's death, Earnford's destruction: these were God's ways of punishing me, of putting me back in my place, of reminding me who I was.

And yet the Tancred who led this desperate and hungry band of folk was an altogether different man to the one who had first arrived in Earnford over a year ago. I could see the change being wrought in myself, could feel fresh determination rising up and filling me. All the bruises I had suffered and all the ruin and slaughter I had witnessed only served to make me stronger.

We came upon others as we travelled: men and women whose lords and stewards, kinsfolk, children and livestock had been killed before their eyes, whose lives had in one stroke been torn away from them. They tended to be wary of us at first, but when they saw how dirt-stained were our clothes, how weary and ill fed our horses, and how few our weapons, they lost their fear and joined us. Probably they thought they were safer travelling in a group rather than alone, and probably they were right.

Thus over the course of the next few days our numbers grew. Some came laden with scraps of food, pots and whatever other goods that they had managed to salvage from their homes; others brought horses and dogs and even on one occasion two scrawny goats, one of which we later killed for its meat, little though there was.

A very few brought rumours of happenings elsewhere. And so we learnt that a great battle had been fought at Scrobbesburh in which the Norman army under Fitz Osbern and the castellan Roger de Montgommeri had been utterly routed. According to some, the enemy had slain the two commanders before reducing the town to ashes, giving no quarter to man, woman or beast. But others had heard differently; they said the commanders still lived, having managed to fall back to and hold out within the castle, and that Bleddyn had left a small force to besiege the town and lay waste the surrounding country while he took the main part of his host to march upon Stæfford to the east.

Whichever version of the tale was true, the news was not good. The only hope I could find came from the mouth of a timid alewife named Mildburg, the only surviving soul from her manor, who had seen a host of horsemen marching north up the old road known as Wæclinga Stræt that led from Lundene.

Ædda glanced at me. 'King Guillaume's army?'

'If it is, it wouldn't be before time,' I muttered. 'Ask her how long ago she saw them, if she knows how many they numbered, and whether she remembers what their banners were.'

He did so, and returned with the answer: 'This happened but two days ago. She says they bore many banners, in all manner of colours and with various beasts emblazoned upon them, but chief among them was the golden lion upon a scarlet field.'

That was what I had been hoping to hear. 'The lion of Normandy.' So the king was indeed marching, though inwardly I couldn't help but wonder if it were too late. 'And their numbers?'

'At least a thousand, she says, though how many more than that she couldn't tell me. She claims she only saw them from a distance, and dared not approach any closer for fear of her life.'

Probably Mildburg had done the right thing, but it frustrated me that she was unable to tell us more. As it was, I had an uneasy feeling in the pit of my stomach. One thousand men would not be nearly enough if we were to drive the enemy out of England and back across the dyke. I only prayed that the real number was much larger, or else that the alewife had merely glimpsed the vanguard or an advance party.

The further we travelled, the more survivors joined us, until our ragtag group had swollen to a band of nearly fifty men, women and children. With every new group of followers came more news; like many hands working together to spin a tapestry, their stories intertwined. Each thread combined with those that had gone before it, so that they often crossed over one another. Some added new colours to the weave or picked out details that the others had missed, until gradually an image began to form in my mind. An image in yellow and orange, brown and black and red. An image of blood; of a kingdom in flames.

Across the rest of Mercia towns were rising in support of the enemy; in many places there had been fighting between English and French and the streets had flowed with blood. In the shires the leading thegns were variously taking up arms in the name of Eadric, the ætheling, or the king, roaming the countryside at the head of their small armies. Travellers were being waylaid on the roads; castles and halls had been burnt to the ground. From the south came stories of a rebellion sweeping through the southern shires of Cornualia, Defnascir and Sumorsæte towards the strongholds of Execestre and Brycgstowe, while from the east flew rumours that the Danish fleet, strengthened by swords-for-hire from Frisia and Flanders, had arrived upon these shores and had raided along the coast, sacking every port between the Temes and the Humbre and leaving only corpses in their wake.

But even that was not the worst part of it. From north of the Humbre came tales that were as bad as anything I had envisioned in my darkest nightmares. Eoferwic had fallen to the ætheling with the help of King Sweyn, the two men having for the moment at least forged an uneasy alliance. The two castles and the great minster church had been put to the torch and the entire city consumed by a raging fire that had blazed for three days and nights. Nearly every one of the Normans, Bretons and Flemings had been cut down in the battle or else had been taken by the flames.

'It's said that those who were spared can be counted on a man's fingers,' said the man who had brought us this news, a travelling monk by the name of Wigheard who hailed from the town of Licedfeld not far to the north and east. He had been on his way to carry the same tale to his brothers in Wirecestre. He recognised my name when I gave it and was familiar with many of the tales that had been told about me, and therefore was only too eager to ingratiate himself and offer what information he could.

'What do you mean, spared?' I asked.

'Taken captive by the Northumbrians and the Danes,' Wigheard explained. 'The rest were killed; none were allowed to escape.'

The Danes were renowned for their ferocity and for the fact that they rarely, if ever, took prisoners. So far as I could see, the only reason they might have for doing so was if these were persons of some standing, whose safe return they could offer to King Guillaume in return for a ransom of silver or some other form of riches.

'Do you know their names of these captives?'

Wigheard shook his head. 'No, lord. I only know what I have heard from others.'

Perhaps it was too much to ask; from what the monk had said it sounded like a massacre. In all likelihood that meant Robert and Beatrice had been killed along with the rest of the garrison in the city. I hoped it was not true, but too often of late had I clung on to faith only to see it dashed.

And so I did the only thing that I could, and prayed.

'What do we do now?' asked Father Erchembald that evening as we stood around the campfire, where I had gathered together the leading men of that small band for counsel.

Among them were the priest, Ædda, Odgar and the others from Earnford, the monk Wigheard and a handful of those we had met on our wanderings: those who looked as if they knew one end of a spear from another. A more feeble and bedraggled group I had seldom seen; they were hardly the kind of men likely to strike fear into the hearts of our enemies. But they were all I had, and so I would have to make do.

'If the Danes and the ætheling have joined forces then they will overrun the north of the kingdom before long,' said Galfrid, a slow-witted Fleming, fond of hearing his own voice, who had been steward of one of the ruined manors we had come across. 'King Guillaume will not be able to fight them off and Eadric and the Welsh as well; not before winter comes at any rate. We would do better to turn south and find safety in Wessex.'

'If Execestre and Brycgstowe fall to the rebels in the south, not even Wessex will be safe,' Ædda said with a snort. 'Wherever we go, it will make no difference. The whole country is rising.'

'Then what would you have us do, Englishman? Would you rather we waited until those of your countrymen who have fallen in with the Welsh finally catch up with us?'

Ædda advanced upon Galfrid. 'What are you suggesting?'

The other man was undeterred, even though he stood a head shorter than the stableman. 'Were it not for the treachery of your kind, none of this would have happened. We would not be roaming the kingdom aimlessly as we are now; instead we'd be keeping warm beside our hearth-fires in our own homes, with food in our bellies and ale-cups in our hands!'

His gaze rested for a moment upon the two seaxes belted to Ædda's waist, one being that which I had given him. The stableman looked every bit the warrior, and perhaps that was what aroused Galfrid's suspicions. Like many of those who had come over since the invasion, he was probably accustomed only to seeing the English as a lesser grade of men, not as equals and certainly not as friends or allies.

'Lord, this man has no place here,' he said, turning to me. 'How do we know he isn't going betray us?'

'He won't,' I told Galfrid. 'Ædda is as loyal a man as I have ever known. Besides, he is right. We cannot guarantee that we will find safety in Wessex.'

'Where do we go, then?' asked Father Erchembald.

I buried my head in my hands as I tried to think. Having brought all these people here to discuss our plans, I still did not know what to suggest. Since hearing the news from Wigheard, a dark mood had overcome me. Truly it was as Fitz Osbern had said all those weeks ago. Everything was falling into ruin, and the more we tried to prevent it, the quicker it seemed to happen.

'Tancred?'

I blinked and looked up. The priest was still waiting for an answer.

'How many men do we have of fighting age?' I said to no one in particular.

'No more than a score,' Ædda replied. 'But they have no weapons or shields—'

'Then we will find them some.'

'From where?' Galfrid challenged me. 'And anyway, do you think they will want to fight, after everything they have seen?'

'If they wish to take vengeance and see justice delivered upon the men who did this, yes.' If they felt anything like I did, they would be only too eager for blood.

I glanced around the circle, at Rædwulf and Dægric and Odgar, at men from other manors and other hundreds whose names I did not know: Frenchmen and Englishmen alike. None of them made a sound, which I took for a sign that they were in agreement. Either that, or else there was no one willing to speak against me.

Ædda nodded solemnly as he gazed into the writhing, twisting flames. I wondered what was running through his mind: whether he could feel any relish at all in the prospect of the fighting to come, or whether it was something he would merely endure. Despite what had happened in his past I hoped he might find some enthusiasm within himself, could summon the battle-fury when it mattered. Often in the fray that was all that kept one going, all that kept one from succumbing to the fear that was always threatening to invade one's mind. For once that had taken hold it did not let go, and when that happened a moment was all it took for a foeman to take advantage. Death came quickly when a man's wits deserted him.

I tried to shut such thoughts from my head. I couldn't afford to lose any more good friends that way. Yet neither could I promise that any or all of them would make it through. In my heart lurked a certain guilt that I would be leading these men, some of them scarcely more than boys, to their graves, as I had led so many before them. But what other choice was there?

'The king is marching,' I said, addressing them all. 'If we are to reclaim the lands that belong to us, he will need every man he can find. Are you with me?'

The priest translated my words for those who did not speak French. One by one they gave their assent, perhaps strengthened by my resolve. A few hesitated, and perhaps their minds were upon the struggles to come, but eventually they too agreed.

Even Galfrid gave his support, though I sensed a certain reluctance in his voice, which I put down to a lack of experience. It did not surprise me. Often the men who spoke the loudest turned out to be those who had the most to prove, their words a mere veil with which they attempted to disguise their shortcomings.

I knew, for not so long ago that had been me.

Twenty-five

W e didn't have long to wait before our first prey presented itself. The sun was not long up, although we had been travelling for the better part of an hour that morning; there was dampness in the air and dew upon the grass. Summer was passing into autumn and all about the leaves were beginning to turn from green to gold, in some places already falling.

Falling, just as shortly the foemen before us would be. I counted four of them, riding from the north and the west. All were mounted upon sturdy ponies and all bore long spears with points that shone beneath the low sun. They came across the pastures and the fields, scattering sheep and tearing up the earth, sending clods of dirt and shredded vegetable leaves flying as they descended upon the small cluster of some five crumbling cottages that stood on the low ground by the water-meadows.

At once the cry was raised amongst the inhabitants, who abandoned their tools and their animals, taking flight in all directions as they made for whatever cover they could find. One long cob and straw house, larger than the rest, stood beside the pig-pens, and the Welshmen made for this first. Outside geese honked a belated warning to their owners, scurrying away with outstretched wings. Two of the enemy burst into the cottage, dragging out a screaming woman by the hair and shoving her to the ground, while the others pulled a large chest they had found into the yard, where one of them proceeded to hack at it with an axe that had been slung across his back.

All this we saw happen from the edge of a copse on the other side of the stream from the houses. The sun was behind us, and perhaps that was why the enemy had failed to notice us approaching, for a party of some four dozen ought to have been enough to frighten them off.

'Wait here,' I said to Father Erchembald, in whose care I had placed the women and the children, then to the menfolk: 'With me. Stay quiet; don't say a word unless you have to.'

We moved slowly so as not to attract attention, making for the rickety-looking bridge that crossed the stream, keeping low to the ground where the long grass would conceal us. The last thing I wanted was to charge upon the enemy only to watch them take to their ponies and escape before we had the chance to kill them. Fortune had seen our paths cross this day, at this hour, but I was determined to make the most of that fortune and ensure that these Devil-sons did not live to return here.

Wisely none of the villagers had dared offer a fight, and so the Welshmen went from house to house, searching for anything of worth that they could find, even breaking into the shabby, moss-covered building that passed for a church, ignoring the protestations of the priest, whom they carried out and cast into a dung-heap piled against a barn. There they left him, though only after kicking him in the side to see that he did not get up.

It was while they were all inside the church that we took our chance. I gave the signal to Ædda and to Galfrid, who were a little behind me, and they passed it on to the rest of the men. As one we rose and dashed across the bridge, which rattled beneath the rush of feet. One group I sent to capture the Welshmen's ponies, which they had left untethered close by the pig-pens. Those who had weapons I took in the direction of the church, breaking into a run across the damp grass and vaulting the low dry stone wall that marked the bounds of the churchyard. Half of them, led by Galfrid, went around the other side of the building while I and six others took up position beside the doorway so that when the enemy came out we could cut them down from both sides.

After that everything happened so quickly that it was almost a blur. Within a few heartbeats the first of the Welshmen emerged, a broad grin upon his face as he dropped a silver candlestick into a sack, and he looked up just in time to see my sword-edge smash into his face and to feel it bite through his skull. Seeing this, the others rushed out with weapons drawn, but we outnumbered them by four to one, and they stood no chance. Despite being dressed for war, they had not come here expecting much of a fight, while we were hungry for blood, hungry for the kill. We tore into them, stabbing and hacking and thrusting, filling the morning with our fury, with their cries and their spilt guts, and when all was done we stripped their limp and battered corpses and flung them into the stream, letting the waters run red so that they carried the evidence of our work here downstream as a warning.

Only when it was clear that we meant them no harm did the villagers approach once more. We returned to them the goods the Welshmen had taken and lifted the priest, a lean, ancient man with a shock of snowy hair, out of the dung-heap where he lay, dazed and somewhat shaken.

'Who are you?' he asked, still eyeing us nervously in spite of our kindness.

'Friends,' I answered simply, though he did not look reassured by that. I supposed he had a right to be nervous, for he had just witnessed four armed warriors slain in quick and brutal fashion on the doorstep of his church and their lifeblood shed over consecrated ground. He had no way of knowing that having dispatched them we wouldn't now turn on him and his people too, and finish what the Welshmen had begun. Only when the rest of our party arrived and he saw that we too had a priest with us was he finally convinced that we did not mean to kill him.

We asked around in case any of the villagers had heard anything of Bleddyn or Eadric's movements, or indeed of King Guillaume's army, which could not be far away either, but met without luck, and I regretted having killed all of the foemen without taking the chance to question them first. Still, we now at least had a little more hope of being able to defend ourselves. To add to the weapons we already possessed, we now had four new round shields, and the same number of spears and knives and leather jerkins of varying sizes reinforced with steel studs, and one sturdy helmet with a chain curtain to protect the neck that I claimed for myself. With us too we took the four ponies. All were headstrong and determined but hardy beasts that I reckoned might well have seen battle before. And so, mounted and armed, we began to look like something resembling a war-band.

Having warmed to us, the old priest bade us stay and share a repast, but I declined. The days were growing shorter, I explained, and we needed to make the most of the light while we had it if we were to catch up with the king and his host. He understood, although he still insisted we take something in return for our good work. Thus we left that place, our packs filled with rounds of cheese and bundles of salted mutton and fish, while their thankful cries rose to the heavens behind us.

But food was not foremost in my mind. No, what I hungered for was the sword-joy, the thrill of battle. This morning had only given me the briefest taste, and I was still far from sated.

We ventured north in search of the ancient trackway known to the English as Wæclinga Stræt, where Mildburg had seen the royal army. Of the people we met along the way few knew anything of the king's progress from Lundene. Occasionally we would find someone who claimed to have glimpsed such a host within the last week, or knew someone else who had, though whether it was Welsh or English or Norman they could not say. Like Mildburg they hadn't dared to approach too closely, but at least she had managed to tell me roughly how many they numbered and the colour of their banners, none of which they knew. I was beginning to think she was the bravest person in all of Mercia, for she had managed to bring us more useful news than anyone.

We reached Wæclinga Stræt late that afternoon and immediately saw the churned-up turf where many hundreds of hooves and feet had passed.

'How recently were they here?' I asked Ædda.

'It's hard to say,' he replied with a shrug as he crouched down and examined some of the tracks. 'As much as a week ago, possibly more.' He rubbed his fingers in a trampled mound of horse shit and then wrinkled his nose as he sniffed at them. 'By the smell of it I'd say this is already several days old.' He glanced about at some of the gouges that the horses' shoes had cut in the mud. 'Whoever came this way, they came upon large animals; you can tell from the depth of the hoof-marks here that these were no mere ponies.' He gestured at the animals we had captured earlier that day. 'Not like those.'

'You think this was King Guillaume's host?'

'Without a doubt, lord.'

That night we camped within the ruins of what I guessed must once have been a Roman house, an arrow's flight from the road. The roof-tiles had long since fallen in, but there were new beams and a layer of thatch over the largest chamber, suggesting someone had been here not long ago, and from the droppings on the floor I guessed it had been used as a barn. We sheltered in there, making a fire close by the entrance where the smoke could escape, warming ourselves beside it and watching flickering light play across the walls with their crumbling plaster and the faded images of people and wild beasts that long ago had been daubed thereon. Ædda, Galfrid, Odgar and myself took it in turns to keep watch through the night, and in the morning we followed the old road for another few miles before, without warning, the tracks veered away to the right.

'In that direction lies Stæfford,' said the monk Wigheard, who alone among all of us had any knowledge of these parts.

Stæfford. According to some of the tales that was where Bleddyn had made for following his victory at Scrobbesburh. We were growing closer. Although if these tracks were a week old as Ædda said, that suggested the battle had already been fought and won without us. Or lost, said a small voice in the back of my mind, and I tried to silence that thought, but over the hours that followed it kept returning.

To that end I kept scouting, riding from copse to copse and ridge to rain-battered ridge, crossing thickly wooded valleys in search of any sign of friend or foe, covering so many miles that by evening my stallion was growing irritable. He was called Fyrheard, which meant 'hardened by fire'. The name, it was said, had been given to him when he was a foal, after a stray spark from a groom's lantern had happened to set the fresh straw in the stables alight. Fortunately the same groom had also neglected to bolt the doors and the young horse had managed to escape the blaze before it consumed the building entirely, though they said he was much changed by his ordeal, and afterwards grew ever more aggressive and wilder in spirit: qualities which made for a good warhorse. I had purchased him in case Nihtfeax should ever become injured or sick, and through the winter had begun to train him to the lance and the mêlée. He had much to learn and was still lacking in the stamina that a destrier needed, but he showed promise.

Now, however, as the sun burnt low in the western sky, Fyrheard was flagging. I coaxed him on, up to the brow of the next hill, promising myself that after this we would turn back. These were not the long evenings of summer, when the light lingered for many hours after sunset; the nights in late September had a way of setting in faster than one expected. I did not trust myself to be able to find the way back to the others in full darkness.

Each step was a struggle; Fyrheard was not in the mood for climbing, but I was determined not to let him have his way and so I urged him on, following a winding deer-track up the hill until we came to the top and I could gaze out over the river plains below—

Where the corpses of men and horses lay in their dozens and their scores and their hundreds, with the shreds of banners and pennons lying blood-stained in the dirt beside them. The dying sun cast a powerful reddish glow upon everything that put me in mind of the wastes of hell as Father Erchembald sometimes described them, and the putrid stench wafting on the breeze only helped to strengthen that impression.

I descended the slope towards the plains. Small fires, long since burnt out, and the remains of tents were scattered across the valley. There had been a camp here, though whether it had belonged to the king's men or the enemy was not easy to discern. The corpses themselves offered little clue, so disfigured were they by wounds and the depredations of the carrion beasts. But as I grew closer to what must have been the heart of the camp I spied wooden plates and drinking cups lying abandoned beside the fires, some with scraps of food still left upon them, as well as a couple of tattered cloaks stitched together from various furs such as were favoured by the Welsh. The stricken banners and pennons were not ones that I recognised, and that I took for a good sign.

That was when I noticed the women – about a dozen of them – moving close to the edge of a copse that ran along the riverbank. Their dark robes marked them out as nuns, and at first I wondered what they were doing, until I saw the wagon piled high with bodies. A great ditch had been dug in one corner of the field, into which they tossed the dead without much ceremony. Elsewhere a pair of oxen had been yoked together, but they were dragging not a plough but the rigid body of a horse. Its side had been carved open by a spear, and out of the wound trailed what was left of its innards; flies swarmed around it.

'Hey,' I called, waving to catch the nuns' attention as I rode towards them. 'Hey!'

Even though I rode alone they were wary of me at first, and understandably so. The scabbard belted to my waist would hardly have escaped their notice, and neither would the helmet upon my head, but I dismounted and spread my arms wide to show that I meant them no harm.

The long sleeves of their habits were rolled up to their elbows and their hands and forearms were covered with blood and dirt. Most of them were young, but there was one who was older than the rest, and who had obviously not been involving in the lifting of corpses, for her hands were unbloodied. She came to greet me, introducing herself as Abbess Sæthryth and asking my business.

I did not answer her question directly, but gave her my name in return. 'What happened here?'

'A terrible battle, lord.'

'I can see that,' I replied stiffly. I had never much cared for men and women of the cloister, nor had much patience around them. 'Which side had the field?'

'King Guillaume, of course. He came upon the Welshmen in the middle of the night while they were sleeping. A vicious ruin he wrought amongst them until they fled. I'm afraid you have arrived too late.'

I ignored that last remark. 'What about the Welsh king, Bleddyn? Did they slay him?'

'Unfortunately he escaped. It's said he retreated back across the dyke, although at what point he abandoned the struggle or which way he fled no one knows.'

It was because of Bleddyn that Byrhtwald was dead and I had spent countless days chained amidst my own piss at that place they called Mathrafal. I cursed loudly. The abbess flinched at my outburst. Normally I wouldn't have thought anything of it, but this time I quickly apologised, knowing that I would get better answers from her if she were well disposed towards me.

'And Eadric?' I asked. 'Did he escape too?'

'Eadric, lord?'

'Called by some the Wild,' I said, thinking that perhaps she hadn't heard of him. 'He was a thegn under the old king; he ravaged these parts some years ago, and this summer joined his cause to the brothers Bleddyn and Rhiwallon.'

'I know who he is,' the abbess answered, her face flushed red with indignance. 'Don't suppose that because we spend most of our days within the cloister that we are entirely ignorant of the world beyond.'

I sighed, trying to hold on to what small patience I had left. 'Then tell me where he went.'

'He was never here,' Sæthryth said, and when she saw my confusion went on: 'They say there was a disagreement between him and the Welsh king. The exact details are a mystery, but what is known is that afterwards he went away into the north, taking his troops with him.'

Of course. When Eadric had come to Mathrafal he had been only too happy to kill Bleddyn's household troops in order to get to me. I ought to have guessed from that, if from nothing else, that some rift had opened between them. And I supposed it was fortunate that it had, or else King Guillaume would have faced an army perhaps half as large again, and the outcome could have been very different.

'You say he went into the north,' I said. 'Where exactly did he go? Does he mean to join the ætheling?'

On that matter Sæthryth was uncertain, although it seemed the most plausible explanation. I asked, too, where King Guillaume had taken his host after the battle. By then the abbess was growing tired of my questions, but I persisted until she answered. She told me that no sooner had the Welsh been routed than the king left for Eoferwic, where he planned to do battle with Eadgar and the Danes.

'How long ago was this?' I asked.

'Six days ago,' she replied. 'My fellow sisters have been working by sun and by lantern-light since then to bury the dead.'

The wind gusted, bringing with it the reek of shit mixed with decaying flesh. Sæthryth lifted a small pouch to her nostrils, no doubt trying to mask the odour with herbs and so stave off the vaporous poisons that some said were carried upon the air. Whether that was true or not I was not knowledgeable enough to be able to judge, but a dozen years and more of breathing in such battle-smells had brought little ill effect upon me. As far as I was aware, at any rate.

With that the abbess left me, having clearly had enough of indulging my questions. Perhaps she thought that by ignoring me I would grow tired and leave her and the rest of the nuns to their work; if so she was wrong. From speaking to a few of the younger nuns I learnt that the king had left behind a small contingent commanded by his half-brother, the Bishop Odo, whom he had tasked with pursuing the Welshmen to the dyke and with relieving Fitz Osbern, who despite some of the rumours we'd heard still held out in the castle at Scrobbesburh. I asked whether any word of Earl Hugues had come from Ceastre, but none had heard anything.

'Are you still here?'

I turned to see Abbess Sæthryth looking sternly upon me, plainly unimpressed by my questioning of her sisters. By then I had all the information I needed, however, and as the sun fell beneath the hills to the west and the light began to fade, I let them be.

Before returning to Fyrheard, I searched the field for anything that might be of use to us that had not already been taken by the victors, and managed to find two sturdy round shields that with a little repair to the leather upon their faces would serve well, together with a pair of fine hunting knives and a mail hauberk that had once belonged to a fellow Frenchman. His body lay part hidden beneath a thorny bush, which was how I supposed such spoils had gone unnoticed. He was a stouter man than I, which meant the hauberk was a little larger than I would have liked, but it was better than no protection at all, and so I pulled it on and tightened the buckles as far as they would go.

With the skies darkening, then, I rode back to the others, eventually making it back some hours later. Father Erchembald chastised me for having been gone so long; he and the others had worried that some ill fate had befallen me, but when I showed them what goods I'd recovered from the place of battle, their moods soon lightened.

'Where now, then?' Ædda asked me after I had related the news of what had taken place close to Stæfford.

That same question had been on my mind as I was riding back, so I had no hesitation in answering it. To my mind there was nothing to be had in joining Bishop Odo's forces in trying to pursue Bleddyn; the Welsh king could be anywhere, and was probably many leagues from here already. No, the main fighting would be in the north, against the ætheling and most likely Eadric too. If I was to have any chance of bringing my sword to bear upon them, that was where I had to be.

Twenty-six

W e set out by way of Licedfeld. I didn't want to take the survivors from Earnford into the wilds of Northumbria, only those who could fight, and so I left behind the older ones, including Nothmund the miller and Beorn the brewer, along with the women and the children, entrusting them into Wigheard's care. He promised he would find shelter for them at the monastery in the town until I returned.

We parted ways outside the gates of the town, where I handed the monk one of the two saddlebags filled with silver from my hoard.

'Give this to your abbot,' I told him.

I hadn't had a chance to weigh or count how much was there exactly, but reckoned it was enough to ensure the monks stayed friendly and provided my people with adequate food and drink for as long as was necessary. As well it should, for it was fully half of all the wealth I had left in the world.

'If he raises any objections, mention my name and tell him whatever you must,' I said. 'Say that I'll build him a new church, or give my eldest child into the service of the Lord, and that if I return he may hold me to those promises.'

'Yes, lord,' Wigheard replied solemnly.

I did not make such oaths lightly, although I sincerely hoped it would not come to such measures. Even before Earnford had been sacked I'd hardly been a rich man, and I was far poorer now. Not only that, but having lost one son before I had even known him, the last thing I wanted was to have to give up my next into holy orders. But having protected these people thus far, I couldn't abandon them now, not while armies ravaged and plundered and burnt their way across this kingdom, and I was resolved to do whatever it took to ensure their safety.

Providing, that was, that I returned. Providing that the Danes and the rebels in Northumbria didn't overrun the kingdom, slaughtering everything in their path. For while the Welsh might have been defeated, Eadgar and King Sweyn and their men were still fresh and eager for battle and glory.

And for Norman blood.

We finally caught up with King Guillaume's army by the banks of the fast-flowing river called by some the Yr, which I was told marked the traditional boundary between the old kingdoms of Mercia and Northumbria. So far he had been unable to effect a crossing, for the enemy had destroyed all the bridges along that stretch and now held the northern side all the way to the Humbre, into which the river emptied some miles to the east.

Raiding-parties patrolled the opposite bank, taunting us from across the water, marked out as Danes by their banners, which displayed runes and skulls, bloodied daggers and wolves' heads, ravens and fire-breathing dragons. While their king purported to be a Christian, many of their kind were godless men, and those were for the most part pagan symbols.

Occasionally some of their horsemen would come within bowshot, and a handful of our archers would try their luck, but the wind usually took their arrows, which only invited yet more jeering and made our men waste even more shafts. And a waste it was, for those scouts were no threat to us and even if we killed them it would be but a small victory. All they wanted was to assess our numbers and try to judge the condition of our men, and it was difficult to stop them for the simple reason that an army as large as ours is almost impossible to hide.

It was a very different host to the one that had marched upon Eoferwic last year: fewer in numbers but for the most part better equipped and better trained, with many more knights and archers and fewer men of the fyrd. To that army I added the six men I'd brought with me: Ædda; Galfrid the steward; the three lads Ceawlin, Dægric and Odgar from Earnford, all of whom had on occasion trained with me and my knights in the yard and thus knew something of fighting, even if it was not much; and Father Erchembald. Reluctant though he'd been to leave those in Licedfeld, I needed him, not for his fighting skills of course, but for his wisdom and advice, which I valued and trusted more than that of anyone else in the world. Nor was there another priest to whom I would rather confess my sins before battle than he, who had come to know me so well over the past year and more. If I died his were the prayers that I wished sent to intercede on my behalf.

There were some faces that I recognised among that army, either because they had been there the last time we had marched on Eoferwic, or because they were influential noblemen and I remembered them from the few times I had attended the king's courts. But those men whom I knew personally or who recognised me were few in number. An oddly despondent feeling came over me as I realised I was no longer the one to whom everyone else looked for instructions, the one who inspired confidence and instilled respect. Instead I was once more merely one stranger among many, with nothing to mark me out as a lord and a leader of men: not a banner or pennon to fly; nor a single household knight to command; nor, apart from the six who were with me, any man there I could even call my friend.

Or so I thought, until that evening as we were setting up camp, when I heard my name being called from a distance. Jolted from my thoughts, I turned and saw two familiar faces I had not expected to see.

'Pons!' I said. 'Serlo!'

We embraced like long-lost siblings. It couldn't have been much more than two months since I had last seen them, but it felt far longer.

'We didn't think we'd see you again, lord,' Pons said. 'We thought you were dead.'

'Well, here I am,' I replied. 'Alive, if only just.'

They had survived the ambush in which I'd been captured, and made it together with Robert to Eoferwic. But as soon as it was heard that the enemy had entered the Humbre and were headed for the city, Robert and his father the vicomte had sent them south to bear the news to King Guillaume, little knowing that he was already on the way at the head of an army.

'Only a few days later we heard that the city had fallen,' Serlo said. 'It was fortunate that they did send us, or else we would have been there when it happened.'

Sometimes God's favour wanes and at other times it shines upon us for reasons we cannot always understand, but it was clear He had chosen to spare them. I could but hope that He had extended the same favour to the Malets themselves.

Still, to add to the unexpected sight of Serlo and Pons came another piece of good fortune in the form of the arrival two days later of Eudo and Wace, who had ridden north from Robert's estates in Suthfolc.

'We thought you had gone with Lord Robert and his sister to Eoferwic,' Wace said. 'When we heard what happened, we feared the worst.'

'Who are these men?' Eudo asked, frowning as he gestured at those seated around our campfire.

To that question there was no simple answer, and so I told them the tale, just as I had told Father Erchembald and Ædda before. Of course Eudo and Wace knew nothing of what had happened to me, and why should they? They had been on the other side of the kingdom entirely, defending Heia and its surrounding manors against King Sweyn.

'Or at least we were, until the Danes brought their fleet up the river,' said Wace. 'Then your countryman Earl Ralph called us to Noruic where we had to fight them off.'

Ralph Guader was the Earl of East Anglia, a man of an age with myself, known as much for his iron will and his lack of humour as for his skill at arms. He had led a contingent of Bretons in the great battle at Hæstinges, and performed his duties admirably from what I'd heard; this battle, however, would have been a sterner test of his abilities for the Danes were determined and unforgiving warriors, who would often rather die than suffer defeat. I had faced them before, and did not much relish the thought of having to do so again.

'I've never known such fighting,' Eudo said. 'We battled them street by street all the way from the walls to the quays, until there was not an inch of mud in the city that was not covered in blood. They throw themselves into the fray without care for their lives, and even when they are surrounded they will not stop.'

He shook his head, unable to say any more. Something in their expressions told me they had both seen things in the past month that they could not bring themselves to relate, not even amongst friends. As had I.

In that moment I understood that the close companionship we once had would never be regained, or at least not in the same form. Before, we had always lived as we had fought, sharing the same tales and the same songs of battle across the feasting-table, bedding down on sodden rushes in distant halls, riding shoulder to shoulder in the charge. Everything that had happened had happened to all of us together. Now, however, we had grown too different; our lives had taken us in separate directions and there would forever be a distance between us that could never be crossed.

'What brought you here?' I asked.

'After we had beaten the Danes off, they sailed on up the coast,' Wace said. 'Earl Ralph thought they might land elsewhere in East Anglia and kept us in Noruic for a while in case they marched overland, but when reports came that they'd gone into the Humbre, he sent some of us north to join the king. We expected to catch up with him some days ago; he must have ridden quickly if he had time to defeat the Welsh at Stæfford first.'

Indeed the word from those close to him was that the king was in a fouler mood than anyone had ever known him. The longer the enemy held us at the Yr and the blacker and thicker grew the smears of smoke on the northern horizon, the worse his temper became. He would lash out at his retainers, one of whom, a manservant by the name of Fulbert, was said to have died after the king had struck him a blow around the head for suggesting that it would be better simply to pay King Sweyn to leave these shores. For the Danes loved gold and silver even more than they did the blood-rush of battle, and nothing pleased them more than obtaining such riches without having to draw steel and risk their lives in its pursuit.

The hapless Fulbert might have been the first to suggest the notion, but he was not the only one, for as October wore on and still our scouts had not found us a crossing over the river, many of the nobles started to offer the same counsel. If the Danes could be paid to depart before winter, the ætheling would be left without allies and would have no choice but to retreat back whence he had come, into the wilds and the moors north of Dunholm. However, so determined was the king to crush his enemies outright, as he had crushed the usurper Harold at Hæstinges, that he refused to listen to such advice. And so for another two weeks we waited for word to return from upriver, where they were looking for a ford by which we might bring our entire host across. By then it was getting late in the campaigning season. Autumn mists shrouded the land, the arms of the trees were growing bare and each day was colder than the last. The minds of the barons were turning to the unrest in the south that was threatening their manors, and beyond that to the gathering of firewood for their hearth-fires and the slaughtering of pigs and cattle in preparation for winter.

'We would do better to let the enemy keep Eoferwic and Northumbria,' said Galfrid one day when we were out on one of our regular foraging expeditions. 'Let them spend the winter there and then in the spring march against them when the troubles elsewhere are settled and we can muster an even greater force.'

'You'd do better to keep your mouth shut if you want your head to stay attached to your neck,' I told him. 'England belongs to King Guillaume and to him alone.'

Though in many ways it was good sense, such talk was close to treason, and if word ever got back to the king that men were openly suggesting he should surrender a part of his realm to pagans and rebels, he would have no hesitation in demanding their heads.

Thankfully Galfrid never discussed it again. Such moments of folly aside, I had begun to warm to him. Indeed, from training with him it was clear he was a far better swordsman than I had expected, if a little overconfident in his abilities. He would have to learn to restrain his excitement if he wanted to survive for long on the field of battle.

And he would have to learn quickly, for the time when our swords would be needed was soon. We returned to camp that same evening with three carts all loaded with supplies, and were greeted with the news that a baron named Lisois had discovered a crossing-place high upstream, some miles to the west. A hundred fyrdmen from the shire of Eoferwic had tried to hold it against him and his knights, but he had succeeded in killing a large number of them before driving the rest off. Even as we rode through the camp men were making ready their horses and donning mail and helmets, the vanguard forming up under the lion banner, even though night was fast falling. Soon the order to march was being passed down to every lord together with his retainers, to every knight and every servant. Only a few remained behind at the king's direction, commanded by his other brother, the Count of Mortain, who was charged with holding the southern bank of the Yr in case the enemy should bring their ships up from the marshes of the Humbre where they lay and try to land on the Mercian side.

'On the march again,' Eudo said wryly as, under the light of the setting sun and rising moon, we mounted up.

'Not a day too soon, either,' I replied. No further news had come from Eoferwic, nor had there been any sign of Lord Robert and Beatrice, and to tell the truth I was growing ever more anxious. I hoped they hadn't been in the city when it fell, and yet if they had escaped then it was strange that they had not made their way south.

The thought that they might be dead was not one that I wanted to entertain. Try as I might, however, I could not stop it preying on my mind, and each time it surfaced what small hope I held out only diminished further.

We reached the ford before the enemy could send any more of their men to hold it and prevent us making the crossing. We rode through the night and the dawn and for several hours into the following day, until our entire host was gathered on the Northumbrian side of the river. A formidable host it was by then, too, for the weeks we had been held at the Yr had allowed other barons to catch up with us. Among them were more than a few English thegns: those who had no love for Eadgar Ætheling, or whose families had suffered at the hands of the Danes in generations past, or who were too afraid to risk their king's wrath by defying him. All of which meant that by the time we marched upon Eoferwic we were many thousands in number.

A few foemen came to stand against our progress and were quickly routed, but mostly they fled at the very sight of us, retreating to rejoin the main host, I didn't doubt. We tried to pursue them, but these lands south of Eoferwic were flat and in many places boggy, not easily penetrable on horseback. They knew the paths through the marshes far better than we did, and it would have been folly to try to face them on unfamiliar ground, where they could easily draw us into ambushes. And so we left them, skirting around those low-lying lands, all the while expecting their banners and their shields to appear upon the ridges and across the fields ahead of us and for the battle-thunder to ring out. But they did not. We saw the evidence of their raiding all around us, but never their entire host.

'They have to be planning something,' Wace said on the second day after we crossed the river. 'Otherwise they would have attacked us before now.'

'Unless they're too afraid to fight us,' Eudo suggested.

He was joking, of course, but Wace had ever struggled to understand Eudo's sense of humour. 'When have the Danes ever been afraid of a fight?' he asked with a snort. 'No, they wouldn't have come all this way if they didn't want a battle. They're drawing us towards Eoferwic, most likely holding out within its walls, inviting us to assault the city just like last year.'

Except that it seemed Eudo had it more right than Wace, for the word from our scouts was that the enemy were abandoning the place altogether, escaping by ship down the Use and by foot and horse into the north. We learnt a fire had spread through the entire eastern quarter of the city, destroying one of the castles and the minster of St Peter, before the wind had carried the ashes and the sparks across the river, where they had settled on the thatch of the houses, leaving almost no building standing. And so, with nothing left to defend, the Danes and the ætheling had quit the place.

Still I did not quite believe it, not until the following day when we arrived at the still-smouldering ruins and I could see everything with my own eyes: the toppled, blackened timbers where the palisades and gatehouses had been; the wisps of smoke rising from the foundations of the great church and the long merchants' houses; the mottes without their towers; the fallen-in roof of the vicomte's palace, where I had recovered from the injuries I'd suffered in the battle at Dunholm and where I had first become indebted to the Malet family and mired in their many struggles.

Seeing how Eoferwic had been ravaged only drove the king to greater fury. The rearguard was only just catching up with the rest of us when he began organising the first of the raiding-parties: conrois of forty or fifty men that he sent both north and south of the Use with orders to harry the surrounding land, pursue those who had fled and drive them out from their hiding places, burn the storehouses and the crops in every village that they came to, seize the people's chattels and put their animals to the sword so that the enemy could find no forage anywhere, and kill every man, woman and child of Northumbria in retribution against all those who would take up arms against him. When the king's own chaplain protested, saying that such wanton slaughter was not God's will, he was promptly stripped of his robes and his cross, his ankle tied by means of a rope to a horse's harness, and then he was dragged naked and howling through the mud for all the army to see.

'He has taken leave of his senses,' Wace said one afternoon while we were patrolling along the riverbank immediately to the south of the city. 'If he destroys everything of worth in this land, why have we come all this way to fight for it?'

I shot him a glance, though he knew as well as I how dangerous such words were. But apart from myself there was no one close by who might hear, and even if they did, such sentiments were already commonplace, to the extent that on the fringes of the camp men were beginning to voice them openly.

'He wants to face the ætheling and King Sweyn in open battle,' I said. 'Nothing else will satisfy him. He hopes that by laying everything waste he might enrage Eadgar and his supporters enough to lure them out.'

By then it was known that they had retreated to their ships amidst the streams and the marshlands of that nook of land by the Humbre known as Heldernesse, though no one could say exactly where they were quartering. Even if they could, the king was not prepared to lead his host into such difficult country. Far better to wait until they broke out, when we might face them on ground that was more advantageous to us. That was the only part of the king's strategy in which I could find any merit.

We followed the river downstream as it wound its way through that flat land, searching for we knew not what. Still, it was better than staying with the rest of the army, where we could only sit on our arses and wait for instructions to arrive from the king, and in the meantime entertain ourselves as bitter scuffles broke out between rival lords and their knights. They had come to fight the enemy, and since they could not do that, they fought amongst themselves instead.

As the light began to fade, we headed back. The city and the encampment outside its broken walls had just come into sight when Wace stifled a cry.

'What is it?' I asked.

About a quarter of a mile off, on a slight rise to the south of the city and the camp, stood a small clump of trees to which Wace directed my gaze. 'There,' he said. 'One of the enemy's scouts, do you think?'

From the branches rose a flock of some dozen or so pigeons, and amidst the trunks and the gently falling orange-gold leaves I caught the faintest trace of movement. The sun was low in the sky and though I thought I could make out the shadowy shapes of a horse and its rider, I was not sure.

'He's adventurous, I'll grant him that,' said Wace. There was precious little cover, and he was so close to our camp that I imagined he must be able to smell the bubbling cooking-pots.

'How long do you think he's been there?'

'All day, maybe. He could have arrived under cover of darkness. He's probably waiting for night to fall before leaving again.'

It didn't seem that he had spotted us, or if he had he clearly did not consider us a threat, for otherwise he would surely not have risked venturing so close. All the same it made sense not to attract attention if we could avoid it, and so, pretending we hadn't seen him, we turned around and rode back along the banks of the Use as if we were patrolling according to a determined pattern. But as soon as that clump was out of sight we left the riverbank, circling around until we had found what we reckoned was the path that he would follow away from there.

There we hid, and waited. Night fell, the stars emerged and still we waited, growing ever more impatient. I was beginning to think this had been a waste of time, that our quarry had somehow slipped away without our noticing, when about an hour past dark I heard the sound of galloping not far away and saw a single horseman, his black cloak flying behind him, riding hard in our direction.

At either side of the path were low bushes, and Wace and I lay low behind them, keeping as still as possible, having already tethered our horses some way off where they would not be easily spotted. Slowly I drew my blade from its scabbard. I did not dare raise my head in case the rider should see us, but as the sound of hooves grew louder I could imagine him approaching ever closer, oblivious, until he was almost on top of us—

'Now!' I shouted to Wace. I burst out from the cover of the brambles and swung my sword into the path of the oncoming horse. The rider had no time to swerve or halt; my blade struck the animal high on the foreleg, slicing through sinew and finding bone and bringing it crashing with a shriek to the ground. Its eyes were white as, unable to stand, it writhed upon the dirt, screaming in pain, blood bubbling from the open wound. At the same time Wace dragged the rider from the saddle, drew the man's knife from its sheath and flung it far into the long grass where he could not reach it. The man gave a shout and tried to struggle, but Wace was much stronger than he, and soon had him pinned with his face against the ground.

'Shut up,' Wace barked at the man, who was whimpering what sounded like a prayer, or else a plea: he spoke too quietly and too quickly for me to make out the words.

I crouched down low so that he could see my face and the moonlight glinting upon my sword-edge. His eyes widened and he fell quiet. At a guess I would have said he was around eighteen in years, like Turold, and of a similar stature too.

'Do you speak French?' I asked him, at the same time trying to work out whether he was one of the ætheling's men or one of King Sweyn's. The Northumbrians wore their hair long in much the same fashion as the Danes; indeed there was much blood shared between the two peoples, and it was often difficult to tell them apart.

When he did not respond I tried in English: 'Whom do you serve?'

'Eadgar,' he said, trembling slightly. 'King Eadgar is my lord.'

At that I recoiled slightly. I knew he had proclaimed himself ruler of this land, but that was the first time I'd actually heard one of his followers refer to him as king.

'What do they call you?' I asked.

'R-Runstan,' he said. 'Runstan, son of Penda.'

'My name is Tancred a Dinant. Does that mean anything to you?'

At that Runstan fell quiet.

'You've heard of me, then,' I said.

He nodded. 'They say . . .' he began, and then mumbled something that I could not make out.

'Speak louder,' I told him, and brought my blade closer to his throat. 'What do they say?'

He swallowed. 'They say King Eadgar is offering a reward to any man who captures you and brings you to him. You were the one who wounded him upon the cheek and gave him his scar.'

So he knew the tales that had been told about me, and that was a good thing, for he knew then that it would not be wise to cross me.

'Tell me where your lord is now,' I said. 'And tell me truthfully, or else I will open your belly, string you up by your guts from the nearest tree and leave you there until you choke to death.'

He faltered, but fortunately he was not the sort of man who was prepared to die for his oath. 'King Eadgar is at Beferlic,' he said at last.

Beferlic. I had heard of that town in passing before, and knew it lay to the east of here, on the edges of Heldernesse.

'And Sweyn?'

'King Sweyn is with him, together with his two sons, his brother Osbjorn and all his jarls.'

It took a while to get all the answers I needed, but eventually Runstan explained to me how they had fortified the old monastery that stood there and were now waiting for King Guillaume to come to fight them by the swamps. Clearly the Danes hoped that the opportunity to destroy in one encounter all the leading men of their realm would be too tempting for us to ignore.

'How many men do they have?'

'In and around Beferlic, close to one thousand English and Danes,' he said. 'Those are the best warriors, the jarls and the hearth-troops. Another five thousand are waiting by their ships in the marshes by the Humbre.'

'Six thousand in all?' We could not hope to fight that many, not unless it was in open country where the might of our conrois could be brought to bear, and even then it would not be easy.

'Yes, lord. And there is more.'

'More?'

'News that will interest you, though it may not please you to hear it.'

I was not in the mood for riddles. 'Go on.'

'Only if you swear to spare my life.'

Another time I might have laughed at his gall, but at that moment I was too intrigued by what he thought he might be able to offer me.

'I swear it,' I said. 'Now tell me.'

He hesitated for a moment as if unsure whether my promise was truly meant, but then he must have seen that if it wasn't then he was a dead man either way.

'When Eoferwic fell there were hostages taken,' he said.

'I know that. What of them?'

'There were five: the only ones who were allowed to survive the battle. Two of them are with the main part of the fleet by the Humbre.'

He gave me the names of the castellan Gilbert de Gand, a man with whom I'd had more than my share of quarrels over the years, as well as his mistress Richildis. Then he paused.

'What about the other three?'

'They were taken to Beferlic.'

With every moment I was growing more impatient. 'Their names,' I said. 'Tell me their names.'

Something was troubling Runstan, as if he did not want to tell me what was next on his mind, but knew that he had to for his own sake. I saw the lump in his throat as he swallowed, and guessed what he was about to say.

'The other three', he said, 'are your lord Robert Malet, his sister Beatrice and their father Guillaume, the vicomte of the shire of Eoferwic.'

Twenty-seven

T hey were alive. In the hands of the enemy and the man I'd sworn to kill, but alive nonetheless.

For a few moments I didn't know what to say, but simply stood rooted to the ground, open-mouthed as thoughts whirled through my head and the faintest glimmer of hope stirred within me, until I heard Wace speaking my name, asking what the Englishman was saying. Somehow I managed to recover my voice enough to tell him.

'We have to take him back with us,' he said afterwards, meaning Runstan. 'We need to deliver him to the king and his advisers.'

'What for?' I asked, glancing at the wide-eyed Englishman, who understood none of what we were saying. Perhaps he guessed that we were discussing his fate, or perhaps not, though he seemed a clever enough lad.

'So he can tell them what he knows,' Wace replied, looking at me as if I were slow-witted. 'So we can raise the ransom for the release of Lord Robert.'

'It won't make any difference. Don't you see? The king won't pay the Danes a single penny to leave these shores. He doesn't want to bargain; he won't even send envoys to parley with them.' My ire was rising and I was aware that I was ranting yet could not stop myself. 'All he wants is to trample their corpses into the earth and let his fuller run with their blood. If he won't so much as talk to the enemy, do you think he'll willingly offer up silver for the lives of Gilbert de Gand and his mistress, or for Lord Robert and his kin?'

Wace did not answer. He knew that I was right. Robert's fool of a father, Guillaume, had failed the king on two occasions in as many years. For all his shrewd governance of Eoferwic, as vicomte the defence of the city and of the shire rested largely upon him. By allowing them to fall into the enemy's hands not once but twice he had demonstrated his ineptitude. There would be no ransom for him, and were that the case it seemed unlikely that the freedom of Robert or Beatrice would be purchased either. It was well known that in the king's eyes the Malet name was tarnished, perhaps irrevocably so. What if he decided it was easier to be rid of them altogether? For if the Danes' price was not met, there would be no advantage in holding them prisoner, and their lives would then be forfeit.

I couldn't let that happen. I couldn't risk the lives of my lord and his family by doing nothing and simply hoping that the king would see sense. I owed my lordship, my reputation and, some would say, my life to the Malets. I had sworn solemn oaths not just to Robert but to his sister too, many months ago.

Beatrice. Despite all our differences I had loved her once, or thought I had. Having already lost Oswynn and Leofrun I was determined not to lose her too.

'What do you suggest we do?' asked Wace, his tone one of resignation.

And I told him.

'This is madness,' said Eudo when we arrived back and Wace told him what I planned. 'Have you lost your mind?'

'I've made my decision,' I replied. 'And I'll do it with or without your help.'

Eudo made a sound halfway between a laugh and a snort. 'And with what army do you propose to do this?'

'With as many as will join me.'

It wasn't much of answer, and we both knew it. Still, I'd had enough time to consider it on the journey back to camp, and knew there was no other choice. Whether it was through silver or some other means, I would find the men. I had to.

'This is the worst folly I have ever heard spew from your mouth in all the years I've known you,' Wace said, scratching at his injured eye as he often did when frustrated. He had ever been the most sober and level-headed of the three of us, and I didn't expect to win him over to my cause now. 'Talk some sense into him, Eudo.'

'If we believe what he says' – Eudo gestured at Runstan, who was sitting in silence with Ædda watching over him – 'Eadgar and Sweyn have between them more than ten hundred warriors in and around Beferlic. They have fyrdmen and huscarls, spearmen and axemen and swordsmen, all of whom will have no hesitation in killing you the moment they find you. And find you they will.'

'Listen to us,' Wace said. He did not often lose his temper, but even in the dim, flickering light of the campfire I could see his face reddening. 'We both want to see Robert alive as much as you do. But you cannot simply march into the heart of the enemy stronghold and expect to walk out again freely. You would give your life for no reason and at the same time lead every one of your men to their deaths.'

I gritted my teeth and turned away. My gaze fell upon the others in our small party, and particularly upon the lads Ceawlin, Dægric and Odgar. Laughing amongst themselves, they were taking it in turns to hurl small stones at the exposed head of a pot-bellied baron who was sitting, oblivious, by one of the other fires some forty or so paces away. Fortunately their aim was poor and each one of their stones disappeared into the night, missing by some distance, or else I might have done something. The last thing I wanted was to begin another quarrel and make yet more enemies: I had enough of those as it was.

'You can't ask them to go with you,' Wace said, mistaking my thoughts. 'They're not much more than pups, barely weaned from their mothers' teats. They will follow you because you are their lord, and because they don't know any better.'

'They trust you,' Eudo added, 'but that same trust will be the end of them if you take advantage of it in this way.'

'I know that,' I said, rounding on them. 'Don't think that I don't.'

Ædda would come with me, and Pons and Serlo, and I would do my best to convince Galfrid too. Apart from those four, who else was there? Five men was no army in anyone's estimation, and I still wasn't sure how such a raid could possibly work, only that it must. Of course we would take Runstan with us, so he could show us the paths through the woods and the marshes, but I still did not trust him, and had no doubt he would try to betray us to his countrymen at the first opportunity unless we kept a close watch over him.

It was more reckless and dangerous than anything I had ever before undertaken, but I didn't see that we had any other choice. Even if this path led only to failure and to death, still we had to follow it. Still we had to try.

'Tell me what else we can do,' I said.

Wace glanced at Eudo, who could only shrug. I had my answer, then.

I'd already divested myself of the hauberk that I'd taken from the field of battle at Stæfford. If we were to cross the marshes into the enemy camp without attracting attention, we would have to travel as lightly and as quietly as possible. The sound of mail was easily heard even at a distance, and besides it was too heavy, too cumbersome. If a man lost his footing and fell into the water it could quickly drag him down beyond the help of his friends. Instead I donned one of the studded leather corselets we had taken from the Welshmen, adjusting the straps so that it fitted me properly, then I buckled my sword-belt and my knife-sheath upon my waist and checked that the blades slid easily out so that I could draw them quickly when needed.

'Will you come with me?' I said to the others. 'This is the last time I'll ask.'

Wace's cold gaze met mine. Eudo would not so much as look at me as he muttered a series of curses. This was how it ended, then. This brotherhood that we had long ago forged now divided. From here we would each venture our separate ways, for good or for ill.

And I would go to Beferlic alone.

'I must be an even greater fool than you,' said Eudo, shaking his head. 'Otherwise I wouldn't even entertain the thought—'

'Eudo,' said Wace in a warning tone, as if sensing what was to come.

'He can't go and meet the enemy alone. If we let him, we'll have as good as killed him by our own hands.'

'Let him die if that's what he wants. What sense is there in giving your life too in pursuit of a hopeless cause?'

'Because it's the honourable thing. If we do nothing and let Robert and his father die, we will be known for ever as the men who forsook their lord and their sworn oaths so that they could protect their own hides.'

'And if we return with the Malets alive,' I added, 'we'll be remembered for having defied the might of the ætheling and the Danes, for risking our necks to fulfil our duty. For doing what other men thought impossible.'

'*If* we return,' Wace muttered, but from that simple phrase I knew that I had won him over, and from one word in particular. *We*.

Some men fight for silver or gold and other kinds of riches; others for women or land or duty to their oaths and their king. But they are lying if they say that is what they crave most of all. For, as I had found, none of those things have the same enduring worth as reputation. All influence and power in this world stem ultimately not from wealth but from fame, and a man lacking in honour can find himself reduced to nothing but the object of ridicule and contempt among his peers. Only for the sake of reputation will a man risk everything, and so it was then.

'I have with me two men,' Eudo said, 'both of them eager for another chance to spill Danish blood after what happened at Noruic.'

'And I bring my two knights,' put in Wace with a sigh. Despite his words, the lingering doubt was clear in his eyes. 'They'll join us, if I so order.'

'Only if they are willing,' I said. 'No one has to come who doesn't wish to.'

As it was, they all agreed, none being willing to abandon their lords to whom they had pledged their loyal service. Added to them were Serlo, Pons and Ædda, and so our number was brought to ten. Galfrid alone would not come, and I did not try to press him, knowing that he was less experienced at arms than the rest of us, but instead left him to take charge of the three lads from Earnford and watch out for them in the shield-wall, if it came to that.

The hour was late but I knew we could not waste a single moment, and so we made ready to leave without delay. I was on my way to seek out Father Erchembald so that he could absolve me of my sins one final time, knowing that there was every chance I might not return from this particular expedition, when there came from nearby a sudden yelp of pain.

The pot-bellied man I'd spotted earlier rose, more suddenly than I might have expected. He rubbed his shoulder-blade as he glanced about, until his gaze fixed upon Ceawlin, Dægric and Odgar. Still laughing, they all fled in different directions as he marched towards our campfire, his eyes filled with rage. And I recognised that plump face, for it belonged to Berengar fitz Warin.

When he saw me he stopped, staring at me as if I could not be real. 'Tancred?' he said, confused and taken aback at the same time. 'They said you'd been taken by the Welshmen. They said you were dead.'

'They were wrong,' I said, not wishing to explain the details at that moment. 'What are you doing here, Berengar?'

'One of those runts struck me—'

I cut him off. 'Not that. Why are you here in Northumbria?'

'Fitz Osbern sent me at the head of four hundred knights,' he said proudly as he struggled to recover his composure, aware of the crowd that was beginning to form. 'As soon as the Welsh had fled back to their country, he went south to deal with the risings in Defnascir and Sumorsæte. Others he sent to Ceastre, where the rebels are holding out against Earl Hugues and Bishop Odo. And I came north. I didn't think I'd find you and your friends here.'

Nor would he have, if he'd been any later. 'Well, you can give thanks to God that you won't have to look upon our faces any longer,' I said.

He frowned and cast his gaze about, at Eudo and Wace and the rest of our men, all dressed and ready to ride out. 'Where are you going? Are you and your lord deserting again? Too afraid to fight, are you?'

I would not rise to Berengar's jibes, not this time. 'Our lord and his family are prisoners of the ætheling and King Sweyn in Beferlic,' I told him. 'I mean to bring them back alive.'

At first he must have thought I was jesting, for he began to laugh, until he saw the solemnity of my expression and those of the men around me.

'You aren't serious, surely?'

I had nothing to lose by asking him; at worst I could expect to receive another barrage of his scorn, and I was well used to that by now.

'To do this I need the best men I can find,' I said. 'I saw how you fought at Mechain; I saw how you captured the banner of King Rhiwallon.'

That was not entirely true, for I had lost sight of him entirely during much of the fray, and had missed the moment when he had killed the enemy's standard-bearer. Nonetheless I hoped that he would accept the flattery.

As it happened I had no need to ask the question, for he understood at once what I meant.

'You think I will follow you, after all the injury you inflicted upon me, after all your insults?'

He spat on the ground at my feet and backed away. My hopes, it seemed, were ill founded.

'You tried to kill me once,' I reminded him, not content to let him heap all the blame upon my shoulders. 'I won't forget that, but I'll gladly forgive it and end this feud between us so long as you're willing to do the same.'

I held out my arm towards him in a gesture of goodwill, much though it pained me to do so. He eyed my hand with suspicion.

'You mock me,' he said. 'I don't know how, but you do. Whatever trickery you have in mind, I will not fall for it.'

He stalked off, still rubbing the back of his shoulder. He had given no less than I had expected from him. Still, a part of me had thought we might at least be able to resolve our differences, even if he couldn't bring himself to offer his sword in our aid.

'An old friend of yours?' asked Erchembald, who had been watching with interest.

'Hardly.'

I was not in the mood for explanations, but thankfully the priest did not enquire further. 'Ten men against a thousand,' he said. 'You realise you do not have to do this, Tancred. There would be no shame if you were to change your mind now.'

We had become good friends over the past year, the priest and I, and it was clear he did not want me to go.

'I made an oath to Robert upon holy relics, under the gaze of our Lord,' I said. 'If I break that oath then I am damned. You know this.'

He sighed. 'God understands it is an arduous task you take upon yourself. He will not punish you for refusing it. He is merciful; He will forgive you.'

'But I may never forgive myself if I let Robert and Beatrice and their father go to their deaths.'

Sadness filled his eyes, though he did his best not to show it by bowing his head. 'Then do what you must.'

'God will protect us,' I said, and hoped that it was true. 'We will meet again.'

Erchembald nodded and clasped my hand. Together we prayed for our safekeeping and that of the Malets, before at last he heard my confession and absolved me of my sins.

'I wish you good luck,' he said. 'God be with you.'

As soon as I left him we mounted up and rode out, leaving the orange dots of the campfires behind us as we traversed that night-shrouded land.

And so we were on our way. To Beferlic, and whatever fate awaited us there.

From Eoferwic Runstan led us south, following the course of the river. Before long we came to a shallow point on the Use where the riverbed was firm and the waters not too fast-flowing. With some coaxing we led our horses across, and from there made for what I supposed was the east, riding hard through the night until we could see the first grey light of dawn rising above low wooded hills.

There we sheltered through the following day. Under the cover of a brown-gold thicket we took it in turns to rest and to keep watch. As soon as night fell we moved on again, descending from the wolds into flatter country towards the swamps that made up Heldernesse. It was a clear, moonlit night and a much colder one than of late. A thick mist soon settled over the low-lying pastures, which was fortunate, for it meant we could ride without fear of being spotted. Before long the shadows of Beferlic came into sight: a cluster of squat houses, workshops, alehouses and halls sitting on a low and narrow promontory of dry land that jutted out into the marshes, with the belfry of a church at its centre, rising towards the sky, and around it the dormitory and other buildings that comprised the monastery. Somewhere amongst all of that were Robert and his family, and Eadgar too.

On the town's eastern flank the land fell away to the marshes and the river Hul, upon the banks of which five small ships had been drawn up. Around the three landward sides, meanwhile, a sturdy palisade had been thrown up, and a deep ditch dug in front of it into which sharpened stakes had been driven. Outside those defences, straddling the roads that led towards the gates, an array of tiny pinpricks of firelight showed where the enemy had made their camp. Often armies would disguise their true numbers by building more fires than needed on the edges of their camp, and yet even with that in mind I could not see how the garrison could be as large as Runstan had told us. Either the enemy were on the move, which seemed strange given the efforts they had made to fortify this place, or else he'd lied. And if he had, what else about his story might be false?

'Surely this is a good thing, though,' said Eudo. 'We won't have to battle our way through so many of them.'

'I'd rather know what I'm fighting before it kills me,' Wace muttered. Now that we saw what we faced, he was probably beginning to have further doubts about this expedition.

Possibly it was a ruse designed to lure King Guillaume and his army to assault the town, when in fact within those walls were gathered scores upon scores of men that we could not see.

Sharing Wace's concerns, I turned to the Englishman. 'You said there were a thousand men in Beferlic. Where are the others?'

'Some among the Danes prefer to sleep by their ships rather than in camp,' Runstan said. 'They've taken a quarter of their force into the marshes a mile or so upstream to guard against an attack from across the hills to the north.'

Or else to catch an unwary foe in the rearguard, and crush them between their swords and the walls of Beferlic. Which meant that in the town itself and the camp surrounding its walls were probably somewhere between seven and eight hundred men.

'From now on you'll tell us everything,' I said, grabbing him by the collar. 'Do you understand?'

He nodded, but I sensed my threats were meaningless to him. He was no longer trembling, no longer afraid; he knew as we did that he was of more use to us alive than dead.

We circled around the town so as to approach it from the south. We left our horses inside what must at one time have been a barn or storehouse, albeit one long abandoned for it was in need of some repair. An ideal hiding place, since there was little reason for the enemy to venture there, though in any case it was well out of sight of both the town and the river. Ædda offered to stay with the animals and wait for our return, and to judge from the anxiety in his eyes that was probably the best thing. He had served me loyally and done more for me than anyone in recent weeks. He had come this far, and I could ask no more of him.

'If first light comes and there is no sign of us, you must get yourself away from here,' I told him. 'Forget about us; make sure you get back safely to Eoferwic and the others.'

He nodded solemnly. How I thought we might escape Beferlic when I didn't even know how to get in, I wasn't sure. With luck an answer would present itself when we needed one; that was the best we could hope for.

Nine of us there were, then, who set out across the sucking bogs.

Nine, that was, not counting our guide. We moved slowly, making our way through the mist: splashing gently over narrow streams; wading across inlets of the river; picking our way through clumps of reeds and tall grass and around pools where the ground had become waterlogged following the rains; staying as low to the ground as we could; keeping our cloaks over our armour so that we would blend in more easily with the night. There would be watchmen upon the walls, and doubtless also atop the monastery's bell-tower, which offered the best vantage of anywhere for miles around. Save for the occasional splashing and calls of waterbirds upon the river, the night was still. The slightest noise or sign of movement and the alarm would quickly be raised. Once or twice I wondered at what point Runstan would try to betray us, as he surely must. Not yet, I thought, when we still had a chance of escaping. Instead he would wait for the right opportunity, perhaps once we were a little nearer.

I followed but a few paces behind him, keeping one hand on my sword-hilt at all times. That way if he did cry out, it would be the last sound he made before my blade was buried in his back. Still, for now at least he seemed to be holding to his word, never rushing on ahead nor, so far as any of us could tell, leading us on any false paths. At the same time he didn't take us too close to the ramparts, the shadows of which I could just make out through the marsh-mist, along with the hulls of the five enemy boats. I could see now that these were cargo vessels, built for the open sea as much as for river-going: broad of beam and with high gunwales. But there were two other ships moored upon the river about a quarter of a mile off that I had not spotted earlier. Larger and sleeker than the others, these ones had to be perhaps twenty-five or even thirty benches in length, sitting high in the water. Ships of war.

I signalled to the others behind me to stop. 'Wait,' I said to Runstan in hushed tones, and pointed in the direction of the ships. 'Whose are they?'

'The nearest is *Ægirulfr*; it belongs to King Sweyn. The other is *Northgar*, King Eadgar's own ship.'

Northgar. The northern spear. No doubt the name had been

chosen to appeal to the Northumbrian families, upon whose support he was greatly reliant.

Hopefully those ships and the men upon them were too far off to make any difference to the plan that was forming in my mind. Upon dry land near to the five wide-bellied boats was a large fire, around which the same number of men were warming their hands; obviously they were the unlucky ones who had been burdened with guard duty this chilly night. Indeed we were fortunate that there weren't more of them, but then what reason did the enemy have to expect an attack from across the marshes?

'Hand me that,' I said to Serlo, pointing to the leather flask he carried: the only drink we had between us.

He frowned but handed it over. 'It's only ale, lord,' he said, perhaps thinking that I wanted something stronger to prepare myself for what was to come. I rarely drank before battle; although it lent courage, it also dulled a man's wits, made him slower and unsteadier on his feet and less deft in his swordplay and spearwork.

What I was thinking of was somewhat different, as I explained to them. I chose Serlo and Pons to watch over our prisoner and sent Wace and Eudo together with their knights to find their way across the muddy ground between the beached ships and the river, and there to wait for my signal.

As soon as they had vanished into the darkness, I began counting under my breath up to one hundred and then back down to nought, before I myself set off in the direction of the ship guards. From so far away I couldn't tell whether they were the ætheling's men or King Sweyn's, but either way I hoped I could fool them. With my straggling and untidy hair there was every chance they would mistake me for an Englishman, while the silver rings upon my arms might suggest to the Danes that I was one of them, from a distance at least. Admittedly it was not much of a disguise, especially since the moment I opened my mouth the entire pretence would be shattered. I knew nothing of the Danish speech, and while I had come to learn many English words and phrases, they did not always come readily to my tongue. And if my hesitation did not betray me then my accent surely would. Still, it was the best I could manage: enough, probably, to confuse the guards for as long as this would take.

Soon I was close enough to hear their voices, though they were too low for me to make out any words. I did not try to hide but ventured openly, trudging heavily through the mud, clutching the ale-flask in one hand and singing a wordless nonsense tune, all the time hoping and praying silently that this ruse would work, or else I was a dead man.

It was not long before one of the guards stepped away from the fire and called out a challenge, his words breaking through the stillness of the night: 'Hwæt eart thu?'

Who are you? That I could understand, which meant these were Englishmen. With any luck that would make this a little easier.

I did not answer, but, my heart pounding in my chest, I began to sing more loudly, affecting what I hoped looked like a drunken stagger. So intent was I on keeping up the ruse, however, that I didn't notice where I was treading, nor see the ground ahead falling away into one of the many streams and channels that crossed those marshes. Losing my footing, I slid with limbs flailing and a great splash into the icy water.

Gasping for breath and inwardly cursing, I managed to right myself and drag myself out on to firmer ground, only to find the Englishmen laughing at me. I had their attention now, at least. Soaked to my skin, my tunic and trews dripping and my jerkin caked in mud, I raised a fist to the heavens as if in appreciation of their cheers; as if their entertainment was my sole purpose. Taking the bottle, I unstoppered it and raised it to my lips, letting the ale cascade into my mouth and down my chin, until I found myself choking. I bent over double, making retching noises and pretending to vomit.

At last their concern got the better of their mirth. Exactly as I'd planned, they left their posts to come to my aid, calling as they did so, asking what I was doing out there, so far from the town and the camp. That was the signal to Wace and Eudo and their knights. I hoped I could keep these men distracted for long enough to allow them to do their work. There were barely one hundred paces between where I stood and the five ships; if they made too much noise and one of the guards happened to notice what was happening, our plan would be finished even before it had begun.

As the Englishmen approached, I fell to my knees, feigning a hacking cough, drawing forth phlegm and spitting it out in gobs on to the ground in front of me. Save for the seaxes at their belts I saw that they were unarmed, with only their tunics and animal-skin cloaks for protection. They were all of them young, about the same age as Runstan, eager for adventure and lacking in wits. Certainly they weren't seasoned warriors, or else they would have had more sense than to abandon their duty and leave their ships unguarded.

'Are you all right, lord?' one of them asked, clearly recognising me by my arm-rings and the weapons on my belt as someone of importance. 'What are you doing out here?'

I pretended not to hear him, but coughed some more for good measure and collapsed on to my side, groaning and clutching my stomach with one hand as if sick, while with the other I held on to the bottle. Of the whole performance, only the shivering was real.

'Perhaps he got lost,' said another with a snigger as they stood over me. Their faces were in shadow and through half-closed eyes I could not make out their features. 'Should we do something?'

'If we leave him, he's only likely to wander into the river and end up drowned,' the first one said. 'Here, Wulf, help me lift him.'

I let my body go as limp as possible, so that it took two of them, one on each side of me, to raise me so that I sat upright.

'Christ, but he's heavy,' said the one called Wulf, who was heavyset with powerful forearms. 'How are we going to get him all the way back to the camp?'

While they pondered this, I decided the time was right for another swig from my ale-flask. Even as I made to upend it, though, Wulf tried to prise it from my fingers. Grunting a warning, I snatched it away so suddenly that his feet slipped on the mud and he lost his balance, tumbling down the bank into the same stream I had fallen in, to the jeers of his friends.

God was with us, for that distraction meant their backs were turned at the very moment when the burning timbers were being drawn from the fire and carried on to the five ships, whereupon Eudo and Wace and the others would take them below decks into the bilges where the oars and spare sailcloth were often stored. If they were lucky they might also find stores of oakum, the unravelled rope fibres that, mixed with pitch, were used to caulk the joints between a ship's timbers, which would help the flames to take hold more quickly. Either way, it would not be long now.

Indeed it happened even more quickly than I expected. As Wulf, sodden and covered in bits of reed, was raising himself from the ditch, I spied the first tendrils of smoke begin to rise quietly into the night sky, so faint that they were probably invisible to anyone who did not know to watch for them, but with every heartbeat growing thicker and blacker, coiling around each other to form five distinct plumes.

It was then that one of the Englishmen, a stout fellow with eyes that seemed too close together, said: 'Is that smoke?'

As his companions turned to look, I rose, in the same movement drawing both my sword and knife, slashing across the back of one man's calves, cleaving through sinew and muscle, bringing him to the ground, then up into the groin of another. So surprised were the other three that they had hardly the chance to make a sound, let alone draw their seaxes, before I'd buried my shorter blade into one's belly and beaten a second across the brow with the flat of the steel, sending him sprawling into the water. That just left Wulf, who lacked the courage to match his stature. A look of desperation upon his face, he tried to flee, but tripped over his own feet as he turned, and was unable to get up in time before I brought the full weight of my weapon crashing into the back of his head.

The first one I had brought down was clutching at his injured leg, shouting out in agony. Standing over him, I briefly met his eyes and saw the fear within them, before driving the point of my blade down upon his neck and through his throat, at once silencing his screams.

All was still again, save for the indignant calling of a pair of moorhens that had been disturbed from their sleep by the commotion. I waited, trying not to breathe too heavily as I listened for any sound from the men on watch upon the town walls, hoping that the shouts of the boat guards had gone unheard. Thankfully there was nothing. In any case they would shortly have more important things to worry about, for as the fires within the ships began to spread, I spied the first glimmers of light emanating from within their hulls.

This was the moment upon which everything depended. I rubbed a palm across my brow; it came away dry and free of sweat. Yet I knew this was only the start, and that much more blood would need to be shed before this night was through.

Twenty-eight

As intended, it wasn't long before the fruits of Eudo and Wace's labours were spotted and the alarm was raised. Of course the five ships by themselves weren't important, but the Danes were known to be as fond of their boats as we Normans were of our destriers, and for this plan to work I was counting on what they would do next.

I wasn't disappointed. We had all gathered by then, all nine Frenchmen and one Englishman, and we watched while the enemy raced in their dozens and their scores out across the mud towards the stricken vessels, trying desperately to douse the writhing, twisting, towering columns of flame, and when they realised that all their efforts were in vain, to retrieve what they could before it was too late. War-horns blasted; from the towers of some of the churches bells pealed out in a great discordant clangour. Soon there were spearmen rushing to defend the ramparts, no doubt thinking that the firing of the boats signified the beginning of an attack. Their helmets and the tips of their weapons gleamed in the reflected light of the blaze, and while they were all transfixed by the light of the fire or else watching the fields and the hills to the west, we crept towards Beferlic, with the mist concealing us.

By the time we reached the storehouses and fishermen's hovels that faced out across the marshes, the flames had engulfed each ship so completely that all one could see of the timber framework within was a black skeleton. The air was filled with panicked shouts and calls to arms and dogs' barking, the whole town rousing from their dreams into confusion. Jarls and thegns barked orders to their hearth-troops, trying to form orderly bands under their pennons and their banners, to little avail. Men wielding torches and spears and seaxes, swords and knives and long-handled axes, some only half-dressed and others wearing mail or leather or hides, emerged from the houses where they were quartering, running in all directions, and in the disorder we managed to slip largely unnoticed from shadow to shadow between the buildings, making in the direction of the minster and the halls surrounding it. Of course, with so many people rushing about it was difficult to stay entirely hidden, and once or twice I thought we would be seen as suspicious by those who were passing, but no one stopped us or questioned what we were doing there. Men will see what they want to see, and at that moment their minds were elsewhere. They were looking for a Norman army numbering in the hundreds or the thousands, and so no one thought anything of a group of just ten men, most of whom were dressed and armed for battle in a similar fashion to them. Like me, the rest had foregone their mail in favour of leather, and instead of their tall kite-shaped shields they bore small, round ones that were both lighter and less cumbersome.

In truth we could have been anyone. Most likely the Danes assumed we were some of Eadgar's men while the English probably took us for hirelings of King Sweyn, or else some of the Flemish or Frisian adventurers and freebooters that had joined his fleet. It almost made me smile to think of it. Almost, but not quite. I was only too aware of how much danger we were in, and how slender were our hopes of escape should we be caught now.

'Which way?' I asked Runstan once the burning ships and the throngs were far enough behind us. Keeping our hands close to our sword-hilts, we hid behind a long storehouse that stank of fish. From here I could see up each one of the main tracks that led across the town: to the monastery ahead, and to the great halls that stood upon the higher ground on the western side. I saw, too, where several houses had been torn down for their timber, so that it could be used in the building of the rampart and palisade.

'I don't know, lord,' the Englishman replied.

I stared at him. 'You don't know?'

We had brought him all this way because of his familiarity with the town, and I had been relying on him to show us to the place where Robert and the other hostages were being held.

'Not exactly,' he said hurriedly, clearly realising that if we had no further use for him then he was no longer worth keeping alive. 'The kings made the monastery their stronghold. That's where your friends will be, although I cannot say in which building.'

A monastery was a large place, and I didn't want to have to spend this entire night searching it when our foes lay at every turn and a single false step spelt death. Still, that small piece of knowledge was better than nothing at all. So long, that was, as it proved true.

'You had better be sure of this,' I said to the Englishman. 'If I find you're lying to us, I will see to it that your death is a painful one.'

He nodded, understanding, but did not change his story. I only hoped he was not leading us into a trap.

We were about to set off when I heard raised voices close by, and gave the signal to retreat further into the shadows between the storehouse and the pig-pens that lay behind it. We were just in time, for a column of horsemen perhaps forty in number rode into sight under two banners. The first was decorated in alternating stripes of purple and yellow, which I recognised as the colours of Northumbria, while the other depicted a white raven in flight clutching a cross in its talons. Beneath them at the head of that column, bellowing instructions, were two figures. One I did not know, although to judge by his haughty bearing, the intricate decoration upon his sword and his shield and the gold-threaded and fur-trimmed cloak that hung about his shoulders, he could be none other than the Danes' king, Sweyn, about whom so much had been spoken. Despite his grey hair and beard, he was still known as a fierce swordsman, unyielding in battle and lacking in any Christian mercy in spite of his professed faith in our Lord.

The other man I recognised in an instant. His features were obscured in large part by his helmet with its gleaming cheek-plates and its gilded nasal-guard, but I knew it was him. A head taller than most of his men, he was possessed of a robust stature and a confident manner. Already he had the look of a seasoned fighter, even though, if one believed the stories told about him, he was then but eighteen years of age. His unkempt, straw-coloured hair trailed from beneath the rim of his helmet, falling to his shoulders. Nephew to the old king, Eadward, he was the last of the ancient English royal house. But all the noble blood had long since run dry in the veins of that vile oath-breaker and murderer. He had sworn his solemn allegiance to King Guillaume in the weeks after Hæstinges and been received with honour and dignity at court, only to reveal his true aspect two winters ago when he had fled and raised an army in rebellion.

Eadgar. The one they called the ætheling: the good and noble, the throne-worthy. The one the Northumbrians dared to acclaim as their king. The one I longed to kill above all others.

This was the first time I had laid eyes upon him since that day at Eoferwic more than a year and a half ago, and I hated him even more now than I had then. I hated him for what he had done, for the injury he had inflicted upon me, for the lives he had taken. Because of him so many lay dead: not just my old lord but so many of my sword-brothers too, and Oswynn—

'Tancred,' Eudo hissed, grabbing my arm and shoulder, dragging me backwards with such force that I almost lost my balance. 'Are you trying to get us all killed?'

Without realising I'd been creeping forward, until I was crouching almost in full view, unhidden by the storehouse and the shadows. Fortunately Eadgar, Sweyn and their huscarls were some thirty or more paces away, or otherwise they would surely have spotted me. My fingers were gripped tightly around my sword-hilt, and my heart was thumping so loudly it seemed a wonder that the whole town didn't hear. Sweat ran off my brow, stinging my eyes.

'Eadgar is there,' I said breathlessly as I blinked and drew a sleeve across my face, trying to clear my sight. 'His huscarls as well. I saw him—'

'And they'll see us too, if you're not careful. Did you think you could fight them all by yourself?'

He was right, of course. Not for the first time, revenge would have to wait.

'We'll have our chance,' Eudo said. 'But not yet.'

I breathed deeply, trying to calm myself while we waited for the band of men to disperse before emerging from our hiding place. Pons kept his knife-edge at Runstan's neck, ready to slit his throat if he so much as coughed, but thankfully the Englishman was not that stupid, and he stayed silent.

Eventually I could make out the sound of hooves upon the hard ground, steadily fading as they receded further and further. I glanced around the corner of the storehouse at the party of horsemen in the distance, riding towards the burning ships. I couldn't spot Eadgar among them, and so whether he had gone with them or not was difficult to say.

'Come on,' I said when it seemed that the way was clear enough. The diversion provided by the burning ships would keep the enemy occupied for a while, but as soon as they realised there was no French host descending upon them from the marshes or the hills, they would return. We had not a moment to spare.

We found the gates to the monastery open and unguarded, which struck me as somewhat careless of the enemy, but rather than pause to dwell upon that fact I took it simply as a sign that luck and God's favour were shining upon us. Of course Eadgar and Sweyn would be expecting a threat from outside, not looking to defend against an enemy within their own stronghold, and so perhaps the men who would usually have been posted there had been ordered elsewhere.

Indeed it was strangely quiet; no one demanding to know our names or what our business was. Forbidding stone walls rose up on all sides, reminding me of the place close to Dinant where I had grown up all those years ago, more like a fortress than a house of God. Outside in the streets men called to one another; boots and hooves thudded upon the dirt as they ran past. Some fifteen or so tents were pitched in the yard close to the well and the workshops that abutted the outer wall. Fires glowed, although whoever had been tending them was no longer there. Neither was there any sign of the monks, and I asked Runstan what had happened to them.

'The Danes captured the town for us, and some of the pagans among them sacked the monastery. They killed the abbot and the monks and looted the church before anything could be done. When King Sweyn found out who was responsible he ordered their right hands cut off and their noses slit as penance, and their leader hanged as a warning.'

And yet Sweyn's respect for this place hadn't prevented him from occupying it and using it for his own ends. Oxen had been allowed to graze in what had once been the monks' cemetery in one corner of the grounds, and there were goats foraging in the herb-garden. Empty ale-cups, flagons and leather flasks lay scattered all about and there was horse dung everywhere, while latrine pits had been dug outside the church, polluting the holy ground. I wondered that Eadgar and his followers, who were Christian, could stomach allying themselves with a people as rapacious and as inconstant in their piety as the Danes.

Nor did it seem as if this was the first time this house had suffered at the hands of the pagans. Most of the buildings looked as though they had been repaired and rebuilt at least once; a few of the walls were in stone but the larger part of the monastery was fashioned either in timber or even in wattle and cob more befitting a peasant's hovel. There was nothing resembling the arches and columns and sheltered walkways of a cloister, but rather three long halls arranged in a rough square, with the nave of the church forming the fourth side, around a yard in the middle of which rose a yew tree.

From within that yard came voices and the softly flickering glow of lantern-light. So the enemy had left someone after all, which meant there had to be something worth guarding in those halls. Maybe I had been wrong to doubt Runstan. We would soon know. Moving as quickly but as silently as we could, taking care to keep to the shadows, we approached. How many there were I couldn't say for sure. From the number of voices I guessed no more than ten, but that was still more than I had bargained on us fighting. Most likely they were Danes, since I didn't recognise their speech.

That was when the barking began: deep-throated and loud enough to fill the night air.

'Hide!' I called, but it was too late, for they had found us. First one, then a second and a third of the animals came racing around the side of one of the halls towards us: large and long-muzzled with rows of fearsomely sharp teeth. They were closely followed by their masters, eight mailed and helmeted huscarls bearing shields that had the raven and the cross emblazoned upon them. They whistled and called to the hounds, and shouted out challenges that I did not understand.

I held up my hands to suggest that we meant no harm, hoping that they understood the meaning behind the gesture, as desperately I tried to think of a plan that would see us through this. We had the slight advantage of numbers, being nine against their eight, but they were much better armed, and I knew what fearsome fighters the Danes could be.

'Call off your dogs,' I shouted out in English above the barks and snarls, hoping they might be able to understand that tongue. 'My name is Goscelin, from Saint-Omer in Flanders, adventurer, sea captain and loyal follower of Eadgar Ætheling, ally of your King Sweyn. I command the ship *Vertu*, the fastest twenty-bencher to weather the German Sea,' I added, as if to make my story seem more credible. The names were invented, being merely the first that came to my mind.

Their leader stepped forward. A giant of a man, he had an axe slung upon his back as well as a sword upon his belt. His face and chin were hidden behind a fair and well-combed beard that clearly marked him out for a Dane. While renowned for their barbarity, as a people they were fastidious in their appearance.

'I don't know you and I've never heard of your ship,' he said. There was a slight slur to his speech, as if he had been drinking. 'What do you want?'

I shouldn't have given a name to my made-up vessel, I thought. If these were Sweyn's huscarls then it was probably their duty to know which ships' crews were here in Beferlic.

I was still trying to think how to answer when Eudo spoke up: 'The ætheling sent us to speak with the captives.'

Perhaps it was a risk to mention them, since we still didn't know they were necessarily here. But it was better than no answer at all.

'Eadgar himself sent you?' the Dane asked doubtfully, glancing first at myself, then at Eudo. His right eye gave a twitch that might have been comical had it not been for his size. 'To speak to them about what?'

The warning bells had ceased tolling by then, although beyond the abbey walls I could still hear men shouting as they ran to defend the palisade and gates against their imagined foe. With all that happening, it was no wonder that the huscarl captain was suspicious. He wasn't as stupid as I might have thought.

'Do you think we're going to tell you?' Eudo countered. He was the tallest among us, but even when he drew himself to his full height he still did not match the Dane.

The three dogs were still growling, despite their masters' hands on their necks trying to calm them, as if somehow they could see our lies for what they were and knew that we were dangerous. One of the huscarls had managed to attach a leash to the collar of the largest, but the animal was too strong, straining at the rope, and the man could barely hold him back.

'Skallagrim! Gunni! Alfketil!' the Dane called to the three men in charge of the dogs, including the one with the leash, then pointed to the animals and said something in his own tongue. He turned back to Eudo. 'If you want to see the hostages then yes, you'll tell me what you want with them, and why it needs ten of you.' He glanced at Runstan. 'And what about you, Englishman?' he asked, clearly recognising him by his dress and his features to be different from the rest of us. 'Are you with these Flemings?'

The Englishman began to open his mouth, and suddenly a cold feeling overcame me as I thought he was about to give us away, when Pons, who was standing not far behind, clouted him about the back of the head, sending him sprawling upon the dirt.

'Keep your mouth shut, slave,' he said. 'Remember your place.'

That was quick thinking, I thought. It took me but a moment to recover my voice.

'He belongs to me,' I told the Dane. 'He speaks only with my permission.'

Pons had obviously hit Runstan harder than I'd realised, for he was crying out in pain, shouting insults at us, calling us sons of whores and even worse. I nodded to Pons, who kicked him in the gut, and that discouraged him from saying anything further.

Still, the Dane seemed convinced by our story. Shouting now to make himself heard over the dogs' barking, which I reckoned loud enough to wake the dead from their graves, he began: 'Tell me what your business is with—'

He didn't get the chance to finish, for at that moment the man holding the leash found himself dragged to the ground by the beast on the other end. Suddenly free, the animal hurled itself at one of Wace's knights, who was not expecting it and fell backwards.

'Harduin!' Wace shouted, drawing his sword and rushing to his retainer's aid even as the other two dogs broke free of their masters' grips and charged, their teeth bared. One made for Wace himself, but he had enough time before it was upon him to raise his sword, plunging the tip of his blade into its breast as it leapt up at his chest. The other sank its teeth into Serlo's ankle, and he swore violently as blood streamed from the wound, soaking into the hem of his trews.

The three huscarls who had been in charge of the hounds came forward, seeking at the same time to restrain them and to stop us from killing them. Most of the others were laughing, enjoying the spectacle as if it were some game, and among them was their captain.

Our ruse wouldn't hold for long, and so this seemed to me as good an opportunity as any we would get.

Roaring through gritted teeth, I pulled my blade free of its scabbard and, with all the might I could muster, heaved it towards the chest of the big man, who all of a sudden was no longer laughing as he saw the sharpened steel glinting wickedly in the light of his men's torches. He ducked just in time, and my strike only succeeded in glancing off his upper arm, failing to penetrate the chain links of his hauberk.

'Kill them,' I shouted. 'Kill them!'

I had thought somehow we might manage to get in and out of this stronghold without having to fight. A hollow hope that seemed in hindsight, since a fight was exactly what we had found.

As I recovered my sword ready for another strike, the giant drew his long-handled axe from over his shoulder, hefting it in both hands, bellowing with fury as he swung it at my head. Having only a buckler with which to defend myself, it was all I could do to throw myself to one side, rolling away from the path of his blade as it clove the air inches from my ear. But he wielded no shield either, which meant he had no protection against the low blow. Even as I scrambled to my feet, I aimed a slice at his shins, hoping to take his feet out from under him or at the very least cripple him so that he would be easier to kill. But rather than cutting through flesh and smashing bone, instead my sword found something like steel, and I realised that under his trews he wore hidden greaves.

The Dane smirked at my surprise and swung his axe again, confident now that he had the better of me. This time, however, rather than stepping back or diving aside I lunged forward, inside the reach of his weapon, seeking an opening higher up as I thrust my knife towards his face. The weight of his weapon and the strength of his swing had drawn him off balance, and that was all the chance I needed as I drove the thin blade up and under his chin, into his throat. Blood bubbled and trickled down the Dane's chest, over my hand, and in an instant his expression changed. The smirk vanished and it was his turn to look surprised as his eyes opened wide and he saw his death approaching. I twisted the knife hard and wrenched it free, and the force of that was enough to pull him off his feet and to the ground, where he lay heavy and still.

The rest of the enemy were by then in disarray. The suddenness of our attack had worked in our favour for I counted only four of them still standing and one of their dogs. Another Dane, who shared the same build and who might well have been a brother or a cousin of the first, rushed towards me, screaming, his eyes filled with hatred and thoughts of revenge. Like his countryman he was not quick, or perhaps it only felt that way because the battle-calm was upon me, that peculiar sense of quietness that often descends during the mêlée. Time itself seemed to slow; suddenly everything seemed so easy, as if I knew even before it happened exactly how and when and where my foe would make his attack. Thus as the Dane lunged with sword drawn I was able to dance around and behind him, landing a kick upon his backside to send him flailing forwards. He rolled on to his back so as to face me, but no sooner had he done so than I laid my foot upon his chest and was thrusting my sword-point with both hands down through his ventail into his neck.

At the same time the last of the three dogs writhed upon the ground, giving a great howl of distress, so terrible as to rent the sky asunder, its lifeblood draining away before at last it was run through by Eudo's hand. Having seen their leader and friends felled, the remaining three Danes preferred not to waste their lives in a hopeless cause and instead tried to flee. Burdened with shields and mail, they didn't get far. One failed to spot a latrine pit in his path and tripped – Pons made short work of finishing him – while the other two threw down their arms, vainly pleading mercy before they were struck down by Eudo and the second of Wace's two retainers, a broad and large-jowled Gascon whose name I had forgotten.

I glanced about to check upon the rest of our party. Wace had dropped his sword and was standing hunched over, clutching his side. Blood, dark and glistening, stuck to his fingers and his expression suggested he was in some pain, although at his feet lay the corpse of the man who must have struck him, so it couldn't have been too grievous an injury.

'Is it bad?' I asked him.

'I'll live, if that's what you mean,' he replied breathlessly, a grimace upon his face. Tears welled in the corners of his eyes as he gestured towards his knight Harduin, who had not got up from where he lay, his face and neck crossed with savage bite marks where the dog had buried its teeth.

This was not the time to mourn him, however. Most of the others looked unhurt save for perhaps some scratches and bruises, although Serlo was limping and cursing violently while one of Eudo's men was nursing a wound to his arm below the sleeve of his hauberk. But still there were eight of us standing.

Eight, when there should have been nine. Our guide, Runstan, had gone. Sheathing my sword and my knife, I glanced about in all directions, hoping to spot him amongst the corpses, but it was a futile hope. He was nowhere to be seen.

'Where's the Englishman?' Pons called as he and Eudo returned from their slaughter.

'I thought you were watching him,' I said, unable to restrain my anger. 'If he's gone—'

'I killed three Danes!' Pons protested, interrupting me. 'How was I supposed to fight them and watch him at the same time?'

I swore. Runstan would take word to his countrymen; they would bring men before long and we would never get out of Beferlic alive. If we'd had little time before, we had even less now.

One of the Danish corpses twitched. At least, I'd assumed it was a corpse. He was lying on his back, his eyes closed and his limbs splayed out on both sides, but then I glimpsed the faintest cloud of mist forming in front of his half-open mouth, and the rise and fall of his chest, so slight as to be almost unnoticeable. I stood over him.

'On your feet,' I said, and when he didn't respond I stamped down hard upon his groin.

That broke his pretence. Howling and shouting curses in his own tongue, he rolled over, clutching his nether regions with both hands.

'Get up,' I said, and with the help of both Eudo and Pons stripped the Dane of his helmet and dragged him to his feet, so that I could look him in the eyes and spit upon his wart-ridden face. 'Where are the hostages?' I asked him in both French and English.

At first he pretended not to understand what I was saying, and began jabbering something in Danish, but the moment my hand went to my knife-hilt he discovered he could understand me after all, and suddenly he was pointing to the smallest of the three halls, on the opposite side of the yard from the church, where the kitchens usually were. I thanked him for his kind help before burying my knife in his gut and slitting his throat.

At the same time the Gascon called to me, brandishing a set of four iron keys attached to a ring that he'd found on the belt of the huscarls' captain. Leaving Wace and Serlo to take charge and keep watch while they tended to their wounds, I took the keys and, signalling for Pons and Eudo to follow, went around the hall to the side facing the yard, where I found the doors lying open. Inside, the only light came from a lantern set upon a large round table beside several flagons of ale. Casks and crates were stacked everywhere; skinned carcasses of deer dangled from hooks fixed into the ceiling-beams; bunches of herbs hung, tied by their stems, upon one wall; logs and kindling had been piled in a corner. At one end of the hall was a wide hearth with a flue above it, though no fire had been lit. At the other, a staircase led downwards towards an ironbound door with a sturdy lock.

'Bring me that lantern,' I said to Pons as I descended the steps and tried each one of the keys in turn. The first and the second didn't fit, and I was beginning to think we would have to break the door down when thankfully the third turned cleanly and the door swung open into darkness.

Pons handed the lantern to Eudo, who passed it down to me, and I shone it into the cellar, lighting the way ahead.

'Lord,' I said. 'Are you there?'

Even as the words left my tongue, I saw him, blinking in the lantern-light, dazed as if half-asleep. He looked considerably thinner than when I'd last seen him. His eyes were heavy, his face was unshaven and his black tunic and trews were torn and frayed.

A flicker of recognition crossed his face, and he found his voice. 'Tancred,' he said. 'I thought—'

'That I was dead,' I finished for him. 'And I almost was.'

His hands were tied behind his back and I went to free them, picking at the knot. The rope was tight around his wrists and ankles, and I could see the marks where it had rubbed his skin raw.

'How did you get here?' he asked. 'Has the king arrived with his army? Or have you come with the ransom?'

I didn't have the heart to tell him that we had come alone, and in any case explanations could wait until later. The sooner we escaped this place, the better.

Instead I said: 'Are your father and sister here?'

'My father's over there,' Robert replied, pointing to the far corner of the cellar and a stack of barrels from behind which I could just see a pair of feet. 'Father!'

In reply there came a low, drawn-out groan. While Eudo saw to the elder Malet's bonds I helped Robert to his feet. He could stand well enough, although it took him a moment to find his balance.

'He's been gripped by fever and sickness for days,' he said. 'They've kept us down here, in the damp and the dark, for I have no idea how long.'

'What about Beatrice?' I asked. 'Where is she?'

Robert shook his head. 'They took her somewhere else. I don't know where.'

I should have known it wouldn't be so easy. I should have kept that wart-faced whoreson of a Dane alive so that he could lead me to her.

I rushed to the door, yanking the ring of keys from the lock. 'Pons, show Robert and his father the way to the others. Find them food and drink and keep the vicomte warm, but be ready to leave as soon as I return.'

'Where are you going?' he shouted after me as I charged up the wooden steps.

'To find Beatrice,' I answered without so much as turning around.

And I prayed to God that she was safe.

Twenty-nine

T here were no other doors leading off from the kitchen. Outside, adjoining the hall, were two small storehouses whose timbers were decaying, and I tried their locks. Both opened on the same key as the cellar; the first was empty while the second held only some mould-ridden sacks of vegetables and flour that provided food for the rats, which scurried away the moment the door creaked and I stepped inside. Which meant that Beatrice was probably being held in one of the other halls: either the large, two-storeyed one that I imagined would have been both the refectory and, on the up-floor, the abbot's chambers; or the one forming the eastern wing opposite from it, which was probably the dormitory. Thinking that the Danes and Eadgar would probably have taken the latter with its large hearth-fire for their chambers, I made instead for the refectory. In truth it was a guess. I had no way of knowing whether she was here at all, and had not been taken to another part of the town entirely.

Unlocking the heavy oak door, I ventured into the blackness, wishing I had a torch or something else to light my way. When my eyes adjusted I could see a long dining table with a dozen stools around it, some of them overturned, and the abbot's chair at the far end. Rotten, half-finished food that no one had cleared away sat on wooden plates, while a clay pitcher lay in fragments on the floor. The rushes and sawdust were stained with what could have been either wine or blood. The monks must have been in the middle of their repast when the pagans stormed the abbey.

'Beatrice!' I shouted. 'Beatrice!'

There was no answer. A flight of stairs led to the up-floor and I ran up them two at a time until I found myself in what must have been a private parlour, hung with richly embroidered drapes, but which now, to judge from the many gilded candlesticks, silver-inlaid plates, bags of coin and fine winter cloaks of wool and fur that had been left here, was being used as a treasure house to store the enemy's plunder.

From the parlour a door led to a chamber beyond, from which I could hear movement: a shuffling that sounded like it came from more than simply vermin.

'Beatrice?' I called. 'Is that you?'

There was no reply, but I was certain that there was someone in there. I tried the door only to find it locked, and I could not open it with any of the keys on the ring. Of course the abbot had probably possessed a separate key to his quarters that was not kept with the others, but it could be anywhere, and I had not the time to search for it.

'Stand back,' I said, and drew my sword. An axe would have been better had I thought of fetching one, but in that moment all I cared about was breaking down that door as quickly as possible by whatever means were at hand. Teeth gritted, I raised the weapon high and brought it down again and again, hacking at the timbers around the lock. At first it did no more than bounce off the surface, but after a couple of strikes the edge began to bite, and shortly splinters were flying, until eventually I cast the blade with a clatter to one side and hurled myself shoulder first at the door. The first time I heard a creak as the wood flexed; the second time I felt it budge. The third time it gave way, flying back on its hinges, and I found myself stumbling forward, breathless, into the chamber.

There she was, sitting huddled in the far corner upon a mattress of straw. Her hands and feet were tied; her knees were drawn up in front of her chest; her mouth was bound with cloth to stop her from speaking. Her fair hair was loose and dishevelled and streaked with dirt, falling across her pale shoulders and breasts. They had stripped her of her clothes, leaving her with nothing so much as a coverlet to hide her modesty.

Her eyes widened in relief as she saw it was me, and I rushed to her, untying the gag from across her lips and freeing her from her bonds.

'Tancred,' she said, gasping and almost in tears. 'Is it really you?'

She threw her arms around me and I held her trembling, naked figure close as a surge of affection coursed through me: affection of a sort and an intensity that I had not expected.

'It's me,' I replied, partly to reassure her and partly because I could think of nothing else to say. My throat was dry. There were bruises upon her arm and upon her face where she had been beaten, and a graze to her forehead too. 'Are you hurt? Did they—?'

I didn't want to finish the question, though she knew well what I meant. 'No,' she said hurriedly. 'No, they didn't.'

That was some relief, although I already knew what fate would befall the men who had done this, if ever I found them. 'Can you stand?'

She nodded, and while she found her feet I brought her one of the winter cloaks I had noticed in the treasure chamber, wrapping it around her to cover her nakedness and keep her warm. It wasn't much, but it would do for now. She was shaking hard, although whether that was born of cold and hunger or of the surprise of seeing me and the anticipation of escape, I couldn't tell.

Having first retrieved my sword, I took Beatrice's cold hand, leading her down the stairs and out through the yard with the yew tree to where the rest of our band were gathered. Father, son and daughter embraced, overjoyed at seeing each other, at being reunited for the first time in what I supposed must be weeks.

I would have liked to allow them more time together, but Wace as ever saw reason. 'Come on,' he said hoarsely, grimacing in pain. He'd wrapped a strip of cloth cut from the tunic of one of the huscarls in an effort to staunch the flow of blood, but the wound was clearly hindering him. 'We can't tarry here.'

He was right. We set off towards the abbey's gates, some of us, like Serlo, limping, others slowed by wounds or hunger. At all times I made sure the Malets remained at the centre of our party, protected at both front and rear. Robert had donned a sword-belt and shield taken from the corpse of one of the huscarls, but he looked far from ready to do much fighting. Still, he looked in better condition than his father, Guillaume, who was more haggard than I had ever seen him, ashen-faced and coughing so hard that he was barely able to speak. When last we had crossed paths his grey hair had already been turning to white, but now he appeared truly old, drained of vigour, no longer the man I'd known. No doubt his sickness had played a part in that, but I wondered whether there was something else behind that change as well: a kind of world-weariness, as if this latest ordeal had proved too much for his spirit to bear. As he stumbled forward I offered him my shoulder to lean upon for support.

'After everything,' he said, his voice barely more than a whisper, 'you come to my aid again. I owe you my thanks, Tancred. We all do.'

Indeed, although the circumstances were very different, this was not the first time I'd had to rescue Malet's hide. But then he was not the main reason I had come here to Beferlic.

'Thank me if we survive this, not before,' I said, more tersely perhaps than I meant, but we had some way to go before we could consider ourselves safe.

An easterly wind blew in biting gusts that pierced my jerkin and my shirt, bringing with it the chill of the marshes and the German Sea, and the frozen homelands of the Danes beyond even that. A thin drizzle was beginning to spit from clouded skies as we left the monastery behind us.

'How did you get inside the town?' whispered Robert. 'And how do you plan to get out? Are there others waiting for us beyond the walls?'

I shook my head. 'I brought every man I could muster. There are no others.'

For a moment he regarded me with a questioning look, as if unsure whether or not I was joking, but as soon as he realised I meant it seriously his expression changed. Still, there was nothing to be done about it now. The only thing that concerned me was escaping this town before Runstan brought an army of English and even more Danes upon us, and then finding our way across the marshes to Ædda, who was waiting with our horses. All without being spotted.

With cries and calls to arms still filling the air across the town, we made our way along the narrow paths between the houses. The fires of the still-burning ships on the edge of the town were our guide, showing us the way towards the marshes. But the main thoroughfares were busy with men, and we would surely be spotted if we ventured out upon them, though at the same time it was impossible to reach the marshes without first crossing at least one of those streets, and that one was the widest for it led towards the marketplace.

'We don't have any choice,' Eudo said. 'If we stay here, they'll find us soon enough. We have to chance it.'

So we did, in small groups, in twos and threes and fours: first Eudo with his man who had the injured arm and the elder Malet; then Wace and Robert followed by Serlo and Pons; and lastly myself with Beatrice, the Gascon and those that remained. And it nearly worked. The last of us had almost made it across when there came a cry come from further up the street. I turned my head and saw, not twenty paces away, Runstan pointing eagerly in our direction. With him were some two score men and more, and bellowing orders to them was a face I had not thought I would see again. A face with small, hard eyes that met mine with a piercing stare, quickly followed by a flicker of recognition.

Wild Eadric.

He had failed to capture me once before, but at that moment he must have thought that God's fortune shone upon him, for he had his chance again.

'Run!' I said, gripping Beatrice's hand and urging her and the others onwards. Eudo and Wace took up the cry, passing it on to those in front: 'Run!'

We raced through the yards behind the houses, ducking past goose houses and butts filled with rainwater, climbing over low fences, until we found ourselves in the middle of a grassy paddock. But it was no use. Half of our party were weakened or hurt, and they could not move as fast as the rest of us, and besides there was nowhere to go. For as well as those behind us there were spearmen running to block our route ahead and also coming around the sides of the houses, as the order to stop us was passed on to some of the other thegns.

And I knew it was hopeless. We could not hope to fight our way through so many, not when we had Beatrice and her father to defend too. After everything, we found ourselves trapped and outnumbered and staring death in the face. To surrender would be to invite a slow and painful demise at the hands of the enemy. Which left us with but one option.

'Shield-ring!' I shouted in desperation, feeling a shiver run the length of my body as I did so.

It was a command that every knight feared, for it was an admission of defeat, the final recourse when all else had failed, when there was no retreat and the end was near. We formed a close circle, each of us overlapping the rim of his buckler with that of the man to his left until we made a continuous wall of limewood and steel, presenting the painted leather faces and the bosses and the points of our blades to our foes, inviting them to come and die. At our backs, inside the ring, stood Malet and Beatrice. I gave a fleeting look over my shoulder and met her eyes: her wide, terrified eyes.

'I'm sorry,' I said, cursing myself for having brought this upon her and her family. But if she said anything in reply I did not hear her above the cries of the enemy, perhaps fifty or sixty of them in all by then, roaring instructions to one another in English and Danish, spreading out so as to entirely encircle us. Five or six spear-lengths separated our wall and theirs, separated us from death. Serlo stood on my left with Pons the other side of him. There were few men I would rather have had beside me in such circumstances. On my right, meanwhile, was Robert, carrying the tall kite shield with the raven and the cross that he had taken from one of the huscarls, and wearing a grim expression.

'I never meant for it to come to this, lord,' I said.

'I know.' He did not look at me but stared directly ahead at the forest of spears and axes upon which our blood would shortly be spilt. 'You have served me well, Tancred, and for everything you have done I thank you. May we send many of them to their graves tonight. May the eternal kingdom greet us both.'

'Yes, lord.'

There was nothing else to be said. I made the sign of the cross upon my breast as, breathing deeply, I glanced about at the gathering hordes and prepared myself for battle for what was undoubtedly the last time, tightening my hold around my shield-straps and the hilt of my weapon, suddenly aware of all the small things: the leather grip pressing into my palm; the blood drying on my fingers; the drizzle falling gently upon my cheeks; the way the light from the still-burning ships in the distance glimmered off my blade and those of the enemy. My only consolation was that at least this way it would be quick.

'Keep to the shield-ring,' Serlo barked to those on the other side of the circle. 'Don't let them draw you out; don't let them break the wall!'

'Let's kill the bastards,' Eudo said. He began to beat his blade against the iron rim of his shield, and then one by one the rest of us joined him, raising the battle-thunder in spite of our small numbers: a warning to the enemy that we would not die easily.

'Kill them!' yelled Pons, and he was joined by Serlo and then by me, our bloods rising until we were all chanting as one: 'Kill them! kill them!'

And then through the ranks of the English and Danes came Eadric, the Wild One himself, marching with the same arrogant bearing that I remembered. Over his mail he wore an embroidered cloak with a golden clasp. He motioned for quiet among his men.

'Tancred a Dinant,' he called, his voice almost lost amidst the roar of our chants. 'Once more our paths meet, only this time you won't be getting away.'

I did not offer an answer, but held his stare.

'Are you the one to blame for all this trouble?' He gestured towards the east where the fires still burnt. 'To have come here you must be more foolish than I'd realised. Do you know what indignities I've suffered because of you?'

'No,' I said, although I sensed he was about to tell me. One by one my knights and companions broke off the battle-thunder.

'Because of you I had to face Eadgar,' he said. 'I had to explain to him how Bleddyn and his men had been careless enough to let you escape before I could bargain with them. This after I'd already sent word promising to deliver you to him. Imagine, then, what happened when I arrived with nothing more than ill tidings to offer. I suffered not just his wrath but also the insults and constant mockery of those who said I'd been a fool to ever trust a Welshman.'

'You should consider yourself fortunate,' I retorted. 'If you'd told the ætheling the truth your fate might have been far worse.'

'He is King Eadgar now,' said Eadric. 'And he will be most pleased when I hand you over to him.'

'A corpse is all you'll be bringing him. You won't take any of us alive.'

I was worth nothing to him dead, and I knew he would much rather atone for his earlier failure and claim his prize than obtain the smaller satisfaction of killing me.

'In that case,' he said, 'I give you two choices. If you choose to stand and fight me, I swear that you will all die. Except for her.' He nodded in the direction of Beatrice, who had frozen where she stood, her face white. 'First I will delight in taking my pleasure from her, before offering her to my men and my fellow thegns, and only then will I kill her.'

At that I saw Robert flinch, his jaw clench and his fingers tighten around his sword-hilt, but thankfully he managed to hold his temper and did not let himself be drawn into a confrontation that he would surely lose.

'What's my other choice?' I asked before Robert could utter a word.

Wild Eadric smiled. 'Give yourself up and I will see to it that your friends, your lord and his kin are allowed to pass freely from this place and return whence they came.'

I considered. If I did as he asked and surrendered myself there was at least the chance that they might all live, whereas if we gave battle in this place we would undoubtedly perish. Yet how could he possibly make such promises, especially if he'd fallen out of favour with the ætheling?

The only answer was that he was lying. He'd already deceived Bleddyn by promising silver in return for handing me over – silver that was never paid – and then sworn falsely that it was the Welshmen's fault I had escaped from Mathrafal. If he was prepared to perjure himself openly before his own liege-lord, how could I trust him?

'You can't do this, Tancred,' said Robert warningly. 'As your lord I forbid it.'

I ignored him but asked Eadric: 'What about Beatrice? Will you allow her to go free as well?'

'I will,' he answered. 'Neither she nor any of the others will be harmed. You have my word.'

'How do I know you'll honour that word?'

Eadric affected a serious tone and tried to conceal his smile, most likely scenting victory close at hand. 'I swear it.'

That in itself meant nothing. I knew as well as any man how easily such a pledge could be broken. And yet it gave me an idea. Casting down my shield but keeping my sword in hand, I stepped forward slowly out of the ring, into the space between the two battle-lines, albeit slightly closer to ours than theirs.

'What are you doing?' shouted Wace. 'He's nothing but a hollow excuse for a man. His oath means nothing; he only says this because he knows if he tries to fight us he'll end up with half of his hearth-troops dead.'

He was probably right, but I had no intention of presenting myself to Eadric without a fight, only of making him think that I did.

Fixing my gaze upon the Englishman, I said: 'In Brittany where I hail from, it is the custom when we swear oaths to do so over the symbol of the cross.'

That was untrue, at least in the manner that I had in mind, but I was relying on him being ignorant enough of Bretons and our ways to believe it. One final attempt to work some cunning; beyond this we had no option but to stand and fight. And die.

With my blade I carved one straight line about six feet in length in the turf, then another to form a cross-piece roughly two-thirds of the distance along the first.

Eadric snorted. 'Must we do this?'

'If you wish me to surrender myself to you, then yes.' I slid my blade back into its scabbard and hoped he did not notice the lump in my throat betraying my apprehension as I swallowed. 'We stand here at opposite ends of the cross, you make your promise to me, and then to solemnise it we embrace as equals. This is how it is done.'

'Tancred!' Beatrice said, and I heard the note of despair in her plea as she began to sob.

A couple of the Englishmen began to object. Eadric raised a hand to silence them. After handing his own shield to a retainer, he paced slowly forward to meet me, frowning in suspicion, as well he might. But I stood alone, with weapons sheathed and arms held away from my body to show I meant no harm as sweat trickled down my back and my chest.

He stopped at the base of the cross as instructed, while I took my position at the other end. If he'd wanted to strike me down at that moment, he could have done, since there was no way I could have drawn my sword in time to parry his blow. But he did not.

'What do I say?' he asked. Probably he was expecting some kind of ritual liturgy.

'You make your oath in whatever form you wish. The exact words don't matter.'

He gave a tired sigh, then said: 'Upon the cross I swear to make certain that, if you submit to me, your companions are set free. Is that sufficient?'

'It is sufficient,' I replied. 'Now we embrace.'

Again Wild Eadric smiled, and this time it was a broad grin that showed his cracked teeth, for in his mind he had won. I spread my arms to receive him and he did likewise as he stepped towards me. He clasped his arms around my back, and I made to do the same, except that with my right hand I seized the hilt of his dagger and in one swift movement tugged it free of its sheath, lifting it to his throat before he was even aware what had happened, while with my other arm I held him firm.

'Move and I will kill you,' I said, and then to his men: 'Stay where you are and lay down your weapons, or else this steel ends up in your lord Eadric's neck.'

At first it seemed they did not hear me, but then I pressed the edge against the underside of his chin, to show that this was no idle threat. A trickle of blood spilt forth where I'd grazed Eadric's skin, and they glanced nervously at each other before doing as I told them. No man wishes to be responsible for the death of his lord, and that holds true no matter whether he is Norman or English or of any other race.

'You wouldn't dare kill me,' Eadric said. 'If you do, they will be upon you before you can so much as blink. They will tear you apart and spit on your corpses.'

'Shut up,' I hissed. Step by step we retreated towards the safety of our shield-ring, where Robert set about relieving him of his sword-belt.

'What do we do now?' muttered Eudo. 'Or is this as far as your plan goes?'

I didn't answer. All I knew was that for the moment at least we held the advantage, and we had to make use of it while we could.

'Make way,' I shouted at Eadric's men. 'Make way!'

It was a long way from here back to the edge of the marshes, though, and even further from there back to the barn where Ædda was waiting with the horses. Even as the Englishmen and Danes cleared a path and we began to move, keeping our ring formation, I saw that we could not maintain this impasse for long. For they would follow us all the way, and sooner or later some of the more hot-headed among Eadric's oath-warriors would decide to try their sword-arms against ours and attempt to rescue their lord. I knew because it was what I would do. When that happened I didn't see how we could manage to fight them all off.

Already a few of them were growing restless, their hands going to the hilts and handles of their weapons as they closed upon us. Behind their shield-rims and their helmets and their long moustaches all I could see of their faces were their cold eyes staring back at me.

'Stay back!' Pons said. 'Stay back or we kill your lord.'

It was an empty threat, and they knew it too, for they kept on coming, faster than we could retreat.

'They are cowards,' Eadric shouted in spite of the sharpened steel at his throat. 'Watch how they run from you!'

And there was nothing more I could do.

'Stop,' I said to the others. We had made barely thirty paces from the spot where Eadric had first trapped us. We hadn't so much as left the horse paddock. For all our efforts, our time had come. I for one would rather meet my maker with sword in hand than running like some pitiful craven. 'We fight here.'

Eadric began to laugh, as well he might. A thundering, triumphant laugh that matched his byname, it seemed to resound off the surrounding buildings and rise to the cloudy heavens, filling the night. Victory belonged to him after all.

But as I cast my gaze around at my loyal companions in arms, I realised that was not the only sound I heard. From somewhere beyond the walls came what sounded like screams, and they were the kind of screams I'd heard many times in my life, for they were screams of pain, of slaughter and the dying. The enemy must have heard them too, for they halted, glancing uncertainly at each other even as I exchanged confused looks with my sword-brothers. Who could be attacking?

Lord Robert grinned. 'When you said these were all the men you could muster, I knew it couldn't be true.'

'I wasn't lying,' I replied, but that was all I had time to say before the sound of war-horns cut me off: two sharp blasts given in quick succession. A signal to rally.

On the main streets all was confusion. Men were running back and forth, some carrying pails filled with water while others seemingly without any purpose at all. And then I realised why, as there was a rush of air from the direction of the walls and the night sky lit up with several long streaks of flame, too many to count, like shooting stars except much lower in the sky and burning more fiercely. They sailed over the top of the palisade: first one volley, then another and another still. Some fell harmlessly on to the mud in the middle of the street, but others landed upon the houses, which quickly caught fire. I glanced back in the direction we had come and saw the thatch of some of the workshops close by the monastery consumed by writhing tongues of red and orange and yellow.

Women fled the houses: wives and camp-followers, slaves and whores alike, wrapping what they could salvage of their menfolk's belongings inside cloaks, or else stuffing them into haversacks. A riderless horse, a mere shadow against the light, galloped towards the market square through streets filled with smoke. Roofs collapsed with a crash of timbers; clouds of still-glowing ash billowed up into the air where the strengthening breeze carried them from one building to the next. And still the rain of fire continued, as if the forces of hell had been unleashed upon this earth.

'Shields up!' I heard Eudo call, although in truth most of those arrows were falling far enough away that they posed little threat.

Then from beyond the palisade, over the cries of the wounded and the dying and the clash of steel upon steel, came the thunder of hooves and the familiar battle-cries: 'For Normandy! For St Ouen and King Guillaume!'

The horns blew once more, this time in long bursts that sounded for all the world like the death throes of some forlorn and stricken beast: the command to retreat. No sooner had it died away than scores of men were pouring in panic through the town's southern gates not a hundred paces away: Danes and English, I assumed, since I didn't recognise the designs on their flags and their shield-faces, all retreating to the protection of the town. And then I saw the purple and yellow stripes of the ætheling, and the raven and cross that belonged to King Sweyn. The two men were mounted next to each other, surrounded by their respective hearth-troops, trying to instil order in their ranks as men ran past to either side of them.

'Attack these bastards, these filth-ridden dogs, these Devil-turds,' Wild Eadric yelled in desperation. 'Attack them now!'

But his orders fell on deaf ears. If his men had wanted to attack, they should have done so already, for their confidence had been allowed to waver and now their numbers were dwindling. Another wave of fire-arrows cascaded down upon the town, much closer this time, falling in the sheepfolds next to the paddock where we stood. That was too close in the eyes of many of the men. They turned and began to run, some seeking cover from those shafts of fiery death, others for safety in numbers beneath the banners of King Sweyn and the ætheling, who even now were falling back, away from the walls and further into the town as they sent their spearmen and fyrdmen and axemen to try to hold the gates. For the enemy had been unable to close them in time to keep their attackers outside, and now a conroi of mailed knights burst through the gap between the ramparts, charging knee to knee in a wedge formation with lances couched under their arms, ready for the kill.

And at the head of that wedge rode the last man I would have expected to see. His banner, decorated in scarlet and blue stripes, marked him out, and even from such a distance, I recognised his stout frame instantly.

'Berengar,' I said under my breath, then to the others, almost laughing in surprise and relief: 'It's Berengar!'

There was no mistaking that standard. Quite why he had followed us to Beferlic, I had no idea, but it was a good thing he had, for the tide of battle was suddenly on the turn, and as dozens upon scores of Norman knights and foot-warriors flooded in through the gates, suddenly I felt my spirits lighten.

'For Normandy,' roared one of the charging knights, and it might even have been Berengar himself. They crashed into the half-formed battle-line, burying their lance-heads in the shields and the chests of the Northumbrians and Danes, riding over those who had fallen as they drew their swords and drove further into the enemy ranks. In their wake rode a dozen more horsemen, then a dozen more after that, and still they kept on coming as Eadgar and Sweyn were pressed ever further back.

Still fifteen or so of Eadric's huscarls remained, enough to outnumber us, although they too had witnessed what was happening, and I could see their resolve breaking. My blood was running hot through my veins, and my sword-arm was itching as renewed confidence filled me.

'Fight us,' I challenged them, roaring as the battle-joy filled me once more and I pressed the flat of Eadric's dagger against his neck. 'Fight us!'

But concern for their own lives overcame that for their oaths and their lord, and they fled. Nor were they the only ones as more and more horsemen swept into the town, cutting down the enemy to left and right. Sweyn and Eadgar must have seen that all would soon be lost if they continued to battle any longer, and now they too were in flight, together with most of the rest of their host, abandoning the town and the monastery they had made their stronghold, making for the marshes and the river Hul where they knew our army would struggle to pursue them, leaving an unlucky few of their thegns and jarls to continue the struggle on foot and face the might of the Norman onslaught alone.

Then I saw Eadgar beneath his gilded helmet turning his mount and making to ride away, with Berengar and his knights in pursuit, and all sense left me. Already I'd let slip one chance to kill the ætheling. Now that fate had brought us to the same place again, I was determined not to fail a second time. His death had been my goal for more than a year and the last thing I wanted was for Berengar to take that from me. Shoving Eadric to the ground, I turned to Pons and Serlo.

'Make sure he doesn't get away,' I said. 'Keep Beatrice and Lord Guillaume safe.'

I heard their protests but paid them no heed, instead waving for the others to come with me as I ran towards the heart of the mêlée, where what remained of the enemy rearguard was rapidly crumbling under the weight of the charge. My feet pounded the streets, which were slick with mud and the blood of the fallen. Once or twice I nearly stumbled over corpses that I did not see, for my mind was solely on keeping that gilded helmet in sight. As it receded into the distance, and as the enemy battle-lines collapsed and the rout began, however, it became ever more difficult to pick him out through the throng.

Ahead, a conroi of knights rode across our path. One of their number noticed us and gave a cry. Hurriedly I called out in French, giving our names so that they would know we were Normans like them. Often in the middle of the fray it can be hard to tell ally and foe apart, especially when ranks have broken and even more so at night. Men will kill before pausing to think, and only after they have struck their imagined adversary down will they realise they've spilt the lifeblood of one of their own closest comrades. I'd seen it happen more often than I cared to remember, and had no wish for us to end up impaled upon their lances that way. Not after all this. Thankfully the captain of that conroi heard me and they wheeled away, chasing a band of fair-haired Danes as they sought refuge with their womenfolk down a narrow alley between two large halls.

We ran on, through the market square and a great plume of black smoke that swirled and rolled across the way, stinging my eyes and burning my throat and my chest. Coughing, blinking to clear my vision, I kept on going. Men on horses raced past us with pennons in all colours flying proudly. They whooped with delight and the thrill of the slaughter, giving cries of Normandy, of God and of victory as they rode down those of the English and the Danes who remained. Others cast aside their spears in favour of brands drawn from the burning houses, with which they set fire to those buildings that had not yet felt the touch of the flames. As the smoke cleared I caught the briefest glimpse in the distance of Eadgar Ætheling's gilded helmet, with Berengar and his men close behind, growing ever more distant with each beat of my heart. In the side streets the staunchest of the enemy still fought on, some preferring to die facing their killers than be struck down trying to flee, others seeking only to hold their ground for as long as it took for their thegns and jarls to mount horses and escape. They formed shield-walls across the ways, standing shoulder to shoulder several ranks deep, in groups as small as a dozen or as large as forty or more—

And I stopped. Mounting a horse behind one of those shield-walls was a face I had never expected to see. Not here.

Not anywhere.

The whole world seemed to slow, and all sense of where I was deserted me. My throat dry, I stood transfixed whilst a spectre rose before me, as if from some half-remembered dream, from a time that had long ago faded into memory. For she was dead.

Her back was turned as she climbed into the saddle, but I knew her nonetheless. Her head was uncovered and her long hair unbound just as I remembered, falling loosely across her shoulders and down her back: as black as jet, black as the night when the moon is new and cloud obscures the stars. It billowed in her face and all around her as the wind caught it. She turned for a moment, and I glimpsed her face.

Oswynn.

It couldn't be, and yet it was. Somehow I had to be imagining this, but for all that I blinked to dispel the image, it would not vanish. My head felt light, my breath caught in my chest, and I felt a chill come over my entire body from my head down to my feet.

She hadn't yet noticed me. Beside her a greying but powerfully built man vaulted into the saddle of a white stallion. Broad-chested, his straggling hair was tied in a braid, while around his arms were rings like mine, made from rods of gold twisted around one another. Upon his shield and those of his hearth-troops was emblazoned a black dragon with eyes of fire and an axe in its claws.

'Oswynn,' I called. 'Oswynn!'

I untied my chin-strap, letting my helmet fall to the ground so that she could see my face. Over and over and over I shouted her name, my throat raw and my voice hoarse, drowned out by the battle-cries and the clash of steel that was all around, and I was beginning to lose hope, when at last she saw me.

Her dark eyes widened as recognition flickered across her face. Open-mouthed, she stared at me, and I at her, as much in joy as in shock that she still lived. For what seemed like an eternity we held each other's gaze, though it could only have lasted a few fleeting moments, since before she had a chance to say anything in reply, the man on the white stallion had grabbed hold of her reins and they were riding away through the alleyways towards the smouldering remains of the ships and the safety of the marshes beyond them. Before I lost sight of her she glanced once more over her shoulder. Her lips moved, and even though her voice was lost amidst the din, there was no mistaking what she was calling.

Tancred.

And then she was gone. Men ran past on all sides; the last of the enemy fled or met their deaths at the touch of Norman steel. Chants of victory rose to the heavens. Beferlic belonged to us.

Drained of all strength, I sank to my knees and closed my eyes, breathing deeply, listening to the heavy beat of my own heart. The bitter easterly wind cut through my corselet and tunic as the rain began to fall harder, lashing my cheeks, biting into the flesh and wounding deep.

I felt a hand upon my shoulder and opened my eyes to find Eudo standing next to me.

'I saw her,' I said simply. Even as the words issued from my lips I could barely believe them. 'I saw Oswynn.'

'It wasn't her,' Eudo replied, and he spoke softly, which after the noise of battle was strange to hear. 'It couldn't have been. She's dead and has been for more than a year.'

So I had thought too. Wasn't that what I'd been told at Dunholm? And yet my own eyes had shown me that was not true. All this time I had thought her murdered, when in fact she lived.

'It was her,' I said through clenched teeth.

'Tancred—'

'I know what I saw.' I tore my arm away from him and rose to my feet. My patience was worn thin, and the words came out more harshly than I meant. I was tired, my limbs were aching, and I was in no mood to argue.

My woman was alive. And yet she was the captive of another man, and no matter how much I tried, I could not rid the image of him from my mind.

Thirty

Beferlic burnt and we fled.
Those of the enemy who had remained with their ships
further up the river Hul were now on their way, sailing
downstream and marching across the open country to the aid of
their leaders. The last thing we wanted was to end up trapped
between the fields and the marshes in a half-destroyed town, whose
very walls were aflame and collapsing around us, and so the order
was given to retreat. We made for the abandoned barn where Ædda
was waiting with our horses, then rode harder than we had ever
ridden before to catch up with the rest of the Norman raiding-army
as it made its withdrawal across the wolds.

We'd left the town not a moment too soon. Even as we in the
rearguard climbed into the hills and slipped away into the night, I
looked back and glimpsed the first band of battle-fresh foemen,
their spears as yet unbloodied, arriving upon the smouldering
remains of what had once been the camp to find their kinsmen
slain in their dozens and their hundreds.

Sweyn and the ætheling had managed to disappear into the
marshlands. Berengar and his conroi had pursued them for a
while, but had struggled to follow them through the maze of
paths across that treacherous ground, and had been forced to
give up. Which meant Eadgar was still out there somewhere. I
couldn't help but feel that if it had been myself chasing him
down, he would not have got away. The moment that thought
crossed my mind, I censured myself for it, and for my lack of
gratitude. I'd never thought it would happen, but Berengar had
come to my aid.

'Why?' I asked when our paths crossed some hours later. 'You risked your life for the sake of me, my friends and our lord.'

For once his persistent scowl was gone, and in its place was a broad smile.

'After what you managed at Eoferwic last year, did you think I'd let you claim all the glory a second time?' he asked. 'If you were prepared to venture into the heart of the enemy camp with a band of just ten men, I reckoned four hundred ought to be enough to do battle with them.'

Even hours after the clash of steel had ended, Berengar's face was still flushed with the exhilaration of battle and the knowledge that he had taken the fight to the ætheling and the Danish king and bested them both, spread panic amongst their troops and forced them to flee, driven them into the swamps and laid waste their only stronghold this side of the Humbre. All with the mere four hundred knights that Fitz Osbern had entrusted to his command: a force barely half the size of the enemy's.

'The king didn't lend you any men, then,' I observed.

'There was no time to ask,' he said. 'I knew you and your friends were travelling lightly; if we were to catch up with you we had to leave quickly. Besides, much larger a force and the enemy would probably have spotted us coming long before we had the chance to attack. By that time they could have further strengthened their defences or else have quit the town entirely.'

'So you took it upon yourself,' I said, shaking my head in disbelief. 'What if you were returning now having led several hundred men to their deaths on a fool's errand? How would you have explained that?'

'No man ever won fame without taking any risks,' he said. 'You know that as well as I do. I had a chance to do something great, something that the poets would sing of, and I knew I had to take it.'

Despite our past quarrels, I admired Berengar's audacity. It was exactly the manner of war we waged out on the Marches: a quick raid in main force to wreak as much damage as possible, followed by an equally swift retreat. This time it had worked better than probably even he had imagined.

'My one regret is that the ætheling still lives,' said Berengar. 'I thought I might be the one to kill him once and for all.'

Once more beaten but not yet defeated, Eadgar would no doubt return in time. I doubted this would be the last we'd see of him.

'We owe you our lives,' I said. 'If you hadn't come when you did, we would all be dead men.'

'I should be the one thanking you,' he replied. 'Without the distraction of the ships, the enemy would have been better prepared, and we might never have broken into the town. That was good thinking, and good work from your comrades.'

I gave him a friendly slap on the shoulder and with that I left him. Others were coming to congratulate Berengar on his victory, whereas my place was with my companions, with Lord Robert and his father.

And Beatrice. She was waiting for my return, and rode to greet me. As well as her cloak, a rough-spun shirt and trews had been found to help keep her warm and preserve her modesty. They were much too big for her slender frame, but she didn't seem to mind.

'I still can't believe you came for us,' she said. 'To lead ten men in such circumstances, knowing that if you were caught it would mean death.'

I shrugged. 'I'd never have forgiven myself had I left you to whatever fates the enemy might have dealt. But it wouldn't have been possible without my friends as well, and Berengar too.'

'I know, and I'm grateful to them as well.'

We rode on in silence, raising our hoods up over our heads as cold rain swept in across the hills.

'I'm sorry about Leofrun,' she said after a while. 'Truly I am.'

'You've heard?'

'Your man Ædda told me what happened. He told me the story of how your manor was sacked; he told me how she died. I know how happy she made you, and I know she's not the first that you've lost either.'

But she was. Hard though it was to believe, Oswynn lived, and I didn't know quite what to make of that fact. In my heart was a swirl of feelings so tangled that it was impossible to tease them all out. On the one hand there was joy at the knowledge that she was out there somewhere, but on the other it seemed a hollow sort of revelation, since I didn't know how I would possibly find her again, only that somehow I had to.

Beatrice of course could know none of this, and yet it was partly because of her that I had gone to Beferlic in the first place. The thought of losing her as well as Leofrun had been too much to bear. While it would have been false to say that I loved her, I did still care for her, even if it wasn't in quite the way that she might have wished.

'Beatrice—' I began, hoping to explain at least some of what was going through my mind.

'You don't need to say anything,' she said, cutting me off. Perhaps she guessed what I was about to say. 'No matter what once passed between us, I understand that it cannot be. I accept that.'

She smiled gently as if to show that she felt no ill will towards me, but her eyes betrayed her pain. I wished there were some words of solace I could offer, some way of easing the hurt in her heart, but knew that anything I tried to say would only make things more difficult, and so I could only smile back.

At least after all this time we understood one another, and that, I supposed, was something.

Rather than kill Wild Eadric we brought him back with us as our hostage. No sooner had we arrived back at Eoferwic than Berengar as the leader of the expedition, together with Robert as the most senior lord among us, took the Englishman to King Guillaume's pavilion to present him in person. The man that Byrhtwald had once described to me as the most unrelenting, cunning and dangerous man I would meet now trembled with dread as he was led away. As one of the rebels' leaders, he had been responsible for the deaths of many Frenchmen in the years since the invasion. I wondered what his fate would be.

At the same time I sought out leech-doctors to tend to Malet and to Wace, whose injury was more serious than at first I'd thought. The same sword that had opened the gash in his side had also smashed more than one of his ribs, driving fragments of bone into his chest, and every breath he took seemed laboured.

'He'll survive,' said Father Erchembald, who was the first to see to him. He sounded confident, and I took that for a good sign. 'He may not be able to fight quite as well as before, but he will live.'

Indeed over the next few days Wace began to recover. He remained in considerable pain, however, and weaker than I had ever known him; while he could walk and even with some difficulty manage to ride a horse, anything more strenuous was beyond him.

'I shouldn't have expected you to come with me,' I said when next I saw him. 'I should never have asked that of you.'

'I knew it would be dangerous,' he replied with a shrug. 'If you were going, though, then so were we. Eudo and I would never have let you go alone. Not after everything we've been through. I only hoped that if anyone was to fall along the way, it wouldn't be me.'

As did we all. No man ever knows whether any given fight will be his last. All he can do is pray, and trust in his resolve and his skill at arms to see him through.

'I don't blame you for what happened, Tancred,' he said. 'And I promise you'll see me wielding a sword and shield again before long.'

So it proved over the weeks to follow as his strength returned, although not entirely. He was slower on his feet than he had been, and more tentative in his sword-strokes, but that was only to be expected and in spite of that he kept in good spirits as October passed into November, and bright autumn faded into biting winter.

All that time we remained with the royal army, ready in case the enemy broke out of Heldernesse or marched upon us. In truth neither they nor King Guillaume wished to give battle and risk ruin unless it was on their own terms, on ground that favoured them. Nevertheless, we held the advantage, for the burning of Beferlic had left much of their livestock dead and destroyed many storehouses' worth of grain and other foodstuffs that they had pillaged from the surrounding country, depriving a large part of their army of the provisions they'd been relying on to help them spend the winter on these shores. Forced to find supplies elsewhere, our foes had little choice but to venture out from their hiding places and seek plunder inland, although by then there was precious little left, as they shortly discovered for themselves. Reinforcements had begun to reach us from the south where the rebellions had been put down, and now King Guillaume sent out ever more bands of knights, both into the north towards Dunholm and also into Lindisse on the southern shore of the Humbre, giving them rein to do whatever they wished. They ravaged the land and seized chattels and everything else they could lay their hands on, defiling the land with fire, rape and the sword and leaving in their wake nothing except blood and ashes.

All of that wasn't enough to incite the ætheling into defending the people of Northumbria, who had lent him their support in all his endeavours and beneath whose purple and yellow banner he fought. The rumour was that he had grown impatient with Sweyn's unwillingness to fight us in open battle, and so he together with his huscarls had gone back into the north, abandoning his allies. By then it was too late in the year and the German Sea too treacherous for the Danes to make the voyage back home, and so they were forced to remain on these shores, albeit half starving and succumbing to sickness and flux. Not that we were faring much better. After several months in the field, our own provisions were running short. Some of the barons had been away from their manors for close to half the year; there was little enthusiasm amongst them for a long-drawn campaign through the cold months to come, and gradually dissent began to grow. And so as November drew to a close our king and theirs saw fit to come to terms at last. Sweyn still held hostage the castellan Gilbert de Gand and his mistress Richildis; he promised both to hand them over and to depart without further trouble in the spring, providing that a generous ransom was paid in silver and gold, that his fleet be allowed to overwinter unmolested on the shores of the Humbre, and that they might in the meantime forage for supplies along the Northumbrian coast, all of which conditions King Guillaume readily agreed to.

Thus with a mutual giving of oaths it was settled, and finally two days before Advent Sunday we were able to take our leave. I bade farewell to both Eudo and Wace, who were due to accompany the Malets south to Suthfolc that same day, and the three of us together made an oath not to let it be long before our paths crossed again. Before we left I also found time to speak to Robert, who had been in despondent mood in the weeks since we had returned from Beferlic. His hearth-knights – oath-sworn and loyal retainers, sword-brothers and friends – had all perished in the last few months, most of them in the fight for Eoferwic during which he, his sister and father had fallen into the enemy's hands. Now he alone was left.

'They were good men,' Robert said. 'Ansculf, Urse, Tescelin, Adso and all the others. Even now I see their faces in my mind and struggle to believe that they're gone. A better band of fighters I have never known.'

I didn't know what to add, and so said nothing. I knew all too well what it meant to live when so many had died. Together we gazed upon the remnants of Eoferwic: upon the houses and churches and the blackened earth of the ramparts and the twin mounds, one on either side of the Use, which were all that survived of the castles.

'How is your father faring?' I asked, feeling that I should break the silence.

'Not well,' Robert replied. 'His sickness keeps returning, and each time it seems worse than before. I worry he might not see through the winter.'

'We can but pray that he does, lord.'

The king had stripped the elder Malet of his role as vicomte of the shire of Eoferwic as punishment for having allowed the city to fall to the enemy a second time. To me it seemed an unnecessary humiliation to inflict upon a man who was already suffering both in body and in spirit. From my dealings with him, I knew Malet as someone to whom honour and respect mattered greatly. The defeat at the hands of the enemy would already weigh heavy upon his heart without this latest insult from the king, although from what Robert was saying it sounded as though that was probably the least of his concerns.

'They say King Guillaume has sent to Wincestre for his crown,' Robert said, and there was a stiffness to his tone that I hadn't heard before. 'He plans to hold a coronation here in the city on Christmas morning.'

'In Eoferwic?' I asked, gesturing at the wreckage of the once-proud city. The perversity of the very idea took me aback. 'Why?'

He looked away, so that I could not see his face, although I could well imagine his expression. 'I have never pretended to understand the king's mind. He wishes it, and so it will be.'

There was clearly much resentment there, and so I decided not to press the matter further. The king's capricious nature was well known. A formidable and awe-inspiring man, he was also bull-headed, determined to have his way by whatever means necessary, and unaccustomed to having his will questioned. I myself had faced him only once in person, but that one brief meeting was enough to know that he was not a man to be crossed.

'Once again you have my sincerest thanks,' said Robert, turning back to face me. 'And I promise that you and all your comrades will be well rewarded. Be safe on your travels. I hope it's not too long before we meet again.'

'I trust that it won't be, lord.'

We embraced, and thus we parted ways. My companions were waiting and I knew it was time to go. The days were growing ever shorter as midwinter approached, and many leagues lay between this place and Licedfeld, where the survivors of Earnford awaited my return, and between there and the Marches. Mounting Fyrheard, I glanced at Serlo and Pons, who were riding alongside me, then over my shoulder at the lads Ceawlin, Dægric and Odgar, at Father Erchembald and Ædda, making sure that they were all ready.

Thus at last we left Eoferwic, and started out on the long road south.

'Do you think the Danes will hold true to their promises?' Ædda asked me later that morning when Eoferwic was some miles behind us. 'Will they leave peacefully in the spring as they agreed?'

We rode through country white with frost. Beneath our mounts' hooves the ground was hard; the puddles on the track had all turned to ice and mist formed before my face with every breath.

'God alone has any idea what King Sweyn is planning,' I said. 'When he and Eadgar made common cause they probably intended to divide England between them. But now that the ætheling's taken his ships back north and we no longer have the Welsh to worry about, I don't see how the Danes think they can defeat us.'

'In which case with any luck they'll see reason and sail back across the sea,' Pons muttered.

'Reason?' Serlo gave a snort. 'When did the Danes ever see reason?'

I smiled at that. Desire for silver and spoils was what drove them above all else. It had brought them to these shores, and if there was one thing we could rely on, it was that they would go wherever they reckoned they had the best chance of obtaining those things. From what I understood of their customs, they saw it as better to die in pursuit of glory and riches than to do the prudent thing and return home alive but empty-handed.

That was why, despite the oaths they'd sworn to King Guillaume and regardless of what good sense suggested was the best course of action, the likelihood was that they would do the opposite. And so we would surely find ourselves fighting them again before too long.

Until then, though, we could only do what we always did: keep our blades and our sword-skills sharp, and wait. Spring was several months away, and in the meantime we had work to do: houses, barns, a hall and a church to build in place of those that had been burnt; fields to till and fresh seed to sow; fish-weirs to repair and vegetable-gardens to replant. A manor to raise from the ashes.

The sun shone in a pale, cloudless sky, while an icy wind gusted at our backs. Ahead of us the way stretched to the distant hills, and across that bright and silent land we rode.

To Earnford, and home.

Historical Note

T he history of the borderlands known as the Welsh Marches is a fascinating one, and shortly after finishing *Sworn Sword* I decided that my second novel would bring Tancred to this treacherous part of Britain. In many ways it presented the ideal setting for him, being a place where Norman control was more tenuous than almost anywhere else in the kingdom, where any gains were invariably hard fought but where at the same time reputations could be forged by those with the necessary ambition.

The idea of Wales as a country united by language, ethnicity and culture was already widely accepted in the eleventh century, by both native and non-native authors. Politically, however, at the time of the Norman Conquest it remained divided into many small and squabbling kingdoms, of which the three most powerful were Gwynedd in the north, Powys in mid-Wales and Deheubarth in the south. Indeed, the one and only time in its history that the various provinces were brought together under the hegemony of a single native ruler was during the brief period from 1055 to 1063 under King Gruffydd ap Llywelyn, described in one Welsh source as 'head and shield and defender of the Britons'. The father of the exiled princes Maredudd and Ithel who appear in *The Splintered Kingdom*, he met his end in 1063 at the hands of his own disaffected followers, having suffered defeat in a fierce campaign directed by a certain Harold Godwineson, then Earl of Wessex, who was approaching the zenith of his power. Following Gruffydd's death, Wales fragmented once more into its constituent kingdoms.

The Marches posed a particular problem for the newly arrived

Normans, whose forces were already dangerously over-extended as they attempted to consolidate their hold over England. For much of this period the default land-boundary between England and Wales was represented by Offa's Dyke, the ancient earthwork traditionally thought to have been built by the eighth-century Mercian king whose name it bears. However, it was never a fixed frontier; as well as the perennial raiding activity there was also considerable movement of peoples in both directions. The districts of Ewias and Archenfield, for example, had largely Welsh populations but are both recorded in Domesday Book (1086) as belonging to Herefordshire, while Radnor on the western side of the dyke was originally a pre-Conquest Saxon manor. Because of this fluidity of movement and the contested ownership of these lands, the Marches proved difficult to hold down. Maps of the distribution of motte and bailey castles built in England after 1066 show a clear concentration along the Welsh border, demonstrating the efforts that were made to impose control upon this chaotic region. Pre-emptive attack, involving widespread pillage and plunder to subdue the enemy, was often regarded as the best form of defence, and the 1070s and 1080s saw many expeditions of the kind led by Tancred as the Normans attempted both to pacify the borderlands and to extend their dominions.

In some ways the protracted battle for mastery of the Marches mirrors on a smaller scale the long struggle for England that took place in the aftermath of the Norman invasion. The Battle of Hastings is rightly regarded as a watershed moment in our island's history, and yet it was merely the opening engagement of the Conquest; effective control of the kingdom was only achieved through a series of bitter campaigns. Indeed, every bit as significant as 1066 itself were the years 1069–70, which witnessed arguably the greatest crisis that the invaders had yet faced. A combination of simultaneous rebellions, invasions, raids and risings, from Cornwall in the south to Yorkshire in the north, brought King Guillaume's newly established realm almost to breaking point, and eventually led to the brutal campaign of retribution known as the Harrying of the North, which systematically devastated Yorkshire and north-east England and left a lasting mark both on the region itself and on our perceptions of the Normans. It is this critical but little-known chapter of the Conquest that forms the backdrop for *The Splintered Kingdom*.

As in *Sworn Sword*, several of the characters in this novel are based on real historical persons. As well as the various kings who ruled during this period, these include Eadgar Ætheling, the various members of the Malet house, Guillaume fitz Osbern, Earl Hugues of Chester – whose byname 'the Wolf' is recorded in contemporary sources – the brothers and princes-in-exile Maredudd and Ithel, the castellan at Shrewsbury (shortly afterwards to become Earl) Roger de Montgommeri, and lastly the dispossessed Shropshire thegn Eadric, commonly known by his soubriquet 'Wild', derived from the Old English *se wilda*, which may in turn have originated from the Latin *silvaticus*, a term that the twelfth-century chronicler Orderic Vitalis uses to describe many of the English rebels of this period. All of the other characters, including Tancred and his brothers in arms, are products of my own imagination.

Establishing a firm chronology for the many tumults that engulfed England in the years following the Norman invasion is no easy task, especially since our principal sources for the period are in many places confused and contradictory. In this novel I confess to having taken a few more liberties with respect to the history. One of the decisions I made early on was to conflate some of the events of 1069 with those of 1070, in order to allow Tancred time to develop as a character and to settle into his newly acquired position on the Marches following the Norman victory at York at the end of the first book. Thus although *The Splintered Kingdom* begins in the summer of 1070, many of the events in fact rightly belong to the previous year, including the rebellion of Wild Eadric in conjunction with his Welsh allies, the Battle of Mechain, the arrival of the Danish fleet (in real life commanded firstly by King Sweyn's sons Harald and Cnut and his brother Osbjorn before he himself came to England to take charge the following spring), the Danes' alliance with Eadgar Ætheling and his army of Northumbrian rebels, the fall of York and its two castles, and of course the Harrying of the North, which continued throughout the winter months. The taking of the Malets as hostages is also recorded in our sources, and from later events we know that they must all have been returned safely, but exactly at what point this took place, and whether they were ransomed or rescued by other means, has not been handed down to us. Into that gap in our knowledge I have woven the fictional tale of Tancred's desperate mission to Beverley.

The extent to which the various rebellions and invasions that plagued England in this period were connected to one another is open for debate, and I have speculatively linked events which in reality may or may not have been related. For example, there is no direct evidence to suggest that the dynastic struggles between the Welsh kings and their rival claimants, the sons of Gruffydd, had anything to do with Wild Eadric's rebellion, but given that the two events took place in the same year it is not implausible. All that we know of the fateful Battle of Mechain comes from the Welsh sources *Brut y Tywysogion* (*The Chronicle of the Princes*) and the *Annales Cambriae* (*The Annals of Wales*), which do not record the circumstances or nature of the encounter, or even the specific location, only the outcome. Neither is there any evidence of Norman involvement in this particular battle. However, in 1072 the *Brut* mentions them coming to the aid of another dispossessed prince by the name of Caradog in his struggles against the King of Deheubarth, whom they succeeded in killing in a battle on the banks of the river Rhymney. The Normans were evidently keen to play an active role in Welsh affairs during this period, engaging in direct military intervention where necessary and helping to install friendly client kings in place of hostile potentates. It is not impossible that a similar arrangement was reached with Maredudd and Ithel, whose long-standing hatred of Harold Godwineson would have made them natural allies in the eyes of the invaders.

Likewise it is unknown whether the rebellion of Wild Eadric was in some way related to the ætheling's campaign, or whether he was operating independently. Indeed Eadric's aims could well have been less grand than I have supposed – possibly no more than the restitution of his lands and those of his followers – and his actions rather more opportunistic. Orderic, who is one of the principal sources for these years, writes in vague terms of large numbers of the leading men of England and Wales meeting together and sending messengers across Britain in order to instigate risings against the Normans. While this particular episode refers to a point in his narrative relating to 1068, his chronology is not always reliable, and so it is entirely possible that this could refer to later events. If that is the case, it implies an element of co-ordination between the various risings that engulfed the kingdom at this time, although it would perhaps be a step too far to suggest that there was any grand strategy.

The motives of the Danes are, like those of Wild Eadric, shrouded in mystery. Sweyn's belief that he had a claim to the crown of England is recorded both by Orderic and by the late-eleventh-century German chronicler Adam of Bremen, who writes that he had been promised the succession by King Edward the Confessor (reigned 1042–66). Regardless of the veracity of this, neither the Danes' alliance with Eadgar Ætheling nor their later actions suggest that they arrived with conquest in mind. Possibly they intended to install Eadgar as a kind of puppet ruler, or perhaps Sweyn merely sought to take advantage of the troubles elsewhere in England and the weakness of the Normans' grip on the kingdom to plunder widely and exact as large a tribute as possible, in which case it could be said that the expedition proved successful, since as the campaigning season came to a close and winter set in, King Guillaume eventually did negotiate with them. The question of exactly what the Danes were trying to accomplish is one of the great unknowns that continues to puzzle historians of this period, and we can only speculate.

The Splintered Kingdom reaches its conclusion as the infamous Harrying of the North, one of the defining episodes of the Conquest, is getting under way. For a novelist such as myself writing from the viewpoint of a Norman knight, this presents an obvious problem, for this was a thoroughly despicable act on the part of the invaders for which there is no defence. The widespread despoliation of land was a tactic that was commonly used in the medieval period to deprive an enemy of resources, although the sheer scale of this particular campaign and the suffering that it inflicted upon the native people mark out the Harrying as exceptionally harsh. We cannot know how many Normans were implicated, but it seems to me that it must have divided opinion among King Guillaume's followers. Orderic, who is otherwise full of praise for the king and his achievements, roundly condemned him for this horrific deed, and doubtless his sentiments were shared by many others both at the time and later.

A similar, long-forgotten atrocity could well have inspired the lines of poetry spoken by Ædda, which come from an Anglo-Saxon text of unknown origin known to scholars of the period as 'The Ruin'. A lament on faded glories, the passage of time and the depredations wrought by *wyrd* (an Old English term for 'fate' or 'destiny'), it uses the image of a decayed Roman city, often identified with the remains of Aquae Sulis in modern-day Bath, as a metaphor for the transitory nature of power and material wealth.

The events depicted in *The Splintered Kingdom* scarred England for years to come. Nevertheless, even after the culmination of the Harrying of the North, the Normans' gains were still far from secure. Thus even as Tancred strives to rebuild that which he has lost, before too long he will find himself called upon to face fresh challenges and new enemies.

Acknowledgements

O ne name appears on the title page of this book, but many other people have contributed at various stages of its development, and without their help it would not be the novel that it is.

The linguistic landscape of eleventh-century Britain was complex, and I am indebted to several members of the Department of Anglo-Saxon, Norse and Celtic at the University of Cambridge for guiding me through it. Dr Richard Dance of St Catherine's College kindly translated several passages of modern English dialogue into Old English, while I have Dr Paul Russell and most especially Silva Nurmio to thank for their time and effort spent providing me with nuanced translations into Middle Welsh.

For their helpful advice, suggestions and support I am grateful to Tricia Wastvedt, Beverly Stark, Liz Pile, Jonathan Carr, Jules Stanbridge and Gordon Egginton, who all read and commented on various sections of the novel in draft form. Their generous feedback has been immensely valuable, and I consider myself fortunate to be a member of such a wonderful and talented circle of writers.

Many thanks also go to my editor, Rosie de Courcy, together with Nicola Taplin, Amelia Harvell, Katherine Murphy and everyone else at Random House for their hard work behind the scenes, as well as to my copy-editor, Richenda Todd, whose insights and close attention to detail have proved enormously helpful in shaping this novel into its final form.

Last but certainly not least, many, many thanks to my friends and family and to Laura for all their support, belief and encouragement along the way.

Now read a chapter from
James Aitcheson's thrilling sequel to
The Splintered Kingdom

KNIGHTS OF
THE HAWK

Coming soon

One

The smoke on the horizon was the first sign that the enemy were nearby. It billowed in great plumes above the fields, spreading like an ink-stain upon the fresh parchment of the sky: a black smudge against the grey-white cloud. Save for the occasional bleating of sheep in the pastures and the warbling of skylarks hovering high above, there was no sound. A thin drizzle fell, the wind had died to almost nothing and everything else was still, which made the sight of those plumes in the distance all the more unnerving.

Straightaway I reined in my destrier, Fyrheard, and raised my hand to those following as a signal to halt. My men, riding to either side of me, responded at once, as did the mounted archers at the rear of our column, but the oxen-drivers were too busy talking between themselves to notice, and only my shout of warning stopped them and their animals from colliding with us. I shouted at them in the English tongue and cast a glare in their direction, but they paid me no heed. Their minds were upon the distant smoke, at which they were pointing and shouting in alarm.

'A hall-burning, do you think, lord?' Serlo asked. One of my two household knights, he was a bear of a man with a fearsome sword-arm and a temper to match: not the kind of man that I would have liked to face in a fight, and I was glad to count him as a friend.

'If it is, it wouldn't be the first,' I replied. Nor, I suspected, was it likely to be the last. In the last fortnight the rebels had done the same thing on half a dozen occasions, always in different places but always following the same pattern: striking as if from nowhere to torch a village or manor, before just as quickly withdrawing to their boats and melting away into the marshes. By the time word of what had taken place had reached us and the king had sent out men to meet them in battle, they were already long gone. Still, it was rare that they should attempt a raid so far from their island stronghold. The castle at Cantabrigie was barely two hours behind us; the rebels were either growing bolder or else more foolhardy, and I couldn't make up my mind which.

'What now?' Pons asked, his voice low. The second of my knights, he possessed a sharp wit and an equally sharp tongue that he often struggled to restrain, but there was nothing light-hearted about his manner now.

'We could try to find another way around,' Serlo suggested.

'Not if we want to reach the king's camp by dusk,' I said. Aside from the main tracks, I wasn't at all familiar with this land: a flat and featureless expanse of pasture and barley-fields, crossed by streams and rivers narrow and wide. What I did know was that there were few well-made ways along which fully laden carts could travel, with bridges and fords that they could cross. We could easily waste several hours if we decided to leave the road and strike out across the country.

Pons frowned. 'Do we go on, then?'

'They could be lying in wait for us,' Serlo pointed out.

I considered. On the one hand I had no wish to lead us all into a trap, but on the other it seemed unlikely the enemy would announce their presence so clearly if an ambush was what they had in mind. Besides, it had been several weeks since the rebels had made any serious attempts to waylay our supply trains. Not since the king had begun sending out parties of knights and other warriors to ward off any would-be attackers.

And that was how I came to be here. I, Tancred the Breton, Tancred of Earnford. The man who had helped win the gates in the battle at Eoferwic, who had led the charge against the pretender, Eadgar Ætheling, faced him upon the bridge and almost killed him. The same man who by night had entered the enemy's camp in

Beferlic, rescued his lord from imprisonment at the hands of the Danes, and captured the feared Wild Eadric, the scourge of the Marches. I had stared death in the face more often than I cared to remember and each time lived to tell the tale. I had done what others thought impossible. By rights I should have been rewarded with vast lands and halls of stone, chests brimming with silver, gilded swords and helmets with which to arm myself, stables of fleet-footed Andalusian horses that I could offer as gifts to my followers. I should have been leading forays against the enemy, hunting down their foraging-parties, training at arms with my companions, or else helping to hone the shield- and spear-skills of those less proficient in the ways of war.

But I was not, and with every day my anger grew. For instead of being allowed to make use of my skills and experience, I found myself reduced to this escort duty, riding back and forth across this featureless country day after day, all to protect a dozen scrawny oxen, their stinking, dung-covered owners and these rickety carts, which were constantly becoming stuck or else collapsing under the weight of the goods they carried. It would have been bearable had the rebels ever dared approach us, since at least then I'd have had the chance to test my sword-arm against them. Probably sensibly, however, they preferred to go where the pickings were easy and where they could wreak the greatest devastation, rather than risk their lives for the sake of whatever goods we guarded, which usually comprised no more than some loaves of bread, barrels of ale and rounds of cheese, timber planks, nails and bundles of firewood – provisions that our army needed to keep it warm and fed, but which, if the reports we received were reliable, they already had in plenty upon their island fastness at Elyg.

'What are you thinking, lord?' Serlo asked.

'I'm thinking that those smoke-plumes are rising thickly,' I said, meaning that those fires hadn't been burning for long, which in turn meant that those who had caused them couldn't be far off. And I was thinking, too, that this was the closest I had come to crossing swords with any of the rebels on this campaign. The battle-hunger rose inside me; my sword-hand tingled with the familiar itch. I longed to hear the clash of steel ringing out, to feel my blade-edge biting into flesh, to let the battle-joy fill me. And as those thoughts ran through my mind, an idea began to form.

'The three of us will ride on ahead,' I said. 'If the enemy are lurking, I want to find them.'

Serlo and Pons nodded. While they were unafraid to speak their minds and while I often relied upon their counsel, they both respected me enough to follow whatever course of action I chose. The same could not be said of the company of archers that had been placed under my command, who guarded the rear of our column. Lordless men, they made their living by selling their services to anyone who would pay, owing allegiance to their purses and their purses alone. Even now I could make out the mutterings of their captain, a ruddy-faced man by the name of Hamo, who possessed a large gut and a sullen manner, and whom I had little liking for.

I turned to face him. At first he didn't notice me, being too busy exchanging snide remarks with his friends about how I was frightened of a little smoke, and how he'd heard it said that Bretons were all cowards, and that was why I'd been tasked with this escort duty, because I was too weak-willed for anything else. Clearly he knew nothing of who I was, or the deeds I had accomplished. He was lucky that I was too poor to afford the blood-price for his killing, or I would have long since struck him down for his insolence.

As it was, I had to wait a few moments before one of his comrades saw that I was watching and nudged him sharply in the side. He looked up; straightaway his tongue retreated inside his head, while his cheeks turned an even deeper shade of red.

'Lord,' he said, bowing extravagantly, which prompted a smirk from a few of the others. 'What are your instructions?'

I eyed him for a few heartbeats, silently daring him to break into a smile, but luckily for his sake he wasn't that stupid. Although he was not averse to muttering behind my back, he knew better than to defy me openly. I reckoned he was probably ten years older than me, which was a good age for someone whose life was lived on the field of battle. I was then entering my twenty-eighth summer, and although no one could yet call me old, I had long ago ceased thinking of myself as a young man.

'Wait for us here,' I told him, trying to hold my temper and my tongue. 'I want to find out what's happened.'

Hamo frowned. 'We were ordered not to leave the carts undefended.'

'I'm not leaving them undefended. You're staying with them.'

Strictly speaking my duties didn't extend to hunting down enemy bands, a fact of which we were both well aware. But if Hamo thought I was going to let this opportunity pass, he was mistaken.

'Lord—' he began to protest, but I cut him off.

'Shut up,' I said, and then pointed to the four of the archers nearest me: a full third of his company. 'You'll come with me.'

The four glanced at their leader, waiting for his assent. He said nothing but for a few moments held my gaze, resentment in his eyes, before nodding and gesturing for them to follow me. No doubt he would add this to his list of grievances, and find some way of using it against me, but I would worry about that another time. For now I had greater concerns.

'Keep a watch out on all sides and have your bows ready,' I said as we began to ride off. 'We'll be back before long.'

'And if the enemy happen upon us while you're gone?' asked Hamo. 'What are we supposed to do then?'

'Kill them,' I answered with a shrug. 'Isn't that what you have arrows for?'

It wasn't much of a reassurance, nor did I expect it to be, but it was all the advice I had to offer. But then I doubted that Hamo and his men would choose to put up much of a fight. Rather, if it seemed they were outnumbered they would most likely turn tail at the first opportunity, abandoning the carts and their contents in order to save their own skins. Were that the case, they needn't worry about ever showing their faces in our camp again, and at least King Guillaume wouldn't need to keep wasting good silver on them. Although I respected their skills with bow and blade, I did not trust them, and in that I was far from alone. Sellswords were considered by many among the lowest class of men; exiles and oath-breakers for the most part, they were entirely lacking in honour and scruple. Many would probably kill their own mothers if they thought they could profit from doing so.

With that we left Hamo and the rest of his company to guard the carts and their contents, striking out across the flat country. Seven men did not make much of an army, if truth be told, especially when I was used to commanding scores and at times even hundreds, but it would have to do. Unlike their captain, the four archers were all young lads. A couple of them were taller even than myself, and I was not exactly short. Each was broad in the chest, with the sturdy shoulders and thick arms needed to draw a string of any great weight. I myself had never mastered the bow, instead preferring as most knights did to hone my skills with sword and lance, mail and helmet. But I knew from experience the slaughter that well-trained bowmen could wreak. They had proven their worth in the great battle at Hæstinges, firstly by inflicting great casualties amongst the English ranks and softening them to our charge, and later, it was said, by wounding the usurper Harold Godwineson, who according to rumour had received an arrow in his eye shortly before he fell to Duke Guillaume's sword. Whether that was true or not, no one knew for certain, although I'd met several men who claimed theirs was the arrow that had struck him.

That was five years ago. Since that day much had changed; I had seen friends and comrades die and gained others from unexpected quarters, had striven hard to win myself lands of my own only for them to be laid waste by my enemies, had found fame and honour and love and come close to losing it all.

One thing, though, remained the same, for even five years after we had triumphed at Hæstinges and King Guillaume had received the crown that belonged to him by right, still many among the English refused to submit to him. And so we found ourselves here in this bleak corner of East Anglia, trying to snuff out the final embers of rebellion, so far without success. We had been in the field for several months now, and what did we have to show for it? A mud-ridden camp in which half the king's army was succumbing to fever and flux, while hundreds more lay dead after earlier attempts to assault the enemy upon the Isle of Elyg had ended in failure. Meanwhile the rebels continued to taunt us with their constant raids on the surrounding land. With every week they held out against us, scores more flocked to their banners, so that they had grown from a paltry couple of hundred to a host reckoned at nearly two thousand strong, and perhaps even larger than that. In truth no one knew for certain, and in the absence of any reliable information, the numbers grew ever wilder. Which meant that if we saw even the slightest chance to inflict some damage upon the enemy, we had to take it.

Keeping a careful watch out on all sides, we rode towards the source of the smoke. Soon I began to make out what only a short time ago would have been barns, hovels and cattle-sheds, though there was little left of them now. Amidst the fallen-in posts and roof-beams I spied glimmers of flame. Carrion birds cawed as they circled above the ruins in pairs and threes and fours; from somewhere came the forlorn bleating of a goat, although I could not see it. There was no other sound, nor any sign of movement, nor any glint of mail or spearpoints, which suggested the rebels had already left this place. Even so, we approached slowly. In my younger days my recklessness had often been my undoing, but experience had taught me the value of caution. The last thing I wanted was to rush in only to find ourselves in a snare, surrounded and outnumbered with no hope of retreat. And so the four archers kept arrows nocked to their bowstrings, ready to let fly if they saw anything that looked like a foeman, while the rest of us gripped our lance-hafts firmly.

The blackened remains of the manor stood upon a low rise. As we climbed, it became clear that we were the only ones around. Anywhere that might have provided a hiding-place for the enemy had been razed to the ground. Livestock had been slaughtered in the fields and the pens, while the corpses of men, women and children alike lay in the yards and the vegetable gardens, their clothes and hair matted with blood. Feathered shafts protruded from the chests and backs of some, while others had gaping wounds to their necks and thighs, and bright gashes across their faces. No one had been spared. The stench of burnt flesh mixed with freshly spilt guts hung in the air: smells at which I might once have retched, but by now had grown only too familiar. In the past year I'd witnessed so many burnings of this kind that it was hard to be much moved by them. Still, it was rare that the enemy left so little in their wake.

'They killed even their own kind,' I murmured, scarcely able to believe it, though it wasn't the first time I'd seen it happen. Usually the rebels would kill the lord and his retainers, if they happened to be French, but leave the English folk alive. Sometimes, though, the battle-rage and the desire for blood consumed them, and they wouldn't stop until all around was ruin and death. Perhaps the villagers had tried to fight back, or else the rebels had judged them guilty of falling subject to a foreign lord. I could only guess the reason. Still, it was rare that the enemy failed to leave at least one person alive. One to tell the tale. One to spread the news of what had happened here. One to foster fear of those who had done this. I knew because it was what I would have done.

We halted not far from what I guessed had once been a church, although there seemed to be little to distinguish it from the remains of the other hovels save for a waist-high stone cross that stood at its western end. One wall alone remained standing, but as we dismounted, that too collapsed inwards, sending a great cloud of dust and still-glowing ash billowing up.

Beside me, Pons shook his head and muttered something that I did not entirely make out but which was most likely a curse.

Serlo turned to me. 'Why do you think they did this, lord?'

To that question there was no simple answer. Even if the lord of this manor had been a Frenchman, as seemed likely, the people living here would have been kinsfolk of the enemy. And apart from a few sheep and goats and chickens, most of which they seemed to have killed rather than take with them, what could there have been in a place like this to make it worth attacking?

Only one explanation came to mind. 'They wanted to send us a message,' I said.

'A message?' Serlo echoed, frowning.

Slowly it was beginning to make sense. The reason why they had come to this place, so far from their encampment upon the Isle.

'The enemy weren't looking for plunder or captives,' I said. 'If they were, they could have chosen to attack any number of manors closer to Elyg.'

'A show of force,' Pons put in, understanding at last. 'That's what they wanted. The more damage they wreak and the more ruthless they appear, the more panic they spread.'

I nodded. 'They want to prove that they don't fear us. That they can strike anywhere, at any time.'

And that was a bad sign, for it suggested that they were not only growing in confidence but also that they had the men to spare on such expeditions. Before, they had preferred to keep to their corner of the marshlands and wait for us to come to them, only raiding occasionally and even then in places where they judged the risks to be fewest. But no longer. Now they laid waste the land with impunity, taunting us, and all the while we were powerless to stop them.

I swore aloud. I'd hoped that we might find some of the enemy still here, but in fact they were probably several miles away by now, which left us nothing more that we could usefully do except return to Hamo and the carts. All we had accomplished was to waste an hour or more on our journey. Back at the king's camp in Branduna the clerks would be waiting: pale, weasel-eyed men who recorded with quill and parchment every last crumb of bread and drop of ale that entered the storehouses and was distributed among the men. They wouldn't thank us if we arrived late and they had to complete their work by candlelight. While I always took a certain pleasure in annoying them – one of the few pleasures afforded by this escort work – it would mean that I'd have to put up with even more of their carping, and I wasn't convinced it was entirely worth it.

Fyrheard pawed restlessly at the ground. I shared his sentiment. I was about to give the order to turn back, when amidst the calls of the crows, which had descended to pick at the bodies, came what sounded like a voice, not far off but weak and indistinct.

'Did anyone else hear that?' I asked.

'All I heard was my stomach rumbling,' muttered one of the archers, whose name I had forgotten but whose gaunt face and large ears I recognised. 'The sooner we return, the sooner we can eat.'

'You'll be going hungry unless you keep quiet,' I snapped. That prompted a snigger from the archer's comrades, but they fell quiet the instant I glared at them, and it was as well that I did, or else I might have missed the voice when it came again: a low moaning, like someone in pain.

'Over there,' said Serlo.

I looked in the direction of his pointed finger. Through clouds of smoke and ash I glimpsed a broken haywain and, lying beside it, what at first I'd taken for a corpse, moving its head, just slightly but enough that I could be sure that my eyes weren't deceiving me.

Keeping one hand close to my sword-hilt just in case, I strode over across the muddy churchyard towards the figure. He lay on his back, coughing up crimson gobs. His tunic and trews were torn, while his face was streaked with mud. An arrow had buried itself in his torso, just above his groin. Around the place where the shaft was lodged his tunic was congealed with so much blood that it was a wonder he still lived. He looked about fifty or so in years; his grey hair was flecked with strands of white and cut short at the back in the French style, which suggested he was a Norman. On a leather thong around his neck hung a wooden cross that suggested he had either been mass-priest here, or possibly chaplain to the local lord.

I knelt down by his side. The others gathered around me and I called for one of them to fetch something for the priest to drink. No sooner had I done so than his eyes opened, only by a fraction but enough that he could see me looking down on him.

'Who—' he began, but faltered over the words. His voice was weak, no more than a croak. 'Who are you?'

'Friends,' I assured him. 'My name is Tancred. We came as soon as we saw the smoke.'

'You came too late.' His face contorted in pain as once more he groaned and clutched at the shaft protruding from his gut. 'Too late.'

I tried to lift his hands away so as to get a better look at the wound. If we could only remove the arrow, I thought, it might be possible to staunch the flow and close up the hole. But no sooner had I prised his trembling fingers from the sticky cloth than I knew it would be no use. In my time I'd seen men recover from all manner of injuries, some worse than this, but not many. I'd learnt a little about wounds and how to treat them from the infirmarian in the monastery where I grew up, and over the years since had often watched leech-doctors at work. That small amount of knowledge was enough to tell me that he was too far gone, even for someone skilled in the ways of healing, which none of us were.

Serlo crouched beside me, holding a leather flask. 'Ale,' he said. 'There's not much left.'

'It'll be enough,' I replied as I took it and removed the stopper. From the weight and the sound it made as I swirled the liquid about I reckoned it was probably about a quarter full. I turned back to the priest. 'Can you sit up?'

He shook his head, teeth clenched in pain. His breath came in stutters, making it hard for him to speak. 'I am beyond the help of ale. Besides, soon there will be no more pain. I shall be with God, and all will be well. There is only one thing you can do for me.'

'What is it, father?'

He gave a great hacking cough and as he did so his whole body shuddered. Thankfully the fit did not last long and, sighing wearily, he lay back once more, at the same time motioning with his fingers for me to come closer. I leant towards him. There were tears in the old man's eyes, running down his cheeks.

'Bring to justice the ones who did this,' he said. 'Their leader too, that spawn of the Devil. The one they call Hereward. Promise me that.'

'Hereward?' I repeated, wanting to make sure I had heard him rightly. 'He did this?'

'So they called him, yes.'

That name was well known to me, as it was to everyone in our army, but I hadn't expected to hear it today, in this place. Hereward was one of the leaders of the rebels; it was he who had instigated this particular rising here in the fens. Some said he was a prominent thegn who had held land in these parts under the old king, Eadward. Others claimed he was a creature of the forest, abandoned at birth by his mother and raised by wolves, which explained his ruthless nature and his lack of Christian mercy. In truth no one knew where he had come from; his name had been first spoken only last autumn. While we had been campaigning with the king in the north, Hereward had raided the abbey at Burh, slain several of the monks and carried away all their treasures, including several shrines and gilded crucifixes, richly bound and decorated gospel-books and even, it was said, the golden crown that had rested upon Christ's head on the rood beneath the chancel-arch. With the help of some Danish swords-for-hire he'd torched the town and monastery, and afterwards had fled by ship across the marshlands to the Isle of Elyg, where he now chose to make his stand against us, bolstered by the hundreds of other English outlaws who had flocked to his banner.

It was because of him that we were here in this godforsaken corner of the kingdom. It was because of him that, barely half a year after we had defeated the Northumbrians and their Danish allies at Beferlic and sent the pretender Eadgar scurrying back to the protection of the King of Alba, we found ourselves once more summoned by King Guillaume to join him on another of his campaigns.

And yet if the old priest was right, and it was indeed Hereward who had done this, and if we could kill or capture him—

A new sense of purpose stirred within me. 'How many of them were there?' I asked.

The priest's eyes were closed again, his skin as pale as snow. His time was near. But if I was to do what he had asked of me, he had to give me answers. I clasped his wrinkled, blood-stained hand, squeezing it firmly to try to keep him with us a little longer. At once he blinked and came to, a look of confusion upon his face, as if he did not quite know where he was.

'How many, father?' I said again.

He groaned as if with the effort of remembering, and after a moment managed to answer, 'A dozen, perhaps fifteen. No more.'

Roughly two men to every one of us, then. Fewer than I had been expecting, but still more than I would have liked to face, especially when one of them was Hereward himself, whose sword-edge had already claimed countless victims, if the stories told about him were true. No warrior ever won himself great fame without some measure of risk along the way, however. The difficulty came in learning which risks to embrace and which to avoid, and this seemed to me one worth taking.

'When did they leave?' I asked the priest.

'Not an hour ago,' he said, his eyelids drooping. 'They went...'

'Where?'

At first I thought he was slipping away and that we wouldn't get an answer, but then I spotted the faintest movement of his lips. I leaned closer.

'North,' he said, barely managing a whisper, and I had to put my ear almost to his mouth in order to hear him. The words came slowly now. 'They went north. That much I know. Now, let me rest.'

I nodded and squeezed the priest's hand one last time, then rested it carefully back upon his chest, which still rose and fell, though so slightly as to be almost imperceptible. Between breaths he whispered something that I could not entirely make out, but which from a couple of Latin words I guessed was probably a prayer for the safe-keeping of his soul. Not that he had the chance to finish it, for he was still in the middle of whatever he was uttering when a pained expression came across his face and a long groan left his lips. His eyes closed once more; moments later his chest ceased moving, and that was when I knew he had left this world and that he was, at last, with God.

I made the sign of the cross across my breast as I got to my feet, and out of the corner of my eye I saw Serlo and Pons do the same. Around us the houses still burned. The wind was rising, tugging at my tunic, blowing the smoke towards us and causing tongues of vibrant flame to flare up amongst what remained of the smoking timbers, wattle and thatch.

'What now?' asked the archer with the gaunt face, his expression now devoid of humour.

'We ride,' I answered.

Hereward and his band couldn't have got far in an hour. No doubt they would be making for wherever they had moored their boats. Since few vessels large and sturdy enough to carry a horse could navigate the marshes, I guessed they would most likely be on foot, which meant that we still had a chance of catching up with them.

Without delay we mounted up. I would have liked to bury the priest if only to save his body from the crows, but there was no time. Instead we left him by the haywain where he lay, his expression serene as if he were simply sleeping.

Only later, when the wreckage of the village was far behind us, did I realise that I hadn't even learnt his name.